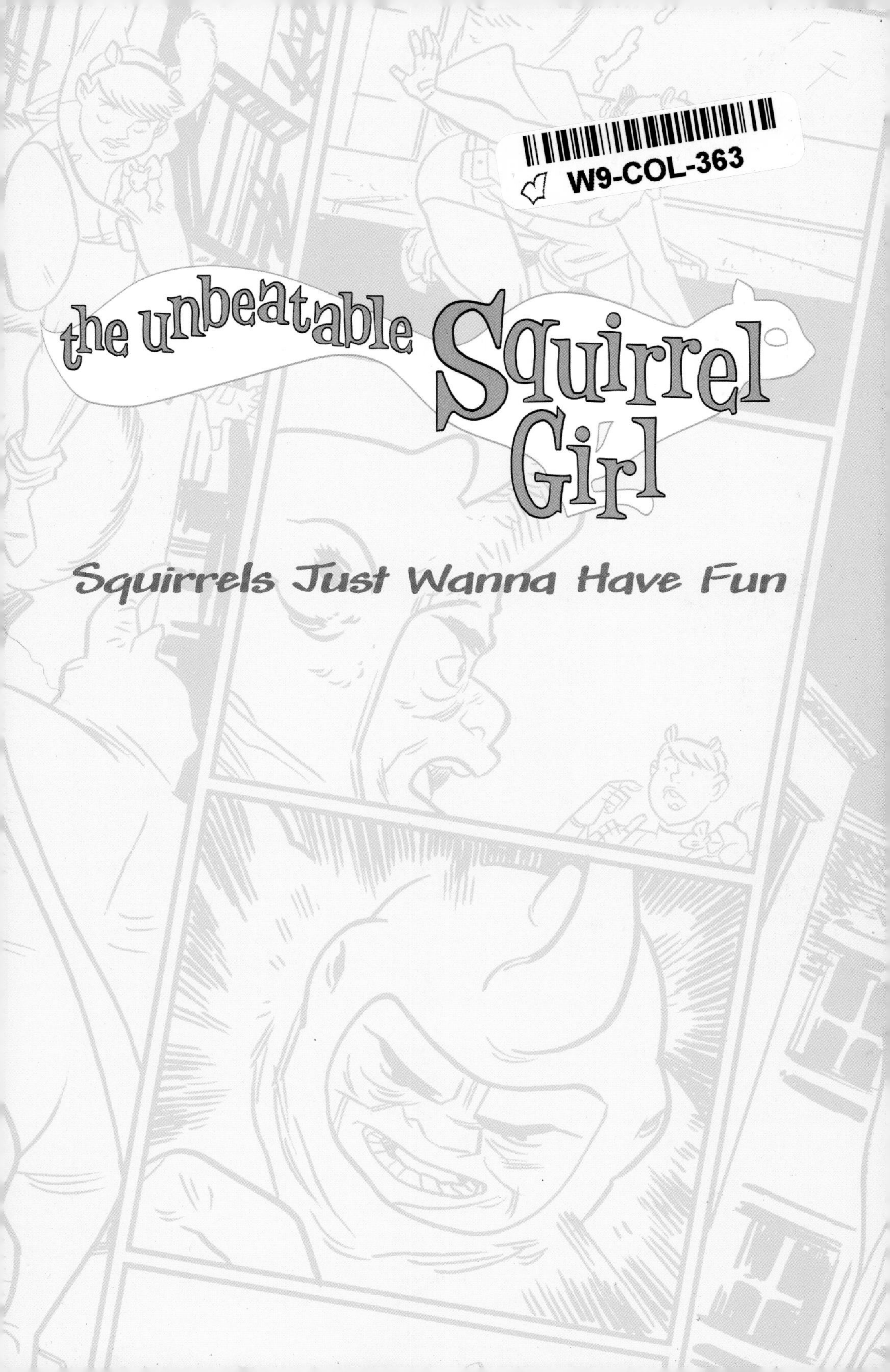

the unbeatable Squirrel Girl

Squirrels Just Wanna Have Fun

Contents

THE UNBEATABLE SQUIRREL GIRL: SQUIRRELS JUST WANNA HAVE FUN. Contains material originally published in magazine form as THE UNBEATABLE SQUIRREL GIRL (2015B) #12-21. First printing 2021. ISBN 978-1-302-92990-9. Published by MARVEL WORLDWIDE, INC., a subsidiary of MARVEL ENTERTAINMENT, LLC. OFFICE OF PUBLICATION: 1290 Avenue of the Americas, New York, NY 10104. © 2021 MARVEL No similarity between any of the names, characters, persons, and/or institutions in this magazine with those of any living or dead person or institution is intended, and any such similarity which may exist is purely coincidental. **Printed in Canada.** KEVIN FEIGE, Chief Creative Officer; DAN BUCKLEY, President, Marvel Entertainment; JOE QUESADA, EVP & Creative Director; DAVID BOGART, Associate Publisher & SVP of Talent Affairs; TOM BREVOORT, VP, Executive Editor; NICK LOWE, Executive Editor, VP of Content, Digital Publishing; DAVID GABRIEL, VP of Print & Digital Publishing; JEFF YOUNGQUIST, VP of Production & Special Projects; ALEX MORALES, Director of Publishing Operations; DAN EDINGTON, Managing Editor; RICKEY PURDIN, Director of Talent Relations; JENNIFER GRÜNWALD, Senior Editor, Special Projects; SUSAN CRESPI, Production Manager; STAN LEE, Chairman Emeritus. For information regarding advertising in Marvel Comics or on Marvel.com, please contact Vit DeBellis, Custom Solutions & Integrated Advertising Manager, at vdebellis@marvel.com. For Marvel subscription inquiries, please call 888-511-5480. **Manufactured between 6/30/2021 and 8/3/2021 by SOLISCO PRINTERS, SCOTT, QC, CANADA.**

10 9 8 7 6 5 4 3 2 1

collection editor JENNIFER GRÜNWALD
assistant editor DANIEL KIRCHHOFFER
assistant managing editor MAIA LOY
assistant managing editor LISA MONTALBANO
vp production & special projects JEFF YOUNGQUIST
vp licensed publishing SVEN LARSEN
svp print, sales & marketing DAVID GABRIEL
editor in chief C.B. CEBULSKI

the unbeatable Squirrel Girl

Squirrels Just Wanna Have Fun

WRITER
RYAN NORTH

WRITER, #16 15-YEAR-OLD DOREEN SEQUENCE **WILL MURRAY**

ARTIST
ERICA HENDERSON

COLOR ARTISTS
RICO RENZI
WITH **ERICA HENDERSON** (#7)

TRADING CARD ART
ANTHONY CLARK (#13), **HANNAH BLUMENREICH** (#13)
& **MICHAEL CHO** (#15)

VULTURE & SANDMAN
PANELS, #17 ART
CHRIS SCHWEIZER

MEW'S DREAM COMICS,
#15 ART
ZAC GORMAN

DOREEN'S COSTUME
DRAWING, #16 ART
STEVE DITKO

LETTERERS
VC'S TRAVIS LANHAM
WITH **CLAYTON COWLES** (#14)

COVER ART
ERICA HENDERSON

ASSISTANT EDITOR
CHARLES BEACHAM

ASSOCIATE EDITOR
SARAH BRUNSTAD

EDITOR
WIL MOSS

SPECIAL THANKS TO CK RUSSELL

SQUIRREL GIRL CREATED
BY WILL MURRAY & STEVE DITKO

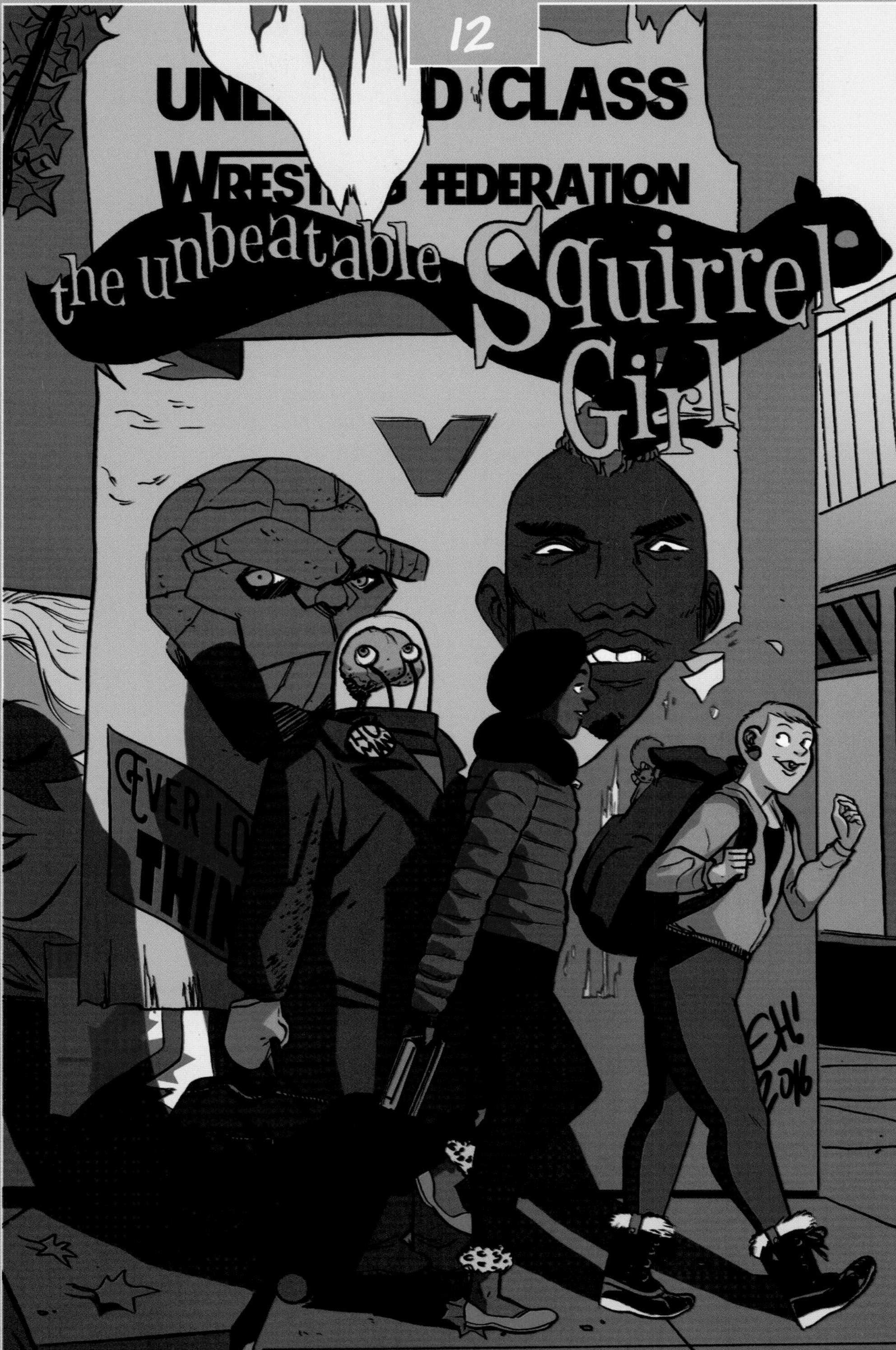

12
CLASS
FEDERATION
the unbeatable Squirrel Girl

Doreen Green isn't just a second-year computer science student: she secretly also has all the powers of both squirrel and girl! She uses her amazing abilities to fight crime **and** be as awesome as possible. You know her as...***The Unbeatable Squirrel Girl!*** Find out what she's been up to, with...

Squirrel Girl *in a nutshell*

Squirrel Girl @unbeatablesg
Whew, I just had THE BEST NIGHT'S SLEEP OF ALL TIME. For some reason I feel like I could take on the world?

Squirrel Girl @unbeatablesg
Like, I woke up energized and jazzed, as if I really had just defeated a super villain and saved the world...IN MY SLEEP!! Felt great tbh

Squirrel Girl @unbeatablesg
But hah hah that's impossible so oh well

Spider-Man @aspidercan
@unbeatablesg actually there's a doctor strange bad guy named "nightmare" that you could've technically fought in your dreams!!!

Spider-Man @aspidercan
@unbeatablesg doc strange isn't on here though otherwise we could ask him

Squirrel Girl @unbeatablesg
@aspidercan A guy with a doctorate in strangeness doesn't hang out online here? WEIRD

Squirrel Girl @unbeatablesg
@aspidercan YOU'D THINK HE'D FIT RIGHT IN

Tony Stark @starkmantony
@unbeatablesg Hey, how's that robot brain in a jar guy you patched up working out?

Squirrel Girl @unbeatablesg
@starkmantony Brain Drain? Great! Well on his way to becoming a real hero, actually! Still mega nihilistic but in a cool way

Squirrel Girl @unbeatablesg
@starkmantony We're going out on patrol together in a bit actually

Tony Stark @starkmantony
@unbeatablesg Shouldn't you not mention when you're going out on patrol, so the criminal element won't know?

Squirrel Girl @unbeatablesg
@starkmantony good point my dude, one sec

Squirrel Girl @unbeatablesg
HELLO CRIMINALS, THIS IS JUST TO ANNOUNCE THAT I AM ON PATROL ALWAYS AND WILL DEFINITELY CATCH YOU DOING A CRIME, SO DON'T DO THEM

Spider-Man @aspidercan
@unbeatablesg holy crap can i use that

Squirrel Girl @unbeatablesg
@starkmantony Tony are you there I just had the best idea!! Tony tony tony

Tony Stark @starkmantony
@unbeatablesg Hey.

Squirrel Girl @unbeatablesg
@starkmantony TONY. BRAINSTORM. What if you changed your name from "Tony Stark" to--HEAR ME OUT--..."Ira."

Tony Stark @starkmantony
@unbeatablesg "Ira Stark"?

Squirrel Girl @unbeatablesg
@starkmantony IRA ONMANN.

Tony Stark @starkmantony
@unbeatablesg oh my god

Squirrel Girl @unbeatablesg
@starkmantony Tony I'm going on vacation so I just wanted to give you something to remember me by

Squirrel Girl @unbeatablesg
@starkmantony just a little memento

Squirrel Girl @unbeatablesg
@starkmantony for my good friend

Squirrel Girl @unbeatablesg
@starkmantony ira onmann

search!

#braindrain

#canada

#nopowernoproblems

#maureengreen

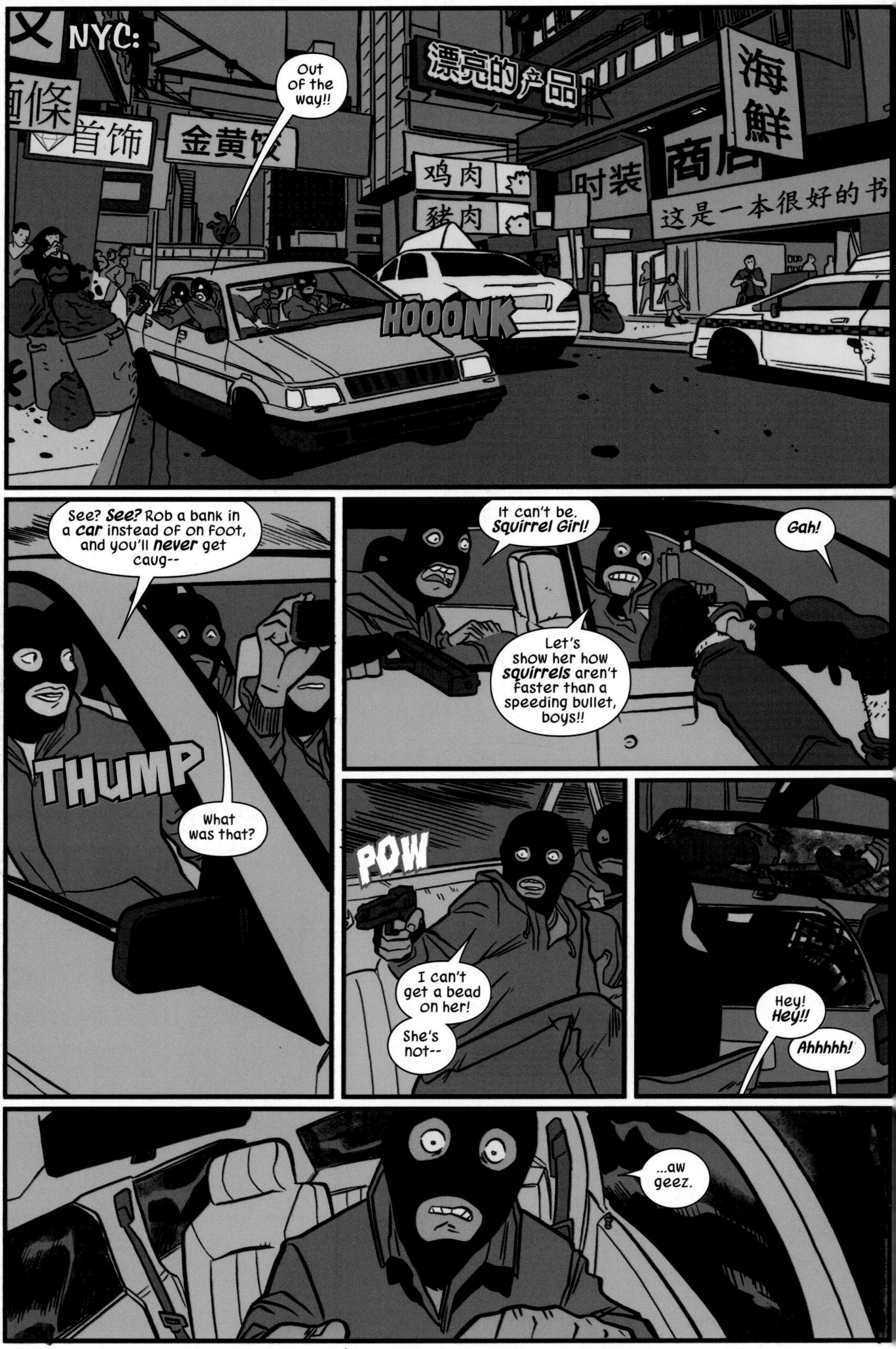
NYC:
漂亮的产品
海鲜
首饰
金黄饺
鸡肉
豬肉
时装
商店
这是一本很好的书
Out of the way!!
HOOONK
See? *See?* Rob a bank in a *car* instead of on foot, and you'll *never* get caug--
THUMP
What was that?
It can't be. *Squirrel Girl!*
Gah!
Let's show her how *squirrels* aren't faster than a speeding bullet, boys!!
POW
I can't get a bead on her!
She's not--
Hey! *Hey!!*
Ahhhhh!
...aw geez.

These are the bank robbers from the first time Squirrel Girl saved a bank! They're back! And they're still robbing banks! Wow, I'd really hoped they'd have worked towards positive change in their own lives but *hah hah hah **guess not!***

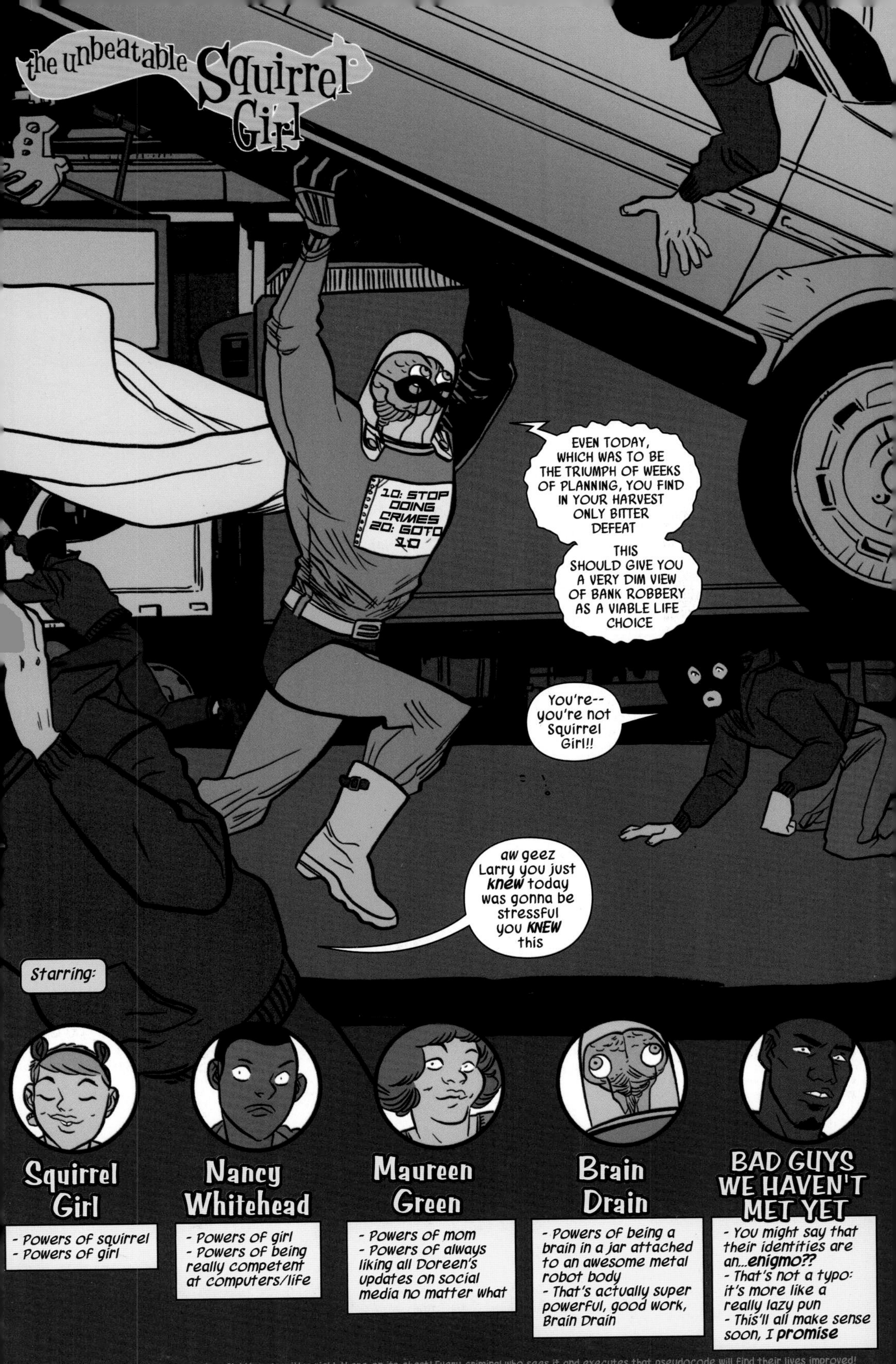

the unbeatable Squirrel Girl
10: STOP DOING CRIMES 20: GOTO 10
EVEN TODAY, WHICH WAS TO BE THE TRIUMPH OF WEEKS OF PLANNING, YOU FIND IN YOUR HARVEST ONLY BITTER DEFEAT
THIS SHOULD GIVE YOU A VERY DIM VIEW OF BANK ROBBERY AS A VIABLE LIFE CHOICE
You're--you're not Squirrel Girl!!
aw geez Larry you just **knew** today was gonna be stressful you **KNEW** this
Starring:
Squirrel Girl
- Powers of squirrel
- Powers of girl
Nancy Whitehead
- Powers of girl
- Powers of being really competent at computers/life
Maureen Green
- Powers of mom
- Powers of always liking all Doreen's updates on social media no matter what
Brain Drain
- Powers of being a brain in a jar attached to an awesome metal robot body
- That's actually super powerful, good work, Brain Drain
BAD GUYS WE HAVEN'T MET YET
- You might say that their identities are an...**enigmo??**
- That's not a typo: it's more like a really lazy pun
- This'll all make sense soon, I **promise**

Brain Drain's costume displays a crime-fighting algorithm right there on its chest! Every criminal who sees it and executes that pseudocode will find their lives improved! This is next-level costume design!!

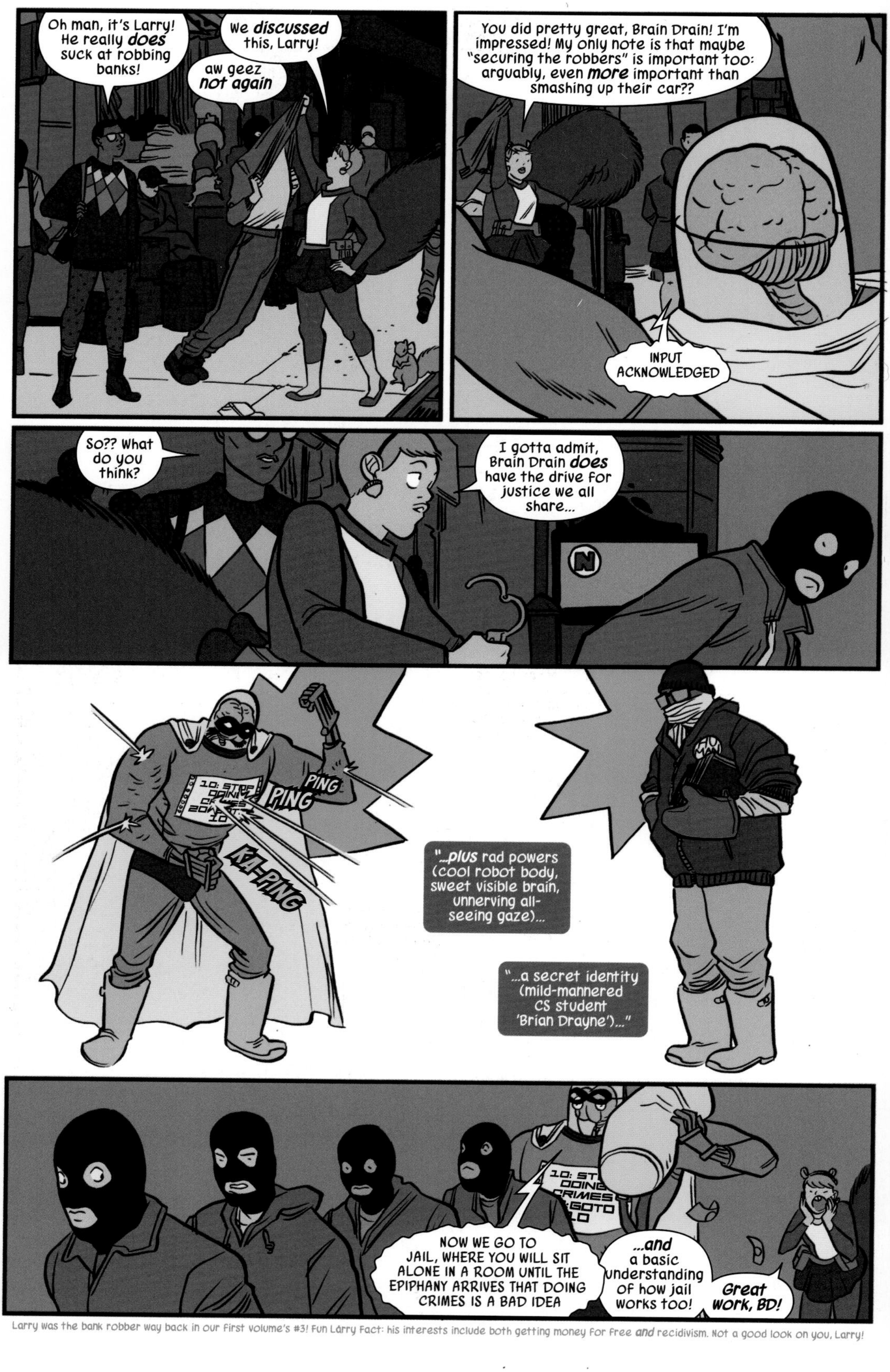

Oh man, it's Larry! He really *does* suck at robbing banks!
aw geez *not again*
We *discussed* this, Larry!
You did pretty great, Brain Drain! I'm impressed! My only note is that maybe "securing the robbers" is important too: arguably, even *more* important than smashing up their car??
INPUT ACKNOWLEDGED
So?? What do you think?
I gotta admit, Brain Drain *does* have the drive for justice we all share...
PING
PING
KA-PING
"...*plus* rad powers (cool robot body, sweet visible brain, unnerving all-seeing gaze)...
"...a secret identity (mild-mannered CS student 'Brian Drayne')..."
NOW WE GO TO JAIL, WHERE YOU WILL SIT ALONE IN A ROOM UNTIL THE EPIPHANY ARRIVES THAT DOING CRIMES IS A BAD IDEA
...and a basic understanding of how jail works too!
Great work, BD!

Larry was the bank robber way back in our first volume's #3! Fun Larry Fact: his interests include both getting money for free *and* recidivism. Not a good look on you, Larry!

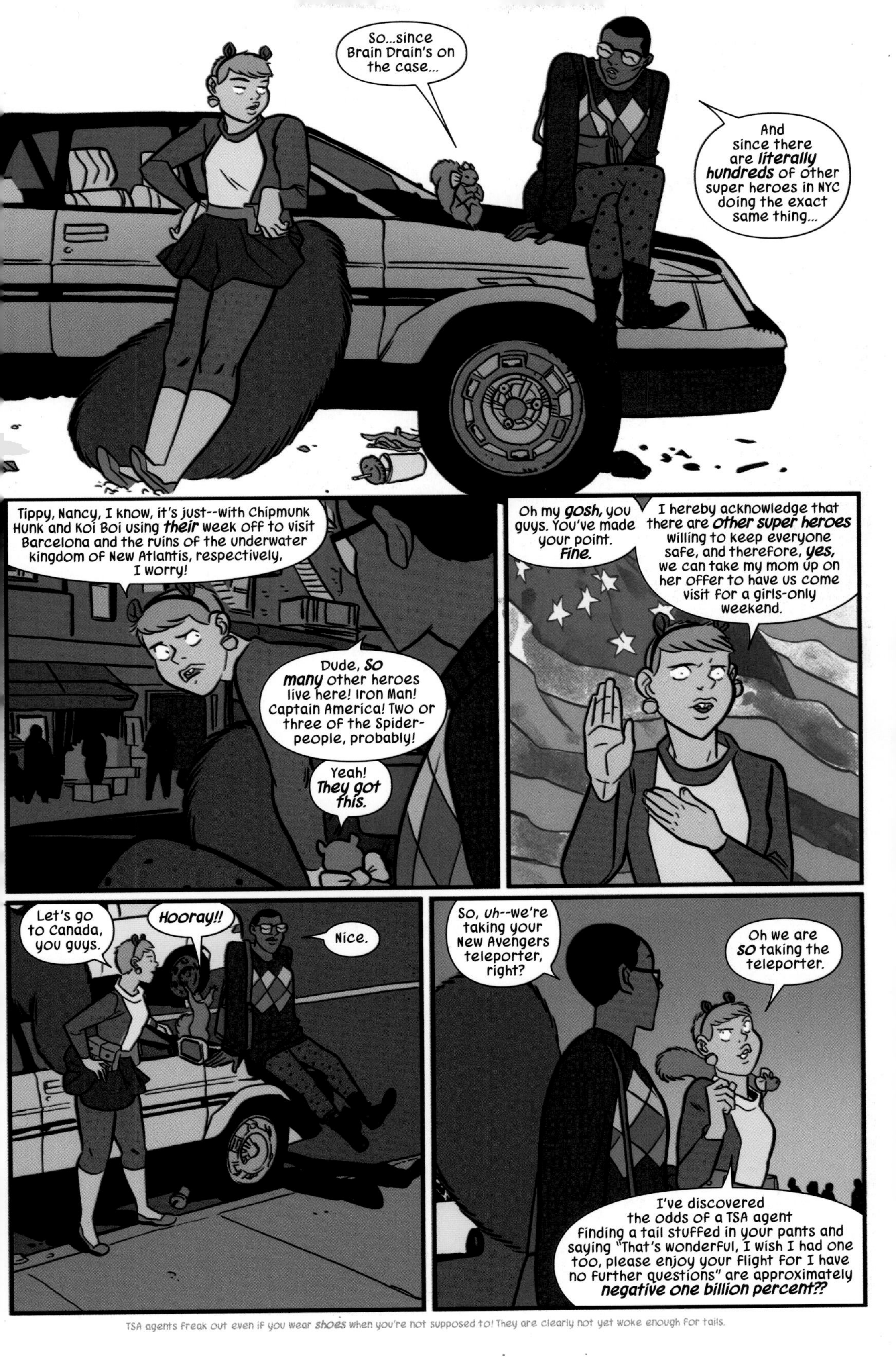
So...since Brain Drain's on the case...
And since there are literally hundreds of other super heroes in NYC doing the exact same thing...
Tippy, Nancy, I know, it's just--with Chipmunk Hunk and Koi Boi using their week off to visit Barcelona and the ruins of the underwater kingdom of New Atlantis, respectively, I worry!
Dude, so many other heroes live here! Iron Man! Captain America! Two or three of the Spider-people, probably!
Yeah! They got this.
Oh my gosh, you guys. You've made your point. Fine.
I hereby acknowledge that there are other super heroes willing to keep everyone safe, and therefore, yes, we can take my mom up on her offer to have us come visit for a girls-only weekend.
Let's go to Canada, you guys.
Hooray!!
Nice.
So, uh--we're taking your New Avengers teleporter, right?
Oh we are so taking the teleporter.
I've discovered the odds of a TSA agent finding a tail stuffed in your pants and saying "That's wonderful, I wish I had one too, please enjoy your flight for I have no further questions" are approximately negative one billion percent??

TSA agents freak out even if you wear *shoes* when you're not supposed to! They are clearly not yet woke enough for tails.

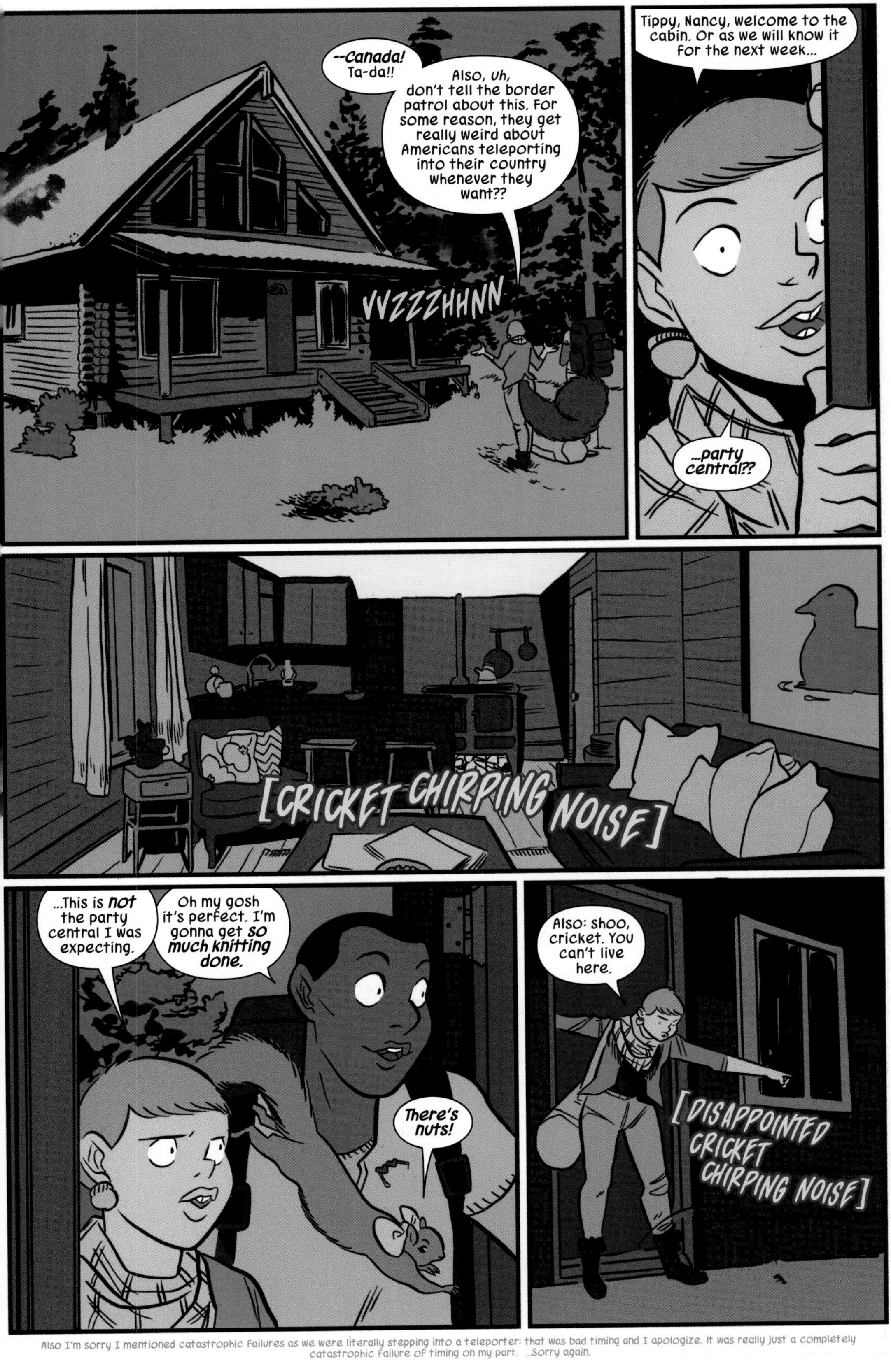
--Canada! Ta-da!!
Also, uh, don't tell the border patrol about this. For some reason, they get really weird about Americans teleporting into their country whenever they want??
VVZZZHHNN
Tippy, Nancy, welcome to the cabin. Or as we will know it for the next week...
...party central!??
[CRICKET CHIRPING NOISE]
...This is not the party central I was expecting.
Oh my gosh it's perfect. I'm gonna get so much knitting done.
There's nuts!
Also: shoo, cricket. You can't live here.
[DISAPPOINTED CRICKET CHIRPING NOISE]

Also I'm sorry I mentioned catastrophic failures as we were literally stepping into a teleporter: that was bad timing and I apologize. It was really just a completely catastrophic failure of timing on my part. ...Sorry again.

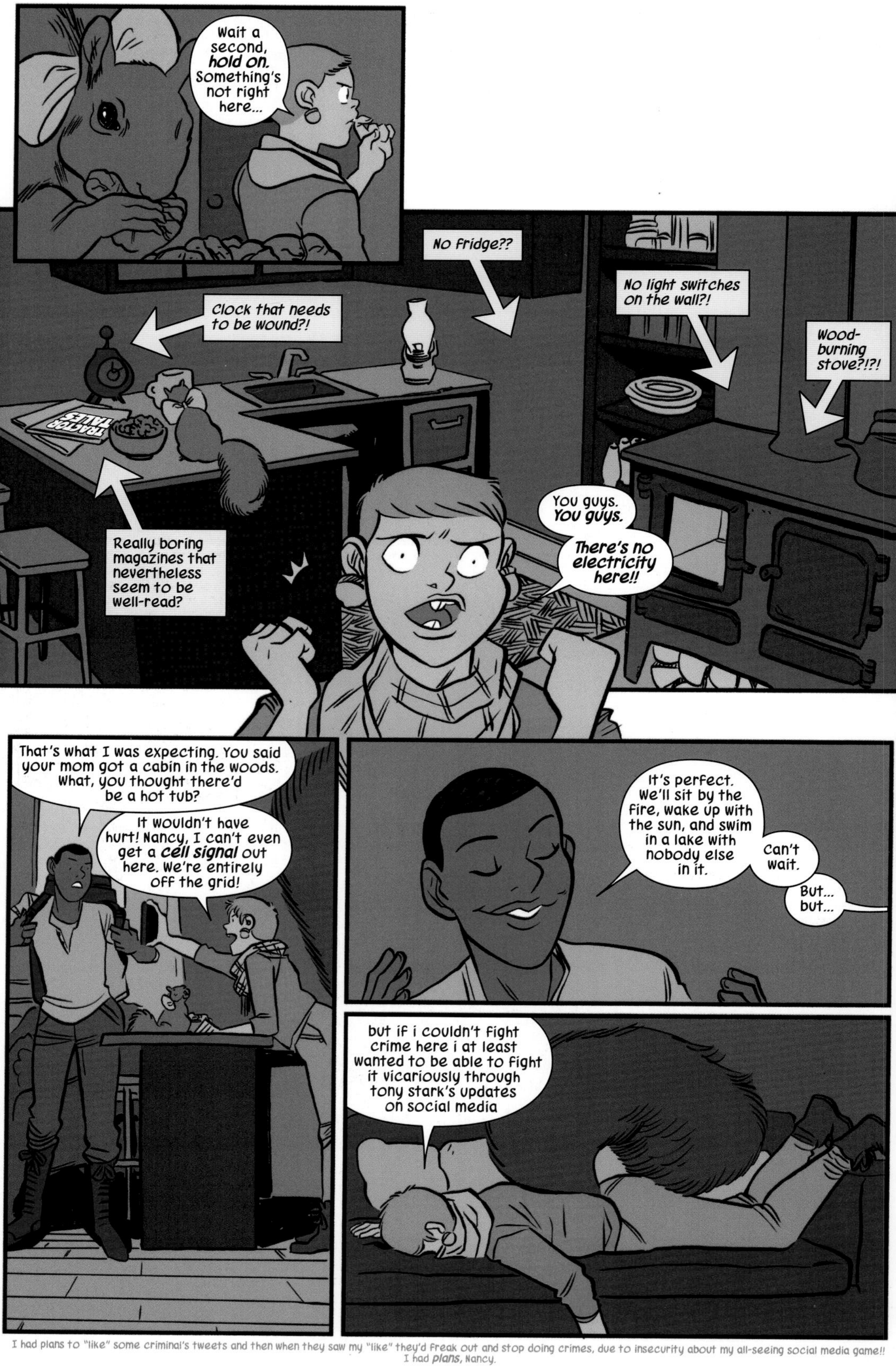
Wait a second, *hold on.* Something's not right here...
No fridge??
Clock that needs to be wound?!
No light switches on the wall?!
Wood-burning stove?!?!
TRACTOR TALES
Really boring magazines that nevertheless seem to be well-read?
You guys. *You guys.*
There's no electricity here!!
That's what I was expecting. You said your mom got a cabin in the woods. What, you thought there'd be a hot tub?
It wouldn't have hurt! Nancy, I can't even get a *cell signal* out here. We're entirely off the grid!
It's perfect. We'll sit by the fire, wake up with the sun, and swim in a lake with nobody else in it.
Can't wait.
But... but...
but if i couldn't fight crime here i at least wanted to be able to fight it vicariously through tony stark's updates on social media
I had plans to "like" some criminal's tweets and then when they saw my "like" they'd freak out and stop doing crimes, due to insecurity about my all-seeing social media game!! I had *plans,* Nancy.

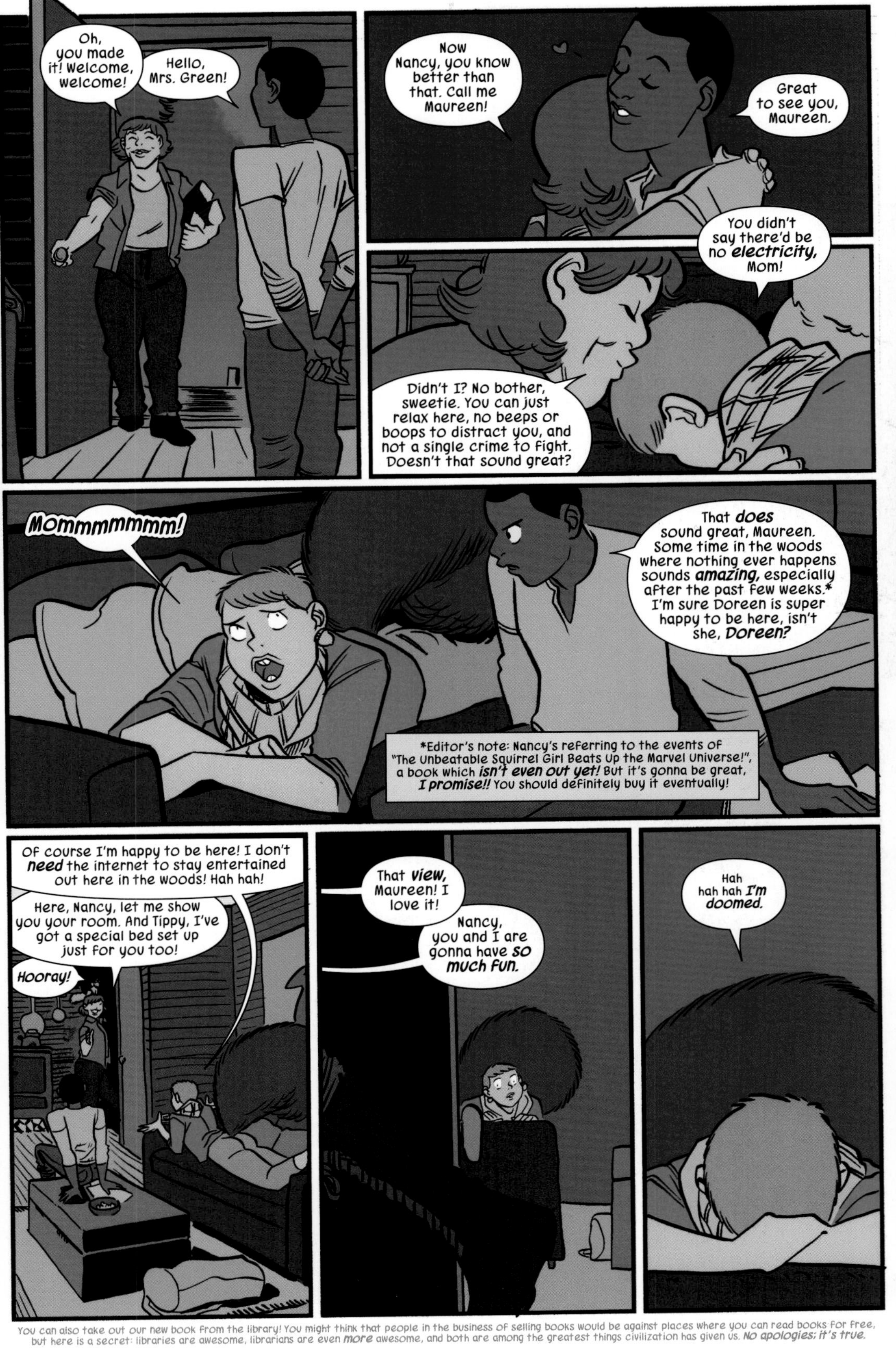

Oh, you made it! Welcome, welcome!
Hello, Mrs. Green!
Now Nancy, you know better than that. Call me Maureen!
Great to see you, Maureen.
You didn't say there'd be no electricity, Mom!
Didn't I? No bother, sweetie. You can just relax here, no beeps or boops to distract you, and not a single crime to fight. Doesn't that sound great?
MOmmmmmmm!
That does sound great, Maureen. Some time in the woods where nothing ever happens sounds amazing, especially after the past few weeks.* I'm sure Doreen is super happy to be here, isn't she, Doreen?
*Editor's note: Nancy's referring to the events of "The Unbeatable Squirrel Girl Beats Up the Marvel Universe!", a book which isn't even out yet! But it's gonna be great, I promise!! You should definitely buy it eventually!
Of course I'm happy to be here! I don't need the internet to stay entertained out here in the woods! Hah hah!
Here, Nancy, let me show you your room. And Tippy, I've got a special bed set up just for you too!
Hooray!
That view, Maureen! I love it!
Nancy, you and I are gonna have so much fun.
Hah hah hah I'm doomed.

You can also take out our new book from the library! You might think that people in the business of selling books would be against places where you can read books for free, but here is a secret: libraries are awesome, librarians are even *more* awesome, and both are among the greatest things civilization has given us. *No apologies; it's true.*

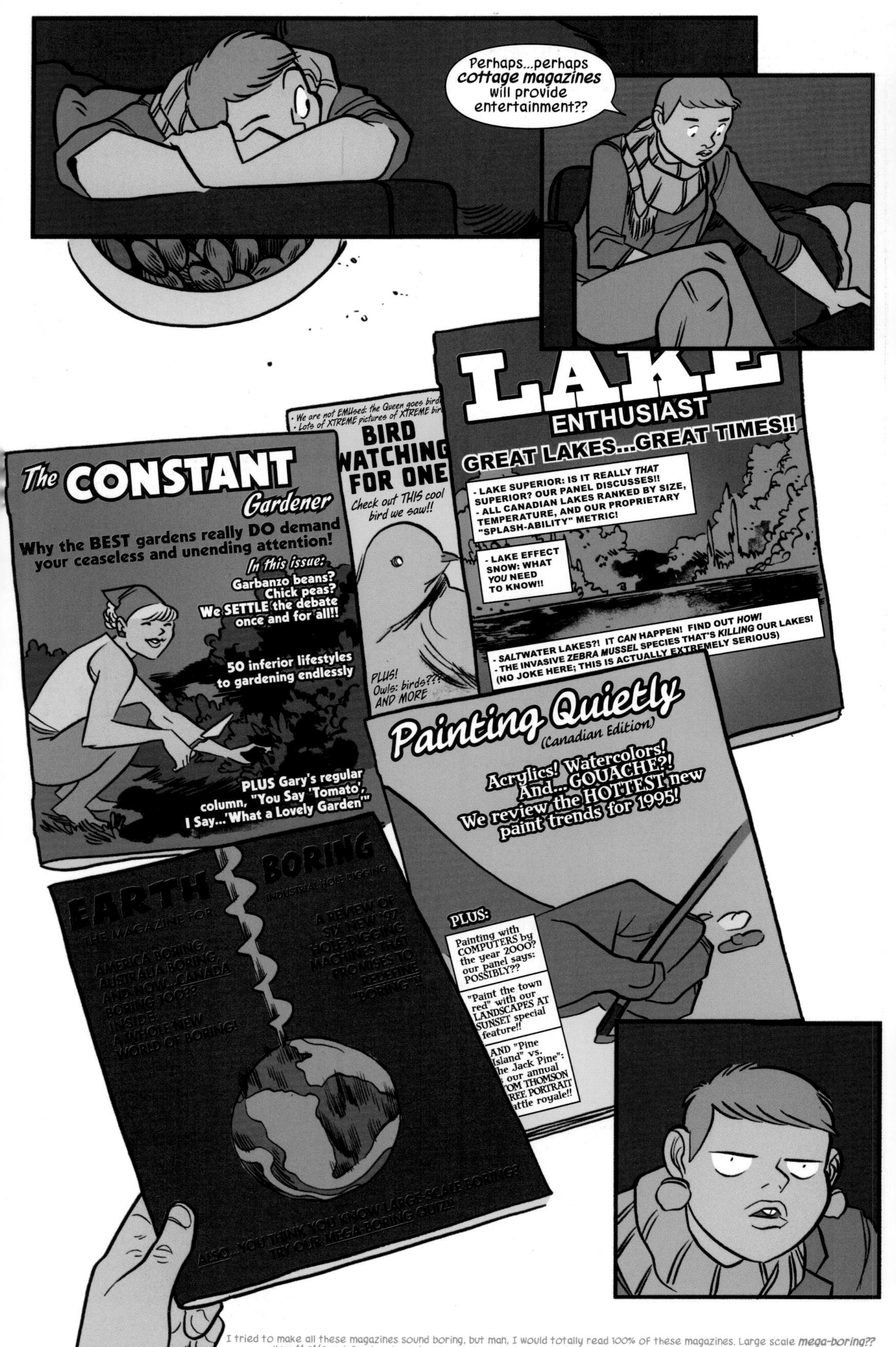

Perhaps...perhaps cottage magazines will provide entertainment??
The CONSTANT Gardener
Why the BEST gardens really DO demand your ceaseless and unending attention!
In this issue:
Garbanzo beans? Chick peas? We SETTLE the debate once and for all!!
50 inferior lifestyles to gardening endlessly
PLUS Gary's regular column, "You Say 'Tomato', I Say...'What a Lovely Garden'"
• We are not EMUsed: the Queen goes bird
• Lots of XTREME pictures of XTREME bir
BIRD WATCHING FOR ONE
Check out THIS cool bird we saw!!
PLUS! Owls: birds??? AND MORE
LAKE ENTHUSIAST
GREAT LAKES...GREAT TIMES!!
- LAKE SUPERIOR: IS IT REALLY THAT SUPERIOR? OUR PANEL DISCUSSES!!
- ALL CANADIAN LAKES RANKED BY SIZE, TEMPERATURE, AND OUR PROPRIETARY "SPLASH-ABILITY" METRIC!
- LAKE EFFECT SNOW: WHAT YOU NEED TO KNOW!!
- SALTWATER LAKES?! IT CAN HAPPEN! FIND OUT HOW!
- THE INVASIVE ZEBRA MUSSEL SPECIES THAT'S KILLING OUR LAKES! (NO JOKE HERE; THIS IS ACTUALLY EXTREMELY SERIOUS)
Painting Quietly (Canadian Edition)
Acrylics! Watercolors! And...GOUACHE?! We review the HOTTEST new paint trends for 1995!
PLUS:
Painting with COMPUTERS by the year 2000? our panel says: POSSIBLY??
"Paint the town red" with our LANDSCAPES AT SUNSET special feature!!
AND "Pine Island" vs. the Jack Pine": our annual TOM THOMSON REE PORTRAIT attle royale!!
EARTH BORING
THE MAGAZINE FOR INDUSTRIAL HOLE DIGGING
AMERICA BORING, AUSTRALIA BORING, AND NOW...CANADA BORING TOO?? INSIDE: A WHOLE NEW WORLD OF BORING!
A REVIEW OF SIX NEW '97 HOLE-DIGGING MACHINES THAT PROMISES TO REDEFINE "BORING"!!
ALSO...YOU THINK YOU KNOW LARGE-SCALE BORING? TRY OUR MEGA-BORING QUIZ!!

I tried to make all these magazines sound boring, but man, I would totally read 100% of these magazines. Large scale *mega-boring??* Now *that's* an infrastructure development project whose industry insider details I'm curious to learn more about!

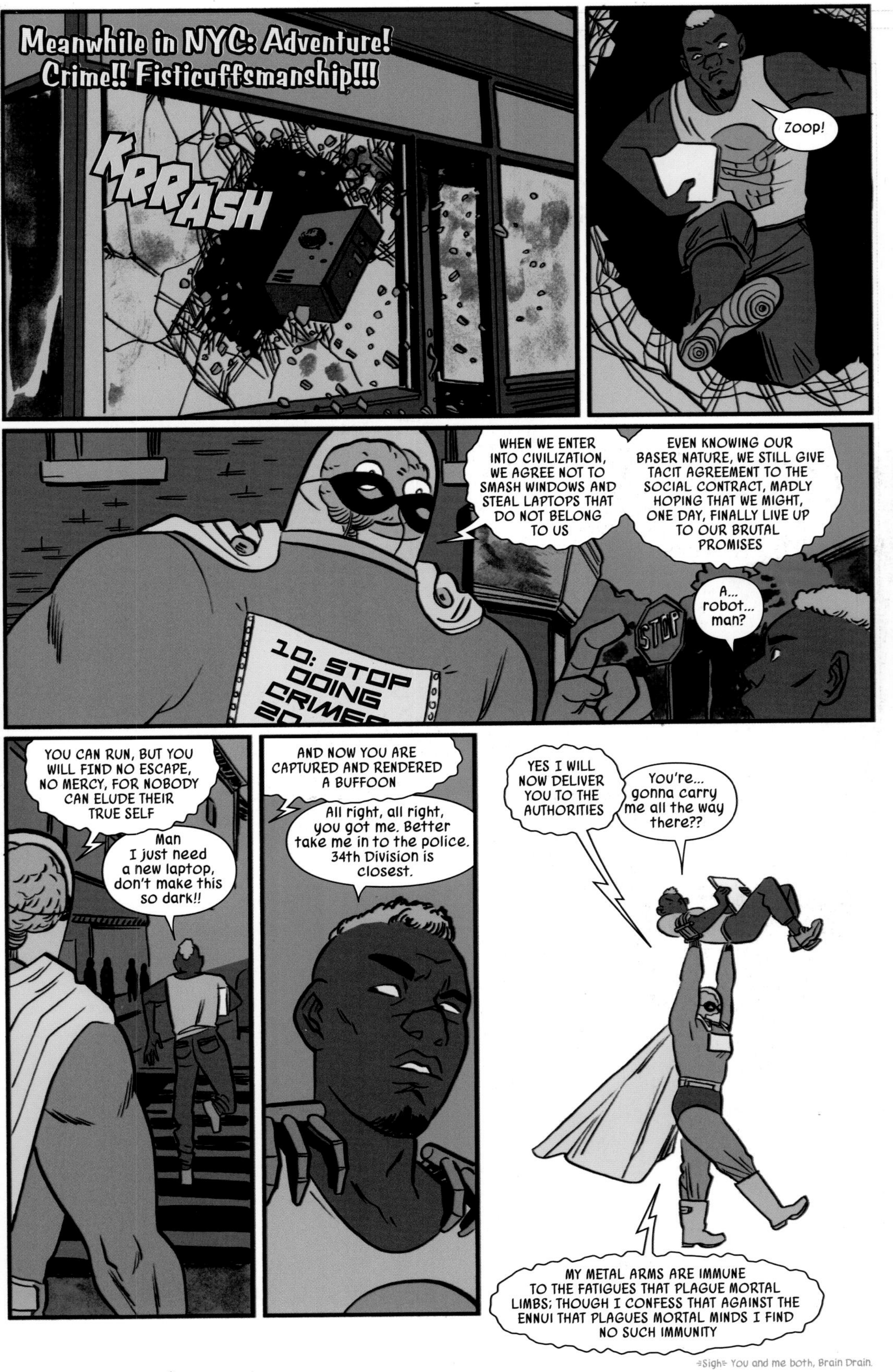

Meanwhile in NYC: Adventure! Crime!! Fisticuffsmanship!!!
KRRASH
Zoop!
WHEN WE ENTER INTO CIVILIZATION, WE AGREE NOT TO SMASH WINDOWS AND STEAL LAPTOPS THAT DO NOT BELONG TO US
EVEN KNOWING OUR BASER NATURE, WE STILL GIVE TACIT AGREEMENT TO THE SOCIAL CONTRACT, MADLY HOPING THAT WE MIGHT, ONE DAY, FINALLY LIVE UP TO OUR BRUTAL PROMISES
A... robot... man?
10: STOP
DOING
STOP
YOU CAN RUN, BUT YOU WILL FIND NO ESCAPE, NO MERCY, FOR NOBODY CAN ELUDE THEIR TRUE SELF
Man I just need a new laptop, don't make this so dark!!
AND NOW YOU ARE CAPTURED AND RENDERED A BUFFOON
All right, all right, you got me. Better take me in to the police. 34th Division is closest.
YES I WILL NOW DELIVER YOU TO THE AUTHORITIES
You're... gonna carry me all the way there??
MY METAL ARMS ARE IMMUNE TO THE FATIGUES THAT PLAGUE MORTAL LIMBS; THOUGH I CONFESS THAT AGAINST THE ENNUI THAT PLAGUES MORTAL MINDS I FIND NO SUCH IMMUNITY

=Sigh= You and me both, Brain Drain.

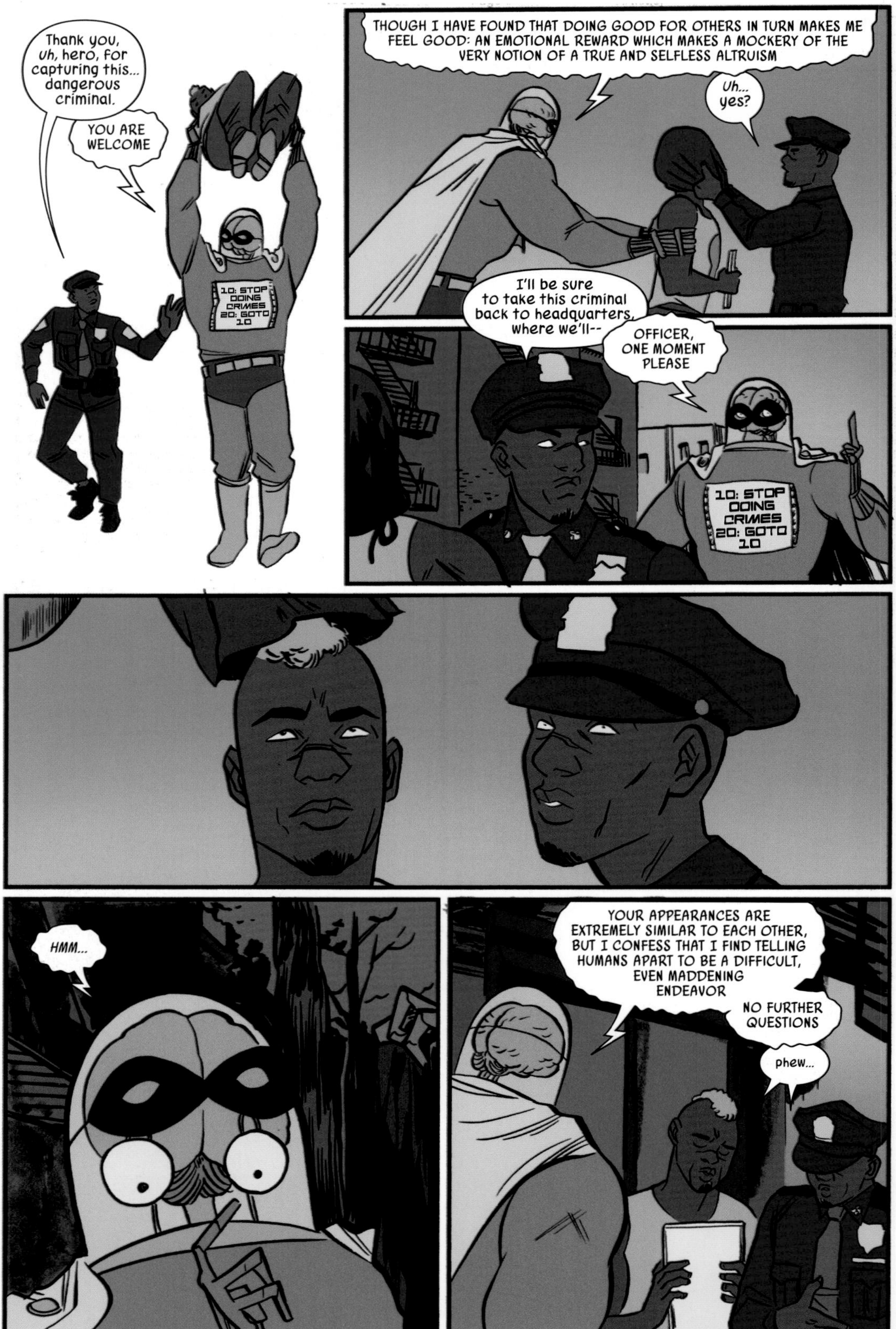
Thank you, uh, hero, for capturing this... dangerous criminal.
YOU ARE WELCOME
10: STOP DOING CRIMES 20: GOTO 10
THOUGH I HAVE FOUND THAT DOING GOOD FOR OTHERS IN TURN MAKES ME FEEL GOOD: AN EMOTIONAL REWARD WHICH MAKES A MOCKERY OF THE VERY NOTION OF A TRUE AND SELFLESS ALTRUISM
Uh... yes?
I'll be sure to take this criminal back to headquarters, where we'll--
OFFICER, ONE MOMENT PLEASE
10: STOP DOING CRIMES 20: GOTO 10
HMM...
YOUR APPEARANCES ARE EXTREMELY SIMILAR TO EACH OTHER, BUT I CONFESS THAT I FIND TELLING HUMANS APART TO BE A DIFFICULT, EVEN MADDENING ENDEAVOR
NO FURTHER QUESTIONS
phew...

Brain Drain has trouble telling humans apart, but can remember their names with the efficiency of a robot man. In contrast, I can distinguish between *thousands* of people whose names I've long ago forgotten and now it's way way ***way*** too late to ask. Life is full of challenges, everyone!!

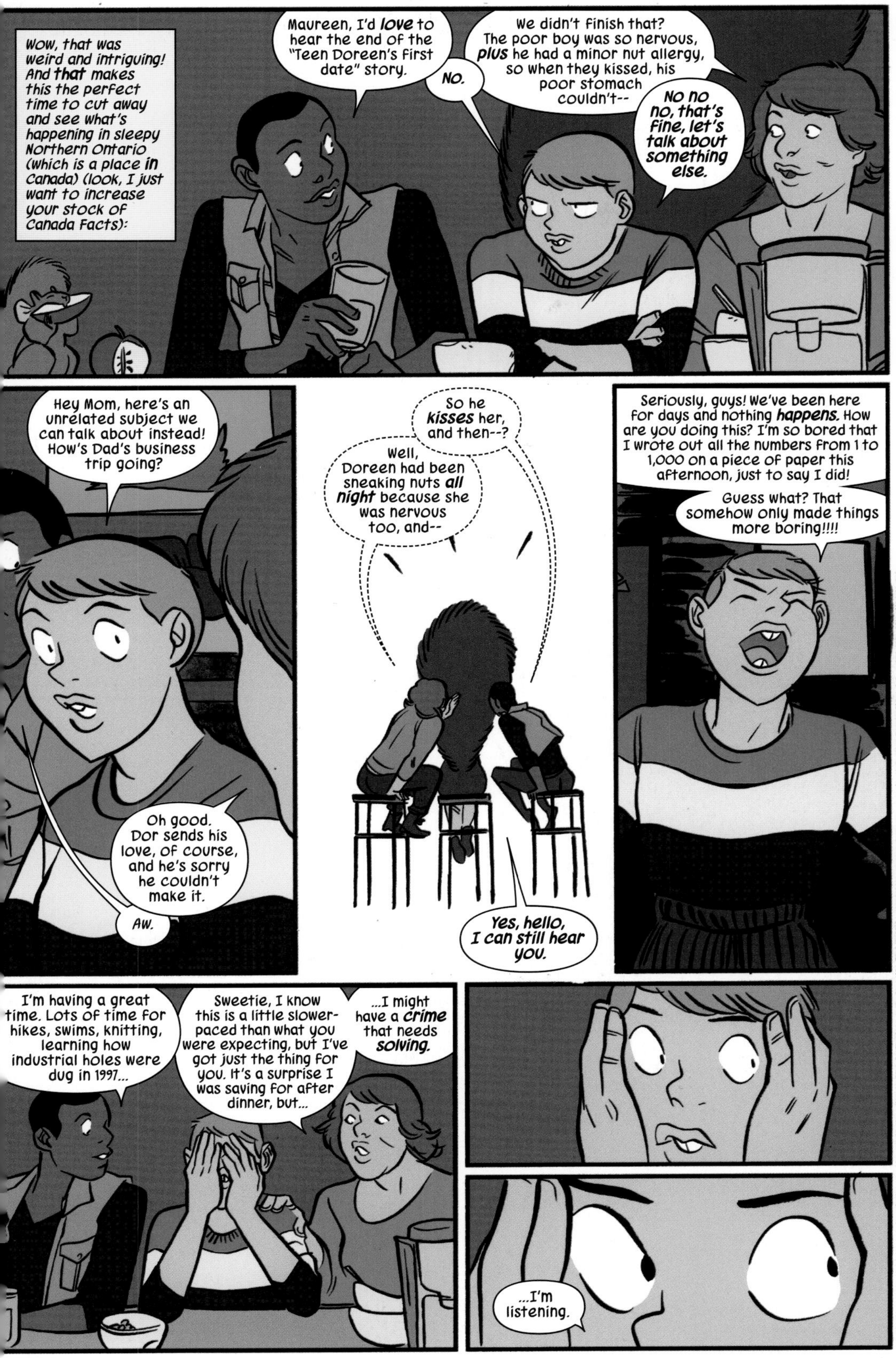

Wow, that was weird and intriguing! And that makes this the perfect time to cut away and see what's happening in sleepy Northern Ontario (which is a place in Canada) (look, I just want to increase your stock of Canada Facts):
Maureen, I'd love to hear the end of the "Teen Doreen's First date" story.
NO.
We didn't finish that? The poor boy was so nervous, plus he had a minor nut allergy, so when they kissed, his poor stomach couldn't--
No no no, that's fine, let's talk about something else.
Hey Mom, here's an unrelated subject we can talk about instead! How's Dad's business trip going?
Oh good. Dor sends his love, of course, and he's sorry he couldn't make it.
AW.
So he kisses her, and then--?
Well, Doreen had been sneaking nuts all night because she was nervous too, and--
Yes, hello, I can still hear you.
Seriously, guys! We've been here for days and nothing happens. How are you doing this? I'm so bored that I wrote out all the numbers from 1 to 1,000 on a piece of paper this afternoon, just to say I did!
Guess what? That somehow only made things more boring!!!!
I'm having a great time. Lots of time for hikes, swims, knitting, learning how industrial holes were dug in 1997...
Sweetie, I know this is a little slower-paced than what you were expecting, but I've got just the thing for you. It's a surprise I was saving for after dinner, but...
...I might have a crime that needs solving.
...I'm listening.

Squirrel Girl has learned a lot about herself on this trip, primarily that she has a super-weakness to getting bored when there's nothing to do and no internet around. Keep it a secret, okay? Friends don't spread their friends' super-weaknesses around!!

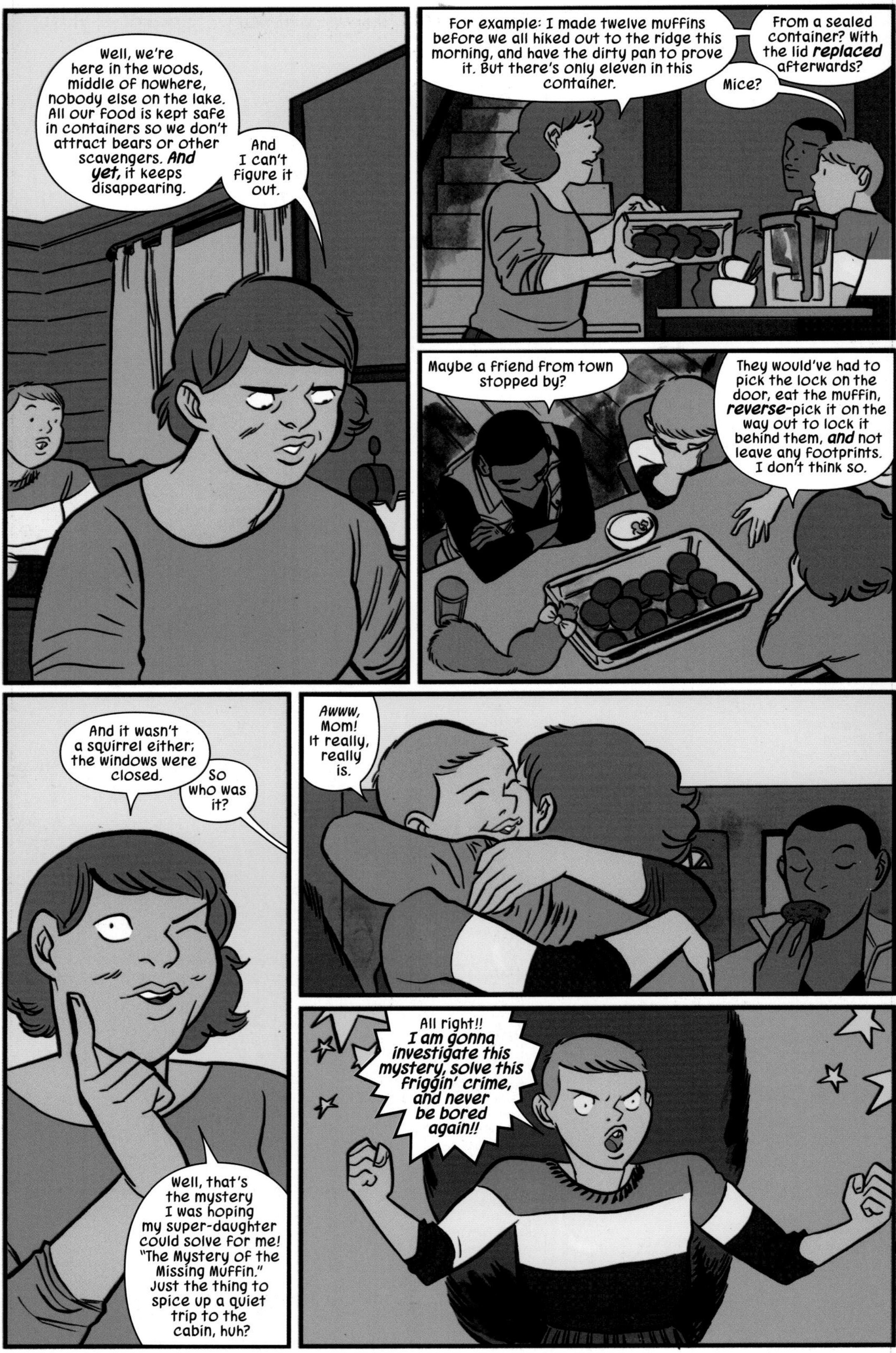
Well, we're here in the woods, middle of nowhere, nobody else on the lake. All our food is kept safe in containers so we don't attract bears or other scavengers. And yet, it keeps disappearing.
And I can't figure it out.
For example: I made twelve muffins before we all hiked out to the ridge this morning, and have the dirty pan to prove it. But there's only eleven in this container.
Mice?
From a sealed container? With the lid replaced afterwards?
Maybe a friend from town stopped by?
They would've had to pick the lock on the door, eat the muffin, reverse-pick it on the way out to lock it behind them, and not leave any footprints. I don't think so.
And it wasn't a squirrel either; the windows were closed.
So who was it?
Well, that's the mystery I was hoping my super-daughter could solve for me! "The Mystery of the Missing Muffin." Just the thing to spice up a quiet trip to the cabin, huh?
Awww, Mom! It really, really is.
All right!! I am gonna investigate this mystery, solve this friggin' crime, and never be bored again!!

Alternative titles for this case: "The Case of the Cupcake Caper," "Just Desserts," and "The Mysterious Muffin of Skellington Bay" (did you know: if a bay doesn't have a name, you can *probably* just name that bay??)

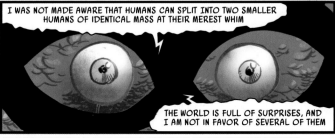

HOWEVER I HAVE BEEN TOLD THAT SOMETIMES THE SURPRISES ARE KITTENS AND ICE CREAM, SO I HOLD OUT HOPE, EVER DREAMING OF THE ICE CREAM KITTEN IN MY FUTURE

Canada:

Local squirrels don't report anyone coming or going for weeks, Doreen, except us. They--

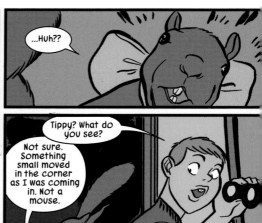

...Huh??

Tippy? What do you see?

Not sure. Something small moved in the corner as I was coming in. Not a mouse.

What was it then?

I wanna say...pants? Red and/or green, possibly?

Pants.

Look, prey animal here. My vision's *so legit* I can see things out of the corner of my eye as clearly as if I was looking right at 'em.

And I'm telling you, I saw *something* in tiny pants slip through this crack.

Well, you're not tearing up the floor, Doreen. This is a rental.

No, that's fair...but there *is* another way. And it's arguably even *more* fun??

All right! Everyone out of the house!!

Most squirrels are red/green colorblind, which means they have trouble telling red and green apart. If you share this property too, then good news! You have at least one *squirrel super-power*, and that's more than most people can say!

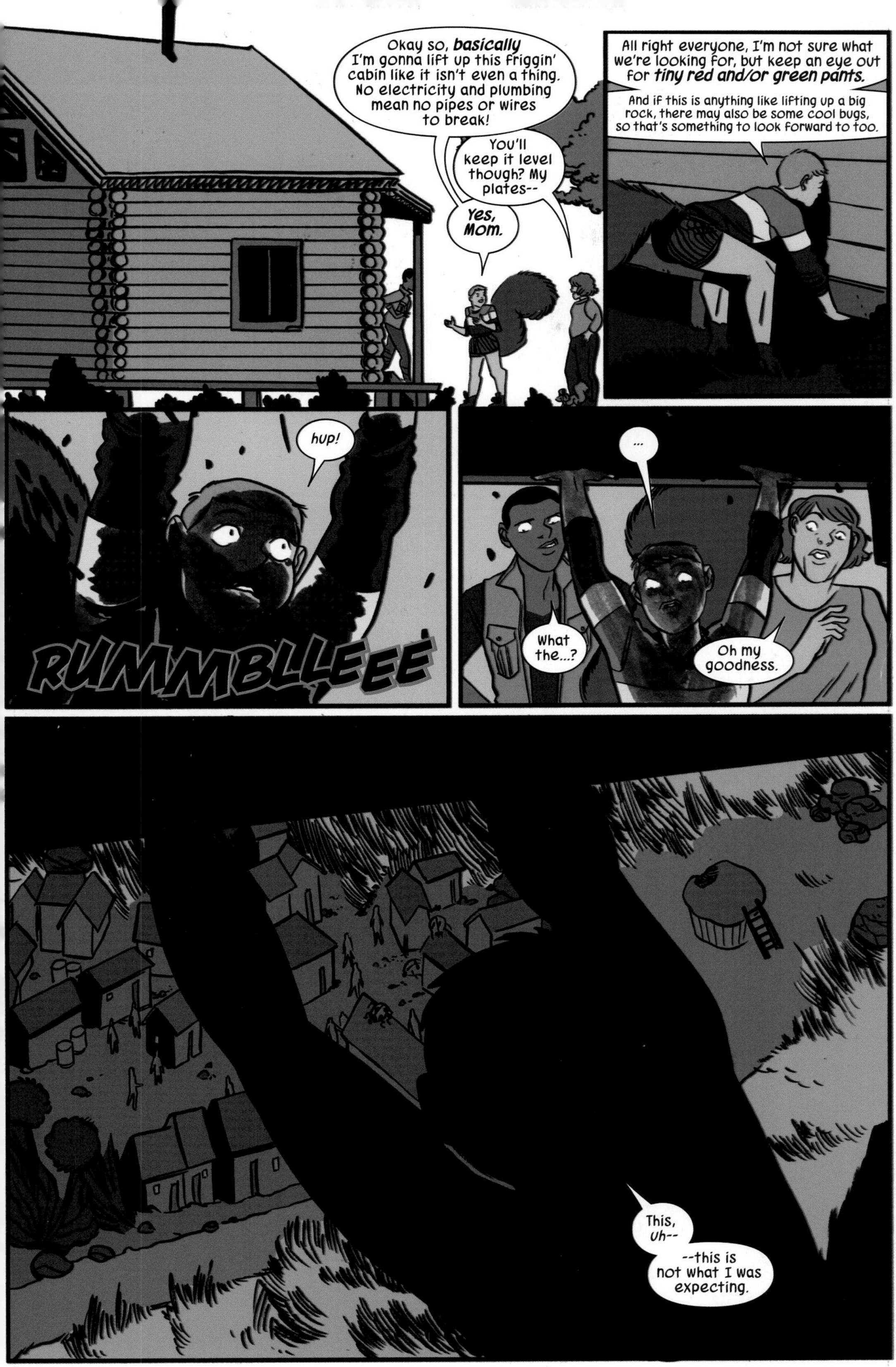
Okay so, **basically** I'm gonna lift up this friggin' cabin like it isn't even a thing. No electricity and plumbing mean no pipes or wires to break!
You'll keep it level though? My plates--
Yes, Mom.
All right everyone, I'm not sure what we're looking for, but keep an eye out for ***tiny red and/or green pants.***
And if this is anything like lifting up a big rock, there may also be some cool bugs, so that's something to look forward to too.
hup!
RUMMBLLEEE
...
What the...?
Oh my goodness.
This, uh--
--this is not what I was expecting.

Honestly: I'm not sure what I was expecting, but I feel confident in saying that "a tiny village beneath the floorboards" is the polar opposite of that.

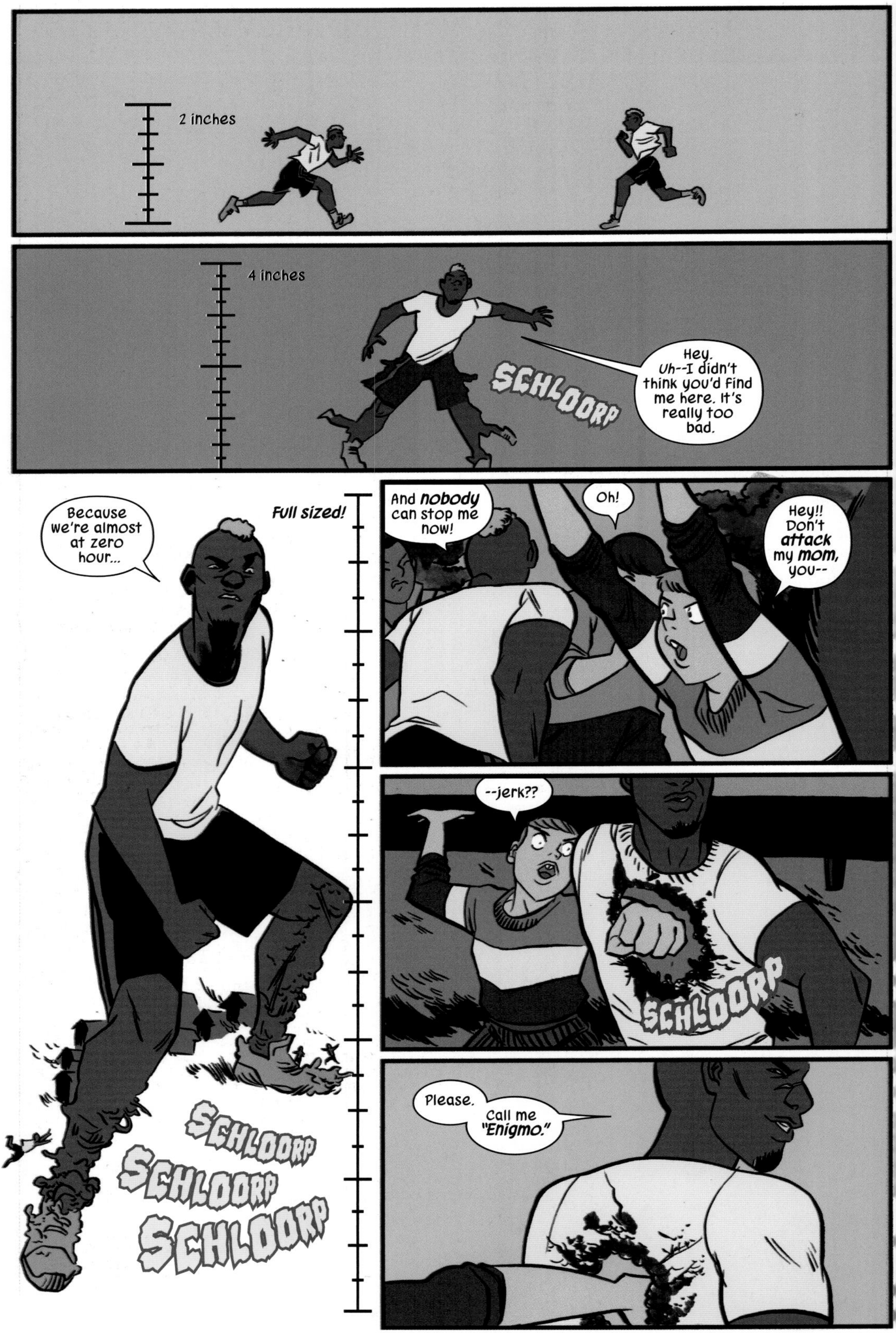
2 inches
4 inches
SCHLOORP
Hey. Uh--I didn't think you'd find me here. It's really too bad.
Because we're almost at zero hour...
Full sized!
SCHLOORP
SCHLOORP
SCHLOORP
And nobody can stop me now!
Oh!
Hey!! Don't attack my mom, you--
--jerk??
SCHLOORP
Please.
Call me "Enigmo."

Enigmo. No, like "enigma," but with an "o." Enigmo. Look, do you have a pen? I can write it--no, it's not "Edward Nigmo"! You're thinking of another guy, and you're not even remembering him that accurately!!

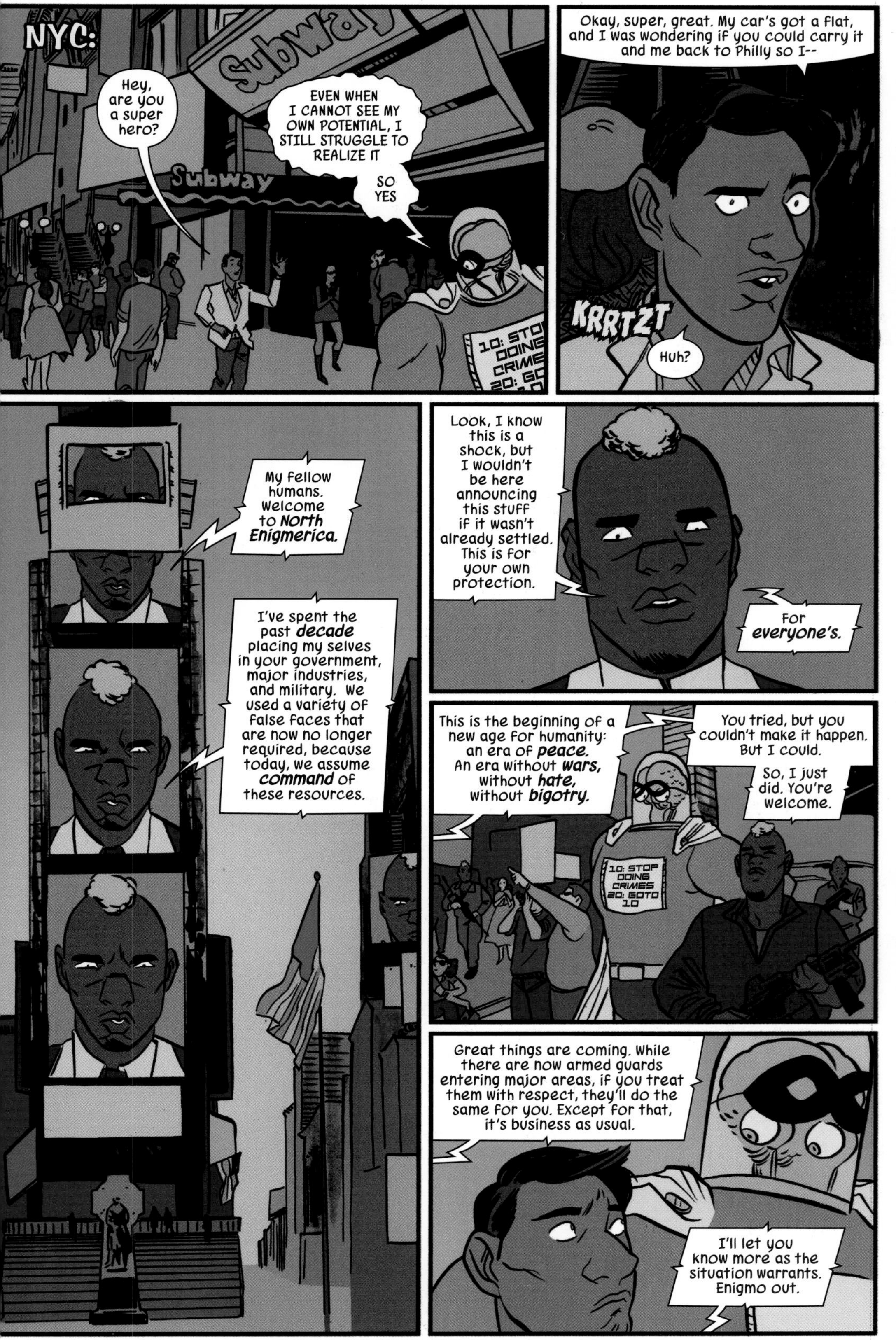
NYC:
Subway
Hey, are you a super hero?
EVEN WHEN I CANNOT SEE MY OWN POTENTIAL, I STILL STRUGGLE TO REALIZE IT
SO YES
Subway
Okay, super, great. My car's got a flat, and I was wondering if you could carry it and me back to Philly so I--
KRRTZT
Huh?
My fellow humans. Welcome to North Enigmerica.
I've spent the past decade placing my selves in your government, major industries, and military. We used a variety of false faces that are now no longer required, because today, we assume command of these resources.
Look, I know this is a shock, but I wouldn't be here announcing this stuff if it wasn't already settled. This is for your own protection.
For everyone's.
This is the beginning of a new age for humanity: an era of peace. An era without wars, without hate, without bigotry.
You tried, but you couldn't make it happen. But I could.
So, I just did. You're welcome.
10: STOP DOING CRIMES 20: GOTO 10
Great things are coming. While there are now armed guards entering major areas, if you treat them with respect, they'll do the same for you. Except for that, it's business as usual.
I'll let you know more as the situation warrants. Enigmo out.

Well, looks like that's it for NYC! But now let's cut back to what everyone's really concerned about: the quiet northern nation of Canada!!

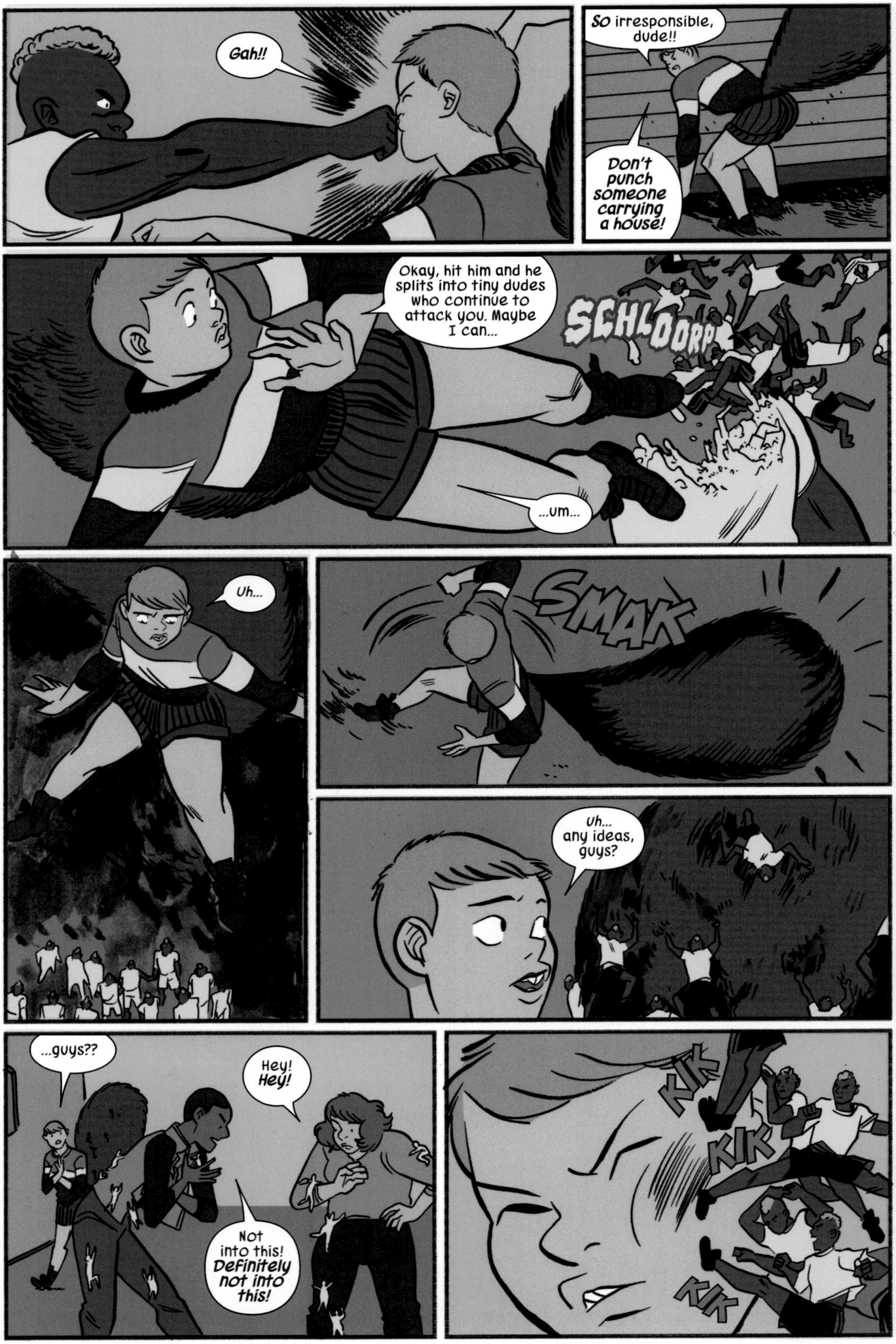
Gah!!
So irresponsible, dude!!
Don't punch someone carrying a house!
Okay, hit him and he splits into tiny dudes who continue to attack you. Maybe I can...
SCHLOORP
...um...
Uh...
SMAK
Uh... any ideas, guys?
...guys??
Hey! Hey!
Not into this! Definitely not into this!
KIK
KIK
KIK

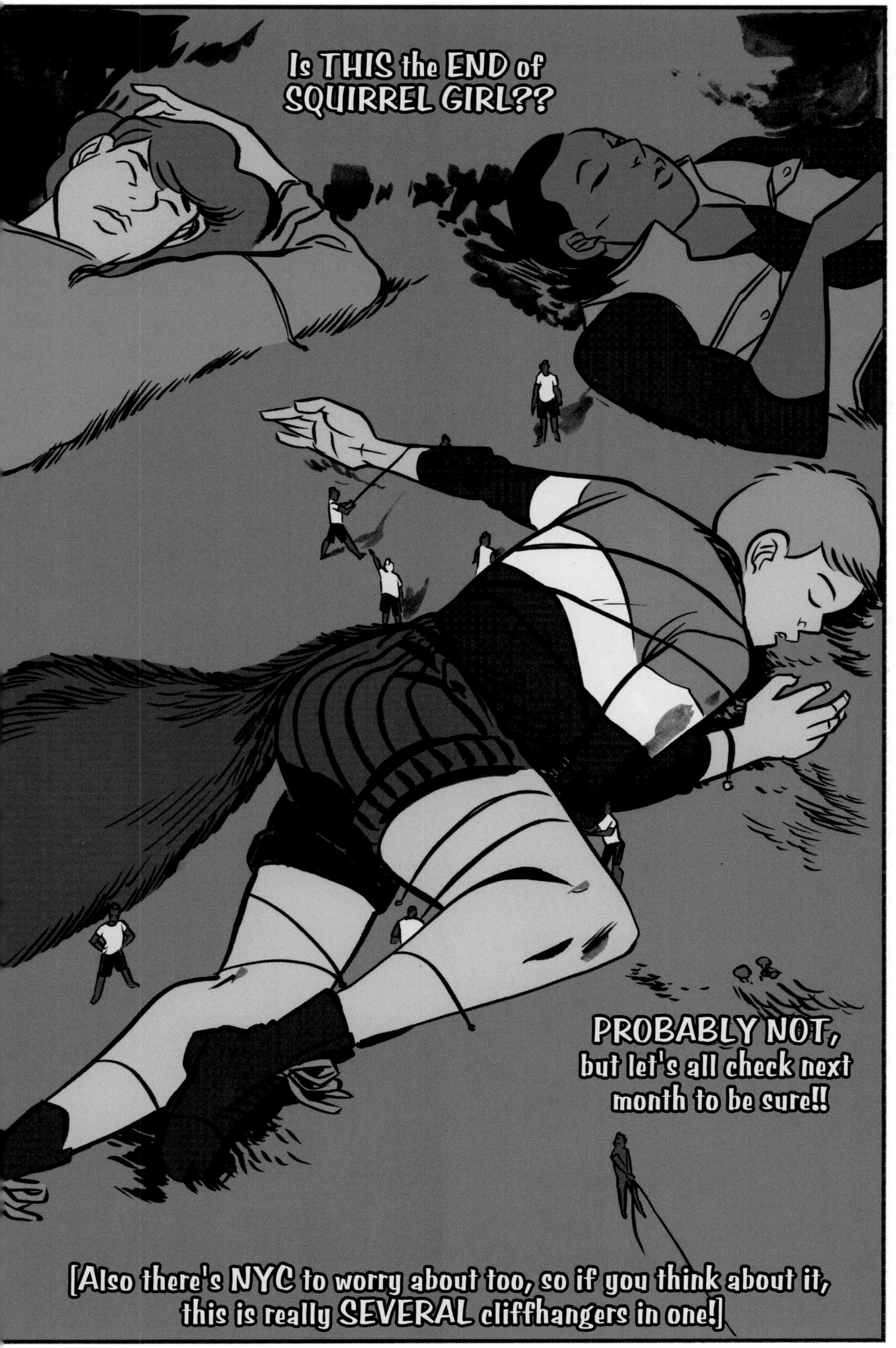
Is THIS the END of SQUIRREL GIRL??
PROBABLY NOT, but let's all check next month to be sure!!
[Also there's NYC to worry about too, so if you think about it, this is really SEVERAL cliffhangers in one!]

Plus we're gonna have a guest star next month! His identity might be a...*tiny* bit surprising?

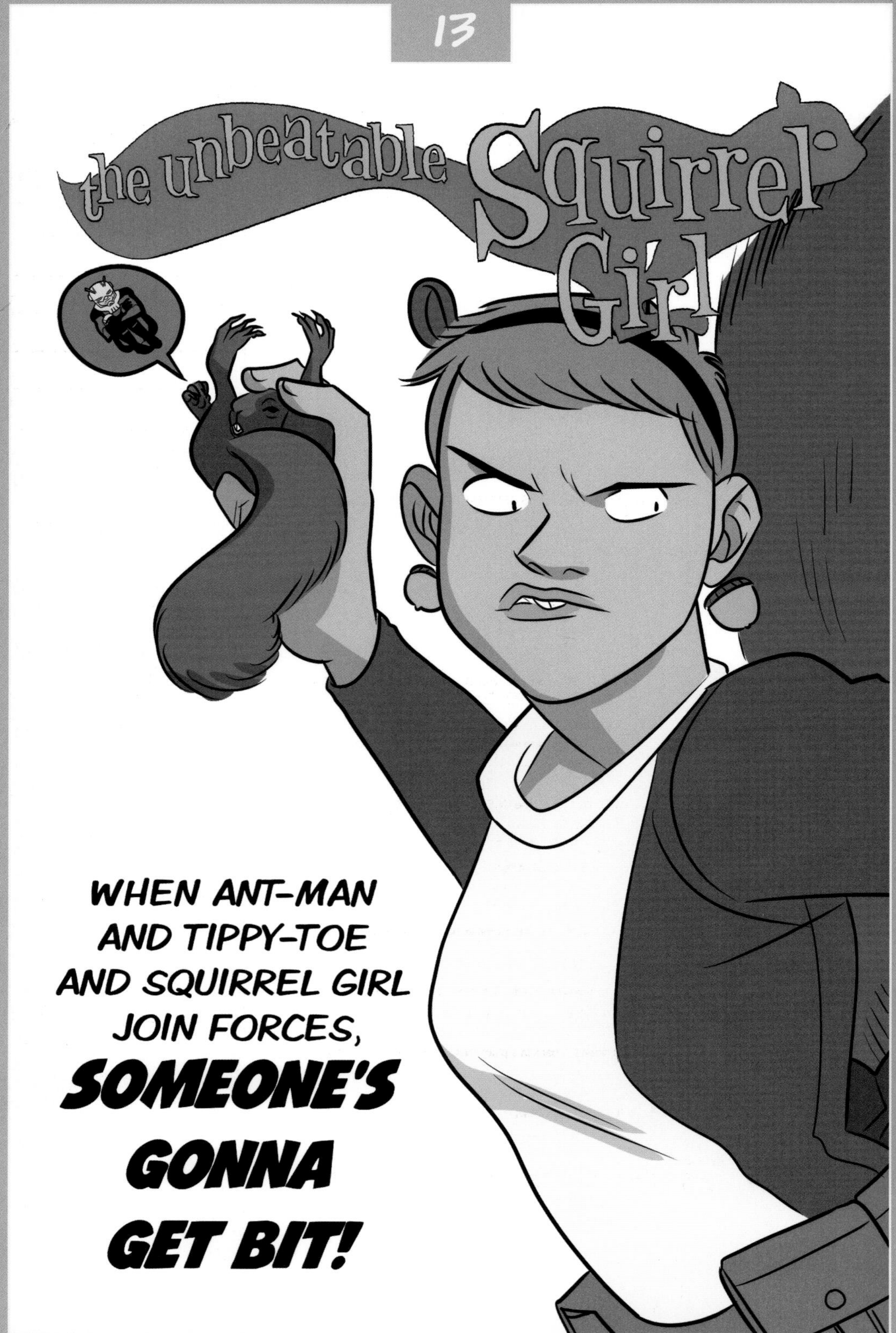
13
the unbeatable Squirrel Girl
WHEN ANT-MAN AND TIPPY-TOE AND SQUIRREL GIRL JOIN FORCES,
SOMEONE'S GONNA GET BIT!

*Doreen Green isn't just a second-year computer science student: she secretly also has all the powers of both squirrel and girl! She uses her amazing abilities to fight crime **and** be as awesome as possible. You know her as...**The Unbeatable Squirrel Girl!** Find out what she's been up to, with...*

Squirrel Girl in a nutshell

Squirrel Girl @unbeatablesg
guys i'm SO BORED, i'm up here in CANADA but there's NOTHING TO DO except read boring magazines

Squirrel Girl @unbeatablesg
and the magazines are SO BORING that i can no longer use punctuation or capital letters

Squirrel Girl @unbeatablesg
boredom has literally sucked the ability to use punctuation out of me

Squirrel Girl @unbeatablesg
science thought it couldn't be done

Squirrel Girl @unbeatablesg
but here we are

Squirrel Girl @unbeatablesg
me with internet: HI I'M COOL AND CAN DISCUSS SEVERAL INTERESTING SUBJECTS!!!
me without internet: i wonder what bark tastes like

Squirrel Girl @unbeatablesg
me with internet: I HAVE SEVERAL HOT TAKES ABOUT TODAY'S NEWS!!
me without internet: so it's decided: i can sneeze at least 3 different ways

Squirrel Girl @unbeatablesg
me with internet: CAN'T WAIT TO CHILL WITH MY PAL TONY STARK ON SOCIAL MEDIA
me without internet: me and that rock are bffs, don't @ me

Squirrel Girl @unbeatablesg
me with internet: WOW SO THAT'S WHAT MY ROBOT PAL BRAIN DRAIN IS DOING IN NYC!
me without internet: i have unsolicited opinions on gardening

Squirrel Girl @unbeatablesg
UPDATE: guys it's a few hours later and things are more interesting now!! There's a CRIME going on!

Squirrel Girl @unbeatablesg
Someone is stealing muffins from my mom!! It's the CASE of the MISSING MUFFINS and I am ON IT

Squirrel Girl @unbeatablesg
also yes I am aware of how pathetic this sounds but listen, I NEED THIS

Squirrel Girl @unbeatablesg
UPDATE 2: okay it turns out there's a whole city of tiny men living beneath our rental cottage who can split apart and back together

Squirrel Girl @unbeatablesg
and who are attacking us on sight for some reason that I don't know!! WHOA!!

Squirrel Girl @unbeatablesg
Anyway I queued these all to post when I'm back in a place that has FRIGGIN' DATA but I should really get back to it

Squirrel Girl @unbeatablesg
Can't fake being knocked out FOREVER, you know?

Squirrel Girl @unbeatablesg
Plus, these tiny Enigmos who are trying to tie me to the ground aren't gonna let me use my phone indefinitely, I'm pretty sure

search!

#canadafacts
#dontatme
#gardening
#thatsapaddlin
#enigmos

This is the Canadian Forest: quiet, peaceful, serene...that is, until *Enigmo the splitty-apart bad guy* wakes up! (He's a bad guy who splits apart into smaller bad guys who can also split apart, and now we're all up to speed.)

See, what happens is he gets so small that air can carry him, and then you breathe in Enigmo dust, and then you've got tiny Enigmos in your lungs that smush together to form a larger but still pretty tiny Enigmo inside your lungs. **Hard pass.**

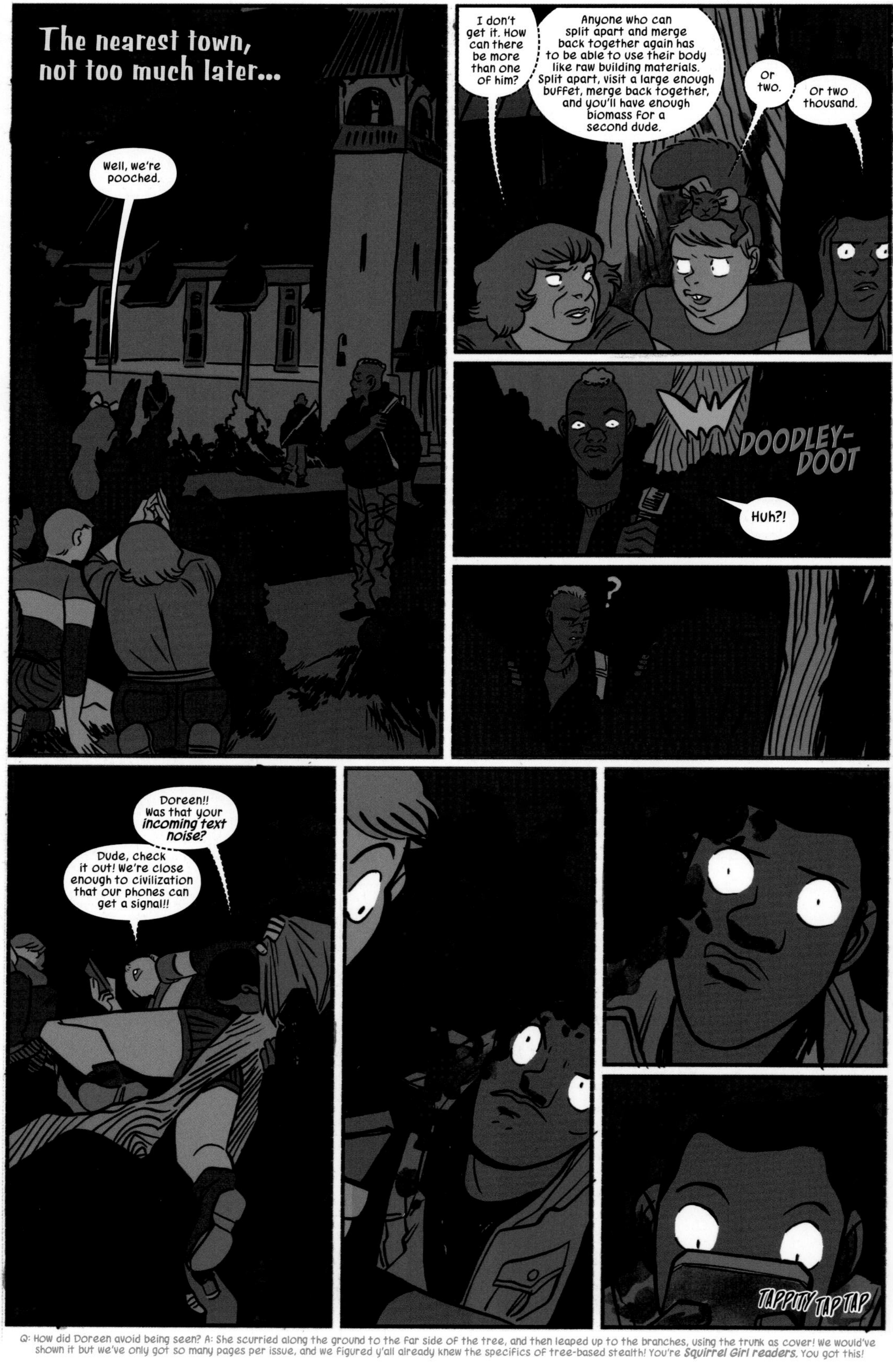
The nearest town, not too much later...
Well, we're pooched.
I don't get it. How can there be more than one of him?
Anyone who can split apart and merge back together again has to be able to use their body like raw building materials. Split apart, visit a large enough buffet, merge back together, and you'll have enough biomass for a second dude.
Or two.
Or two thousand.
DOODLEY-DOOT
Huh?!
?
Doreen!! Was that your incoming text noise?
Dude, check it out! We're close enough to civilization that our phones can get a signal!!
TAPPITY TAP TAP

Q: How did Doreen avoid being seen? A: She scurried along the ground to the far side of the tree, and then leaped up to the branches, using the trunk as cover! We would've shown it but we've only got so many pages per issue, and we figured y'all already knew the specifics of tree-based stealth! You're ***Squirrel Girl readers.*** You got this!

Uh, guys, I think you'll want to read this.

The news sites aren't doing much better.

SPIDER-MAN
hey anyone know what's going on?? same guy is everywhere at the same time? if it's cloning i'm gonna flip a table, omg

TONY STARK
Doreen, message me when you get this. We, uh, could use a hand.

THOR (LADY ONE <3)
Squirrel Girl, your digits come to me from Stark. I message now as we face an emergency of legendary proportions. Verily, hit me back.

HOWARD
soem guy calleld "enigom" juts toko over new yokr cityq but espelcicayly my ofifce, can u coem hepl me get ti back k thnkas!!!!1

HULK (AMADEUS CHO ONE):
SQUIRREL GIRL!! HULK whoa caps lock sorry! Squirrel Girl, Hulk here. We need you. We're being overwhelmed. Where are you?

GLOBAL MESSAGING SYSTEM:
ATTENTION CITIZENS: OUTGOING TEXT MESSAGING SERVICES ARE NOW PROVIDED BY AND TO ENIGMOS ONLY. WE THANK YOU FOR YOUR UNDERSTANDING IN THIS TIME OF TRANSITION. ENIGMO OUT.

NEW YORK ✷ BULLETIN
TOP HEADLINES:

Everyone In Power Is Enigmo Now...And That's Great!!	Vigilantism Is Now Illegal, All Remaining "Super Heroes" To Happily Stand Down Any Minute Now

Military Taken Over By Engimo! Public Relieved, Because It Was Actually Really Dangerous To Have All Those Weapons In The Hands Of Strangers

BREAKING: Enigmo Objectively a Better Leader than All Other Leaders Combined	Public Unanimous: New State-Controlled Media "Endlessly Perfect"!

PLUS: New "Life's a Laff with Enigmo" Special Comics Section

See, Mom? See?

This is what we get for staying in a place without internet!!

So are we--

Yes okay fine let's go fix it

alos he kcikde me in teh btutt adn caleld me "quackres," whikc, like, *heollo* I've hearfd rthem all ebfore! I've herads thme alol befoer, sqyulkrel guril!! waugh!!! anywya hti me bakc

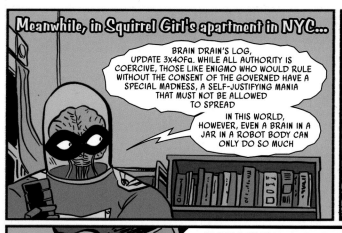

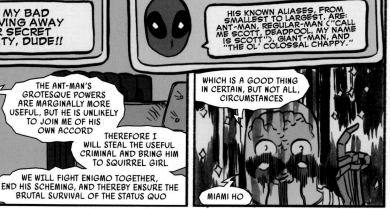

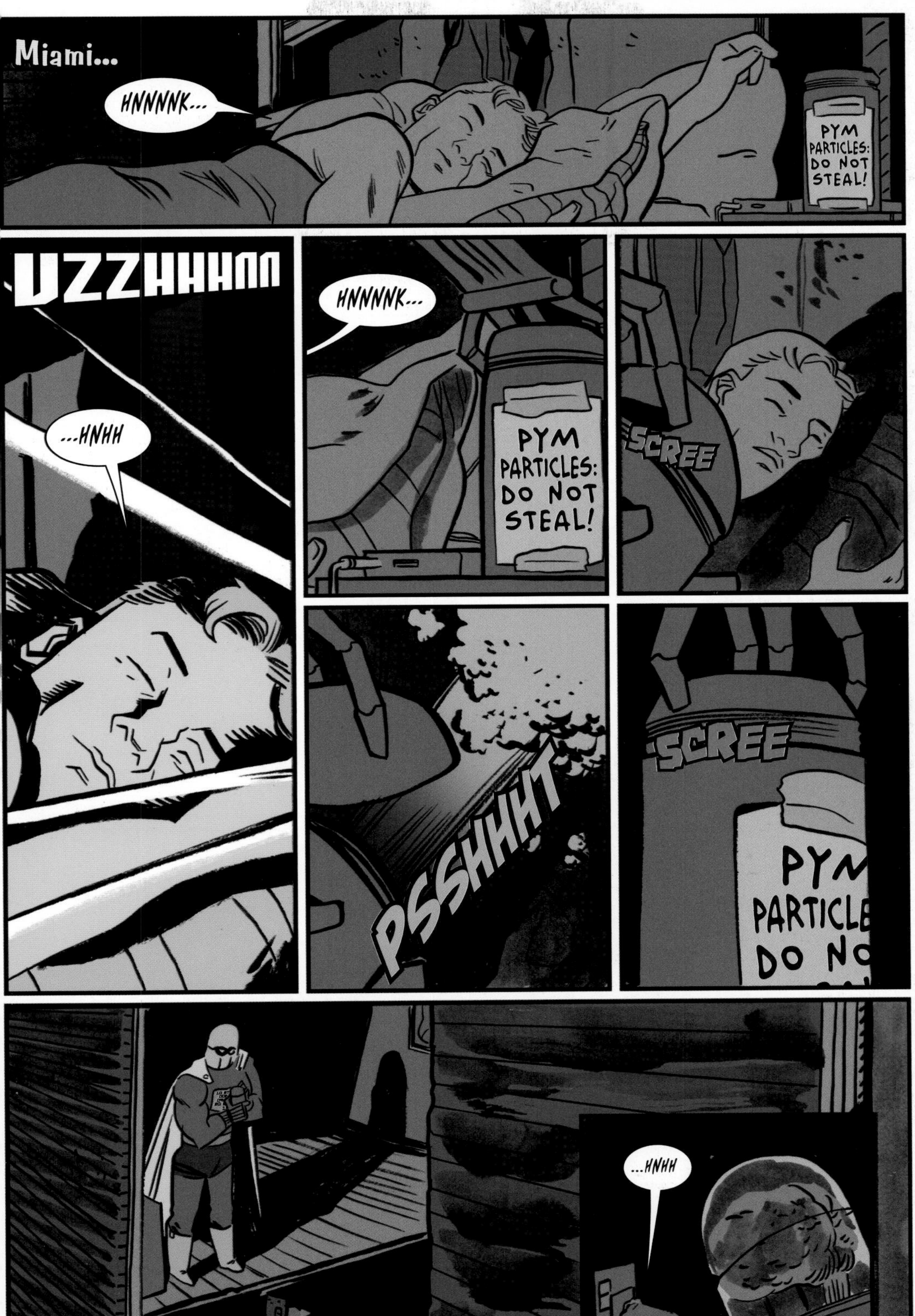
Miami...
HNNNNK...
PYM PARTICLES: DO NOT STEAL!
VZZHHHNN
...HNHH
HNNNNK...
PYM PARTICLES: DO NOT STEAL!
SCREE
PSSHHHT
SCREE
PYM PARTICLE DO NO
...HNHH

Those "HNNNNK" and "HNHH" are snoring sound effects. I created them by listening to someone snore as they slept while taking detailed notes!!

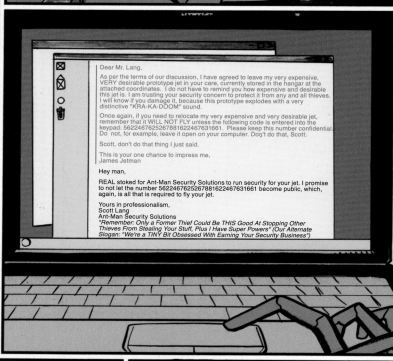

Our Backup Alternate Slogan: "You CAN'T Steal What You CAN'T See (We Shrink Down Things To Ant Size So Criminals Can't Steal Them, So That's Why That Capitalization Makes Sense)

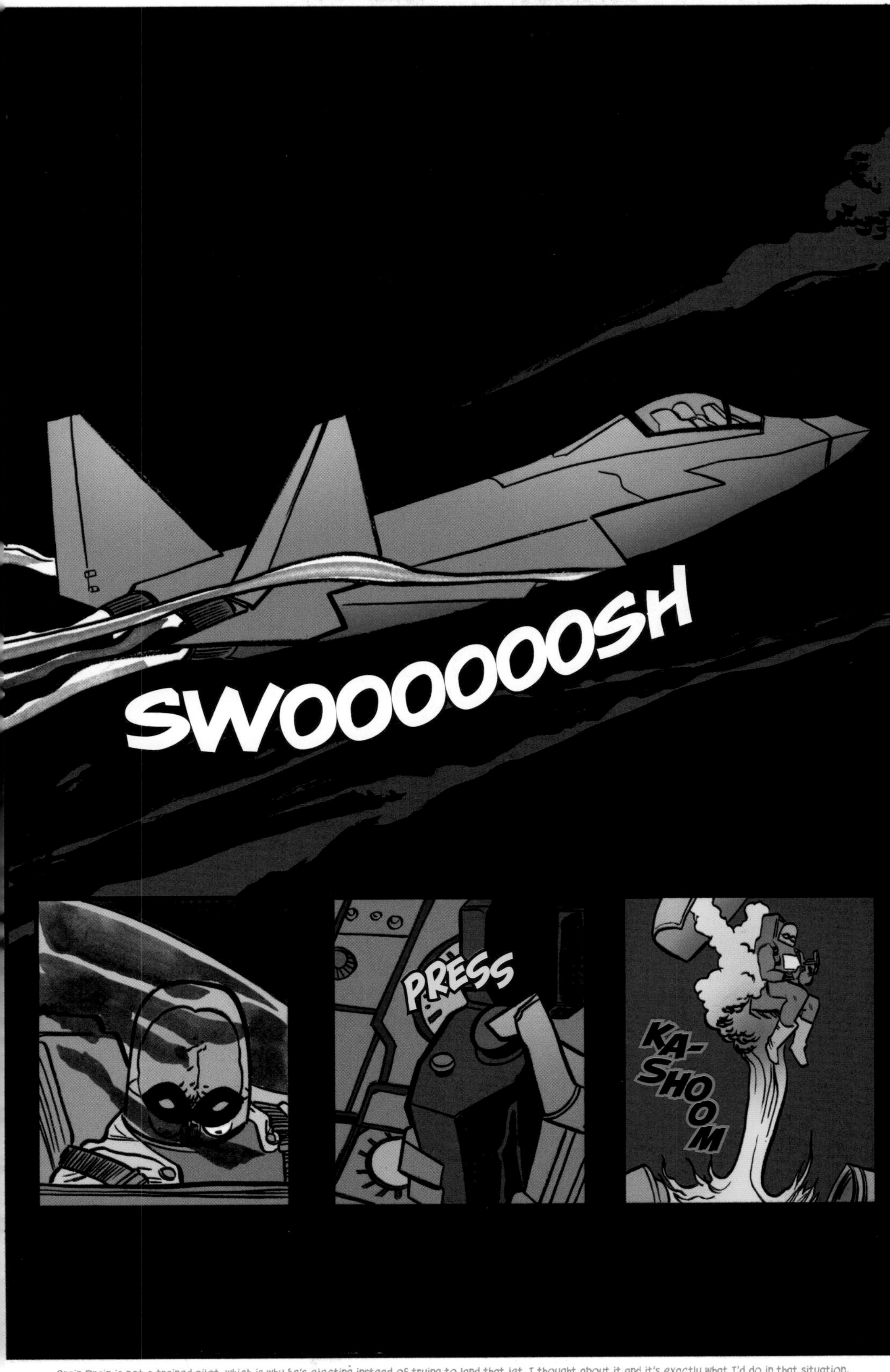
SWOOOOOOSH
PRESS
KA-SHOOM

Brain Drain is not a trained pilot, which is why he's ejecting instead of trying to land that jet. I thought about it and it's exactly what I'd do in that situation, which means it is extremely realistic, because I myself am also extremely realistic!!

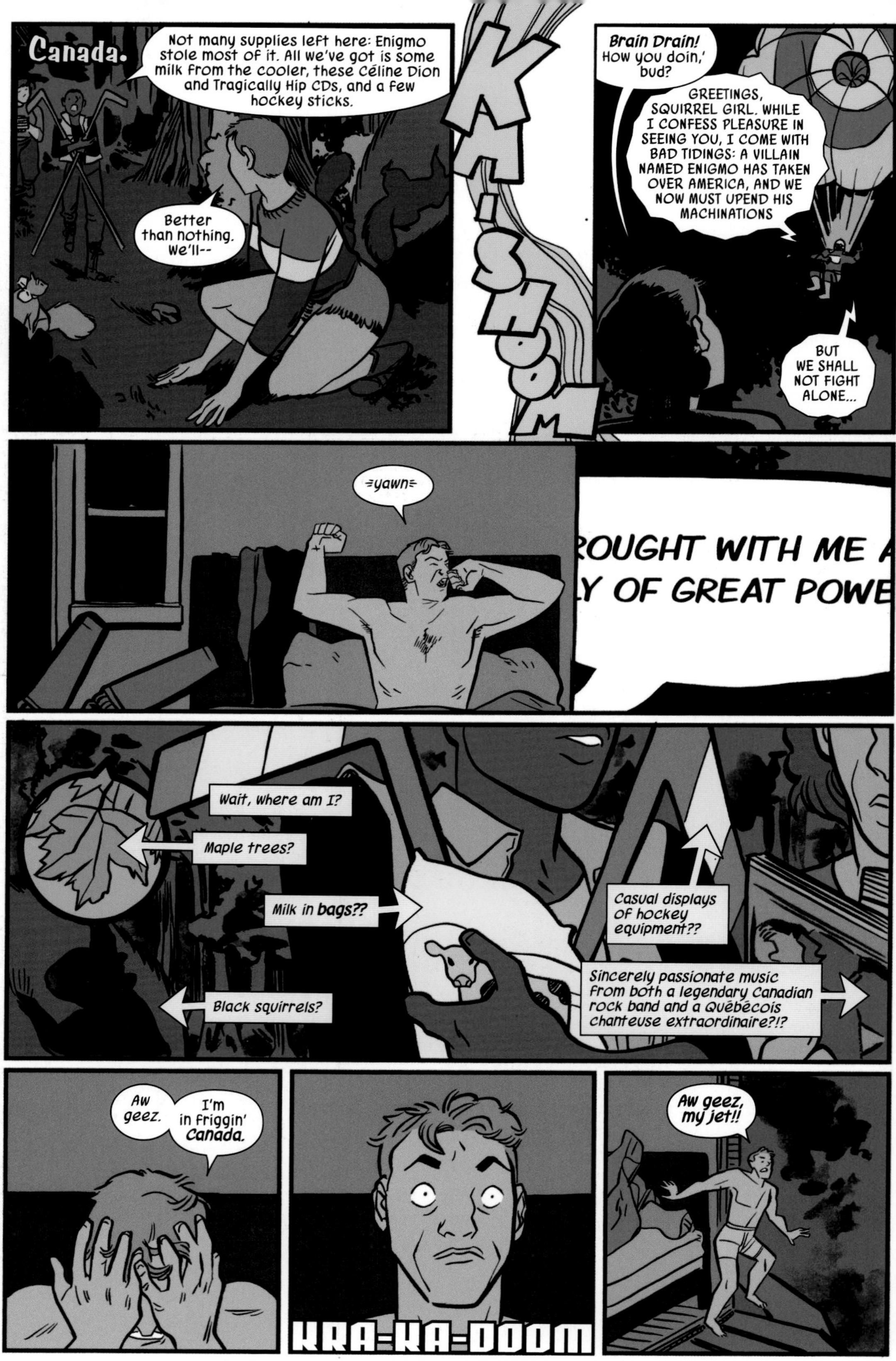
Canada.
Not many supplies left here: Enigmo stole most of it. All we've got is some milk from the cooler, these Céline Dion and Tragically Hip CDs, and a few hockey sticks.
Better than nothing. We'll--
KA-SHOOM
Brain Drain! How you doin,' bud?
GREETINGS, SQUIRREL GIRL. WHILE I CONFESS PLEASURE IN SEEING YOU, I COME WITH BAD TIDINGS: A VILLAIN NAMED ENIGMO HAS TAKEN OVER AMERICA, AND WE NOW MUST UPEND HIS MACHINATIONS
BUT WE SHALL NOT FIGHT ALONE...
ROUGHT WITH ME A
LY OF GREAT POWE
=yawn=
Wait, where am I?
Maple trees?
Milk in bags??
Casual displays of hockey equipment??
Black squirrels?
Sincerely passionate music from both a legendary Canadian rock band and a Québécois chanteuse extraordinaire?!?
Aw geez.
I'm in friggin' Canada.
KRA-KA-DOOM
Aw geez, my jet!!

Scott's just lucky that Maureen left all the cod, fiddle music, poutine, and dulse inside.

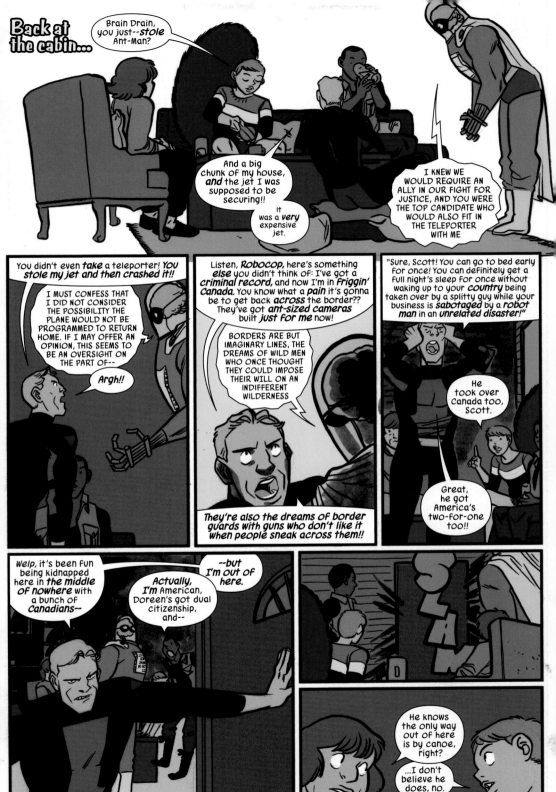

Brain Drain, you just--*stole* Ant-Man?

And a big chunk of my house, *and* the jet I was supposed to be securing!!

It was a *very* expensive jet.

I KNEW WE WOULD REQUIRE AN ALLY IN OUR FIGHT FOR JUSTICE, AND YOU WERE THE TOP CANDIDATE WHO WOULD ALSO FIT IN THE TELEPORTER WITH ME

You didn't even *take* a teleporter! *You stole my jet and then crashed it!!*

I MUST CONFESS THAT I DID NOT CONSIDER THE POSSIBILITY THE PLANE WOULD NOT BE PROGRAMMED TO RETURN HOME. IF I MAY OFFER AN OPINION, THIS SEEMS TO BE AN OVERSIGHT ON THE PART OF--

Argh!!

Listen, *Robocop*, here's something *else* you didn't think of: I've got a *criminal record*, and now I'm in *friggin' Canada*. You know what a *pain* it's gonna be to get back *across* the border?? They've got *ant-sized cameras* built *just for me* now!

BORDERS ARE BUT IMAGINARY LINES, THE DREAMS OF WILD MEN WHO ONCE THOUGHT THEY COULD IMPOSE THEIR WILL ON AN INDIFFERENT WILDERNESS

They're also the dreams of border guards with guns who don't like it when people sneak across them!!

"Sure, Scott! You can go to bed early for once! You can definitely get a full night's sleep for once without waking up to your *country* being taken over by a splitty guy while your business is *sabotaged* by a *robot man* in an *unrelated disaster!*"

He took over Canada too, Scott.

Great, he got America's two-for-one too!!

Welp, it's been fun being kidnapped here in *the middle of nowhere* with a bunch of *Canadians*--

Actually, I'm American, Doreen's got dual citizenship, and--

--but I'm *out* of here.

He knows the only way out of here is by canoe, right?

...I don't believe he does, no.

There are some international borders that go right through the middle of cities, even buildings! Borders are *crazy!* Nobody tell Brain Drain though, it sounds like he's got enough opinions about them already.

That Canadian human-powered pleasure craft law is legit. Also, yes, Canadian lawyers call canoes "human-powered pleasure craft," which should tell you all you need to know about Canadian lawyers.

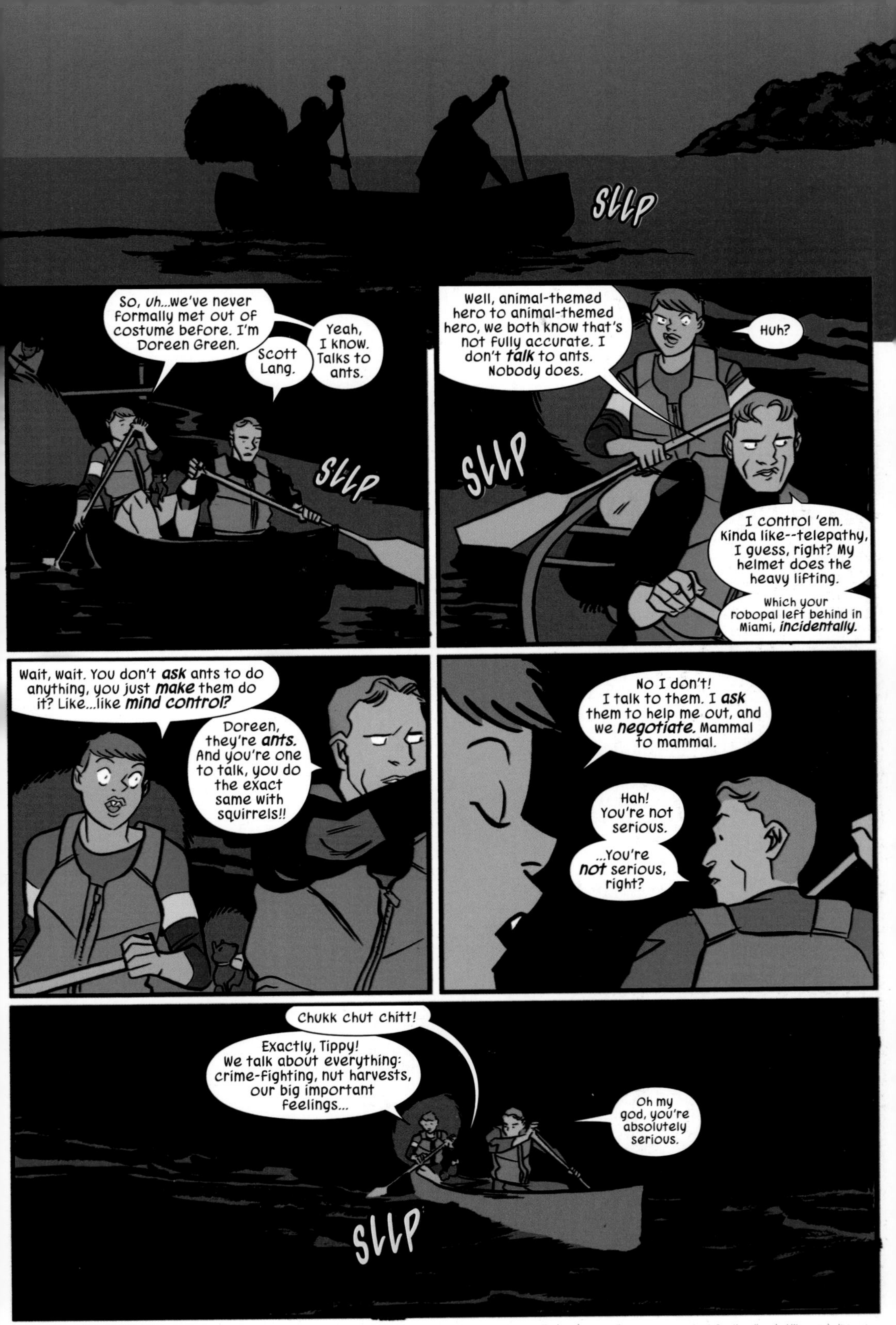
SLLP
So, uh...we've never formally met out of costume before. I'm Doreen Green.
Scott Lang.
Yeah, I know. Talks to ants.
SLLP
Well, animal-themed hero to animal-themed hero, we both know that's not fully accurate. I don't talk to ants. Nobody does.
Huh?
SLLP
I control 'em. Kinda like--telepathy, I guess, right? My helmet does the heavy lifting.
Which your robopal left behind in Miami, incidentally.
Wait, wait. You don't ask ants to do anything, you just make them do it? Like...like mind control?
Doreen, they're ants. And you're one to talk, you do the exact same with squirrels!!
No I don't! I talk to them. I ask them to help me out, and we negotiate. Mammal to mammal.
Hah! You're not serious.
...You're not serious, right?
Chukk chut chitt!
Exactly, Tippy! We talk about everything: crime-fighting, nut harvests, our big important feelings...
Oh my god, you're absolutely serious.
SLLP

When my dog cries I ask him about his big important feelings, and he never replies, possibly because it's ***really hard*** to say "your big important feelings" and still sound sincere.

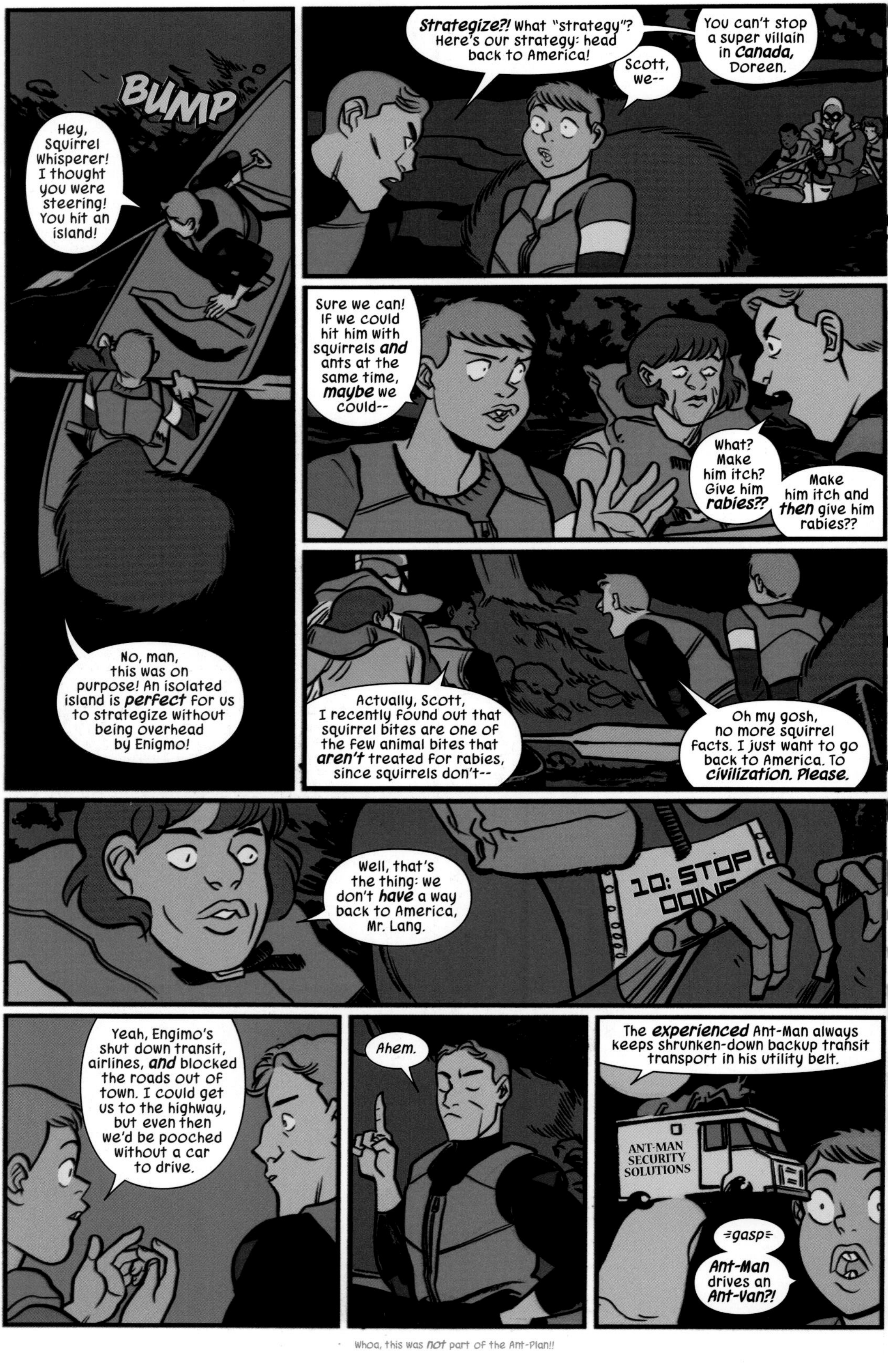
BUMP
Hey, Squirrel Whisperer! I thought you were steering! You hit an island!
No, man, this was on purpose! An isolated island is perfect for us to strategize without being overhead by Enigmo!
Strategize?! What "strategy"? Here's our strategy: head back to America!
Scott, we--
You can't stop a super villain in Canada, Doreen.
Sure we can! If we could hit him with squirrels and ants at the same time, maybe we could--
What? Make him itch? Give him rabies??
Make him itch and then give him rabies??
Actually, Scott, I recently found out that squirrel bites are one of the few animal bites that aren't treated for rabies, since squirrels don't--
Oh my gosh, no more squirrel facts. I just want to go back to America. To civilization. Please.
Well, that's the thing: we don't have a way back to America, Mr. Lang.
10: STOP DOING
Yeah, Engimo's shut down transit, airlines, and blocked the roads out of town. I could get us to the highway, but even then we'd be pooched without a car to drive.
Ahem.
The experienced Ant-Man always keeps shrunken-down backup transit transport in his utility belt.
ANT-MAN SECURITY SOLUTIONS
gasp
Ant-Man drives an Ant-Van?!

Whoa, this was *not* part of the Ant-Plan!!

Chht! Chhit chukk?

Tippy's right. So how *do* we beat this guy anyway?

I have an idea.

Please, Nancy. I'm all ears.

ANT-MAN SECURITY SOLUTIONS

So, Argentine ants. Invasive species. And in 2000, Japanese scientists discovered what they *thought* were a bunch of smaller colonies but were actually one *giant* ant colony, with 300 million workers and over a million queens.

Supercolonies! I read about these. Ants in one won't fight each other, because they're all on the same team, even if they're in different nests!

Exactly. But then we discovered another colony in the Mediterranean, this time spanning 3,700 *miles* of coast. And later scientists found the same thing in California. But here's the kicker: take ants from these different supercolonies, put them in a jar together, and guess what?

They won't fight each other either.

These ants, with an ocean between them, still behave like they're in a world-spanning *megacolony.* Sound familiar?

That's Enigmo's whole plan! If *he's* in charge everywhere, he won't fight *himself,* and hey presto: world peace.

Right. At the cost of everyone's freedom.

Wait, hold up. How do *you* guys know so much about ants?

General interest science reporting.

GENERAL INTEREST SCIENCE REPORTING FOR ME TOO

Dude, you never heard of this? Scott, buddy, you *gotta* read up on your animal familiars!

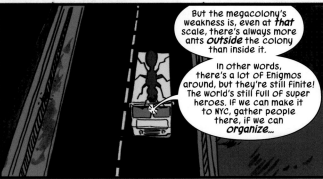

But the megacolony's weakness is, even at *that* scale, there's always more ants *outside* the colony than inside it.

In other words, there's a lot of Enigmos around, but they're still finite! The world's still full of super heroes. If we can make it to NYC, gather people there, if we can *organize...*

Look, I'm not saying ants are organizing themselves into a world-spanning superorganism. I'm just saying that when they *do,* y'all have no excuse for acting surprised.

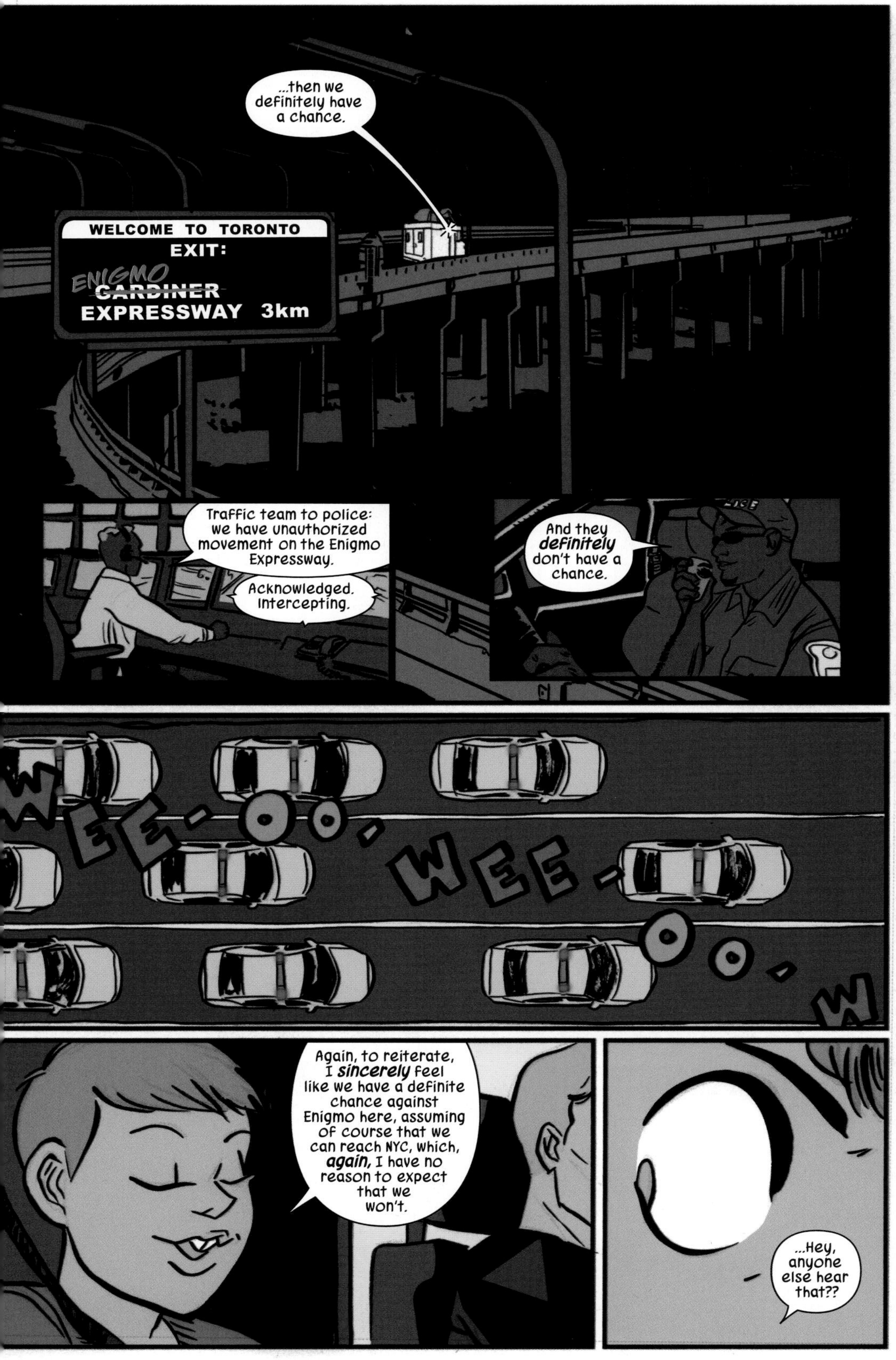
...then we definitely have a chance.
WELCOME TO TORONTO
EXIT:
ENIGMO
GARDINER
EXPRESSWAY 3km
Traffic team to police: we have unauthorized movement on the Enigmo Expressway.
Acknowledged. Intercepting.
And they *definitely* don't have a chance.
WEE-OO-WEE-OO-W
Again, to reiterate, I *sincerely* feel like we have a definite chance against Enigmo here, assuming of course that we can reach NYC, which, *again,* I have no reason to expect that we won't.
...Hey, anyone else hear that??

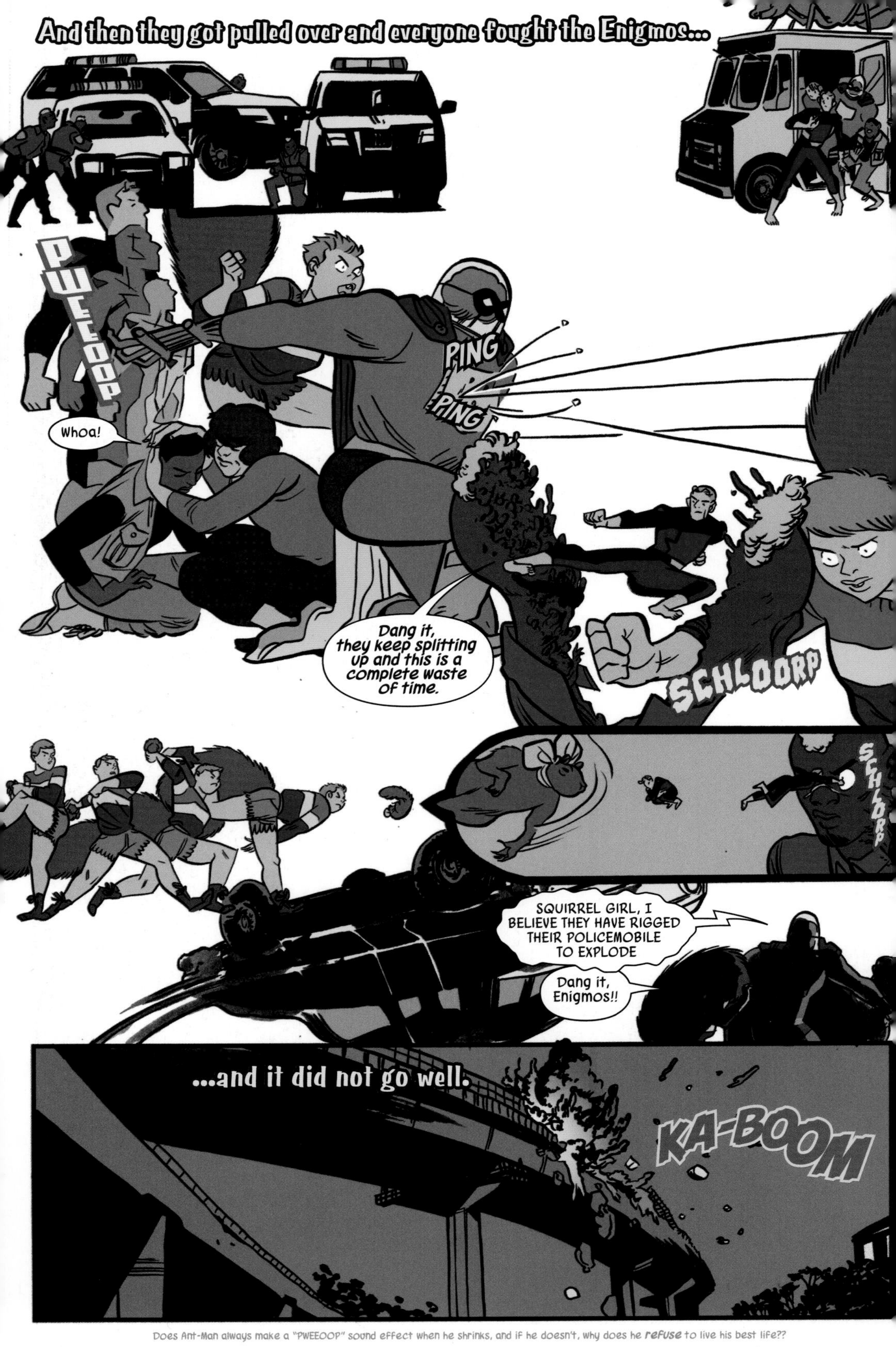
And then they got pulled over and everyone fought the Enigmos...
PWEEOOP
PING
PING
Whoa!
Dang it, they keep splitting up and this is a complete waste of time.
SCHLOORP
SCHLOORP
SQUIRREL GIRL, I BELIEVE THEY HAVE RIGGED THEIR POLICEMOBILE TO EXPLODE
Dang it, Enigmos!!
...and it did not go well.
KA-BOOM

Does Ant-Man always make a "PWEEOOP" sound effect when he shrinks, and if he doesn't, why does he *refuse* to live his best life??

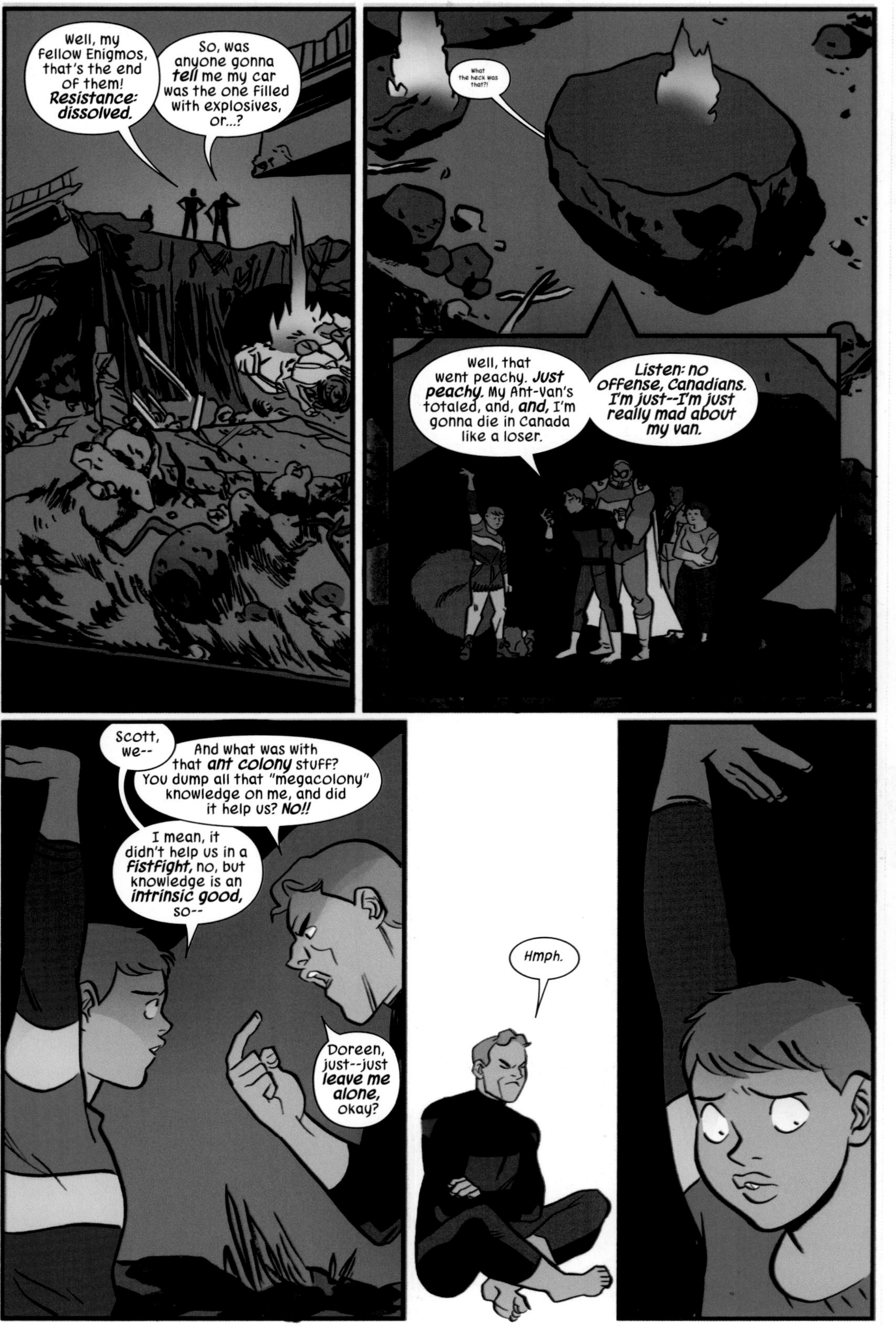
Well, my Fellow Enigmos, that's the end of them! Resistance: dissolved.
So, was anyone gonna tell me my car was the one filled with explosives, or...?
What the heck was that?!
Well, that went peachy. Just peachy. My Ant-Van's totaled, and, and, I'm gonna die in Canada like a loser.
Listen: no offense, Canadians. I'm just--I'm just really mad about my van.
Scott, we--
And what was with that ant colony stuff? You dump all that "megacolony" knowledge on me, and did it help us? NO!!
I mean, it didn't help us in a fistfight, no, but knowledge is an intrinsic good, so--
Doreen, just--just leave me alone, okay?
Hmph.

Here Lies Ant-Van, 1975-2016. Beloved Friend of the Kra-Van, the Stilt-Van, and the Iron Van. She Will Be Missed.

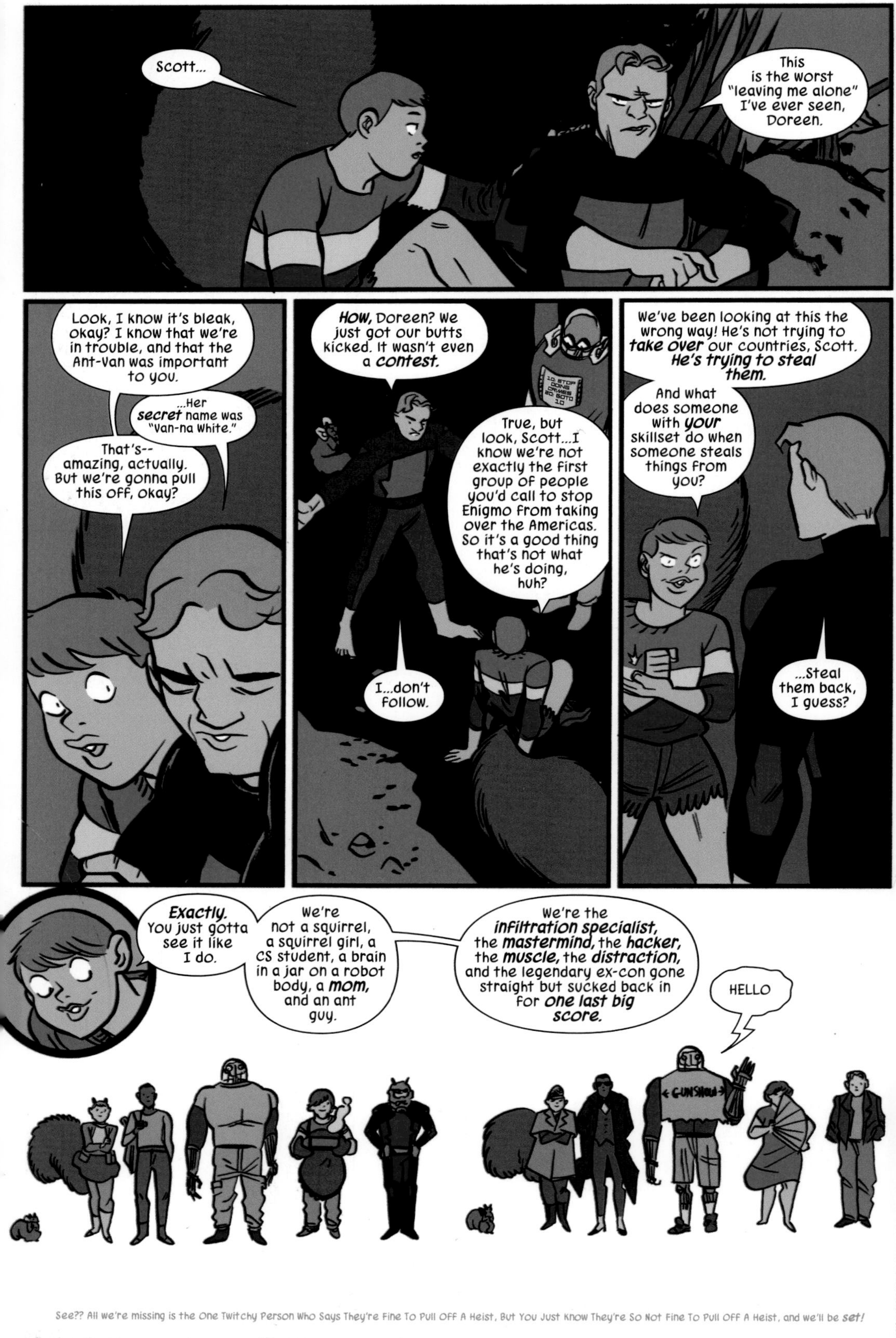
Scott...
This is the worst "leaving me alone" I've ever seen, Doreen.
Look, I know it's bleak, okay? I know that we're in trouble, and that the Ant-Van was important to you.
...Her *secret* name was "Van-na White."
That's--amazing, actually. But we're gonna pull this off, okay?
HOW, Doreen? We just got our butts kicked. It wasn't even a *contest.*
10: STOP DOING CRIMES 20: GOTO 10
True, but look, Scott...I know we're not exactly the first group of people you'd call to stop Enigmo from taking over the Americas. So it's a good thing that's not what he's doing, huh?
I...don't follow.
We've been looking at this the wrong way! He's not trying to *take over* our countries, Scott. *He's trying to steal them.*
And what does someone with *your* skillset do when someone steals things from you?
...Steal them back, I guess?
Exactly. You just gotta see it like I do.
We're not a squirrel, a squirrel girl, a CS student, a brain in a jar on a robot body, a *mom,* and an ant guy.
We're the *infiltration specialist,* the *mastermind,* the *hacker,* the *muscle,* the *distraction,* and the legendary ex-con gone straight but sucked back in for *one last big score.*
HELLO
GUNSHOW

See?? All we're missing is the One Twitchy Person Who Says They're Fine To Pull Off A Heist, But You Just Know They're So Not Fine To Pull Off A Heist, and we'll be *set!*

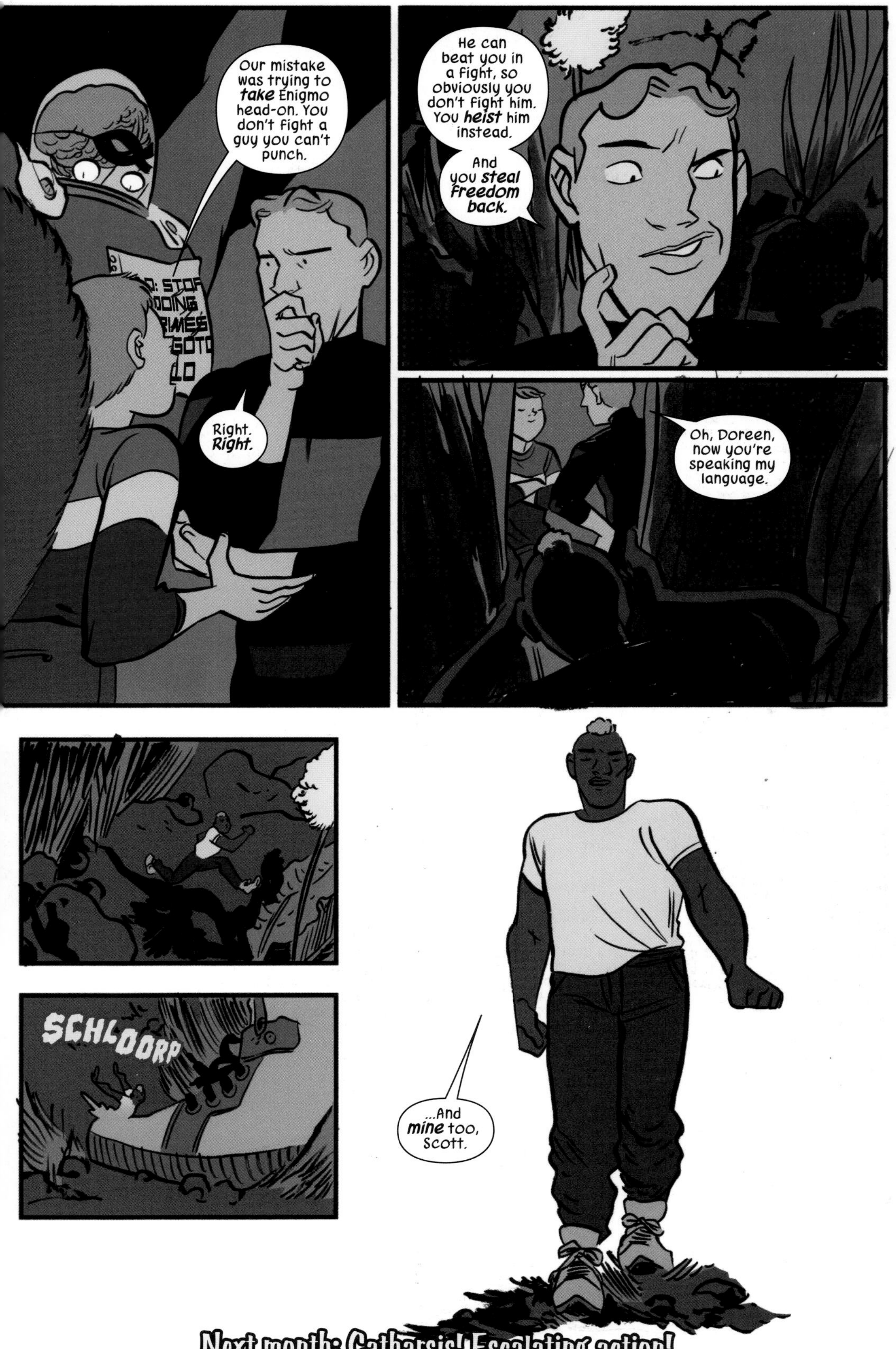
Our mistake was trying to *take* Enigmo head-on. You don't fight a guy you can't punch.
Right. *Right.*
He can beat you in a fight, so obviously you don't fight him. You *heist* him instead.
And you *steal Freedom back.*
Oh, Doreen, now you're speaking my language.
SCHLOORP
...And *mine* too, Scott.

Next month: Catharsis! Escalating action!
Finding out why this one Engimo has been stalking our gang! AND MORE??

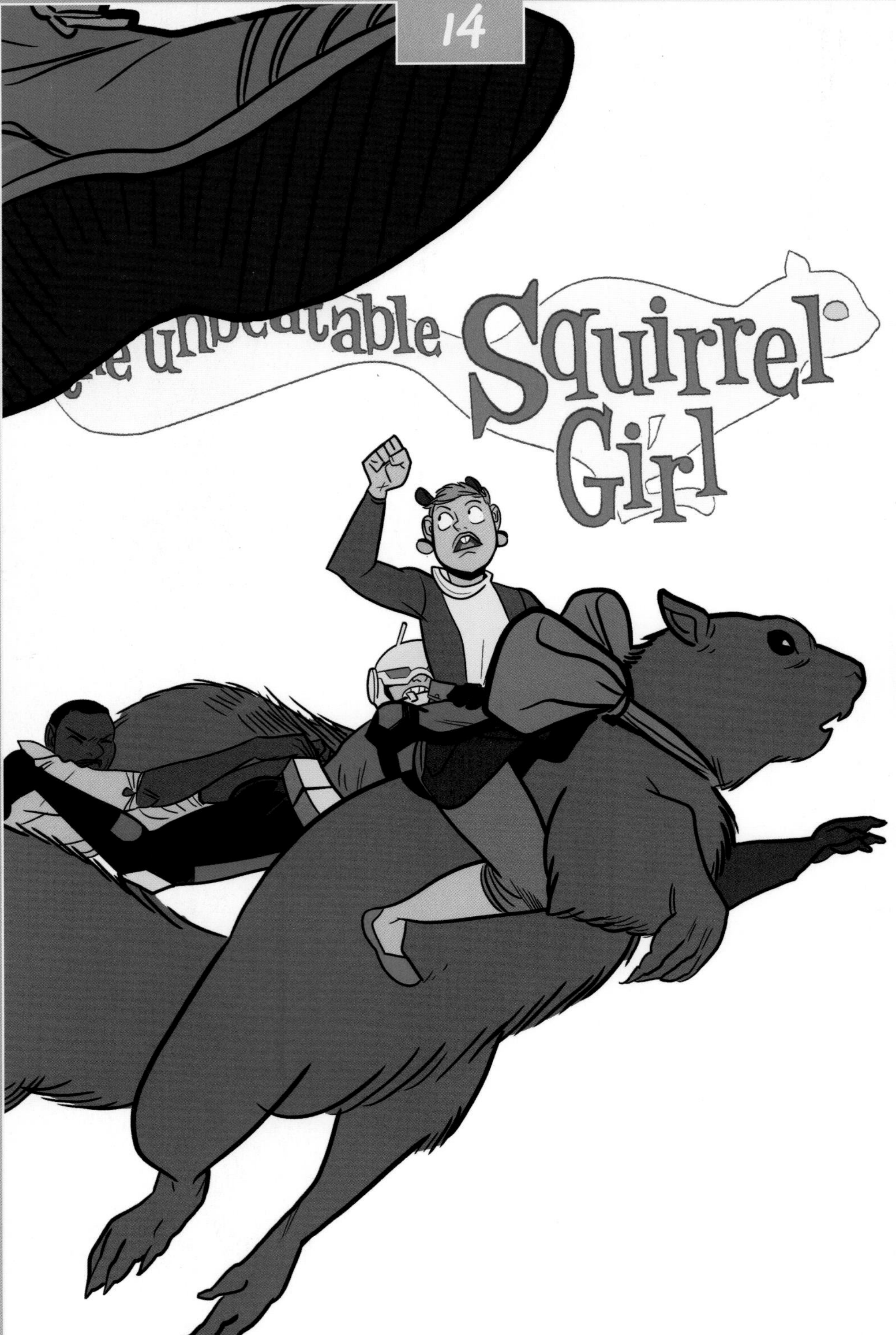
14
Squirrel
Girl

Doreen Green isn't just a second-year computer science student: she secretly also has all the powers of both squirrel and girl! She uses her amazing abilities to fight crime and be as awesome as possible. You know her as...**The Unbeatable Squirrel Girl!** Find out what she's been up to, with...

Squirrel Girl in a nutshell

search!

#toronto
#cityhall
#heistmusic
#parentalleave
#physics

Squirrel Girl @unbeatablesg
Hey everyone guess who's back from her vacation in Northern Canada where she couldn't get a cell signal?

Squirrel Girl @unbeatablesg
And now she's in SOUTHERN Canada where she can easily get a cell signal, only this dude named Enigmo has taken over??

Squirrel Girl @unbeatablesg
And so now she's gotta deal with THAT baloney RIGHT AWAY even though she never got more than a few pages into Lake Enthusiast Magazine???

Squirrel Girl @unbeatablesg
Anyway yeah it's me. HELLO ENIGMO YOU SHUT DOWN SMS MESSAGING BUT WE CAN STILL HANG OUT HERE ON SOCIAL MEDIA

Squirrel Girl @unbeatablesg
anyway send me your freshest anti-Enigmo memes, as far as we know that could be his only weakness so it's good to be prepared I guess

Egg @imduderadtude
@unbeatablesg omg ive waited my whole life for this moment

Tony Stark @starkmantony
@unbeatablesg Good to have you back. We, uh, haven't had much luck defeating this guy in NYC. He splits apart into other guys.

Squirrel Girl @unbeatablesg
@starkmantony Not a problem, Tony!! I once beat a guy made of a bunch of bees who could split apart into regular bees! NO BIG DEAL.

Tony Stark @starkmantony
@unbeatablesg I can use this. What'd you do?

Squirrel Girl @unbeatablesg
@starkmantony Oh, bees can't fly when they're wet so I got him wet and then took bags of wet bees to the police. ANOTHER CRIME WELL FOUGHT

Tony Stark @starkmantony
@unbeatablesg This...helps me precisely 0%.

Squirrel Girl @unbeatablesg
@starkmantony I'm on it, dude!! Me and Ant-Man came up with a plan to save everything! I can't tell you it publicly but let me just say

Squirrel Girl @unbeatablesg
@starkmantony WE ARE GONNA HEIST FREEDOM BACK

Squirrel Girl @unbeatablesg
@starkmantony ME and TIPPY and ANT-MAN and BRAIN DRAIN and MY MOM and MY GOOD FRIEND are gonna HEIST FREEDOM BACK

Squirrel Girl @unbeatablesg
@starkmantony AND IT'S DEFINITELY GONNA WORK

Squirrel Girl @unbeatablesg
@starkmantony AND WE'RE GONNA GO DO IT RIGHT NOW SO WHEN YOU NEXT HEAR FROM ME IT'LL BE ME SAYING "GLAD MY PLAN WENT PERFECTLY, LOL"

Squirrel Girl @unbeatablesg
@starkmantony I'm not sure if I'll say "lol" or not yet though

Tony Stark @starkmantony
@unbeatablesg Yeah you always gotta play that by ear lol

Squirrel Girl @unbeatablesg
@starkmantony Tony

Squirrel Girl @unbeatablesg
@starkmantony It's weird when you do it

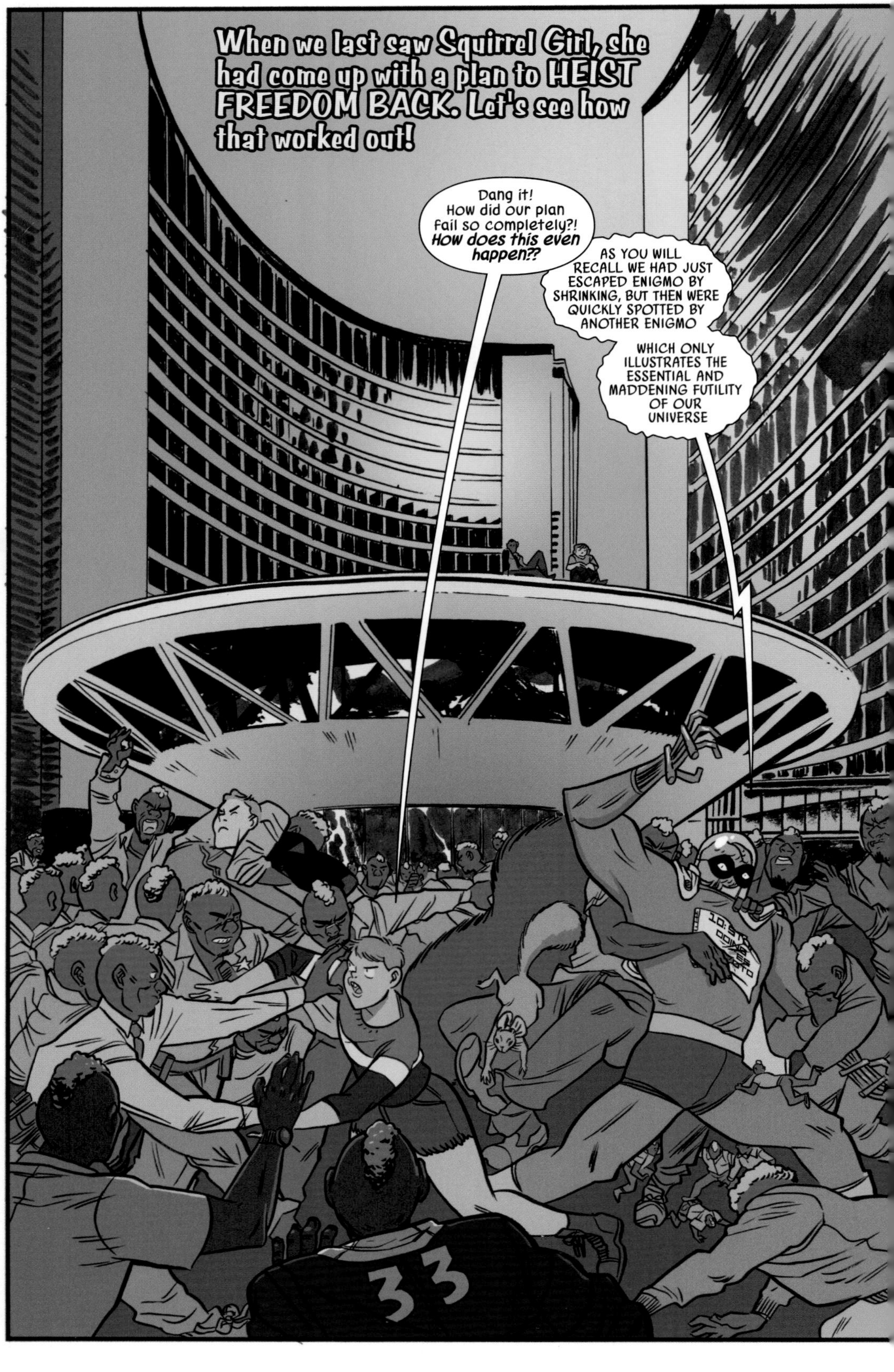
When we last saw Squirrel Girl, she had come up with a plan to HEIST FREEDOM BACK. Let's see how that worked out!
Dang it! How did our plan fail so completely?! How does this even happen??
AS YOU WILL RECALL WE HAD JUST ESCAPED ENIGMO BY SHRINKING, BUT THEN WERE QUICKLY SPOTTED BY ANOTHER ENIGMO
WHICH ONLY ILLUSTRATES THE ESSENTIAL AND MADDENING FUTILITY OF OUR UNIVERSE
33

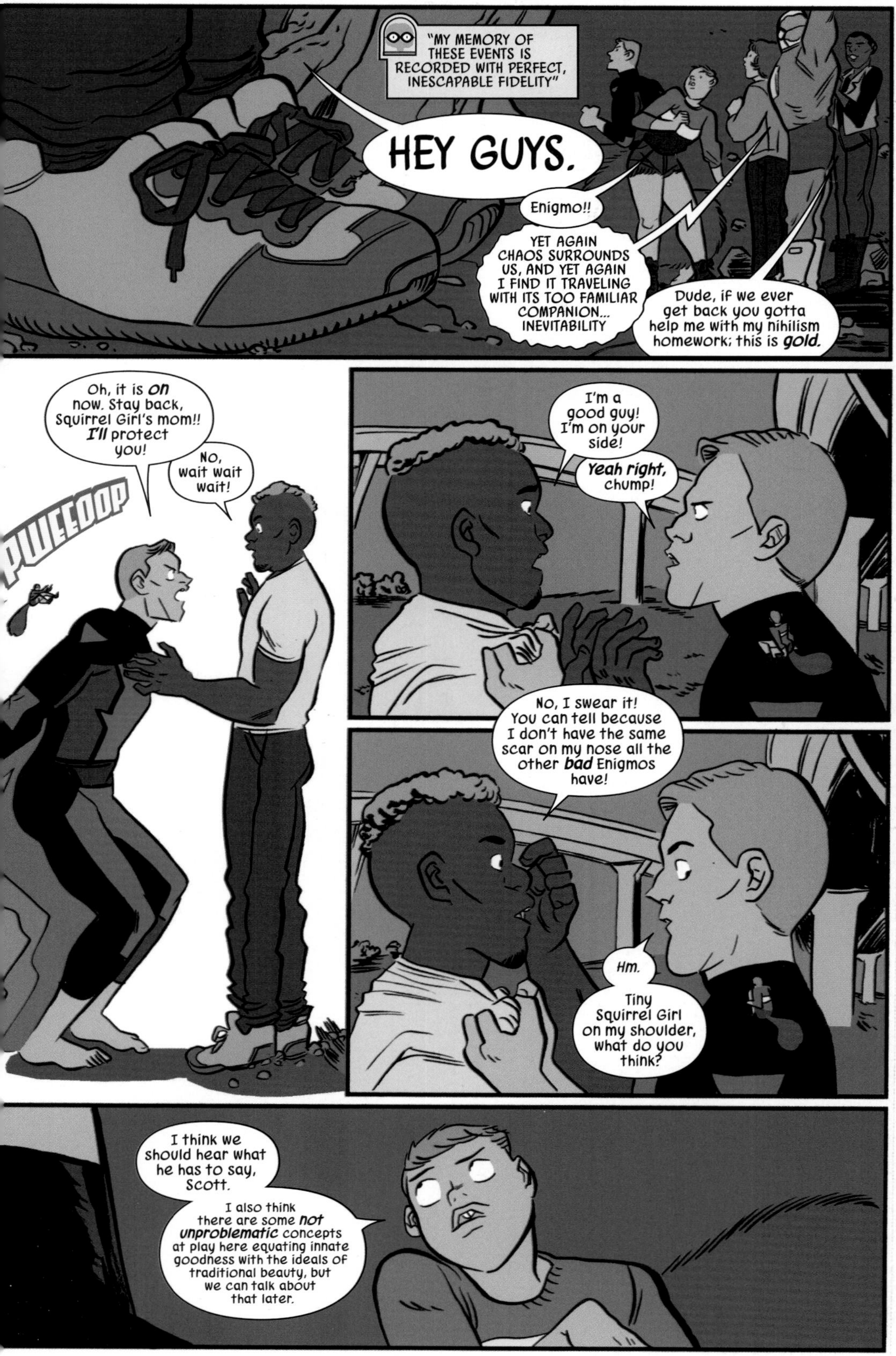
"MY MEMORY OF THESE EVENTS IS RECORDED WITH PERFECT, INESCAPABLE FIDELITY"
HEY GUYS.
Enigmo!!
YET AGAIN CHAOS SURROUNDS US, AND YET AGAIN I FIND IT TRAVELING WITH ITS TOO FAMILIAR COMPANION... INEVITABILITY
Dude, if we ever get back you gotta help me with my nihilism homework; this is gold.
PWEEOOP
Oh, it is on now. Stay back, Squirrel Girl's mom!! I'll protect you!
No, wait wait wait!
I'm a good guy! I'm on your side!
Yeah right, chump!
No, I swear it! You can tell because I don't have the same scar on my nose all the other bad Enigmos have!
Hm.
Tiny Squirrel Girl on my shoulder, what do you think?
I think we should hear what he has to say, Scott.
I also think there are some not unproblematic concepts at play here equating innate goodness with the ideals of traditional beauty, but we can talk about that later.

OF *COURSE* there's an Empire State University course on nihilism. OF *COURSE* Nancy took that as her mandatory English elective.

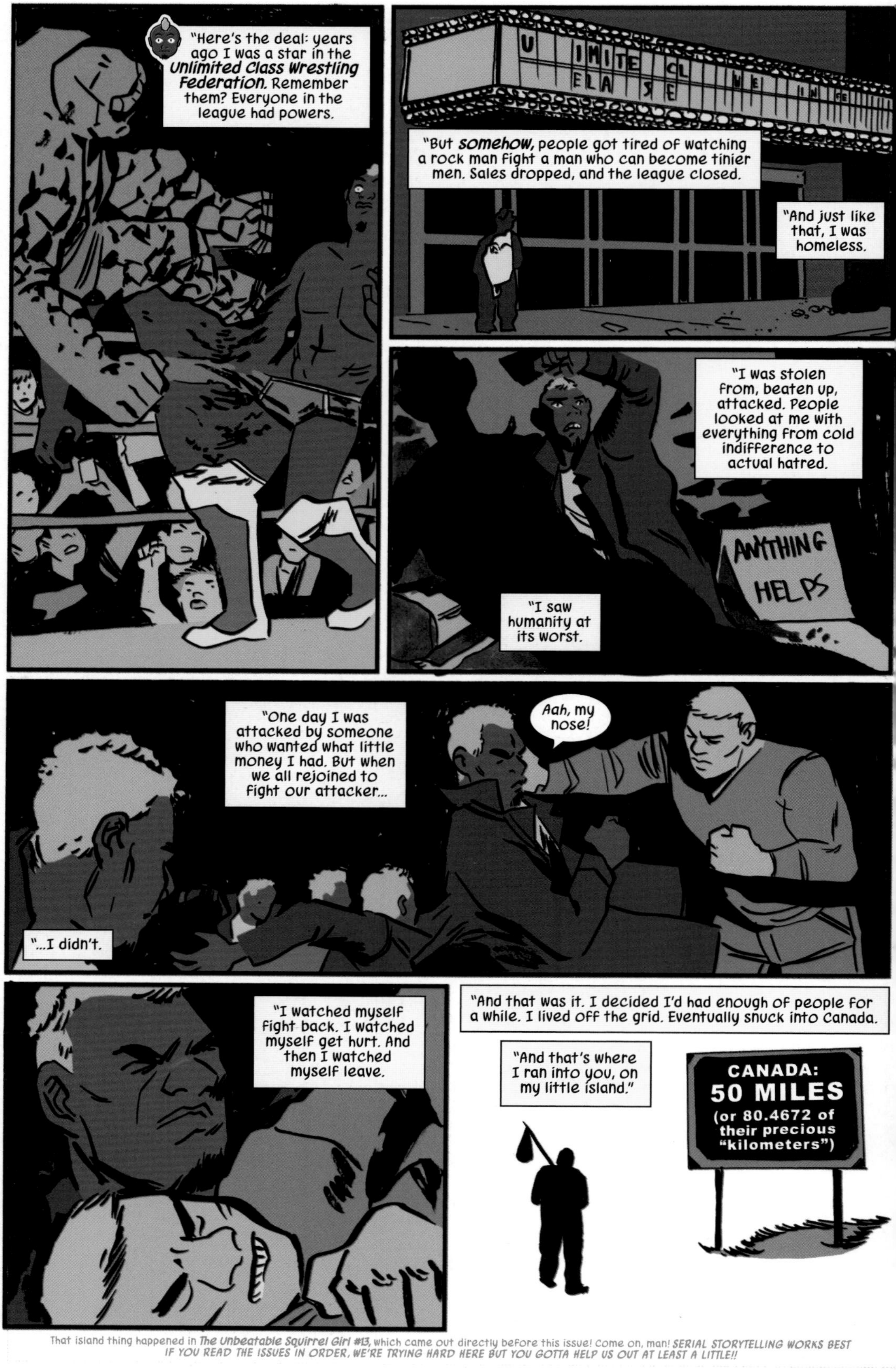
"Here's the deal: years ago I was a star in the Unlimited Class Wrestling Federation. Remember them? Everyone in the league had powers.
"But somehow, people got tired of watching a rock man fight a man who can become tinier men. Sales dropped, and the league closed.
"And just like that, I was homeless.
"I was stolen from, beaten up, attacked. People looked at me with everything from cold indifference to actual hatred.
ANYTHING HELPS
"I saw humanity at its worst.
"One day I was attacked by someone who wanted what little money I had. But when we all rejoined to fight our attacker...
Aah, my nose!
"...I didn't.
"I watched myself fight back. I watched myself get hurt. And then I watched myself leave.
"And that was it. I decided I'd had enough of people for a while. I lived off the grid. Eventually snuck into Canada.
"And that's where I ran into you, on my little island."
CANADA:
50 MILES
(or 80.4672 of their precious "kilometers")

That island thing happened in *The Unbeatable Squirrel Girl #13*, which came out directly before this issue! Come on, man! *SERIAL STORYTELLING WORKS BEST IF YOU READ THE ISSUES IN ORDER, WE'RE TRYING HARD HERE BUT YOU GOTTA HELP US OUT AT LEAST A LITTLE!!*

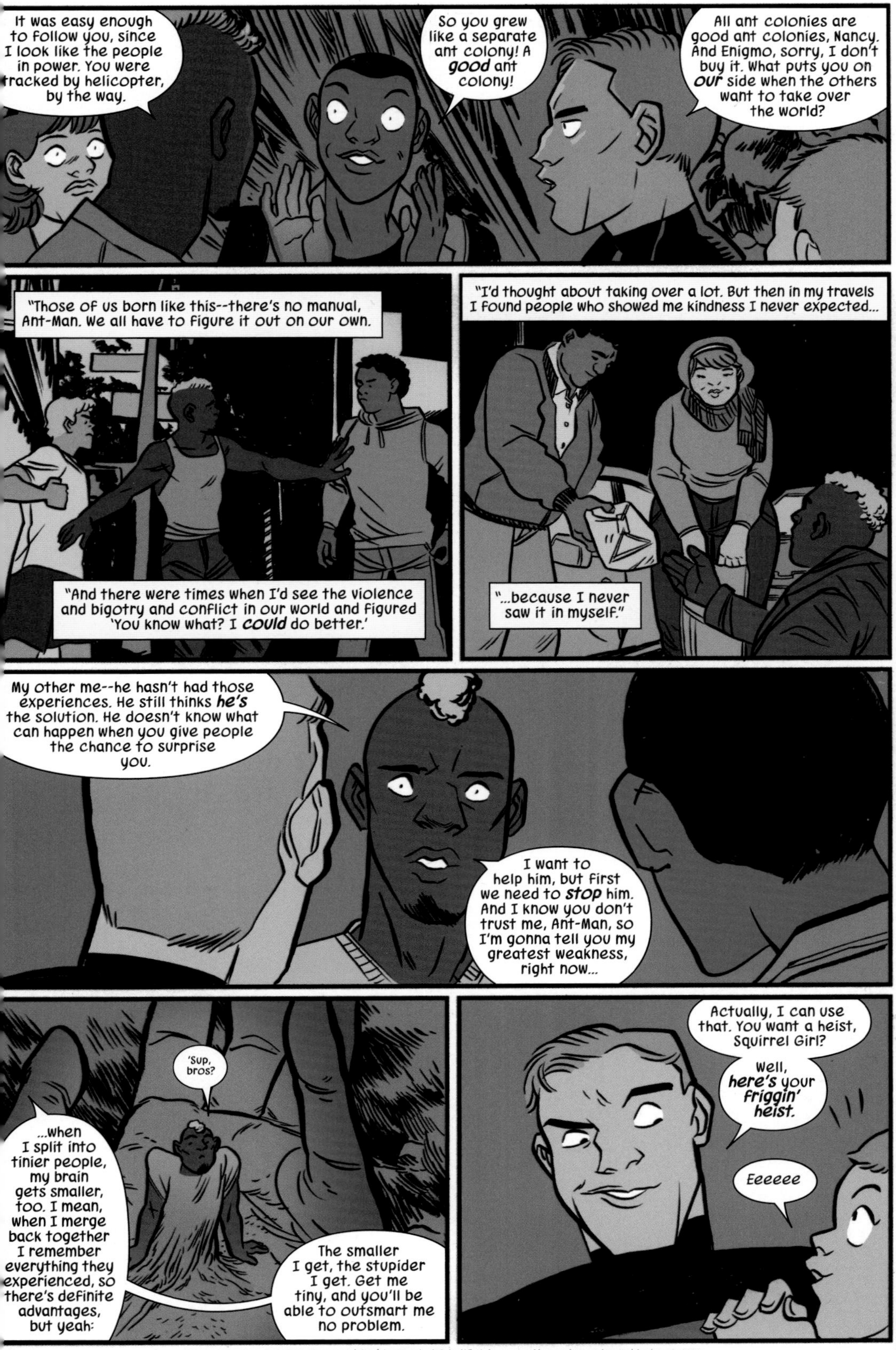
It was easy enough to follow you, since I look like the people in power. You were tracked by helicopter, by the way.
So you grew like a separate ant colony! A *good* ant colony!
All ant colonies are good ant colonies, Nancy. And Enigmo, sorry, I don't buy it. What puts you on *our* side when the others want to take over the world?
"Those of us born like this--there's no manual, Ant-Man. We all have to figure it out on our own.
"And there were times when I'd see the violence and bigotry and conflict in our world and figured 'You know what? I *could* do better.'
"I'd thought about taking over a lot. But then in my travels I found people who showed me kindness I never expected...
"...because I never saw it in myself."
My other me--he hasn't had those experiences. He still thinks *he's* the solution. He doesn't know what can happen when you give people the chance to surprise you.
I want to help him, but first we need to *stop* him. And I know you don't trust me, Ant-Man, so I'm gonna tell you my greatest weakness, right now...
'Sup, bros?
...when I split into tinier people, my brain gets smaller, too. I mean, when I merge back together I remember everything they experienced, so there's definite advantages, but yeah:
The smaller I get, the stupider I get. Get me tiny, and you'll be able to outsmart me no problem.
Actually, I can use that. You want a heist, Squirrel Girl?
Well, *here's* your *friggin' heist.*
Eeeeee

Can you tell an Ant-Man story and *not* have a heist in it? It is a question science is unable to answer, because the second someone tries, they're like, "Man, what if I just put a fun heist in here though??"

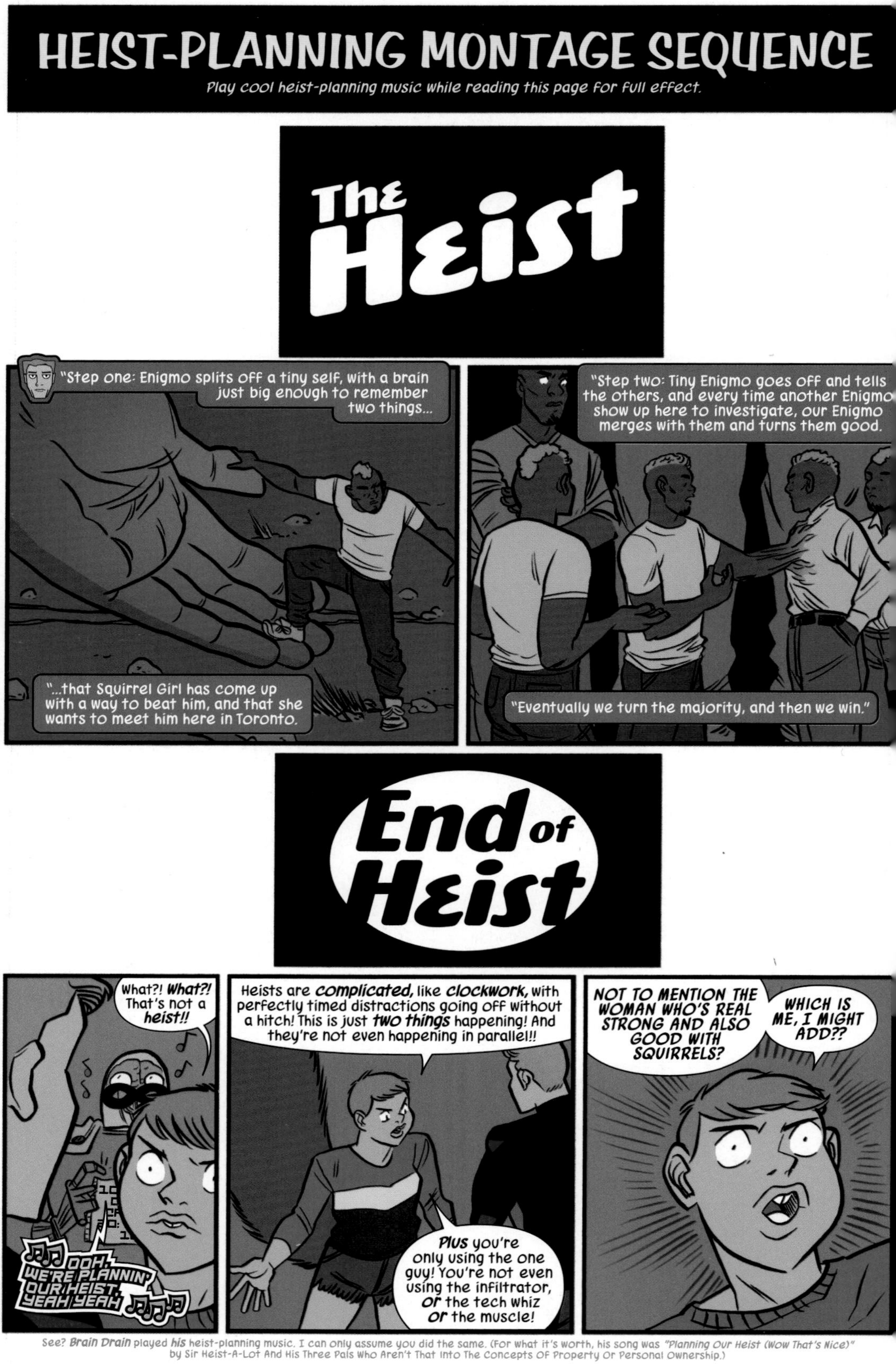
HEIST-PLANNING MONTAGE SEQUENCE
Play cool heist-planning music while reading this page for full effect.
The Heist
"Step one: Enigmo splits off a tiny self, with a brain just big enough to remember two things...
"...that Squirrel Girl has come up with a way to beat him, and that she wants to meet him here in Toronto.
"Step two: Tiny Enigmo goes off and tells the others, and every time another Enigmo show up here to investigate, our Enigmo merges with them and turns them good.
"Eventually we turn the majority, and then we win."
End of Heist
What?! What?! That's not a heist!!
OOH, WE'RE PLANNIN' OUR HEIST, YEAH YEAH
Heists are complicated, like clockwork, with perfectly timed distractions going off without a hitch! This is just two things happening! And they're not even happening in parallel!!
Plus you're only using the one guy! You're not even using the infiltrator, or the tech whiz or the muscle!
NOT TO MENTION THE WOMAN WHO'S REAL STRONG AND ALSO GOOD WITH SQUIRRELS?
WHICH IS ME, I MIGHT ADD??

See? *Brain Drain* played *his* heist-planning music. I can only assume you did the same. (For what it's worth, his song was *"Planning Our Heist (Wow That's Nice)"* by Sir Heist-A-Lot And His Three Pals Who Aren't That Into The Concepts Of Property Or Personal Ownership.)

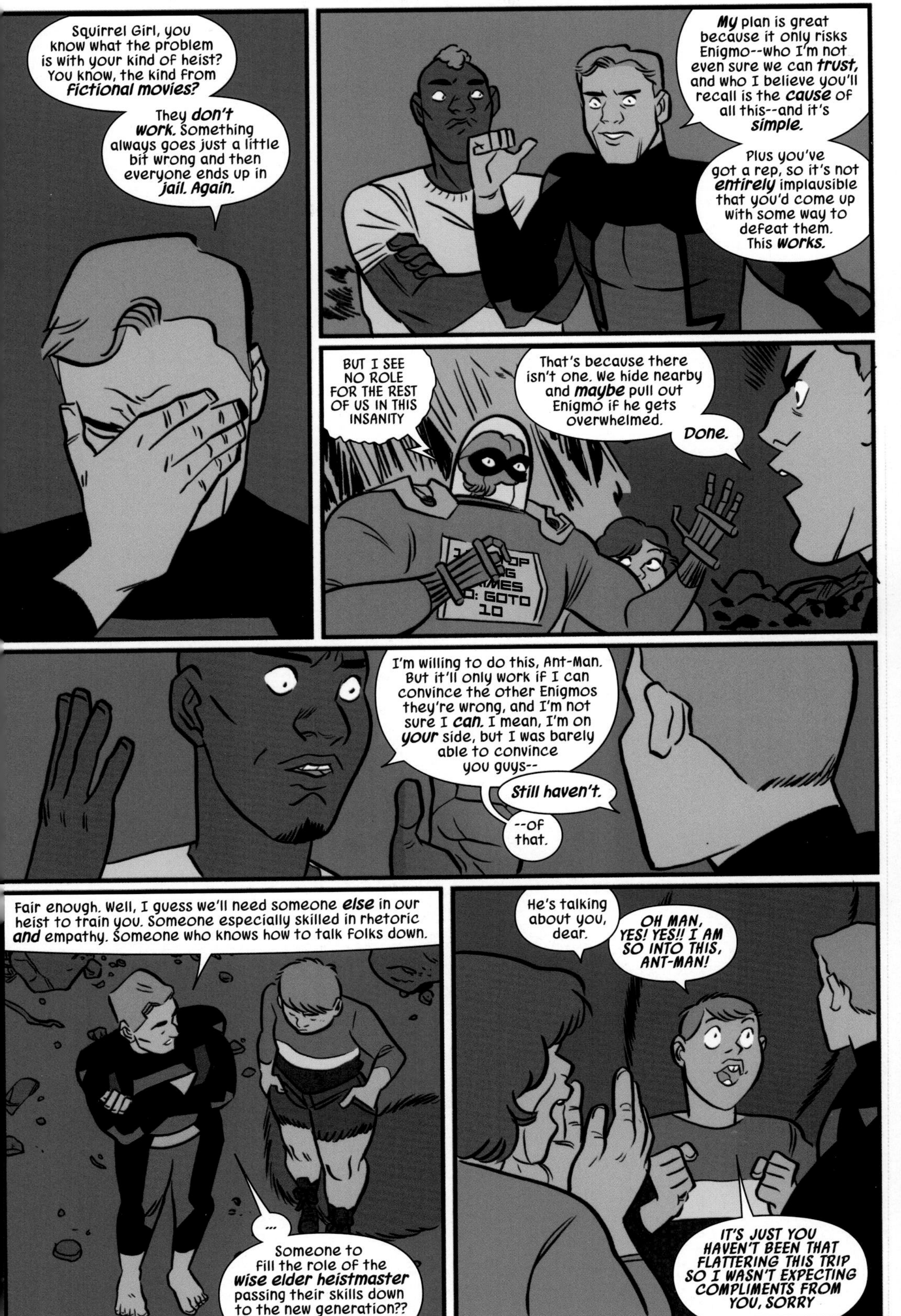
Squirrel Girl, you know what the problem is with your kind of heist? You know, the kind from fictional movies?
They don't work. Something always goes just a little bit wrong and then everyone ends up in jail. Again.
My plan is great because it only risks Enigmo--who I'm not even sure we can trust, and who I believe you'll recall is the cause of all this--and it's simple.
Plus you've got a rep, so it's not entirely implausible that you'd come up with some way to defeat them. This works.
BUT I SEE NO ROLE FOR THE REST OF US IN THIS INSANITY
That's because there isn't one. We hide nearby and maybe pull out Enigmo if he gets overwhelmed.
Done.
I'm willing to do this, Ant-Man. But it'll only work if I can convince the other Enigmos they're wrong, and I'm not sure I can. I mean, I'm on your side, but I was barely able to convince you guys--
Still haven't.
--of that.
Fair enough. Well, I guess we'll need someone else in our heist to train you. Someone especially skilled in rhetoric and empathy. Someone who knows how to talk folks down.
...
Someone to fill the role of the wise elder heistmaster passing their skills down to the new generation??
He's talking about you, dear.
OH MAN, YES! YES!! I AM SO INTO THIS, ANT-MAN!
IT'S JUST YOU HAVEN'T BEEN THAT FLATTERING THIS TRIP SO I WASN'T EXPECTING COMPLIMENTS FROM YOU, SORRY

I JUST ASSUMED YOU WERE TALKING ABOUT SOME OTHER WISE ELDER HEISTMASTER! I DUNNO, MAYBE MY MOM?

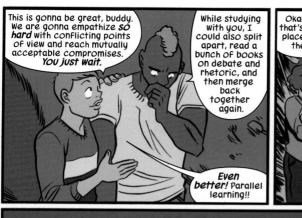

This is gonna be great, buddy. We are gonna empathize *SO hard* with conflicting points of view and reach mutually acceptable compromises. *You just wait.*

While studying with you, I could also split apart, read a bunch of books on debate and rhetoric, and then merge back together again.

Even better! Parallel learning!!

Okay, so all that's left is a place to lure them to.

We'll need a place that's got a large public square, in case several Enigmos arrive at once.

How about City Hall?

Welcome to TORONTO!

Our city hall has a large open public space out front.

Not to mention lots of convenient food trucks and souvenir stands!

Perfect. We'll also need a library, preferably nearby, so Squirrel Girl can help Enigmo complete his education as quickly as possible.

Billboard just to the right of the other one, dude.

Additionally, our city hall ALSO has a free library!

We're very proud of our socialized public services!!

Plus, like all of Canada, we offer up to 50 weeks paid time off if you have a baby.

That's compared to the mere 12 weeks available in America, and that's UNPAID leave!

So what the heck, America??

These billboards are getting pretty sassy.

Sorry.

I don't think we expected Americans to see them.

So... heist is go?

Heist is go.

I'm not holding my breath, but there is at least a *chance* this plan will work and not fall apart almost immediately.

America, I don't think having a baby is as cheap or as easy as your social safety net would seem to imply!! SORRY, AMERICA, BUT BABIES EAT, LIKE, 100% OF THE TIME THEY AREN'T SLEEPING OR CRYING.

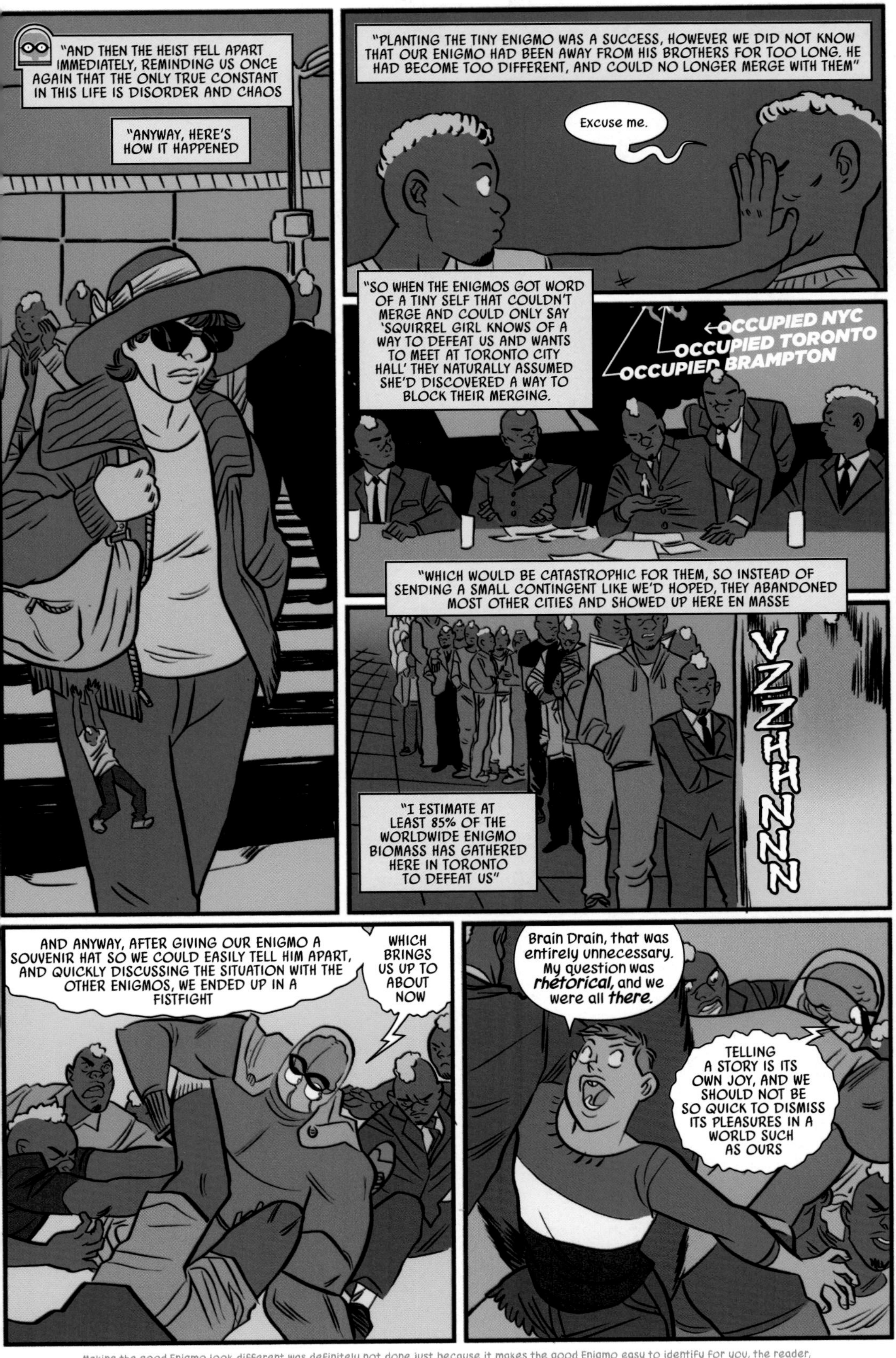
"AND THEN THE HEIST FELL APART IMMEDIATELY, REMINDING US ONCE AGAIN THAT THE ONLY TRUE CONSTANT IN THIS LIFE IS DISORDER AND CHAOS
"ANYWAY, HERE'S HOW IT HAPPENED
"PLANTING THE TINY ENIGMO WAS A SUCCESS, HOWEVER WE DID NOT KNOW THAT OUR ENIGMO HAD BEEN AWAY FROM HIS BROTHERS FOR TOO LONG. HE HAD BECOME TOO DIFFERENT, AND COULD NO LONGER MERGE WITH THEM"
Excuse me.
"SO WHEN THE ENIGMOS GOT WORD OF A TINY SELF THAT COULDN'T MERGE AND COULD ONLY SAY 'SQUIRREL GIRL KNOWS OF A WAY TO DEFEAT US AND WANTS TO MEET AT TORONTO CITY HALL' THEY NATURALLY ASSUMED SHE'D DISCOVERED A WAY TO BLOCK THEIR MERGING.
←OCCUPIED NYC
OCCUPIED TORONTO
OCCUPIED BRAMPTON
"WHICH WOULD BE CATASTROPHIC FOR THEM, SO INSTEAD OF SENDING A SMALL CONTINGENT LIKE WE'D HOPED, THEY ABANDONED MOST OTHER CITIES AND SHOWED UP HERE EN MASSE
"I ESTIMATE AT LEAST 85% OF THE WORLDWIDE ENIGMO BIOMASS HAS GATHERED HERE IN TORONTO TO DEFEAT US"
VZZHHHNNN
AND ANYWAY, AFTER GIVING OUR ENIGMO A SOUVENIR HAT SO WE COULD EASILY TELL HIM APART, AND QUICKLY DISCUSSING THE SITUATION WITH THE OTHER ENIGMOS, WE ENDED UP IN A FISTFIGHT
WHICH BRINGS US UP TO ABOUT NOW
Brain Drain, that was entirely unnecessary. My question was *rhetorical,* and we were all *there.*
TELLING A STORY IS ITS OWN JOY, AND WE SHOULD NOT BE SO QUICK TO DISMISS ITS PLEASURES IN A WORLD SUCH AS OURS

Making the good Enigmo look different was definitely not done just because it makes the good Enigmo easy to identify for you, the reader, when he shows up four pages from now. It *also* lets us draw and write about cool hats!!

Uh, clearly that guy does, Ant-Man. It's *right there*. Also, that's not the good Enigmo! *His* ball cap is red and has a maple leaf on it. We almost tricked you, huh??

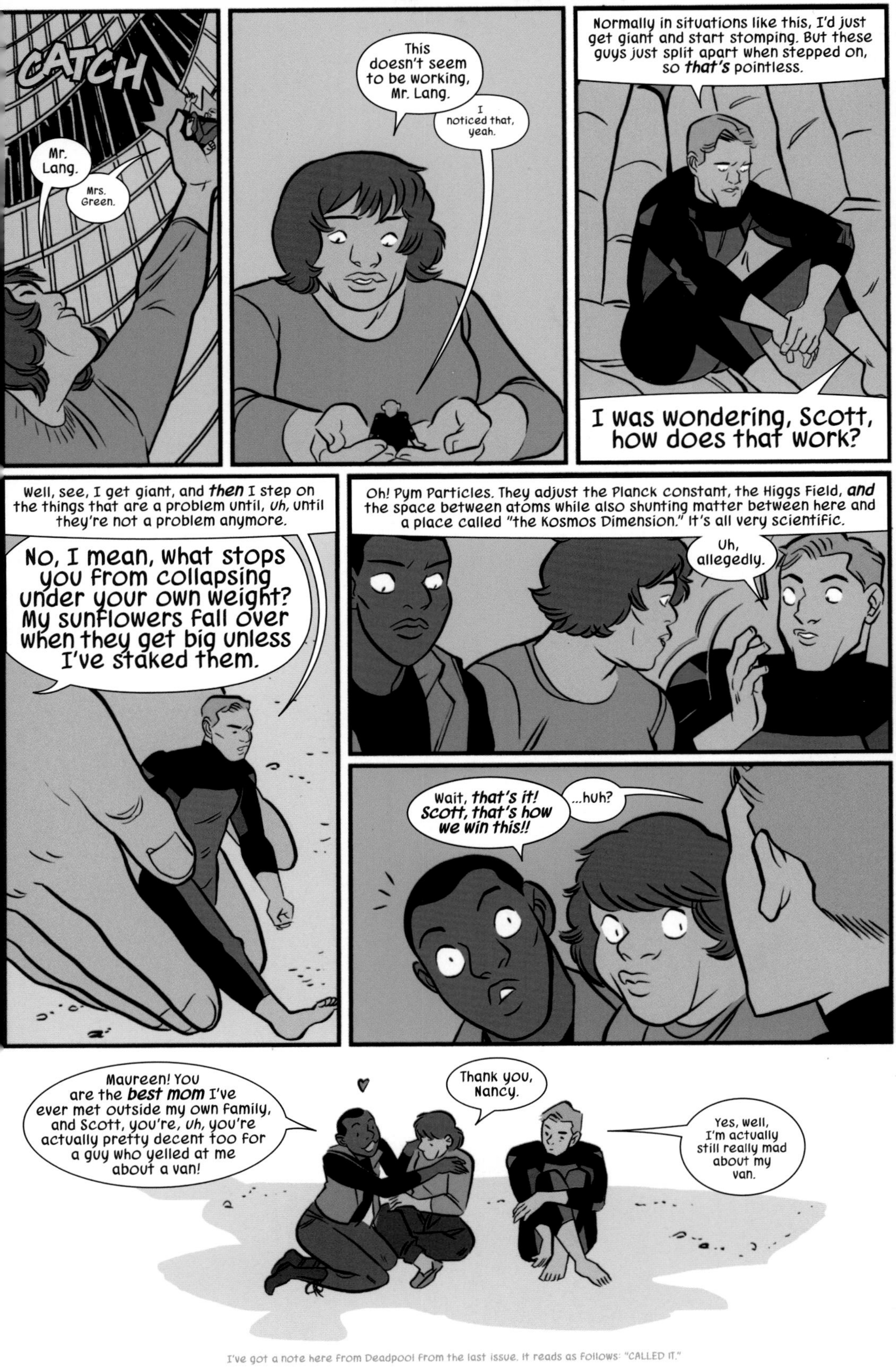
CATCH
Mr. Lang.
Mrs. Green.
This doesn't seem to be working, Mr. Lang.
I noticed that, yeah.
Normally in situations like this, I'd just get giant and start stomping. But these guys just split apart when stepped on, so that's pointless.
I was wondering, Scott, how does that work?
Well, see, I get giant, and then I step on the things that are a problem until, uh, until they're not a problem anymore.
No, I mean, what stops you from collapsing under your own weight? My sunflowers fall over when they get big unless I've staked them.
Oh! Pym Particles. They adjust the Planck constant, the Higgs Field, and the space between atoms while also shunting matter between here and a place called "the Kosmos Dimension." It's all very scientific.
Uh, allegedly.
Wait, that's it! Scott, that's how we win this!!
...huh?
Maureen! You are the best mom I've ever met outside my own family, and Scott, you're, uh, you're actually pretty decent too for a guy who yelled at me about a van!
Thank you, Nancy.
Yes, well, I'm actually still really mad about my van.

I've got a note here from Deadpool from the last issue. It reads as follows: "CALLED IT."

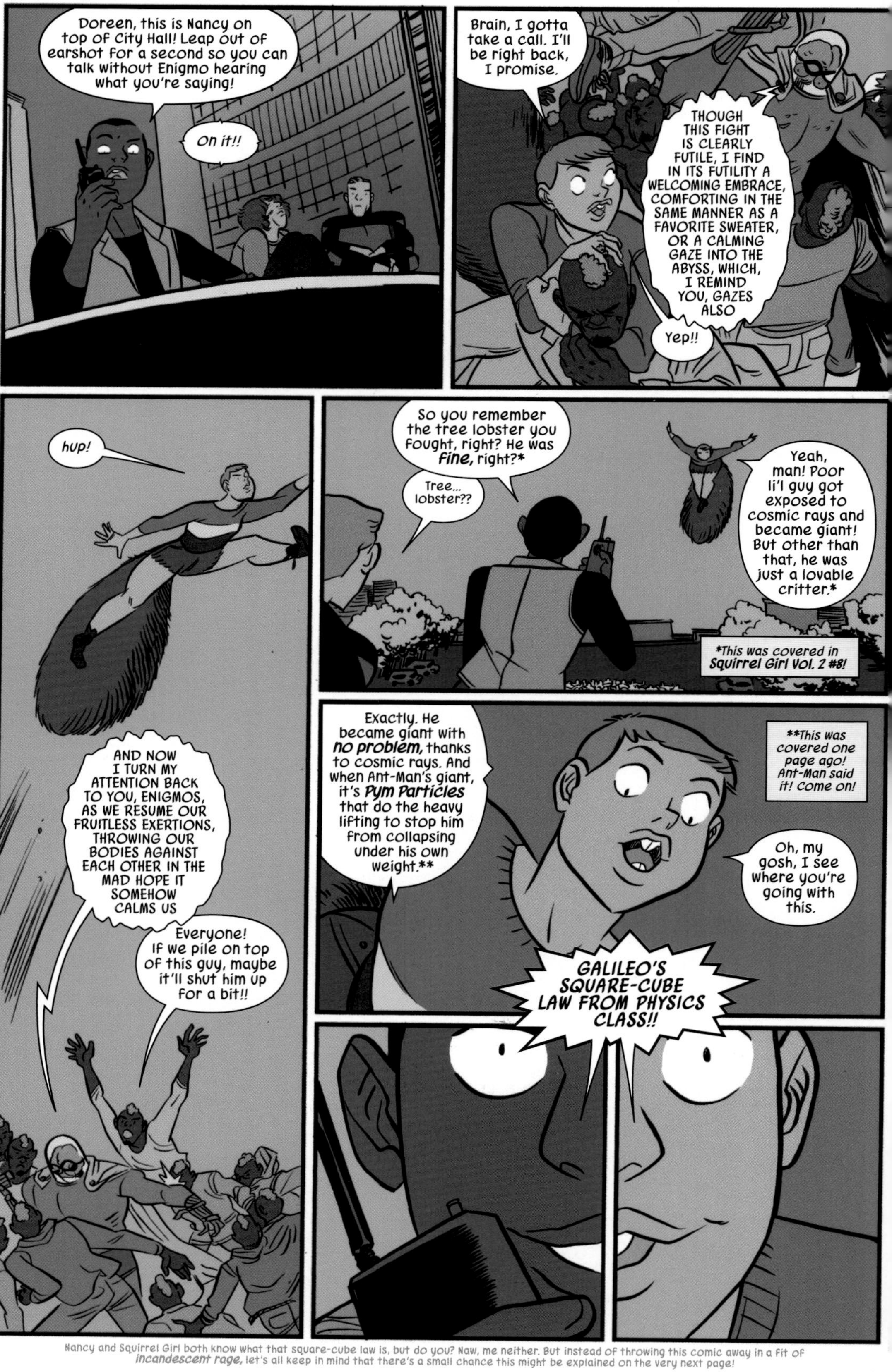
Doreen, this is Nancy on top of City Hall! Leap out of earshot for a second so you can talk without Enigmo hearing what you're saying!
On it!!
Brain, I gotta take a call. I'll be right back, I promise.
THOUGH THIS FIGHT IS CLEARLY FUTILE, I FIND IN ITS FUTILITY A WELCOMING EMBRACE, COMFORTING IN THE SAME MANNER AS A FAVORITE SWEATER, OR A CALMING GAZE INTO THE ABYSS, WHICH, I REMIND YOU, GAZES ALSO
Yep!!
hup!
So you remember the tree lobster you fought, right? He was *fine*, right?*
Tree... lobster??
Yeah, man! Poor li'l guy got exposed to cosmic rays and became giant! But other than that, he was just a lovable critter.*
*This was covered in Squirrel Girl Vol. 2 #8!
AND NOW I TURN MY ATTENTION BACK TO YOU, ENIGMOS, AS WE RESUME OUR FRUITLESS EXERTIONS, THROWING OUR BODIES AGAINST EACH OTHER IN THE MAD HOPE IT SOMEHOW CALMS US
Everyone! If we pile on top of this guy, maybe it'll shut him up for a bit!!
Exactly. He became giant with **no problem,** thanks to cosmic rays. And when Ant-Man's giant, it's *Pym Particles* that do the heavy lifting to stop him from collapsing under his own weight.**
**This was covered one page ago! Ant-Man said it! Come on!
Oh, my gosh, I see where you're going with this.
GALILEO'S SQUARE-CUBE LAW FROM PHYSICS CLASS!!

Nancy and Squirrel Girl both know what that square-cube law is, but do you? Naw, me neither. But instead of throwing this comic away in a fit of *incandescent rage,* let's all keep in mind that there's a small chance this might be explained on the very next page!

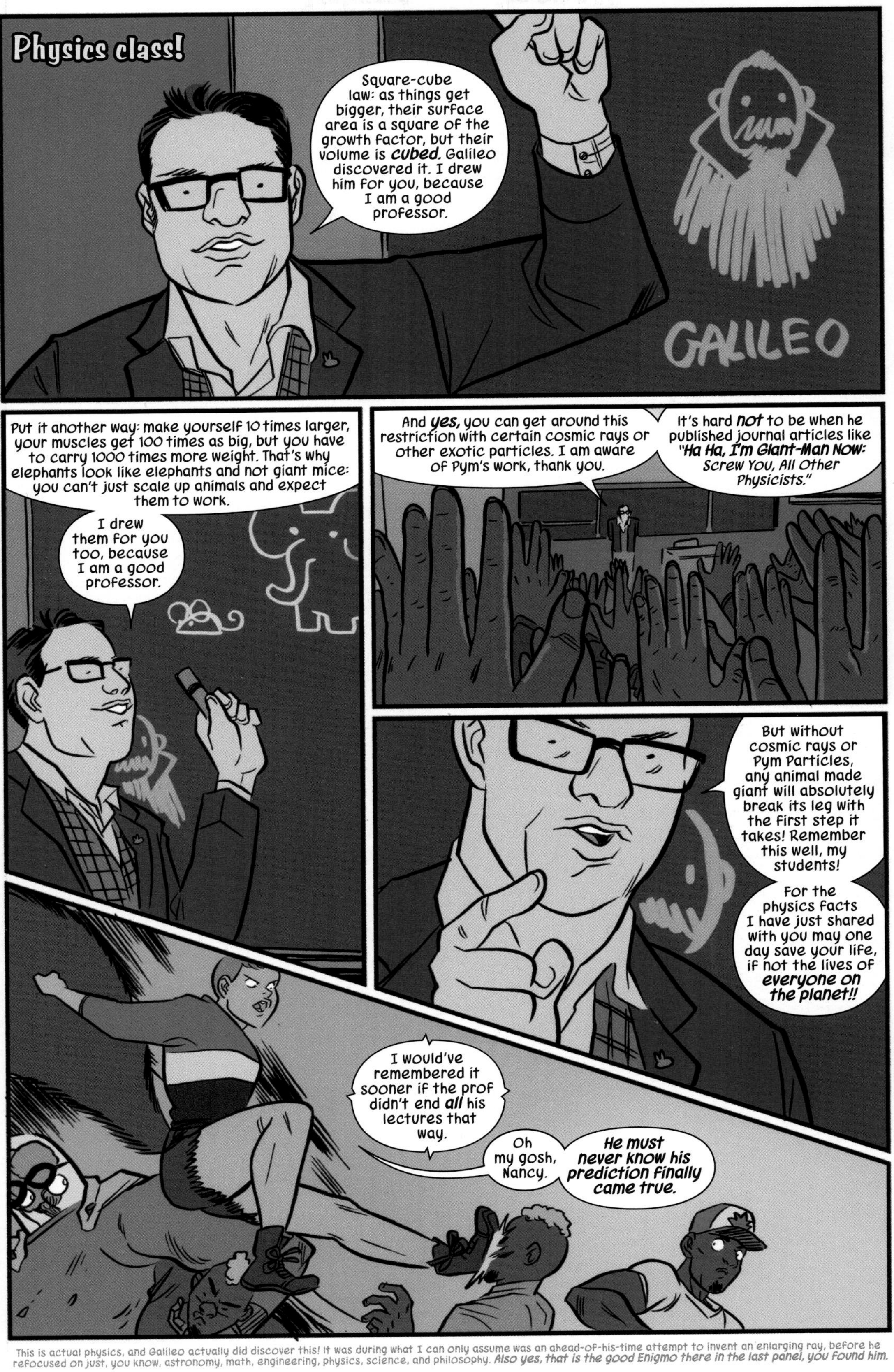
Physics class!
Square-cube law: as things get bigger, their surface area is a square of the growth factor, but their volume is ***cubed.*** Galileo discovered it. I drew him for you, because I am a good professor.
GALILEO
Put it another way: make yourself 10 times larger, your muscles get 100 times as big, but you have to carry 1000 times more weight. That's why elephants look like elephants and not giant mice: you can't just scale up animals and expect them to work.
I drew them for you too, because I am a good professor.
And ***yes,*** you can get around this restriction with certain cosmic rays or other exotic particles. I am aware of Pym's work, thank you.
It's hard ***not*** to be when he published journal articles like ***"Ha Ha, I'm Giant-Man Now:*** *Screw You, All Other Physicists."*
But without cosmic rays or Pym Particles, any animal made giant will absolutely break its leg with the first step it takes! Remember this well, my students!
For the physics facts I have just shared with you may one day save your life, if not the lives of ***everyone on the planet!!***
I would've remembered it sooner if the prof didn't end ***all*** his lectures that way.
Oh my gosh, Nancy.
He must never know his prediction finally came true.

This is actual physics, and Galileo actually did discover this! It was during what I can only assume was an ahead-of-his-time attempt to invent an enlarging ray, before he refocused on just, you know, astronomy, math, engineering, physics, science, and philosophy. *Also yes, that is the good Enigmo there in the last panel, you found him.*

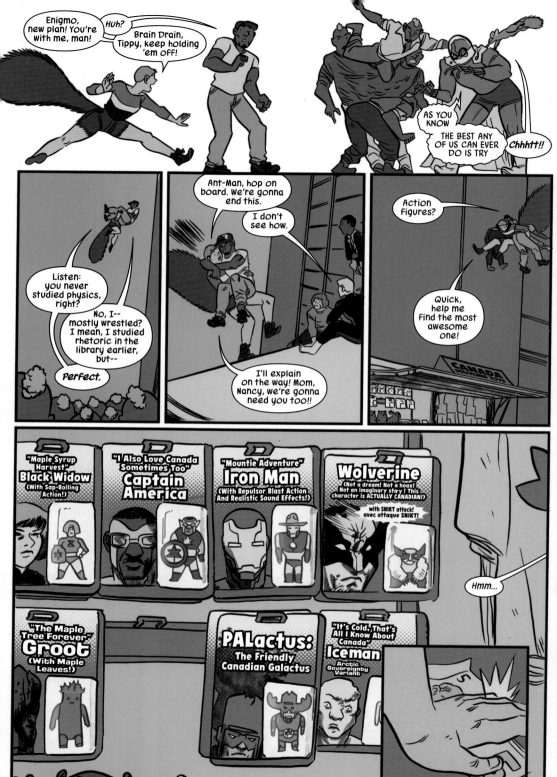

Action Figures not pictured include: "Hellcat (But in Canadian Clothes)," "Howard the Canadian Duck (So I Guess That Means He's A Northern Shoveler Duck Or Something)," and "Angela: Queen of Halifax."

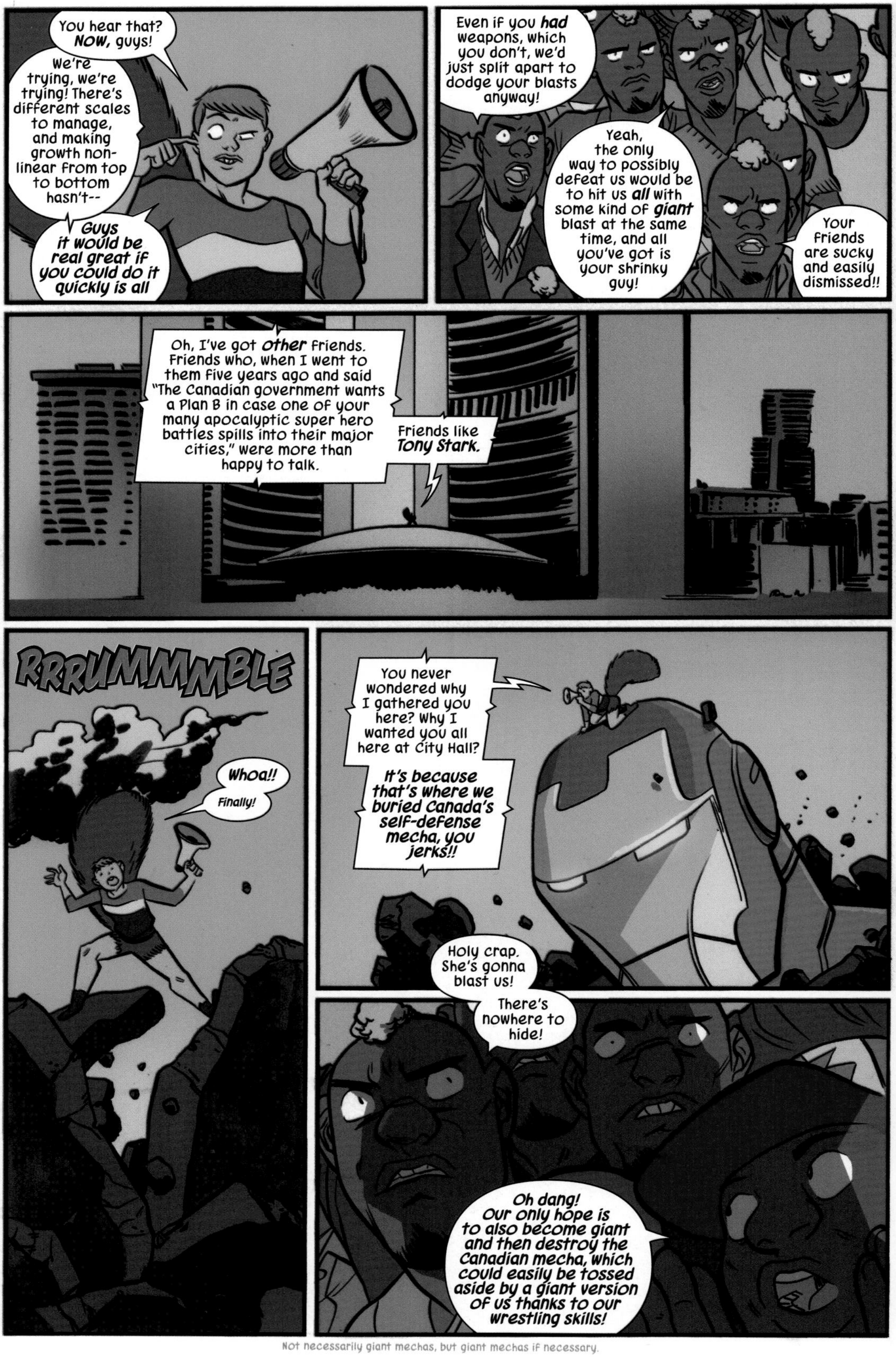
You hear that? NOW, guys!
We're trying, we're trying! There's different scales to manage, and making growth non-linear from top to bottom hasn't--
Guys it would be real great if you could do it quickly is all
Even if you had weapons, which you don't, we'd just split apart to dodge your blasts anyway!
Yeah, the only way to possibly defeat us would be to hit us all with some kind of giant blast at the same time, and all you've got is your shrinky guy!
Your friends are sucky and easily dismissed!!
Oh, I've got other friends. Friends who, when I went to them five years ago and said "The Canadian government wants a Plan B in case one of your many apocalyptic super hero battles spills into their major cities," were more than happy to talk.
Friends like Tony Stark.
RRRUMMMMBLE
Whoa!!
Finally!
You never wondered why I gathered you here? Why I wanted you all here at City Hall?
It's because that's where we buried Canada's self-defense mecha, you jerks!!
Holy crap. She's gonna blast us!
There's nowhere to hide!
Oh dang! Our only hope is to also become giant and then destroy the Canadian mecha, which could easily be tossed aside by a giant version of us thanks to our wrestling skills!

Not necessarily giant mechas, but giant mechas if necessary.

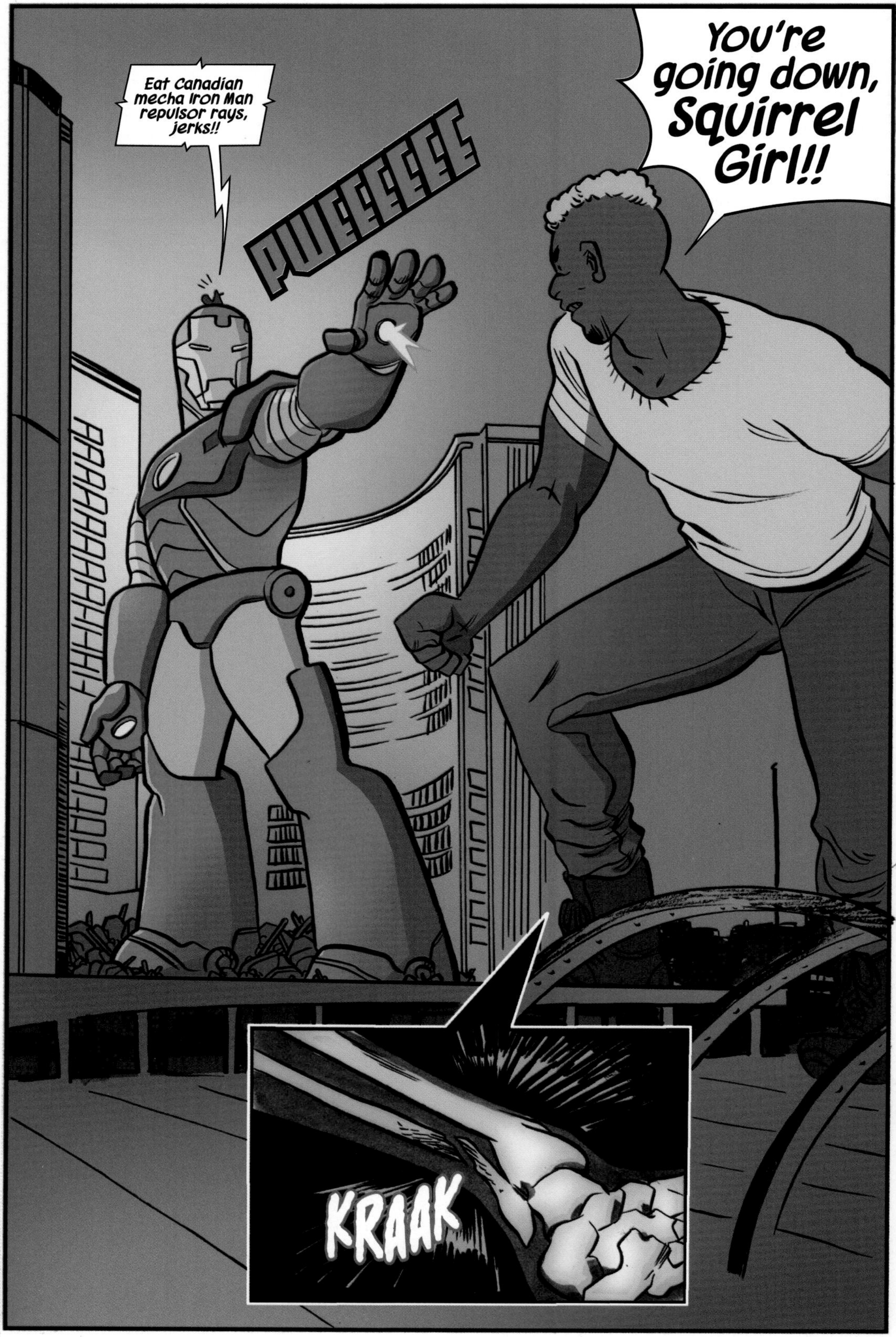

Eat Canadian mecha Iron Man repulsor rays, jerks!!
PWEEEEEEE
You're going down, Squirrel Girl!!
KRAAK

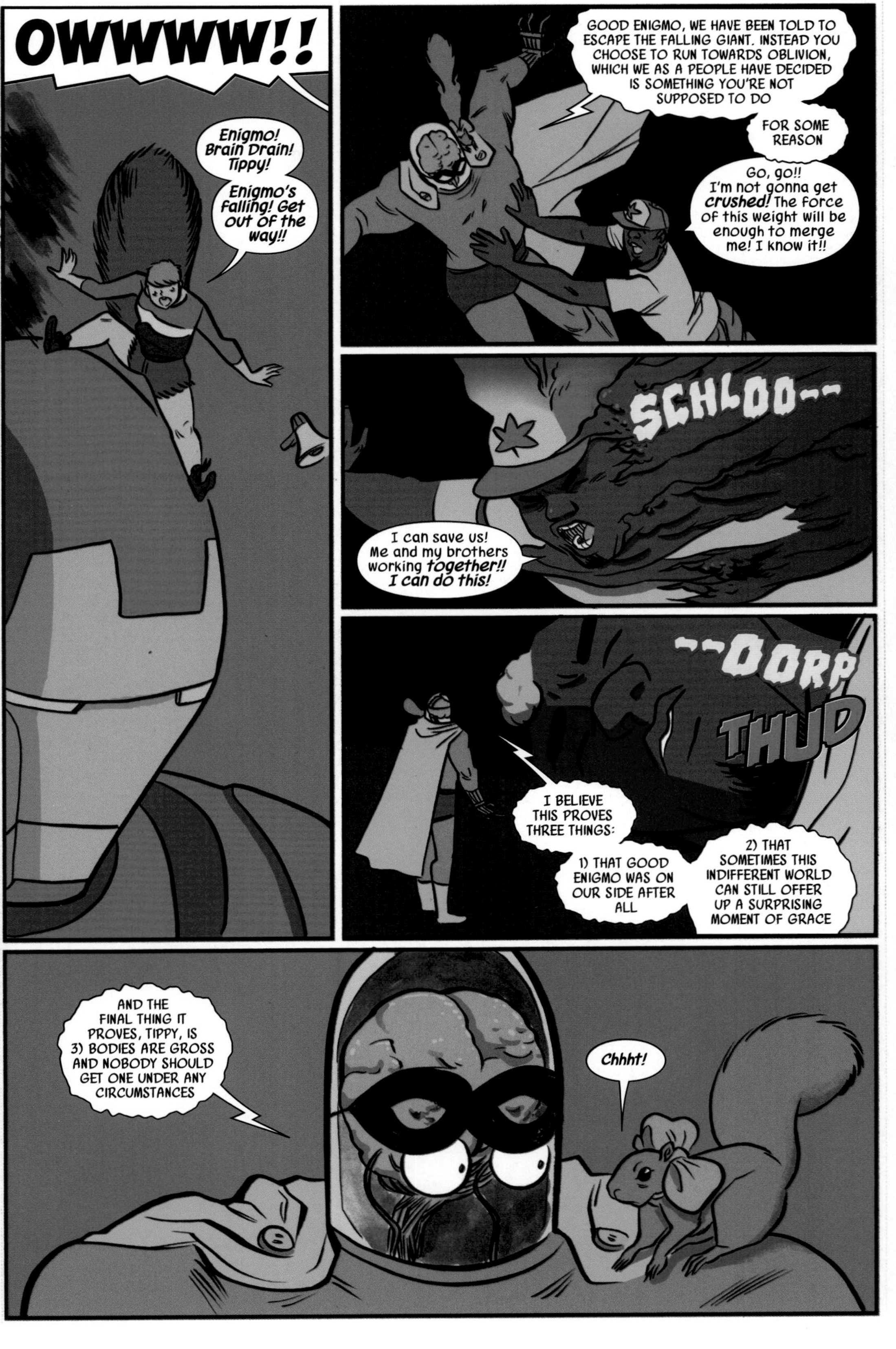
OWWWW!!
Enigmo! Brain Drain! Tippy!
Enigmo's falling! Get out of the way!!
GOOD ENIGMO, WE HAVE BEEN TOLD TO ESCAPE THE FALLING GIANT. INSTEAD YOU CHOOSE TO RUN TOWARDS OBLIVION, WHICH WE AS A PEOPLE HAVE DECIDED IS SOMETHING YOU'RE NOT SUPPOSED TO DO
FOR SOME REASON
Go, go!! I'm not gonna get crushed! The force of this weight will be enough to merge me! I know it!!
SCHLOO--
I can save us! Me and my brothers working together!! I can do this!
--OORP
THUD
I BELIEVE THIS PROVES THREE THINGS:
1) THAT GOOD ENIGMO WAS ON OUR SIDE AFTER ALL
2) THAT SOMETIMES THIS INDIFFERENT WORLD CAN STILL OFFER UP A SURPRISING MOMENT OF GRACE
AND THE FINAL THING IT PROVES, TIPPY, IS 3) BODIES ARE GROSS AND NOBODY SHOULD GET ONE UNDER ANY CIRCUMSTANCES
Chhht!

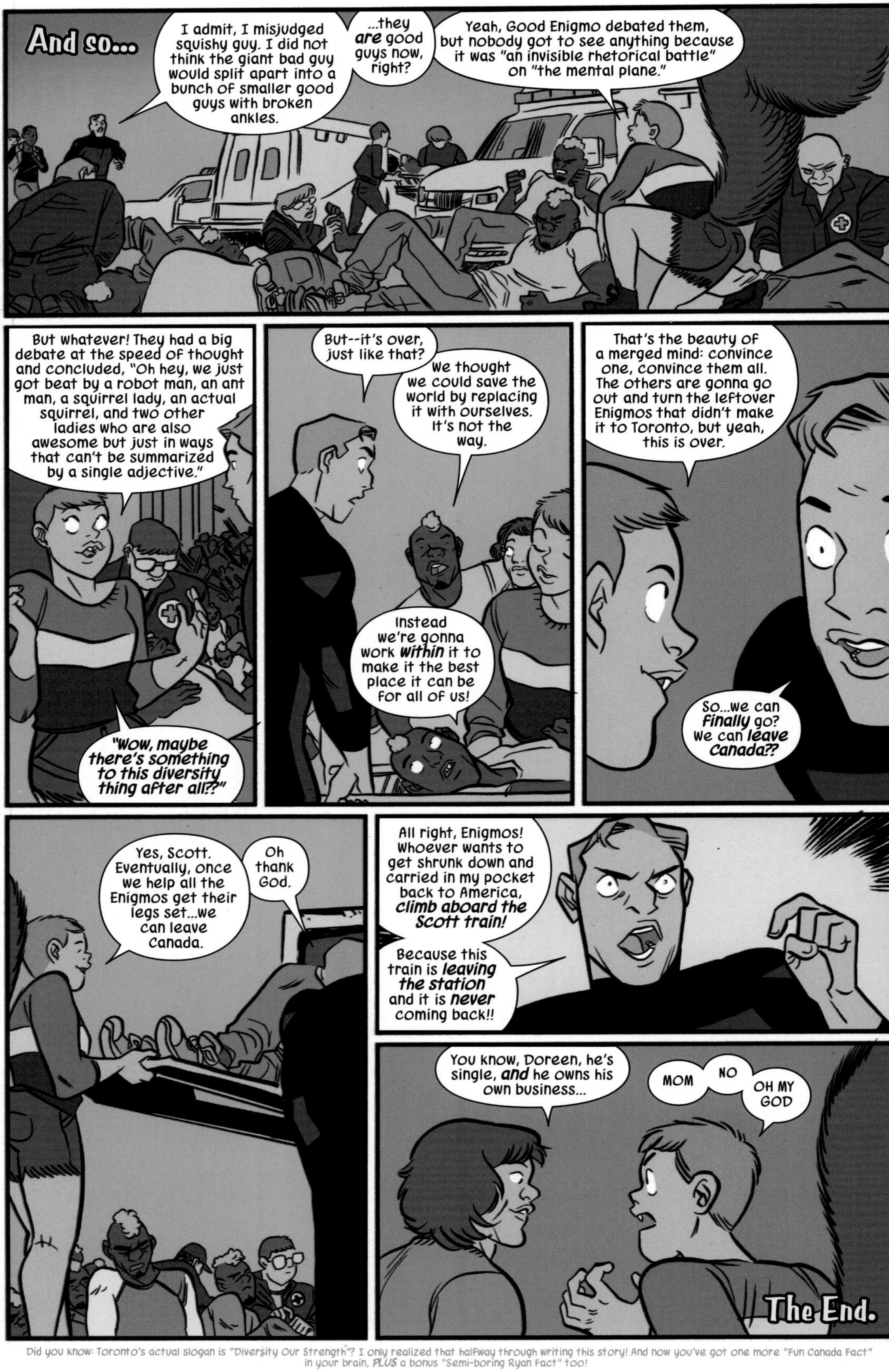

And so...
I admit, I misjudged squishy guy. I did not think the giant bad guy would split apart into a bunch of smaller good guys with broken ankles.
...they *are* good guys now, right?
Yeah, Good Enigmo debated them, but nobody got to see anything because it was "an invisible rhetorical battle" on "the mental plane."
But whatever! They had a big debate at the speed of thought and concluded, "Oh hey, we just got beat by a robot man, an ant man, a squirrel lady, an actual squirrel, and two other ladies who are also awesome but just in ways that can't be summarized by a single adjective."
"Wow, maybe there's something to this diversity thing after all??"
But--it's over, just like that?
We thought we could save the world by replacing it with ourselves. It's not the way.
Instead we're gonna work *within* it to make it the best place it can be for all of us!
That's the beauty of a merged mind: convince one, convince them all. The others are gonna go out and turn the leftover Enigmos that didn't make it to Toronto, but yeah, this is over.
So...we can *finally* go? We can *leave Canada??*
Yes, Scott. Eventually, once we help all the Enigmos get their legs set...we can leave Canada.
Oh thank God.
All right, Enigmos! Whoever wants to get shrunk down and carried in my pocket back to America, *climb aboard the Scott train!*
Because this train is *leaving the station* and it is *never* coming back!!
You know, Doreen, he's single, *and* he owns his own business...
MOM
NO
OH MY GOD
The End.

Did you know: Toronto's actual slogan is "Diver$ity Our Strength"? I only realized that halfway through writing this story! And now you've got one more "Fun Canada Fact" in your brain, *PLUS* a bonus "Semi-boring Ryan Fact" too!

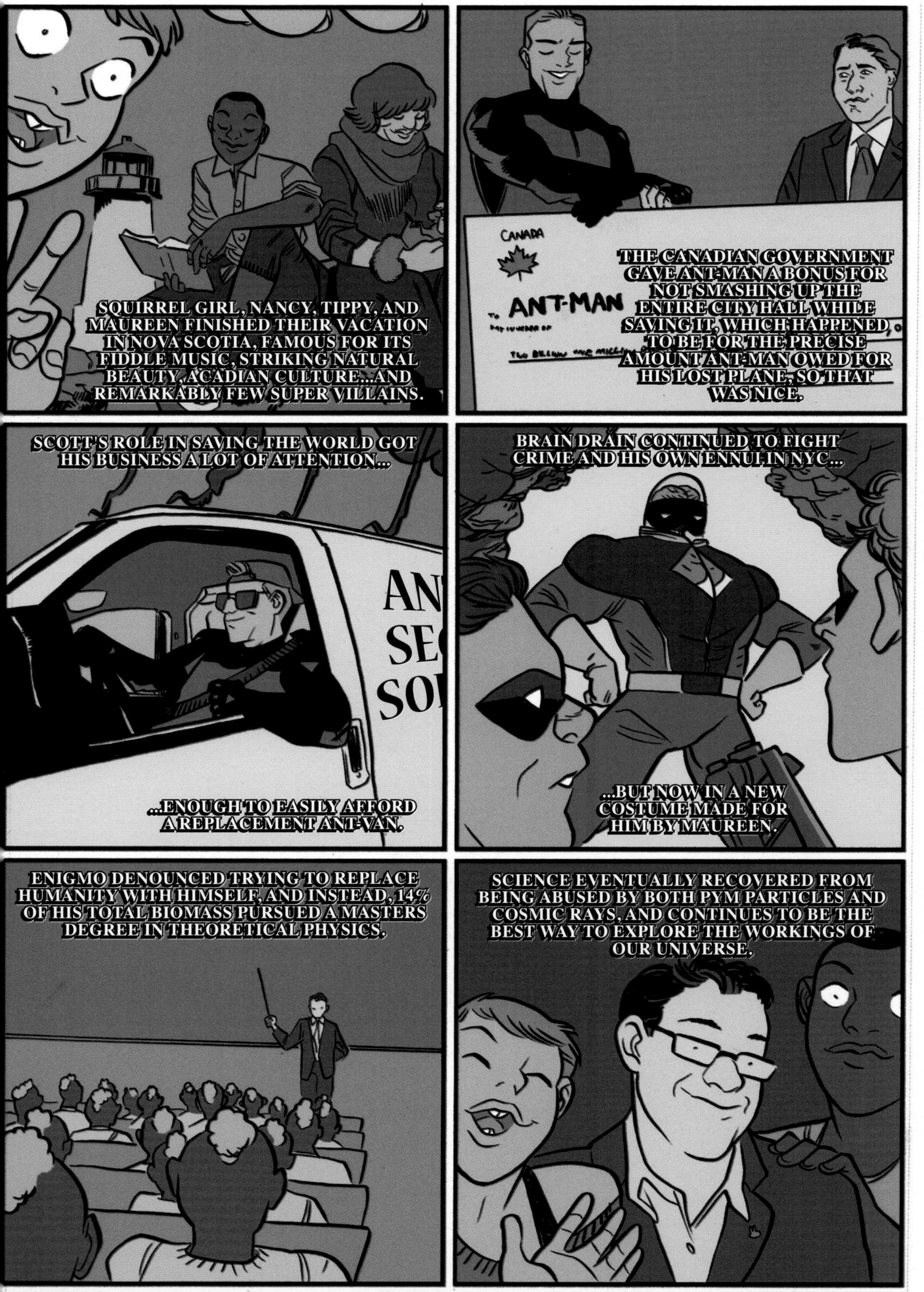
SQUIRREL GIRL, NANCY, TIPPY, AND MAUREEN FINISHED THEIR VACATION IN NOVA SCOTIA, FAMOUS FOR ITS FIDDLE MUSIC, STRIKING NATURAL BEAUTY, ACADIAN CULTURE...AND REMARKABLY FEW SUPER VILLAINS.
CANADA
ANT-MAN
THE CANADIAN GOVERNMENT GAVE ANT-MAN A BONUS FOR NOT SMASHING UP THE ENTIRE CITY HALL WHILE SAVING IT, WHICH HAPPENED TO BE FOR THE PRECISE AMOUNT ANT-MAN OWED FOR HIS LOST PLANE, SO THAT WAS NICE.
SCOTT'S ROLE IN SAVING THE WORLD GOT HIS BUSINESS A LOT OF ATTENTION...
...ENOUGH TO EASILY AFFORD A REPLACEMENT ANT-VAN.
BRAIN DRAIN CONTINUED TO FIGHT CRIME AND HIS OWN ENNUI IN NYC...
...BUT NOW IN A NEW COSTUME MADE FOR HIM BY MAUREEN.
ENIGMO DENOUNCED TRYING TO REPLACE HUMANITY WITH HIMSELF, AND INSTEAD, 14% OF HIS TOTAL BIOMASS PURSUED A MASTERS DEGREE IN THEORETICAL PHYSICS.
SCIENCE EVENTUALLY RECOVERED FROM BEING ABUSED BY BOTH PYM PARTICLES AND COSMIC RAYS, AND CONTINUES TO BE THE BEST WAY TO EXPLORE THE WORKINGS OF OUR UNIVERSE.
THE (REAL, FINAL) END.

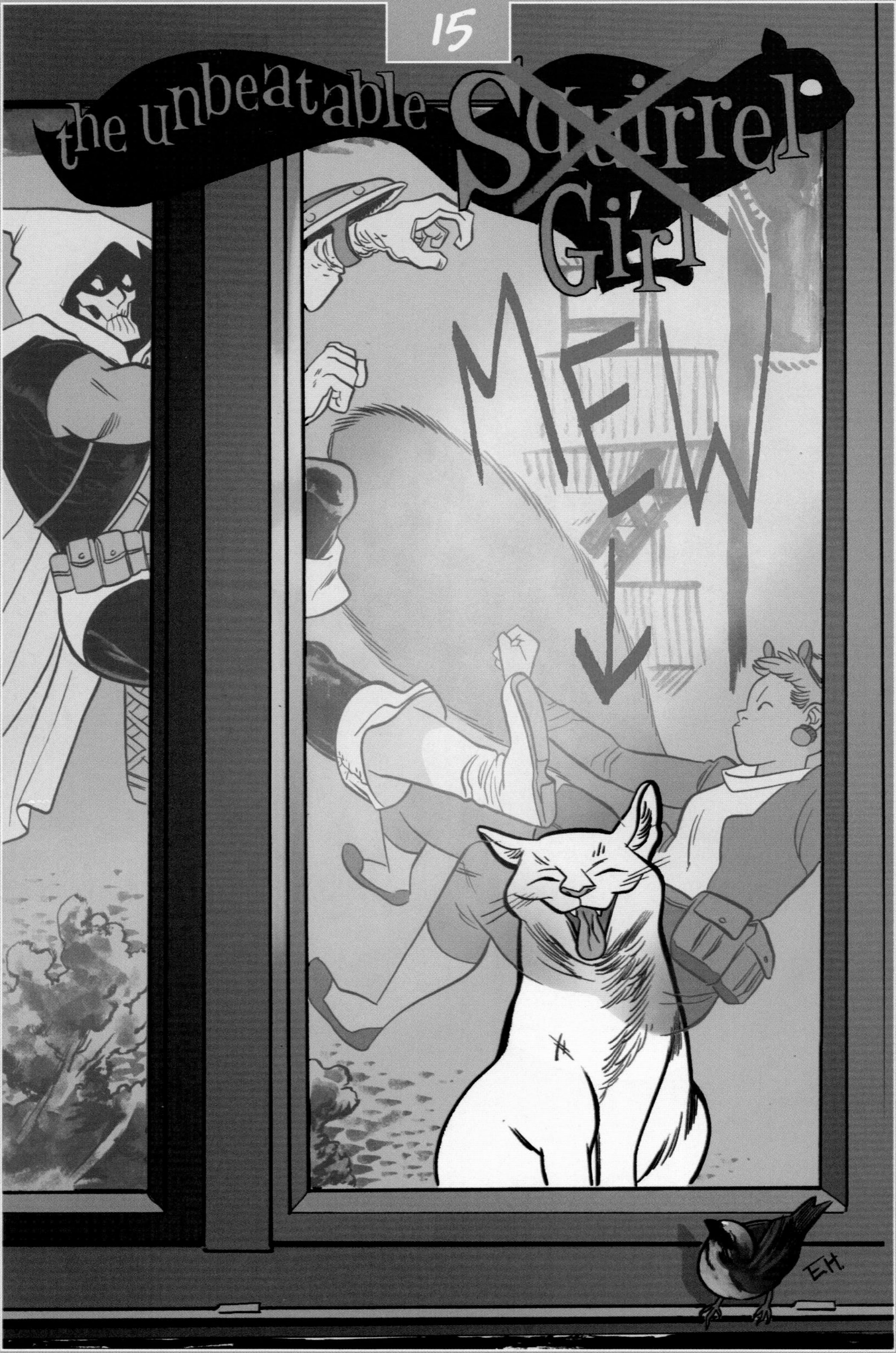
15
the unbeatable Squirrel Girl
MEW
E.H.

Doreen Green isn't just a second-year computer science student: she secretly also has all the powers of both squirrel and girl! She uses her amazing abilities to fight crime **and** be as awesome as possible. You know her as...*The Unbeatable Squirrel Girl!* Find out what she's been up to, with...

Squirrel Girl *in a nutshell*

Nancy Whitehead @sewwiththeflo
zcadfewg5ttyniu,o;

Nancy Whitehead @sewwiththeflo
Hey everyone, sorry, my cat got on my keyboard and somehow posted that. Pretty cute though, right? Anyway, test post please ignore.

Nancy Whitehead @sewwiththeflo
';,l;joih87t67r5d4dsaqzdx

Nancy Whitehead @sewwiththeflo
Once more, sorry, Mew walked on my laptop again. Less cute the second time. I'll keep it closed from now on.

Nancy Whitehead @sewwiththeflo
hrzayus5f3iu6t54h76p8k70[k98;'--]\

Nancy Whitehead @sewwiththeflo
Okay okay she got on my phone this time but I PROMISE Mew will stop posting on my account.

Nancy Whitehead @sewwiththeflo
Thank you all for following me on social media today and I hoped you enjoyed this unscheduled #content.

Nancy Whitehead @sewwiththeflo
fmgnsjkbehrftyqu27334dfd5yn7c5jmikn,ob,lm;n9',

Nancy Whitehead @sewwiththeflo
Mew, how is this happening

Nancy Whitehead @sewwiththeflo
How is this happening, Mew

Nancy Whitehead @sewwiththeflo
XSCDV32CDN43KJ54HK6LUUMIK9OP97LKI

Nancy Whitehead @sewwiththeflo
Sorry, I'm sorry, I don't know how this keeps being a thing. I put my laptop under the bed WHILE LOGGED OUT, and yet here we are??

Nancy Whitehead @sewwiththeflo
VDSABCwvce32j43t56hy86jk98..l;jk

Nancy Whitehead @sewwiththeflo
Look all I can say is: if you followed me on this site then you knew the risks.

Squirrel Girl @unbeatablesg
@sewwiththeflo Maybe you should ask Mew to put her social media posts on... PAWS

Nancy Whitehead @sewwiththeflo
@unbeatablesg xacf435hy6gngj7ti7tj

Nancy Whitehead @sewwiththeflo
@unbeatablesg OKAY SHE'S REPLYING TO YOU NOW, HOLY COW, THIS IS CRAZY, WHAT IS GOING ON

Squirrel Girl @unbeatablesg
@sewwiththeflo I agree it's...CLAWS for concern

Nancy Whitehead @sewwiththeflo
@unbeatablesg I THINK I FIGURED IT OUT, YOU HAVE TO HIT CTRL+ENTER TO POST AND HER NATURAL GAIT REACHES THOSE TWO KEYS

Squirrel Girl @unbeatablesg
@sewwiththeflo but how is she getting the laptop open though??

Nancy Whitehead @sewwiththeflo
@unbeatablesg Listen, Mew is the best cat and therefore I'm sure she has her ways, but I'm CERTAIN now I've figured it out.

Nancy Whitehead @sewwiththeflo
@unbeatablesg It won't happen again. EVER.

Nancy Whitehead @sewwiththeflo
zwdreh4u7oi98p-['9=-=;p0lomnybtcdexweaq

Nancy Whitehead @sewwiththeflo
MEW

Nancy Whitehead @sewwiththeflo
WHY

Nancy Whitehead @sewwiththeflo
WHY, MEW

search!

#zcrg5ju7,i;

#lknmjguifte4w3q

#zcdvtnmukil;;;;;;;;;;

#8dfuetryt3#4

#cyuu6ui7jjmmm

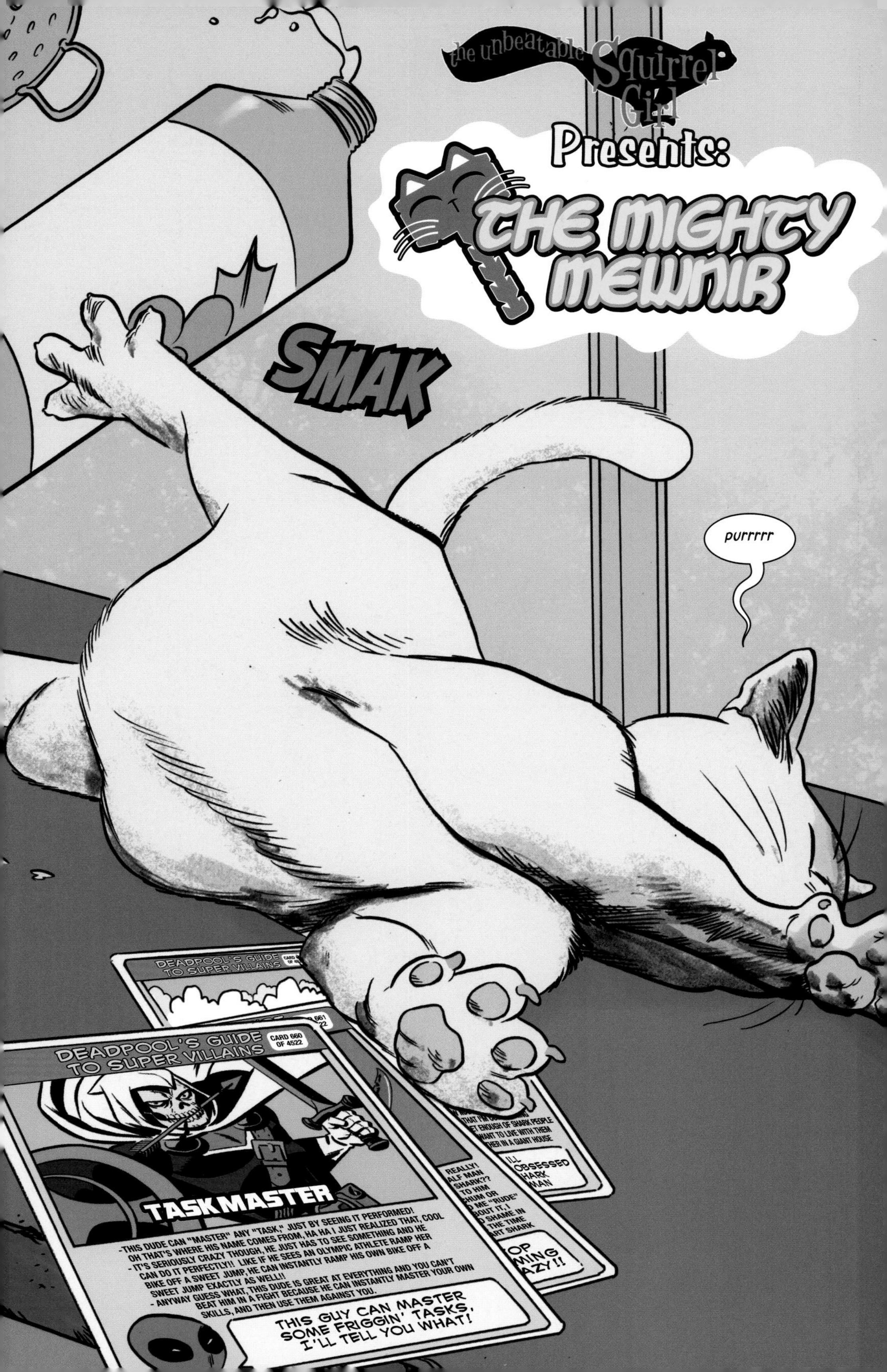
the unbeatable Squirrel Girl
Presents:
THE MIGHTY MEWNIR
SMAK
purrrrr
DEADPOOL'S GUIDE TO SUPER VILLAINS
CARD 660 OF 4522
TASKMASTER
-THIS DUDE CAN "MASTER" ANY "TASK," JUST BY SEEING IT PERFORMED! OH THAT'S WHERE HIS NAME COMES FROM, HA HA I JUST REALIZED THAT, COOL
- IT'S SERIOUSLY CRAZY THOUGH, HE JUST HAS TO SEE SOMETHING AND HE CAN DO IT PERFECTLY!! LIKE IF HE SEES AN OLYMPIC ATHLETE RAMP HER BIKE OFF A SWEET JUMP, HE CAN INSTANTLY RAMP HIS OWN BIKE OFF A SWEET JUMP EXACTLY AS WELL!!
- ANYWAY GUESS WHAT, THIS DUDE IS GREAT AT EVERYTHING AND YOU CAN'T BEAT HIM IN A FIGHT BECAUSE HE CAN INSTANTLY MASTER YOUR OWN SKILLS, AND THEN USE THEM AGAINST YOU.
THIS GUY CAN MASTER SOME FRIGGIN' TASKS, I'LL TELL YOU WHAT!

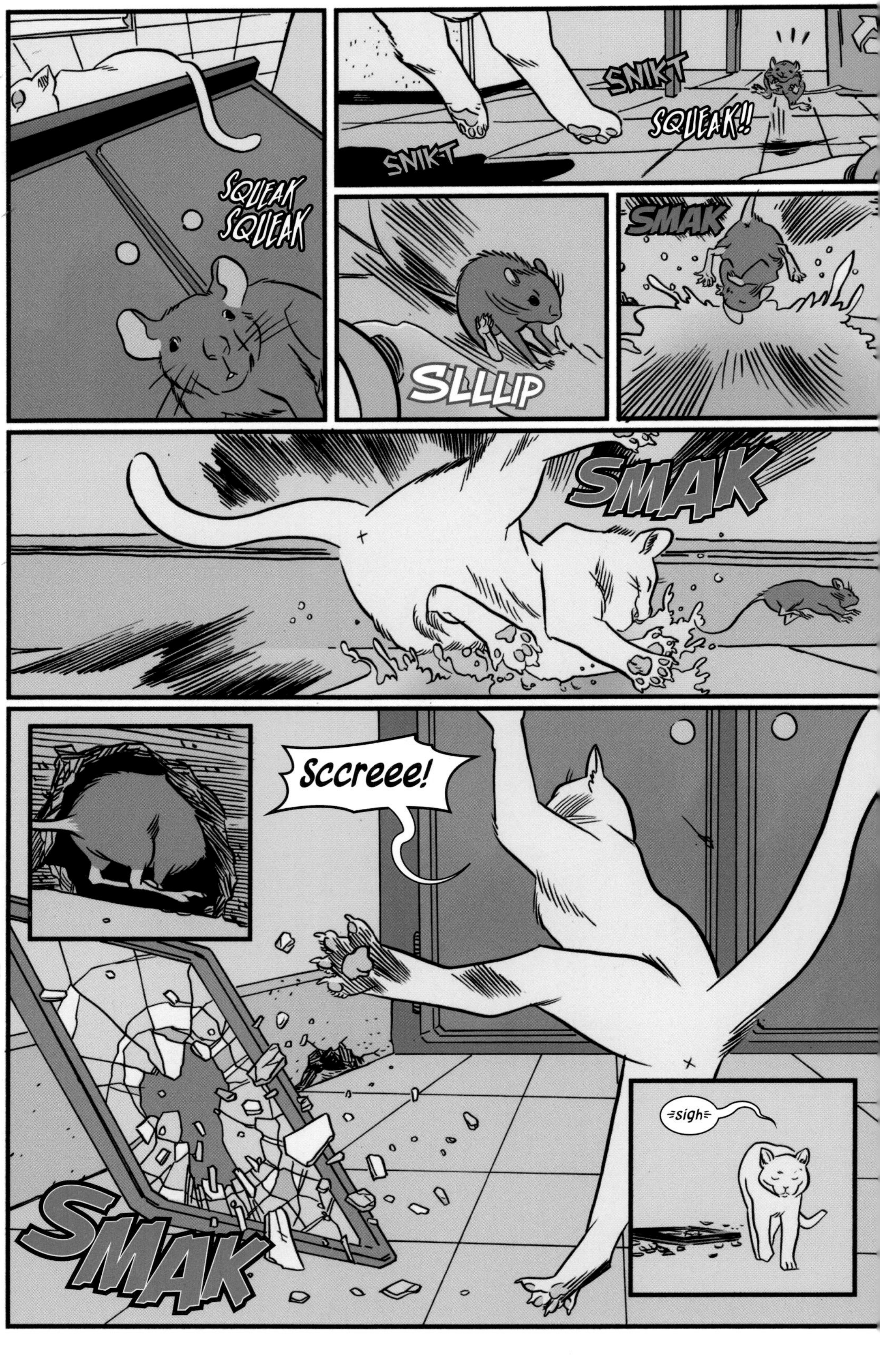
SQUEAK
SQUEAK
SNIKT
SNIKT
SQUEAK!!
SLLLIP
SMAK
SMAK
Sccreee!
SMAK
sigh

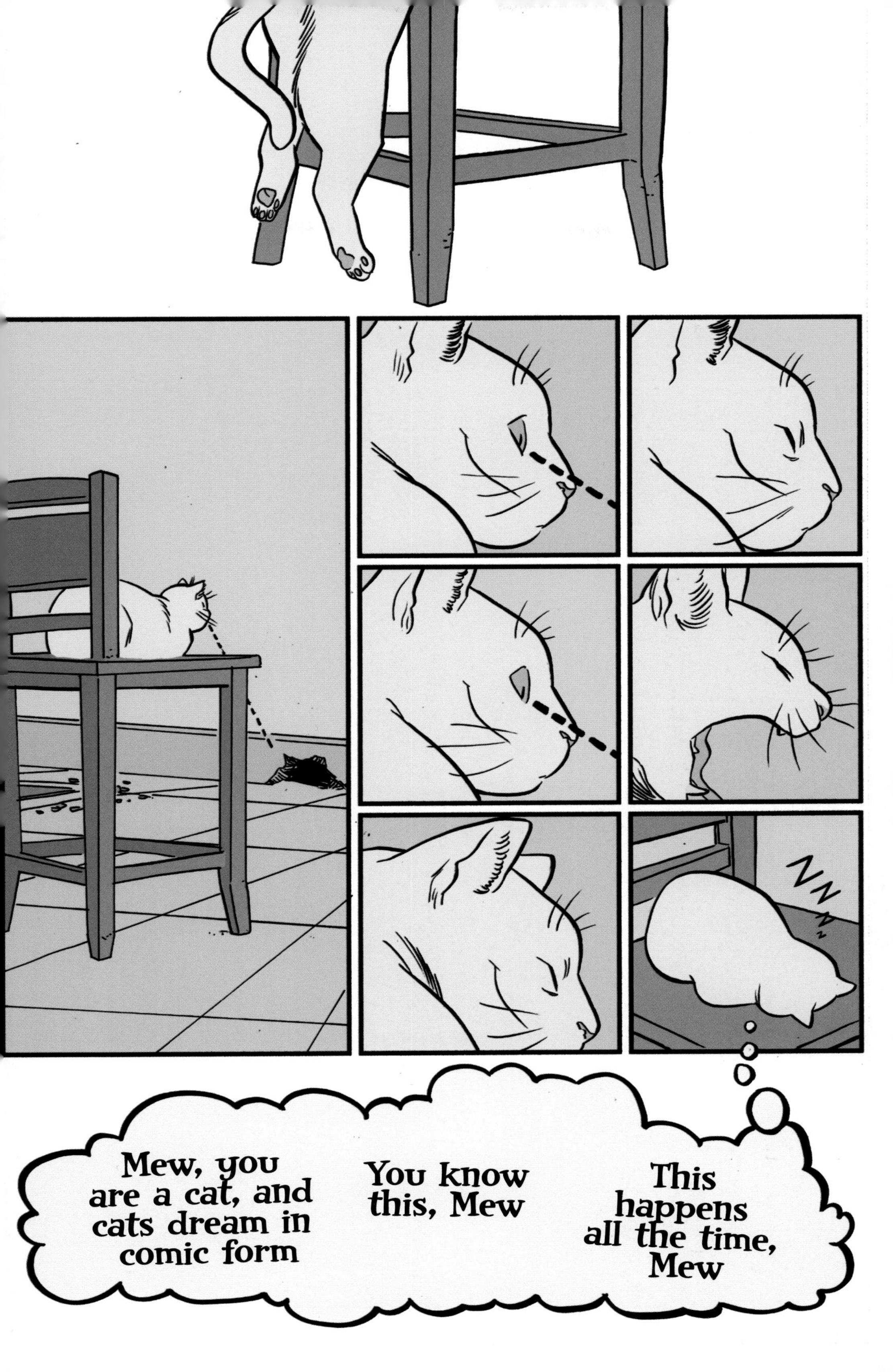
ZZZ
Mew, you are a cat, and cats dream in comic form
You know this, Mew
This happens all the time, Mew

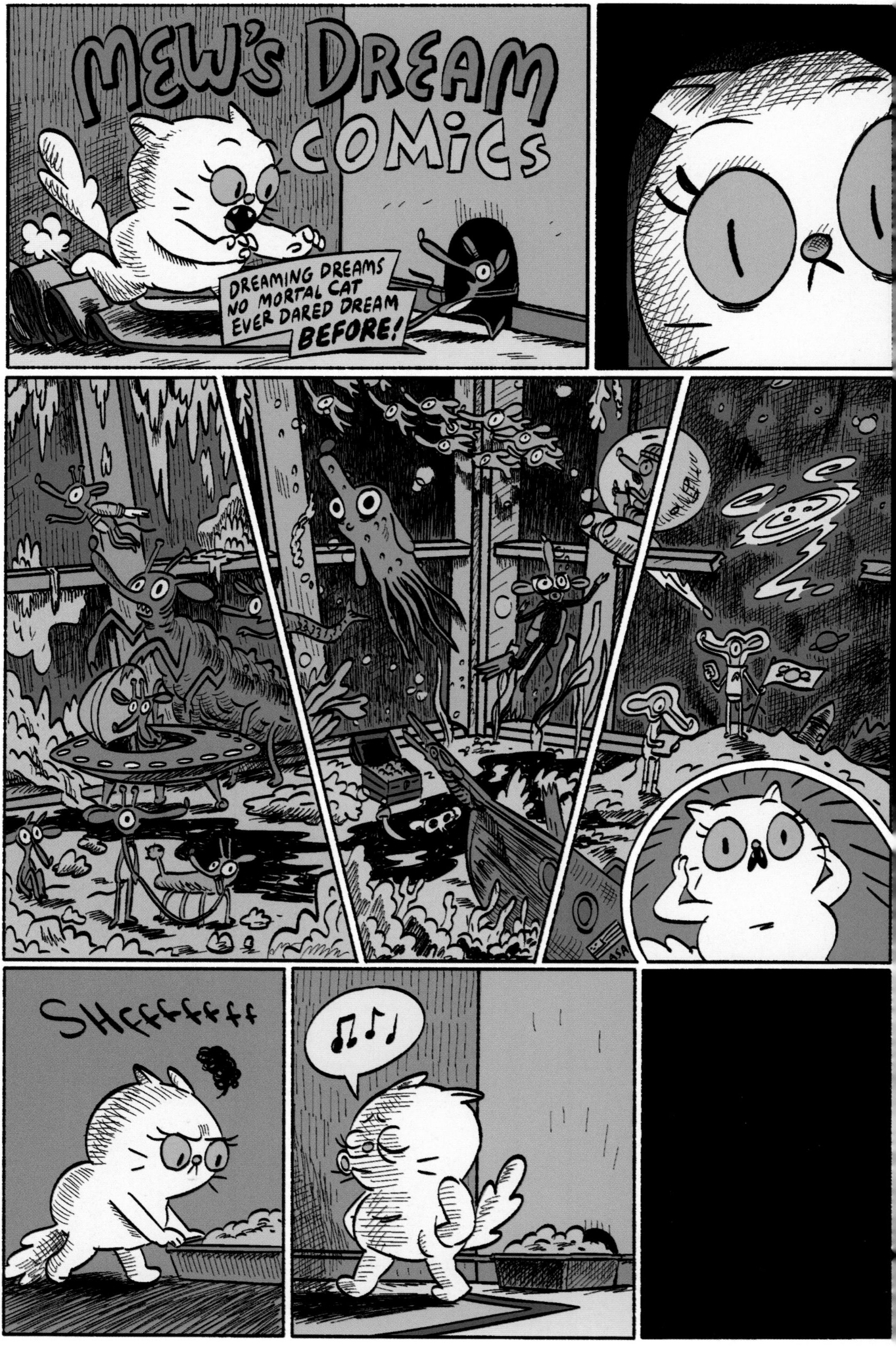
MEW'S DREAM COMICS
DREAMING DREAMS NO MORTAL CAT EVER DARED DREAM BEFORE!
SHFFFFFFF

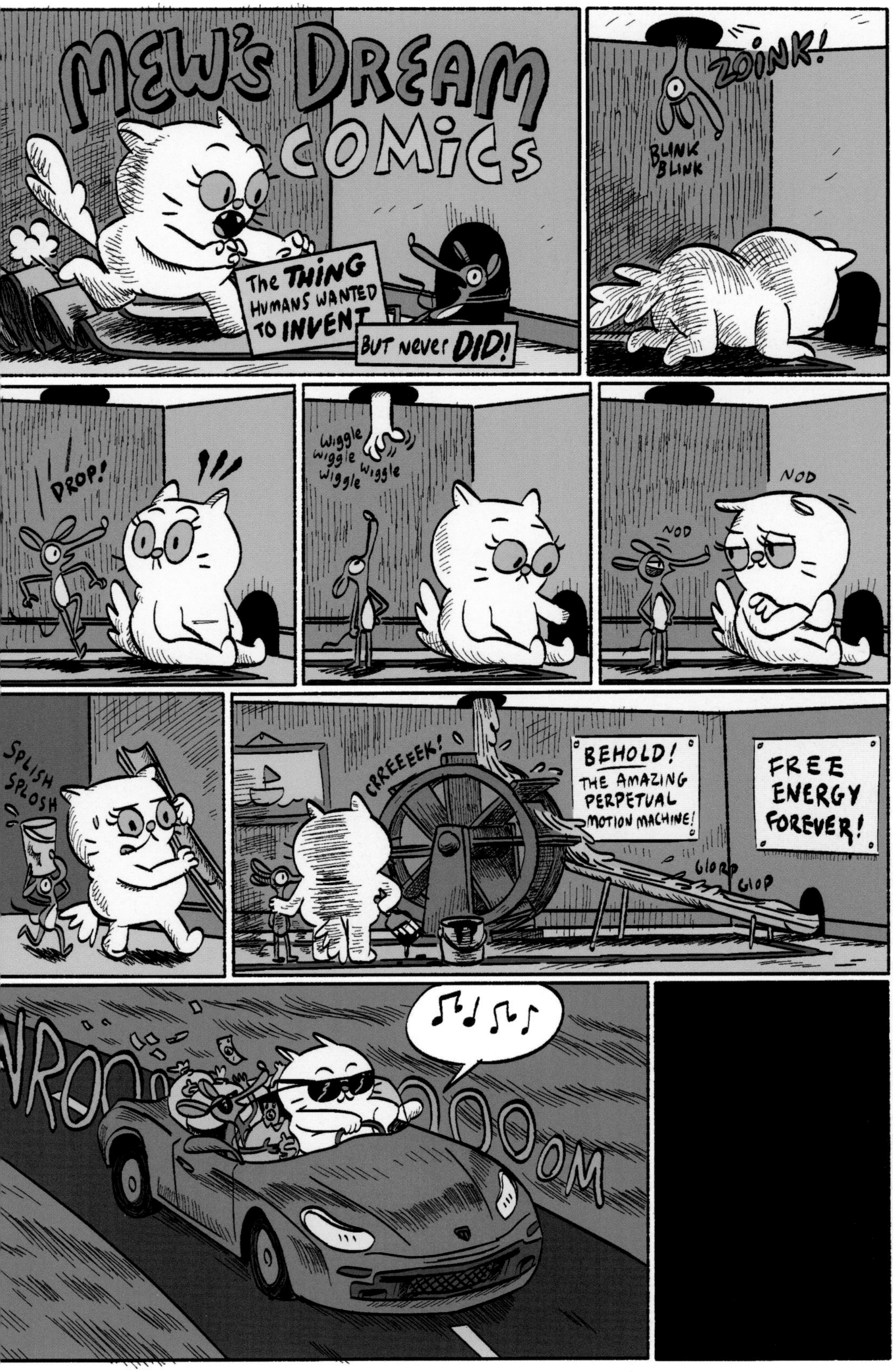
MEW'S DREAM COMICS
The THING HUMANS WANTED TO INVENT
BUT never DID!
ZOINK!
BLINK BLINK
DROP!
Wiggle wiggle wiggle wiggle
NOD
NOD
SPLISH SPLOSH
CREEEEK!
BEHOLD! THE AMAZING PERPETUAL MOTION MACHINE!
FREE ENERGY FOREVER!
GLORP GLOP
VROOooooOOOM

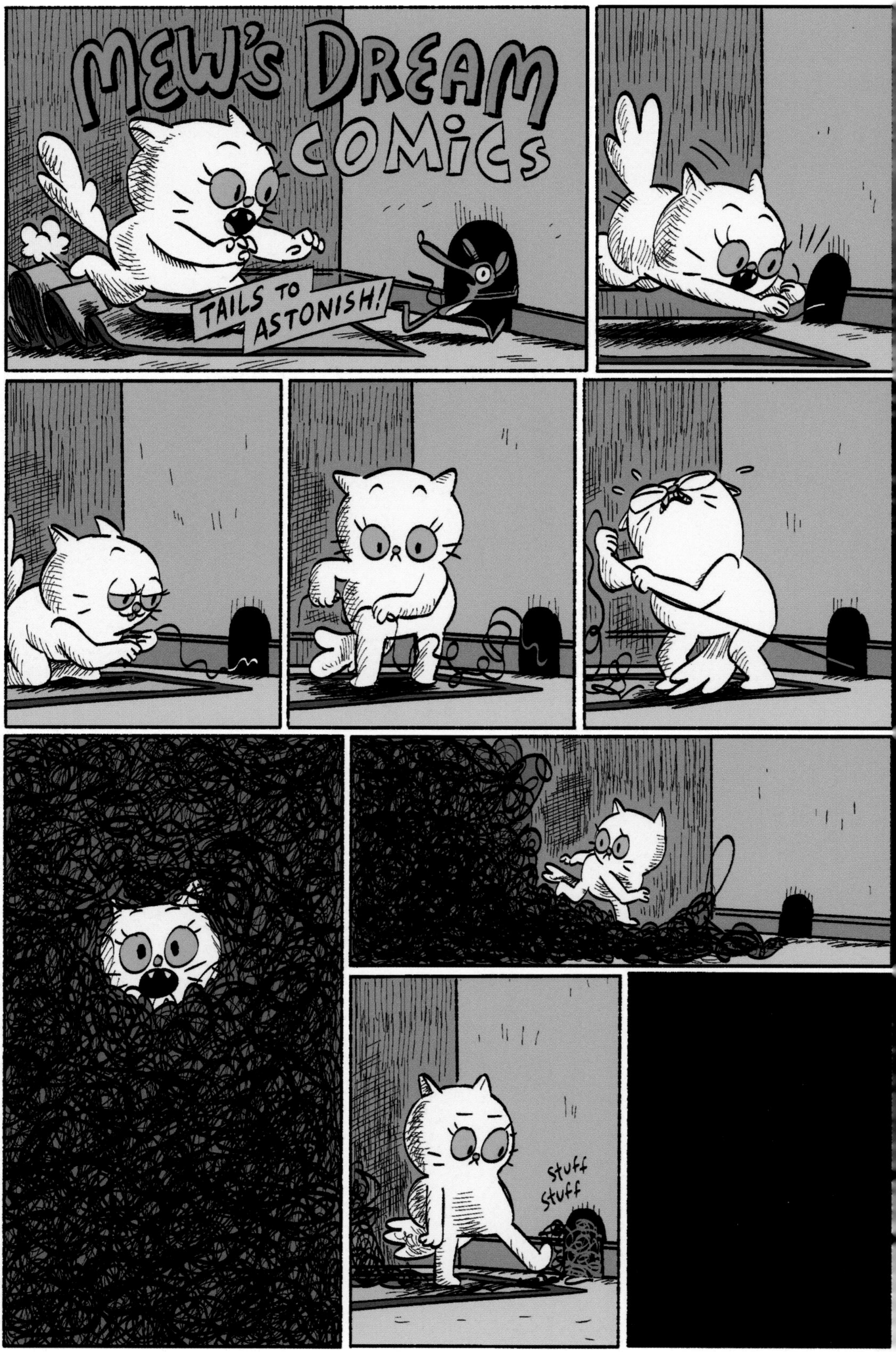
MEW'S DREAM COMICS
TAILS TO ASTONISH!
stuff
stuff

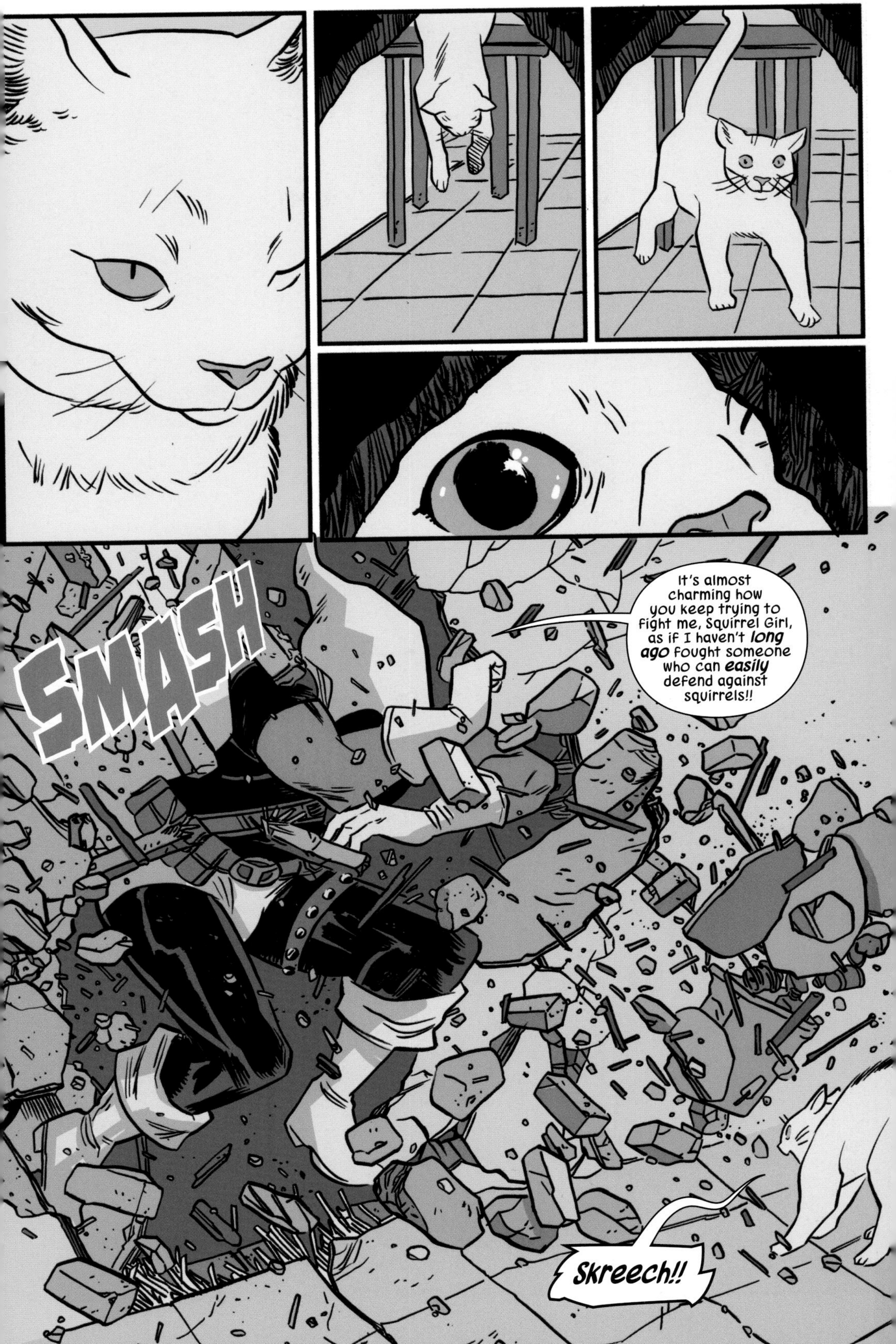
SMASH
It's almost charming how you keep trying to fight me, Squirrel Girl, as if I haven't long ago fought someone who can easily defend against squirrels!!
Skreech!!

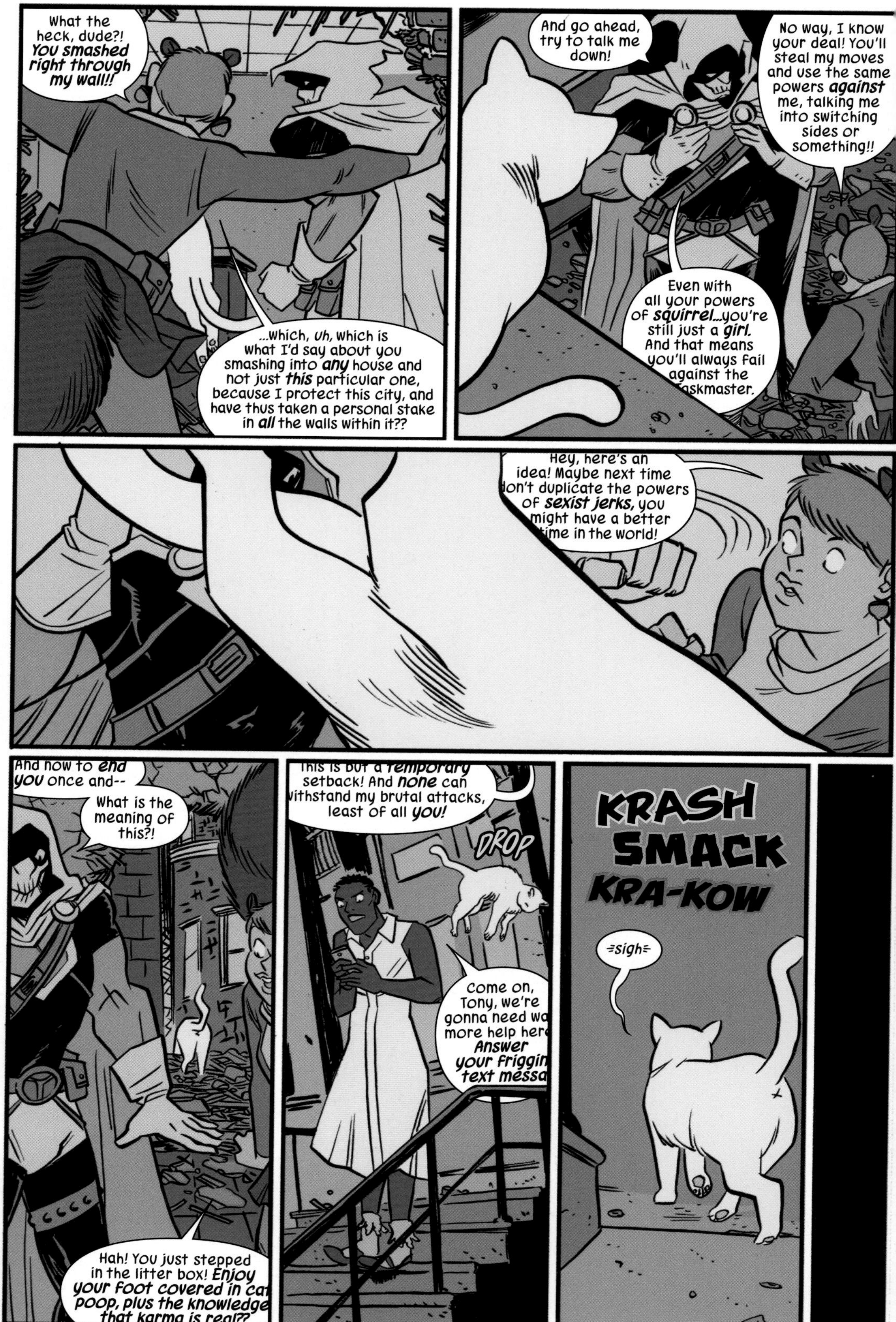

What the heck, dude?! You smashed right through my wall!!
...Which, uh, which is what I'd say about you smashing into any house and not just this particular one, because I protect this city, and have thus taken a personal stake in all the walls within it??
And go ahead, try to talk me down!
No way, I know your deal! You'll steal my moves and use the same powers against me, talking me into switching sides or something!!
Even with all your powers of squirrel...you're still just a girl. And that means you'll always fail against the Taskmaster.
Hey, here's an idea! Maybe next time don't duplicate the powers of sexist jerks, you might have a better time in the world!
And now to end you once and--
What is the meaning of this?!
Hah! You just stepped in the litter box! Enjoy your foot covered in cat poop, plus the knowledge that karma is real??
This is but a temporary setback! And none can withstand my brutal attacks, least of all YOU!
DROP
Come on, Tony, we're gonna need wa more help here Answer your friggin text messa
KRASH
SMACK
KRA-KOW
=sigh=

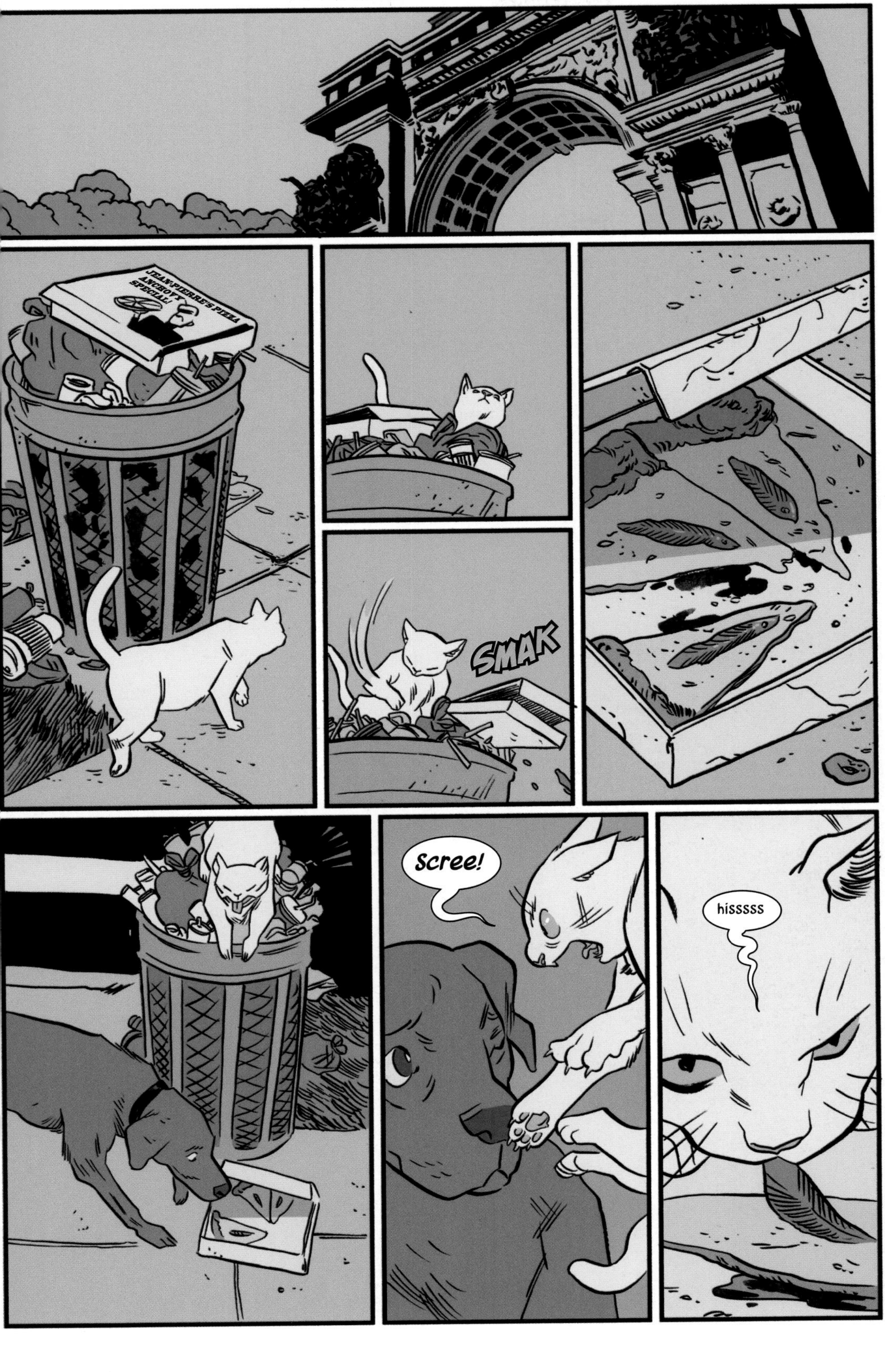

JEAN-PIERRE'S PIZZA
ANCHOVY SPECIAL!
SMAK
Scree!
hisssss

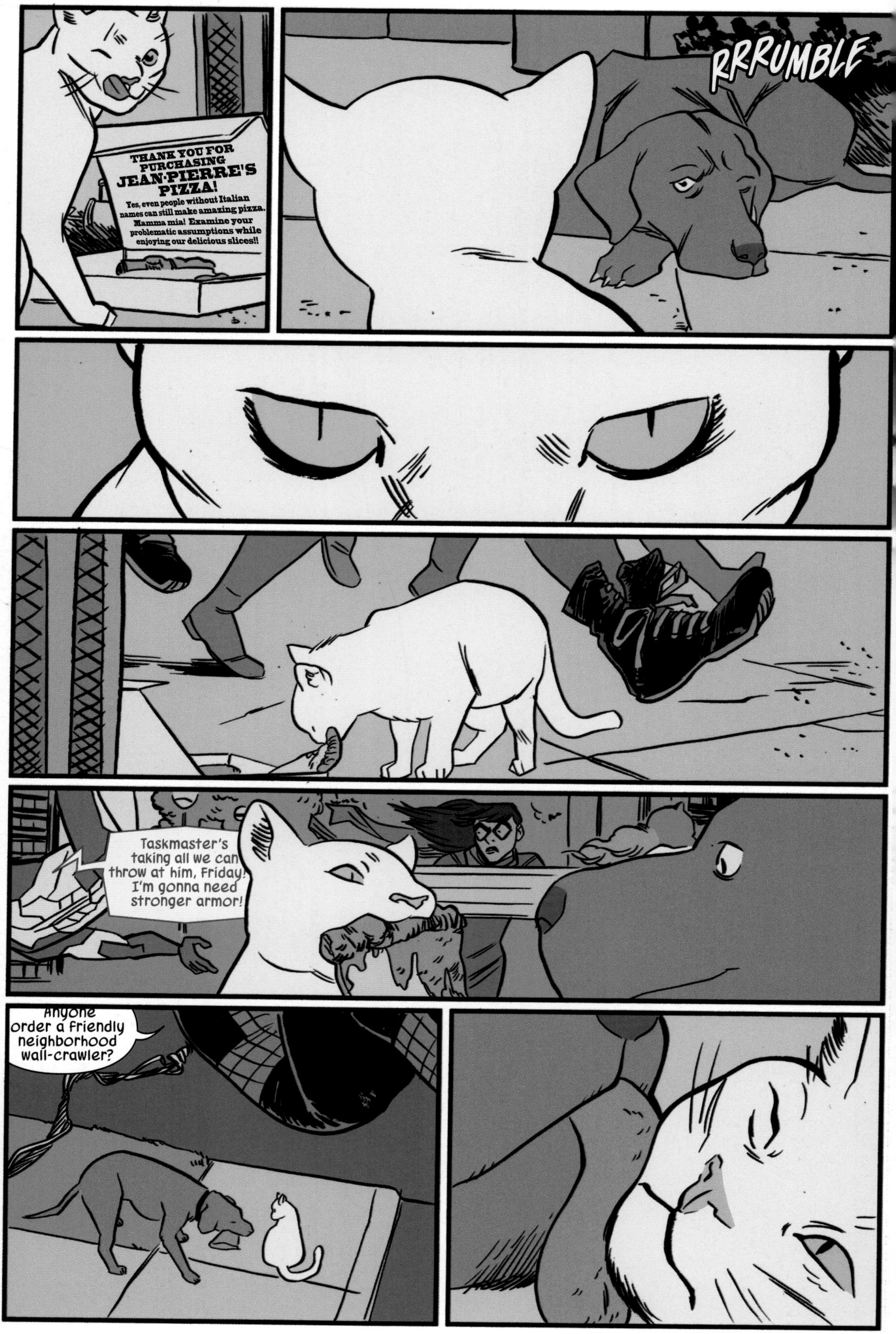
THANK YOU FOR PURCHASING JEAN-PIERRE'S PIZZA!
Yes, even people without Italian names can still make amazing pizza. Mamma mia! Examine your problematic assumptions while enjoying our delicious slices!!
RRRUMBLE
Taskmaster's taking all we can throw at him, Friday! I'm gonna need stronger armor!
Anyone order a friendly neighborhood wall-crawler?

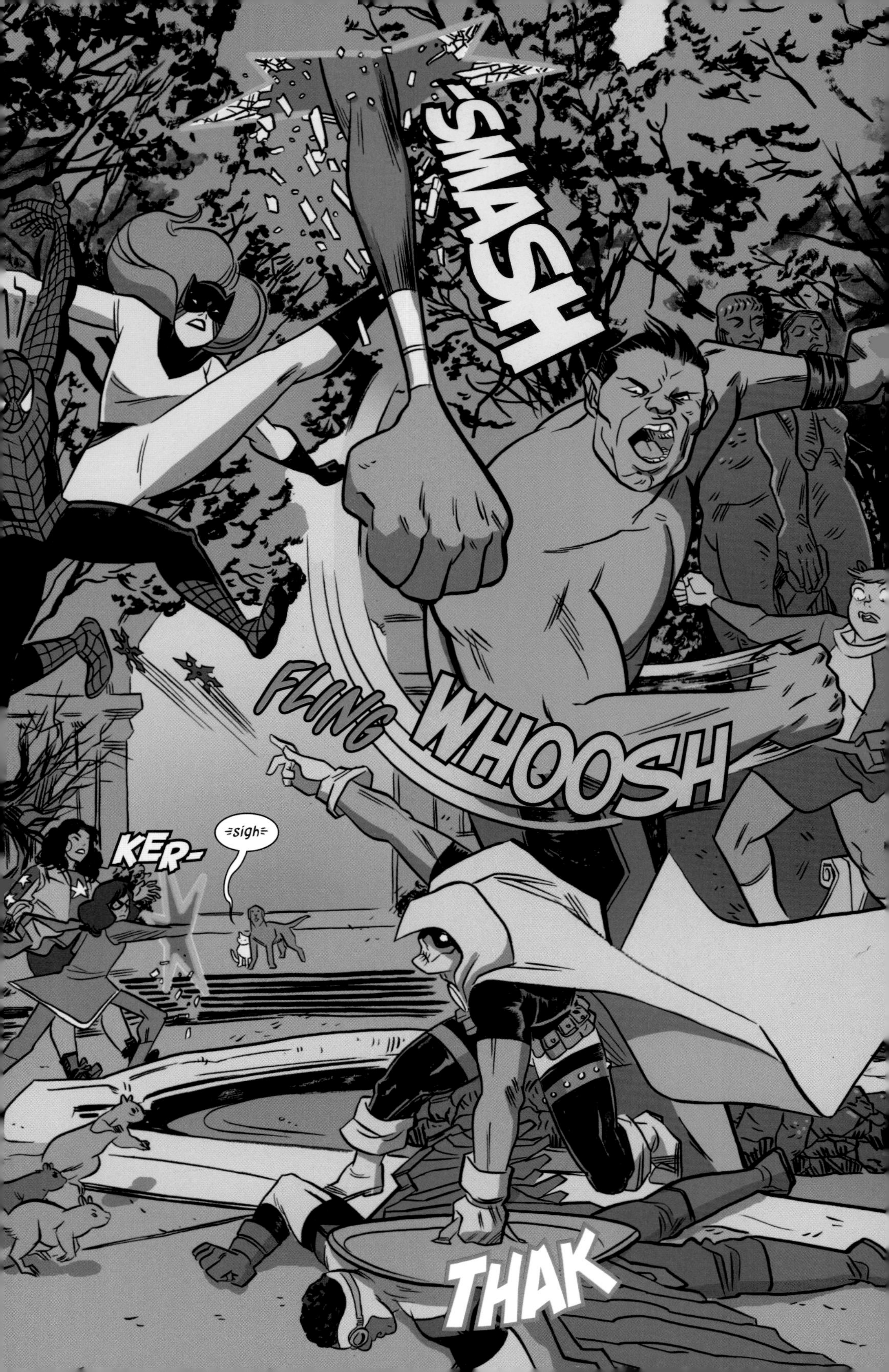
SMASH
FLING
WHOOSH
KER-
=sigh=
THAK

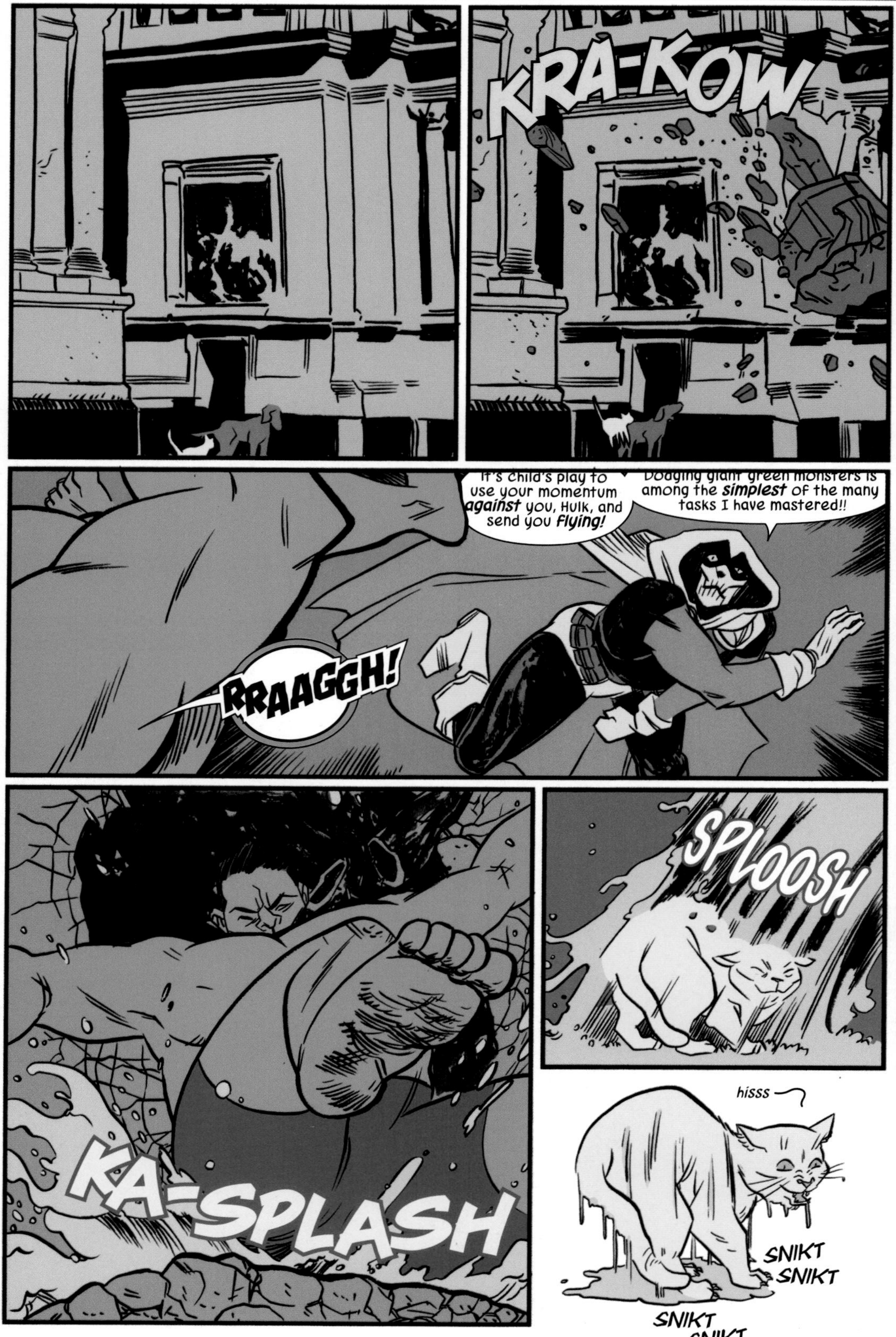
KRA-KOW
It's child's play to use your momentum *against* you, Hulk, and send you *flying!*
Dodging giant green monsters is among the *simplest* of the many tasks I have mastered!!
RRAAGGH!
KA-SPLASH
SPLOOSH
hisss
SNIKT
SNIKT
SNIKT
SNIKT

Even *all* your strength can't stop e! *Surrender* and I might

GR EAAK

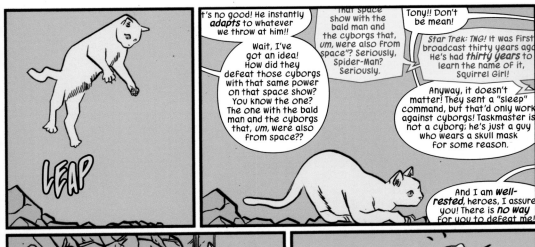

It's no good! He instantly *adapts* to whatever we throw at him!!

Wait, I've got an idea! How did they defeat those cyborgs with that same power on that space show? You know the one? The one with the bald man and the cyborgs that, *um*, were also from space??

That space show with the bald man and the cyborgs that, *um*, were also from space"? Seriously, Spider-Man? Seriously.

Tony!! Don't be mean!

Star Trek: TNG! It was first broadcast thirty years ago! He's had *thirty years* to learn the name of it, Squirrel Girl!

Anyway, it doesn't matter! They sent a "sleep" command, but that'd only work against cyborgs! Taskmaster is not a cyborg; he's just a guy who wears a skull mask for some reason.

And I am *well-rested*, heroes, I assure you! There is *no way* for you to defeat me!

LEAP

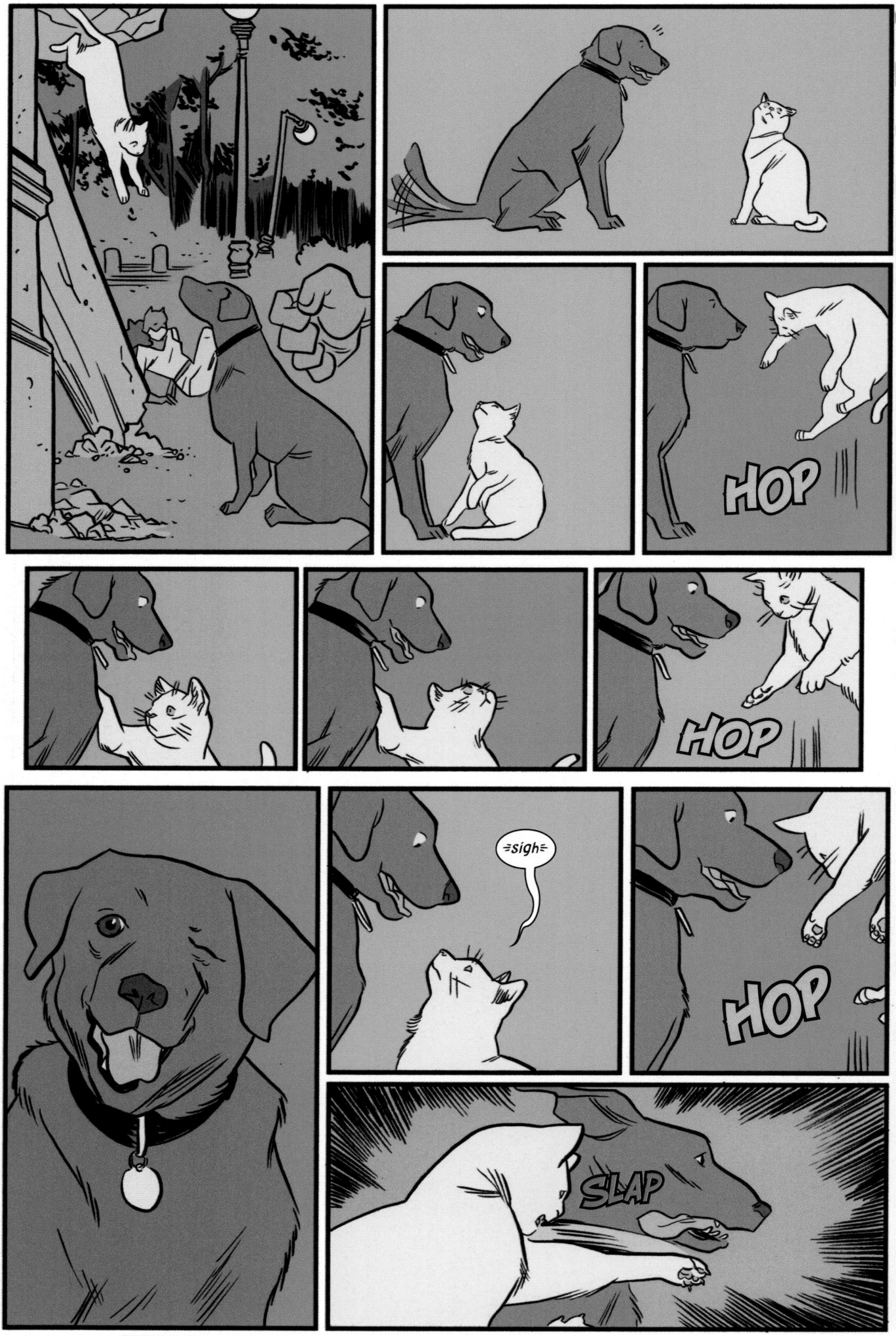
HOP
HOP
sigh
HOP
SLAP

Rarr rarr rarr!

Rarr rarr!

HOP

CRRRREEEEEEEAK

HOP

Rrrrarrr?

Oh, I've learned from the best. Including you, Spider-Man, and how you keep general situational awareness at all times!

POW

THWIP

PLOP

And it will take more than *falling stone* to hit me!

KA-SMASH

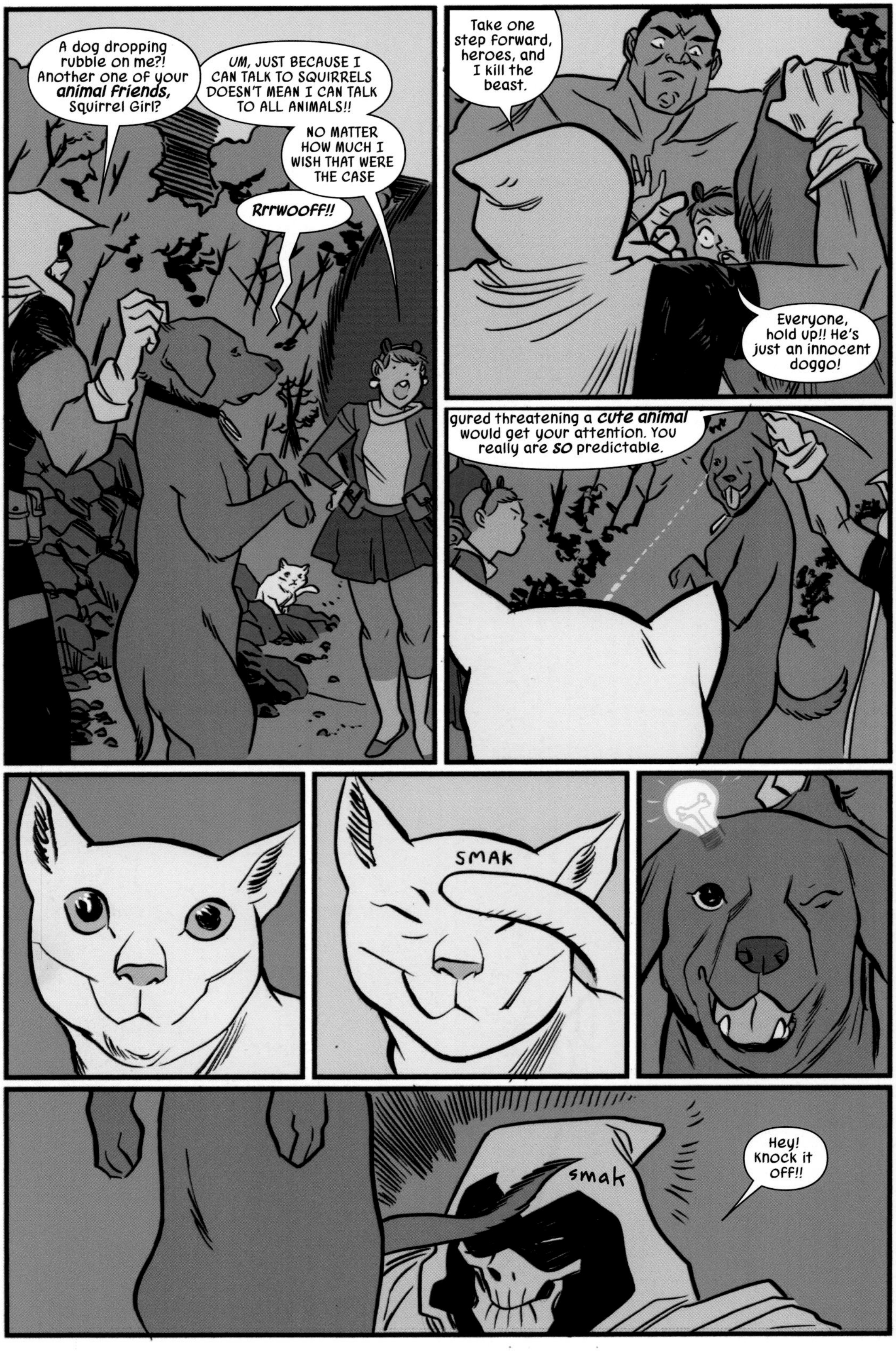

A dog dropping rubble on me?! Another one of your *animal friends,* Squirrel Girl?
UM, JUST BECAUSE I CAN TALK TO SQUIRRELS DOESN'T MEAN I CAN TALK TO ALL ANIMALS!!
NO MATTER HOW MUCH I WISH THAT WERE THE CASE
Rrrwooff!!
Take one step forward, heroes, and I kill the beast.
Everyone, hold up!! He's just an innocent doggo!
gured threatening a *cute animal* would get your attention. You really are *so* predictable.
SMAK
smak
Hey! Knock it OFF!!

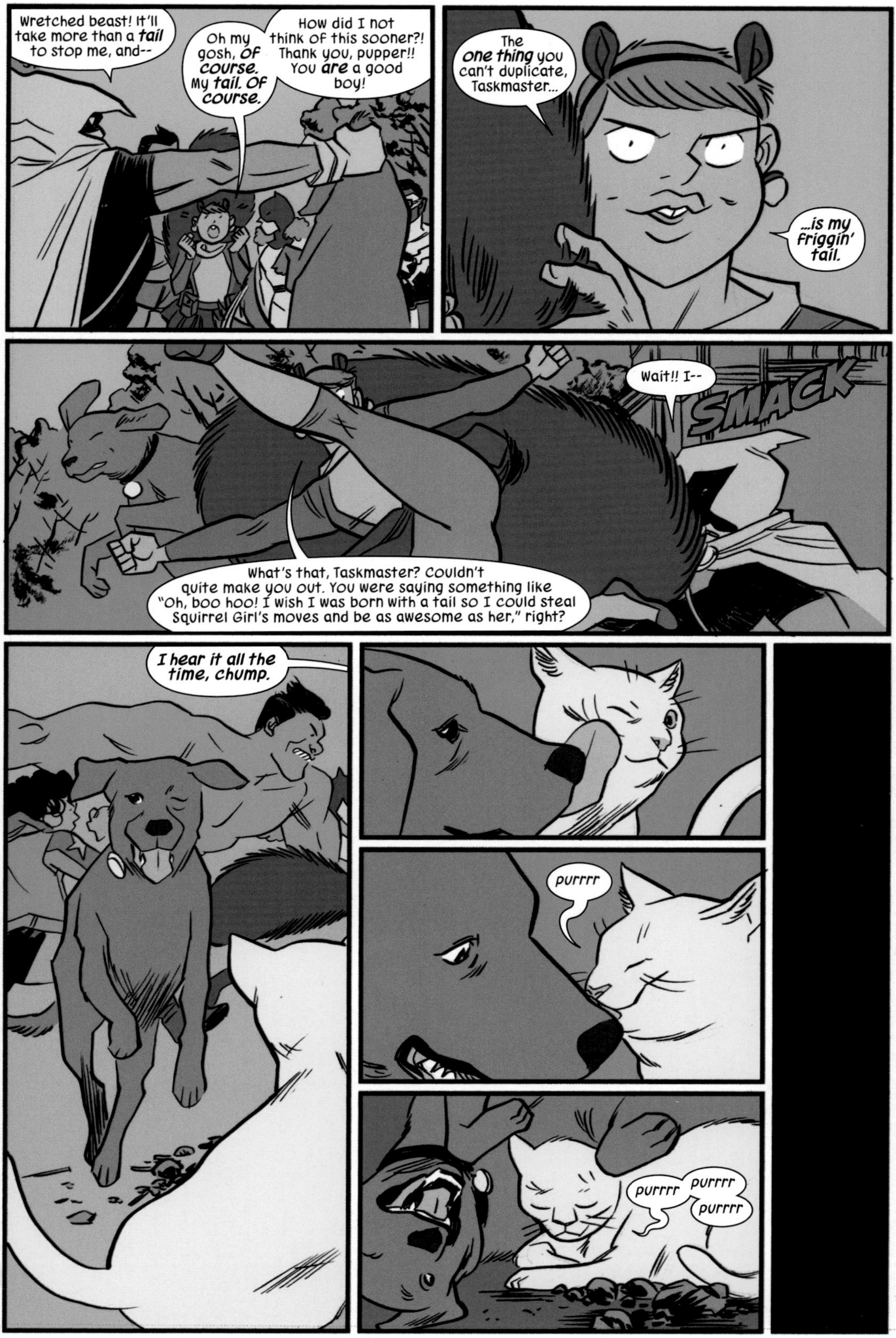
Wretched beast! It'll take more than a *tail* to stop me, and--
Oh my gosh, *of course.* My *tail. Of course.*
How did I not think of this sooner?! Thank you, pupper!! You *are* a good boy!
The *one thing* you can't duplicate, Taskmaster...
...is my friggin' tail.
Wait!! I--
SMACK
What's that, Taskmaster? Couldn't quite make you out. You were saying something like "Oh, boo hoo! I wish I was born with a tail so I could steal Squirrel Girl's moves and be as awesome as her," right?
I hear it all the time, chump.
purrrr
purrrr
purrrr
purrrr

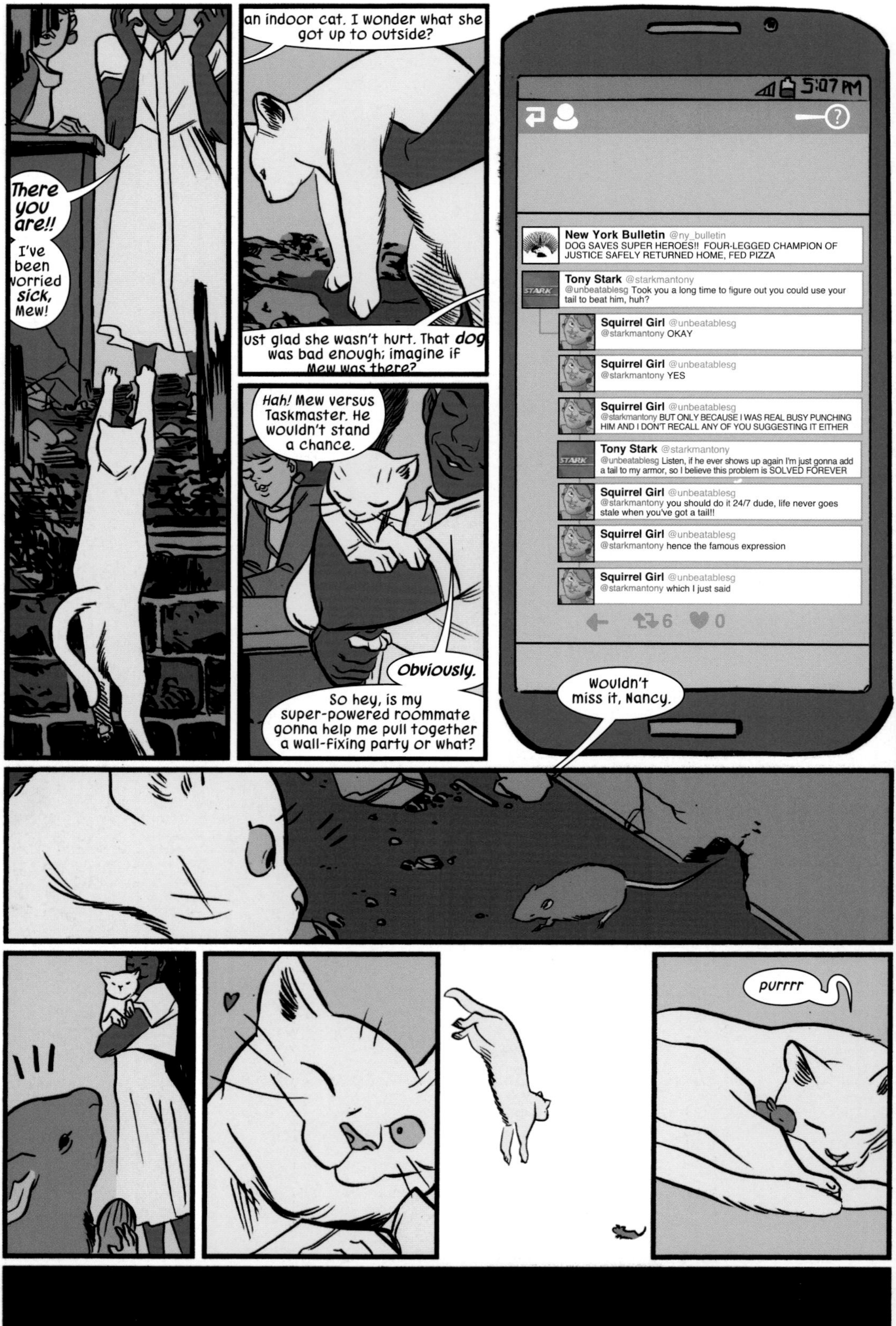
There you are!!
I've been worried sick, Mew!
an indoor cat. I wonder what she got up to outside?
ust glad she wasn't hurt. That dog was bad enough; imagine if Mew was there?
Hah! Mew versus Taskmaster. He wouldn't stand a chance.
Obviously.
So hey, is my super-powered roommate gonna help me pull together a wall-fixing party or what?
5:07 PM
New York Bulletin @ny_bulletin
DOG SAVES SUPER HEROES!! FOUR-LEGGED CHAMPION OF JUSTICE SAFELY RETURNED HOME, FED PIZZA
Tony Stark @starkmantony
@unbeatablesg Took you a long time to figure out you could use your tail to beat him, huh?
Squirrel Girl @unbeatablesg
@starkmantony OKAY
Squirrel Girl @unbeatablesg
@starkmantony YES
Squirrel Girl @unbeatablesg
@starkmantony BUT ONLY BECAUSE I WAS REAL BUSY PUNCHING HIM AND I DON'T RECALL ANY OF YOU SUGGESTING IT EITHER
Tony Stark @starkmantony
@unbeatablesg Listen, if he ever shows up again I'm just gonna add a tail to my armor, so I believe this problem is SOLVED FOREVER
Squirrel Girl @unbeatablesg
@starkmantony you should do it 24/7 dude, life never goes stale when you've got a tail!!
Squirrel Girl @unbeatablesg
@starkmantony hence the famous expression
Squirrel Girl @unbeatablesg
@starkmantony which I just said
6
0
Wouldn't miss it, Nancy.
purrrr

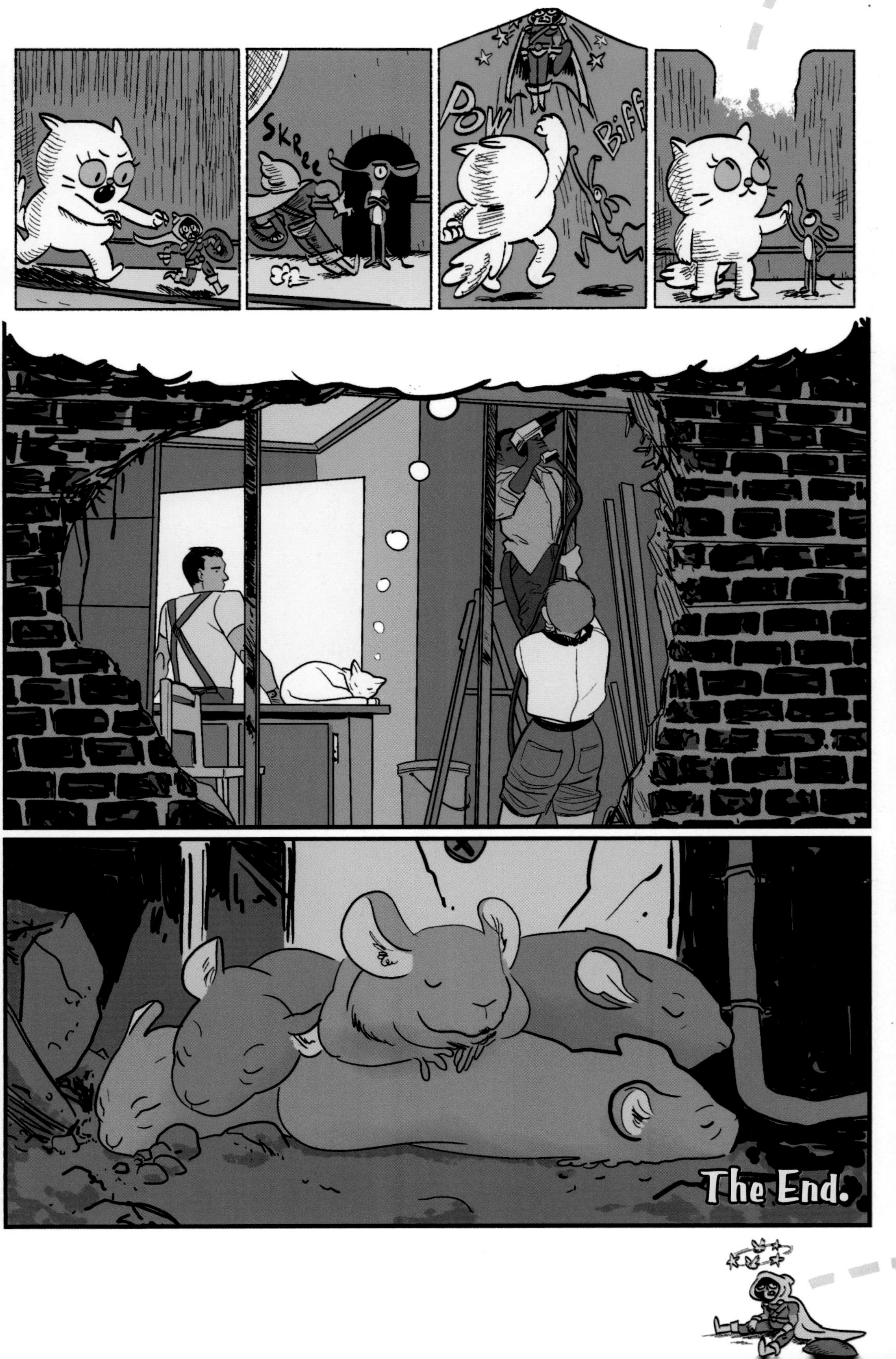
SKREee
POW
BiFF
The End.

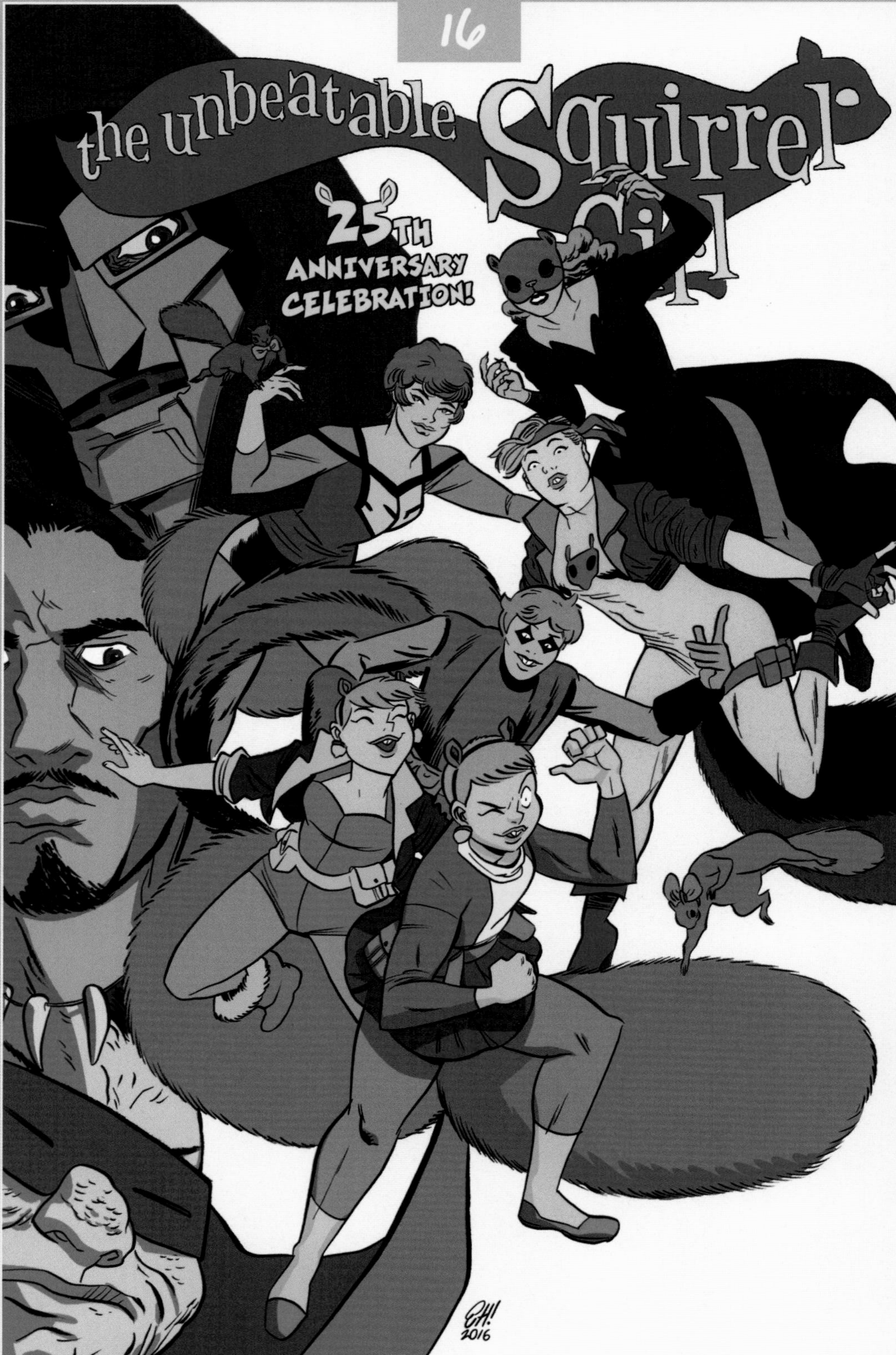
16
the unbeatable Squirrel Girl
25TH ANNIVERSARY CELEBRATION!
EH! 2016

Doreen Green isn't just a second-year computer science student: she secretly also has all the powers of both squirrel and girl! She uses her amazing abilities to fight crime **and** be as awesome as possible. You know her as...**The Unbeatable Squirrel Girl!** Find out what she's been up to, with...

Squirrel Girl *in a nutshell*

Squirrel Girl @unbeatablesg
IT'S MY BIRTHDAY!! I'M 20 YEARS OLD!! EVERYONE GET REAL EXCITED BECAUSE I WAS BORN...TWENTY YEARS AGO...THIS VERY NIGHT!

Squirrel Girl @unbeatablesg
Fav to wish me happy birthday, RT to wish me an EXTRA happy birthday

Nancy W. @sewwiththeflo
@unbeatablesg Have we worked out the etiquitte of wishing YOURSELF a happy birthday on social media?

Squirrel Girl @unbeatablesg
@sewwiththeflo what if YOU wished me happy birthday, then I could RT that? what if that was a thing we made happen

Nancy W. @sewwiththeflo
Happy birthday to Squirrel Girl, who is both one of my favorite super heroes AND one of my favorite people.

Squirrel Girl @unbeatablesg
@sewwiththeflo aww Nancy!! <3 <3 <3

Tony Stark @starkmantony ✓
@unbeatablesg Are you having a party? Assuming you are having a party, can I come?

Squirrel Girl @unbeatablesg
@starkmantony YES BUT YOU HAVE TO WEAR THE ARMOR

Tony Stark @starkmantony ✓
@unbeatablesg Is this a setup to get me so hepped up on cake that you can convince me to let YOU wear the armor?

Squirrel Girl @unbeatablesg
@starkmantony haha no

Squirrel Girl @unbeatablesg
@starkmantony it's my birthday

Squirrel Girl @unbeatablesg
@starkmantony i'm definitely ending up in that armor tony

Squirrel Girl @unbeatablesg
@starkmantony none can deny me my one true birthday wish

Odinson @num1odinson
@unbeatablesg I pray thee, might Asgardians come to thy party??

Nancy W. @sewwiththeflo
@num1odinson YES BRING LOKI

Odinson @num1odinson
@sewwiththeflo Though I may no longer wield Mjolnir, that does not mean I have been demoted to my brother's secretary service.

Nancy W. @sewwiththeflo
@num1odinson Hmm wow that's a super weird way to spell "yes I will absolutely bring Loki to this party and also Thor, excellent idea Nancy"

Nancy W. @sewwiththeflo
@unbeatablesg I'd be interested in knowing how that little baby born 20 years ago became Squirrel Girl.

Squirrel Girl @unbeatablesg
@sewwiththeflo YES! YES. It is an amazing story.

Nancy W. @sewwiththeflo
@unbeatablesg ...And?

Squirrel Girl @unbeatablesg
@sewwiththeflo And it goes...a little something...A'LIKE THIS.

Nancy W. @sewwiththeflo
@unbeatablesg ...

Nancy W. @sewwiththeflo
@unbeatablesg ...so were you going to post something after that, or

search!

#meetcute

#followtheleaper

#monkeyjoe

#properconcussiontreatment

#fishyhulk

#avengersassemble

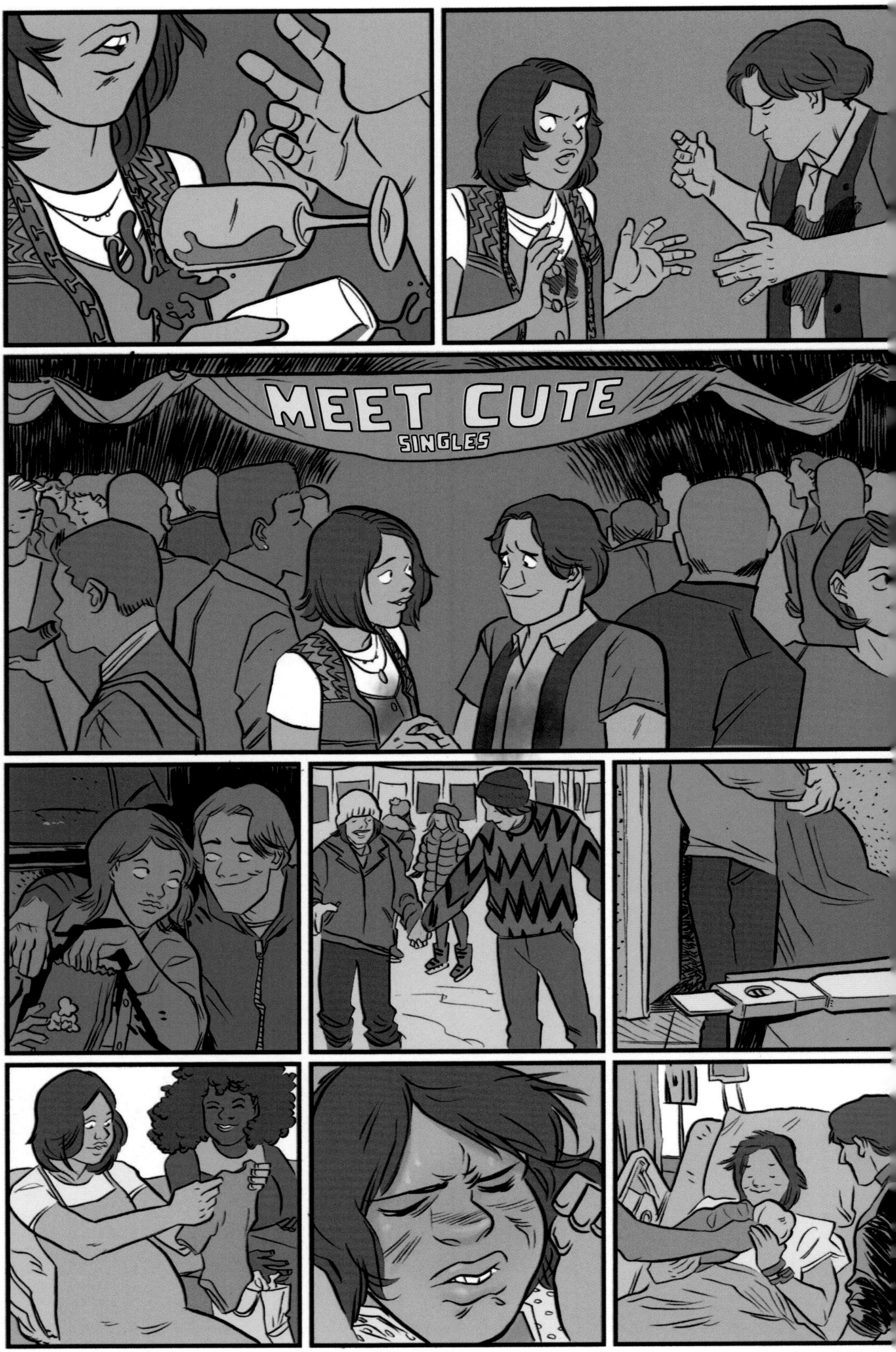
MEET CUTE
SINGLES

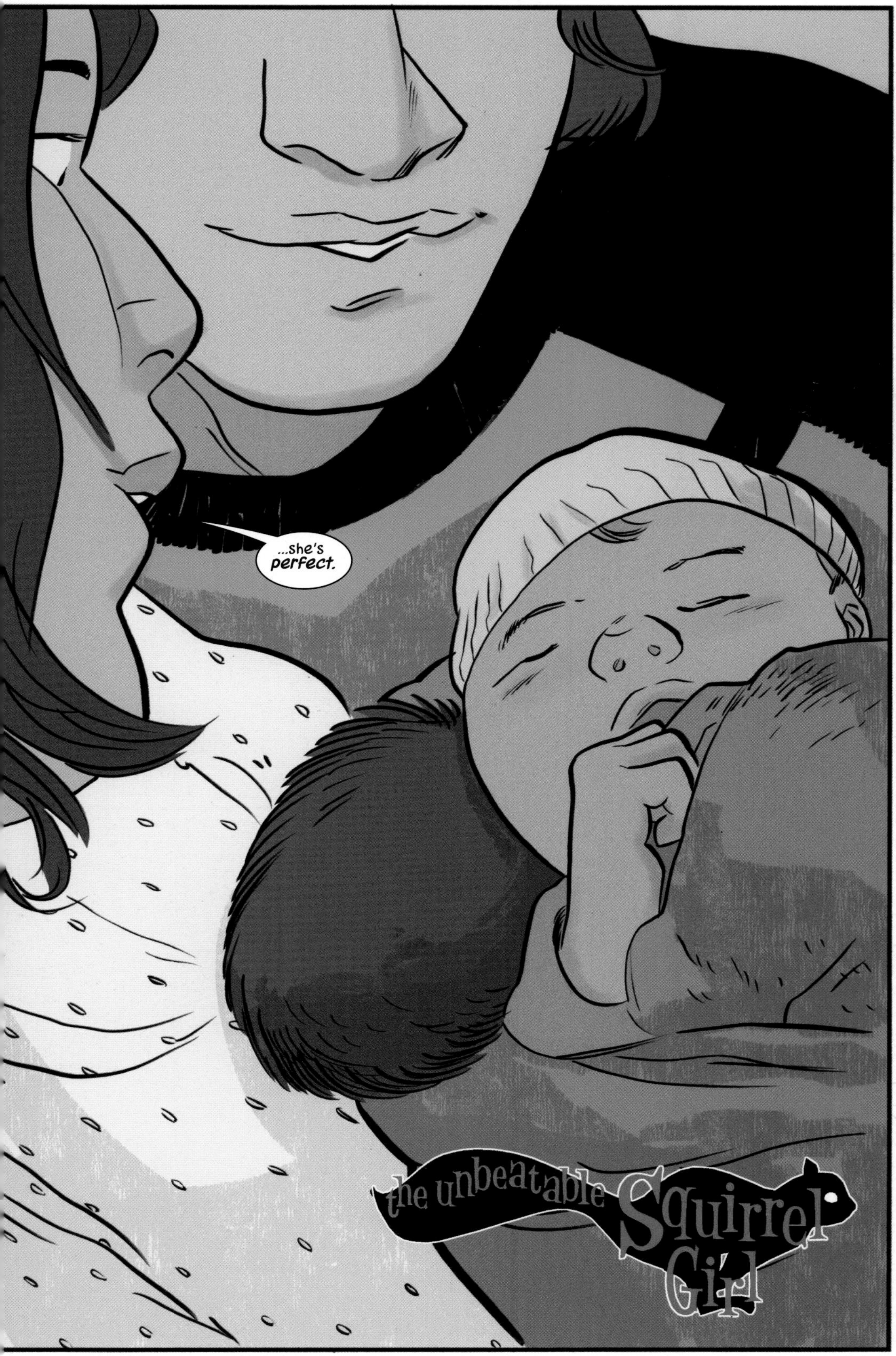
...she's perfect.
the unbeatable Squirrel Girl

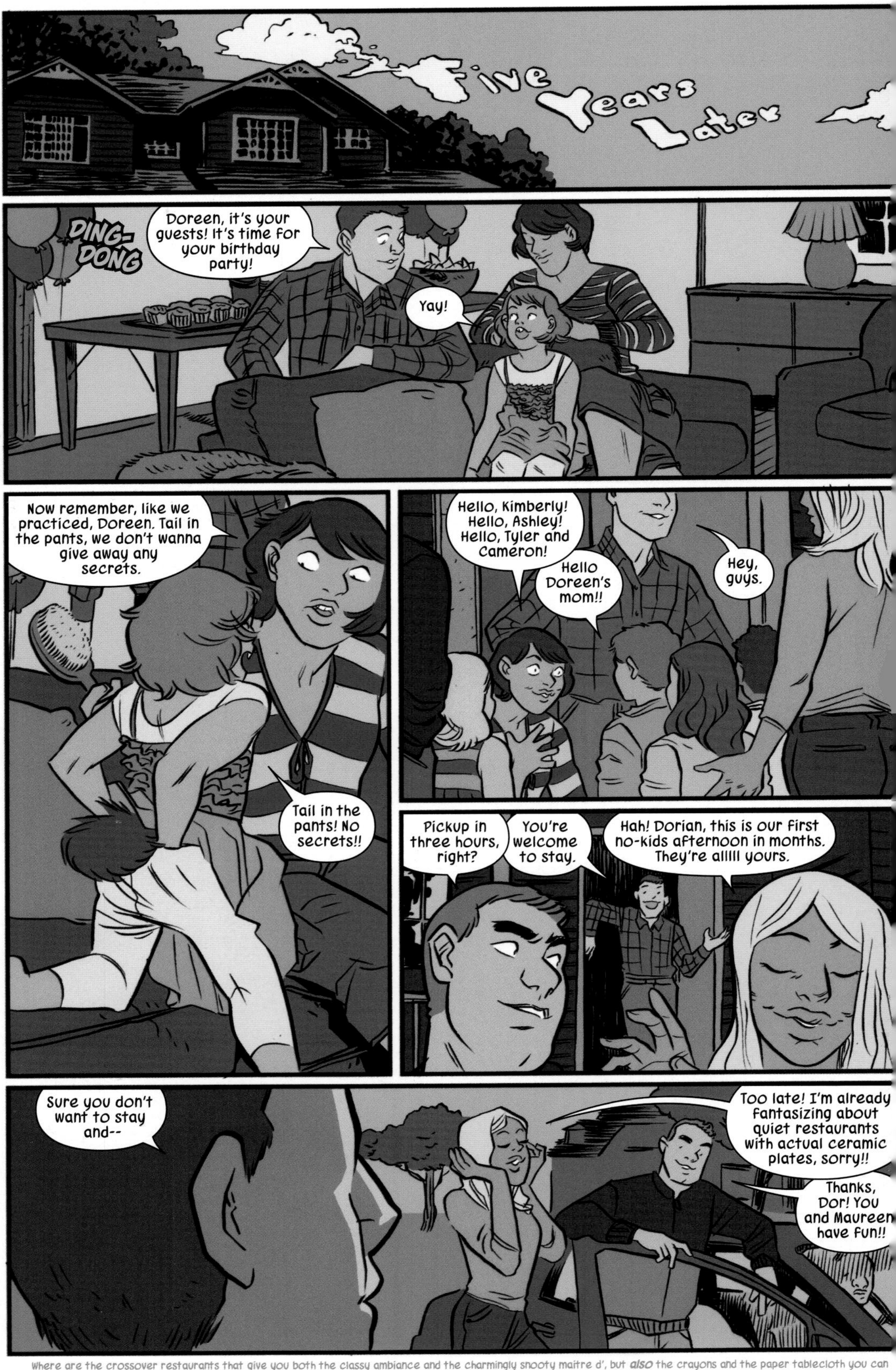
Five Years Later
DING-DONG
Doreen, it's your guests! It's time for your birthday party!
Yay!
Now remember, like we practiced, Doreen. Tail in the pants, we don't wanna give away any secrets.
Tail in the pants! No secrets!!
Hello, Kimberly! Hello, Ashley! Hello, Tyler and Cameron!
Hello Doreen's mom!!
Hey, guys.
Pickup in three hours, right?
You're welcome to stay.
Hah! Dorian, this is our first no-kids afternoon in months. They're allll yours.
Sure you don't want to stay and--
Too late! I'm already fantasizing about quiet restaurants with actual ceramic plates, sorry!!
Thanks, Dor! You and Maureen have fun!!

Where are the crossover restaurants that give you both the classy ambiance and the charmingly snooty maitre d', but *also* the crayons and the paper tablecloth you can draw on? "No idea," you whisper, as we both smuggle our crayons and coloring books past the charmingly snooty maitre d'.

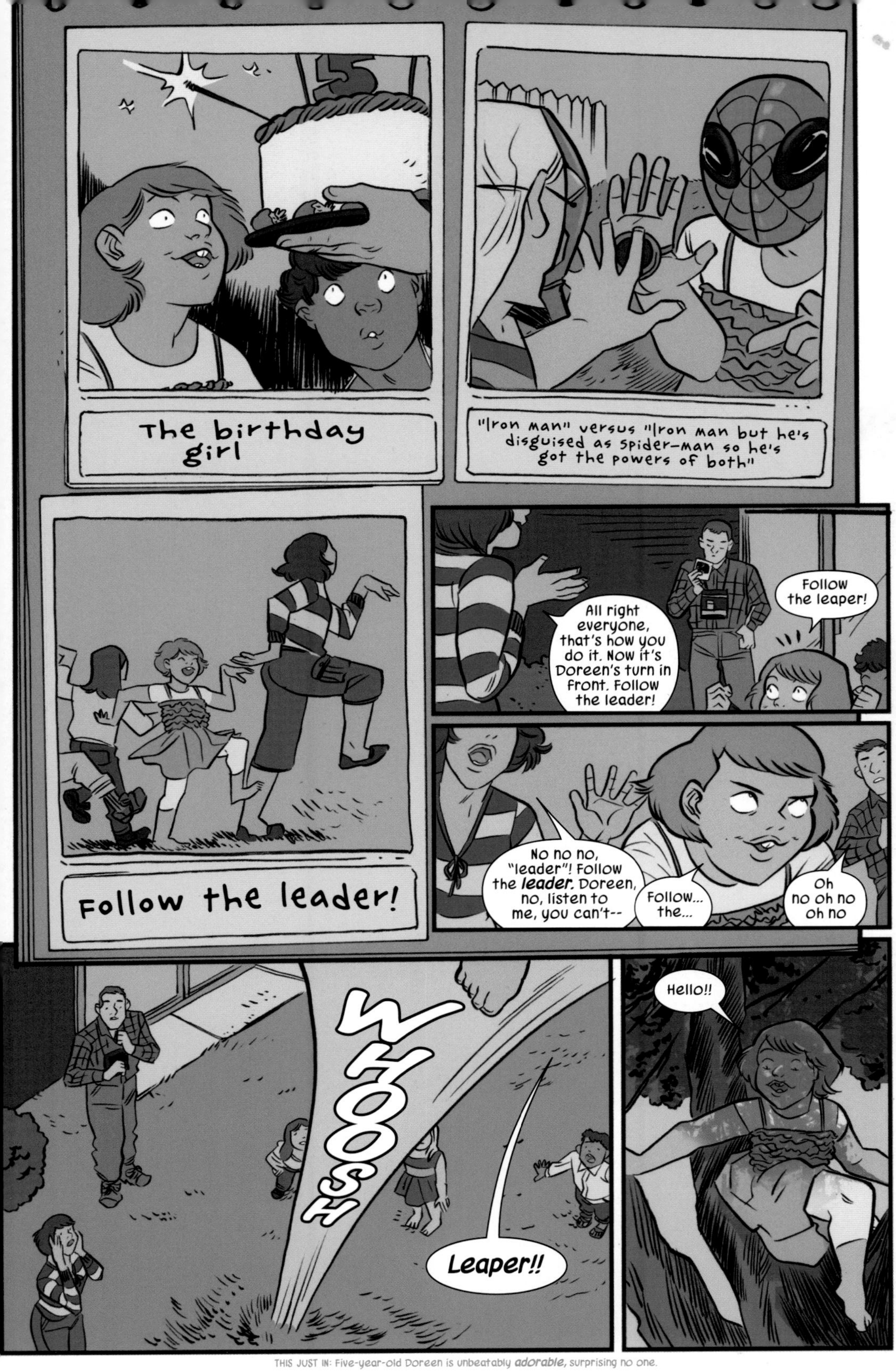
The birthday girl
"Iron Man" versus "Iron Man but he's disguised as Spider-Man so he's got the powers of both"
Follow the leader!
All right everyone, that's how you do it. Now it's Doreen's turn in front. Follow the leader!
Follow the leaper!
No no no, "leader"! Follow the *leader.* Doreen, no, listen to me, you can't--
Follow... the...
Oh no oh no oh no
WHOOSH
Leaper!!
Hello!!

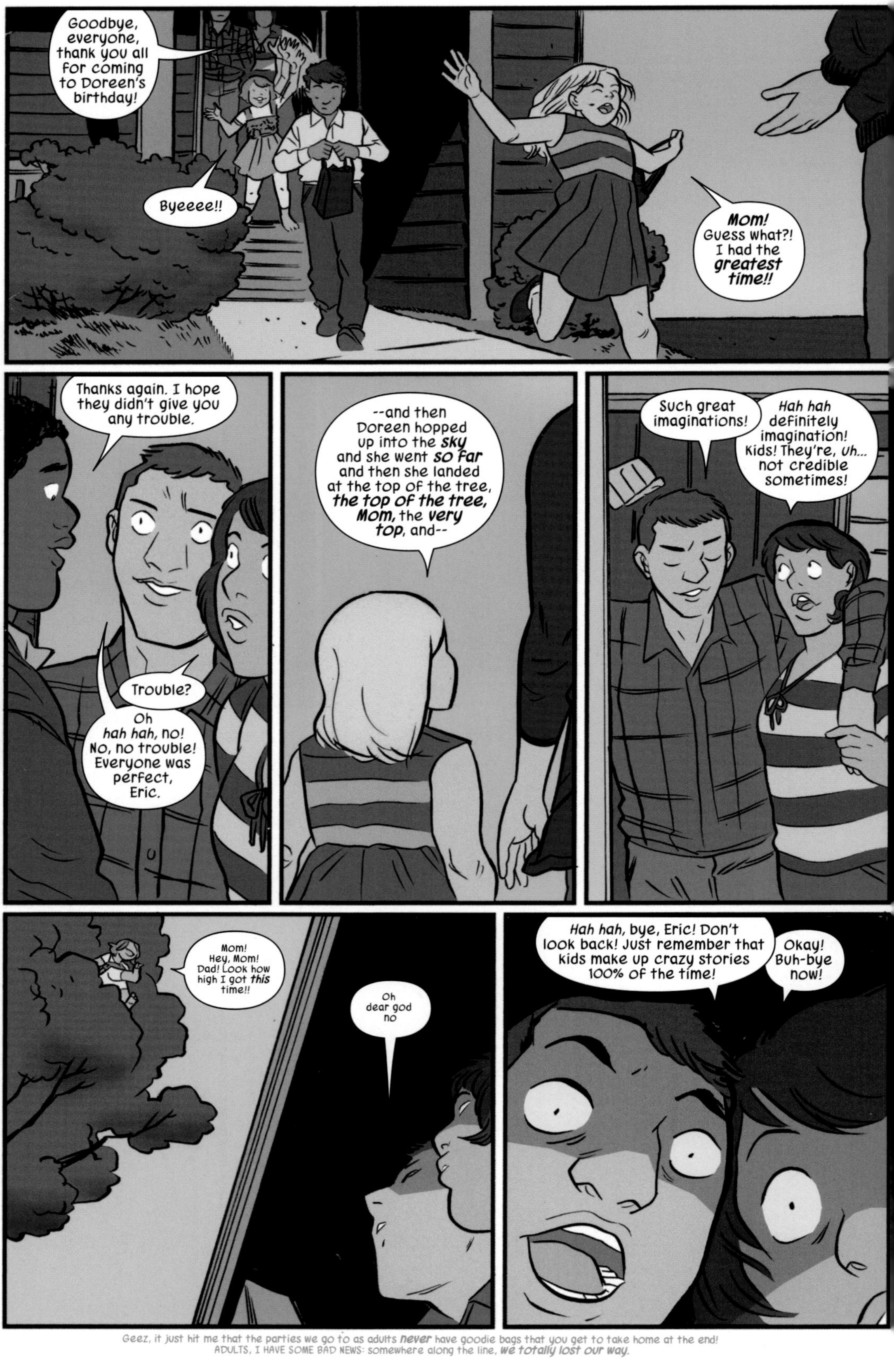
Goodbye, everyone, thank you all for coming to Doreen's birthday!
Byeeee!!
Mom! Guess what?! I had the greatest time!!
Thanks again. I hope they didn't give you any trouble.
Trouble?
Oh hah hah, no! No, no trouble! Everyone was perfect, Eric.
--and then Doreen hopped up into the sky and she went so far and then she landed at the top of the tree, the top of the tree, Mom, the very top, and--
Such great imaginations!
Hah hah definitely imagination! Kids! They're, uh... not credible sometimes!
Mom! Hey, Mom! Dad! Look how high I got this time!!
Oh dear god no
Hah hah, bye, Eric! Don't look back! Just remember that kids make up crazy stories 100% of the time!
Okay! Buh-bye now!

Geez, it just hit me that the parties we go to as adults ***never*** have goodie bags that you get to take home at the end!
ADULTS, I HAVE SOME BAD NEWS: somewhere along the line, ***we totally lost our way.***

Five years later...

I am happy to report that close reading of Doreen's Thing clock suggests that it's *always* clobbering time. Please, govern yourselves accordingly.

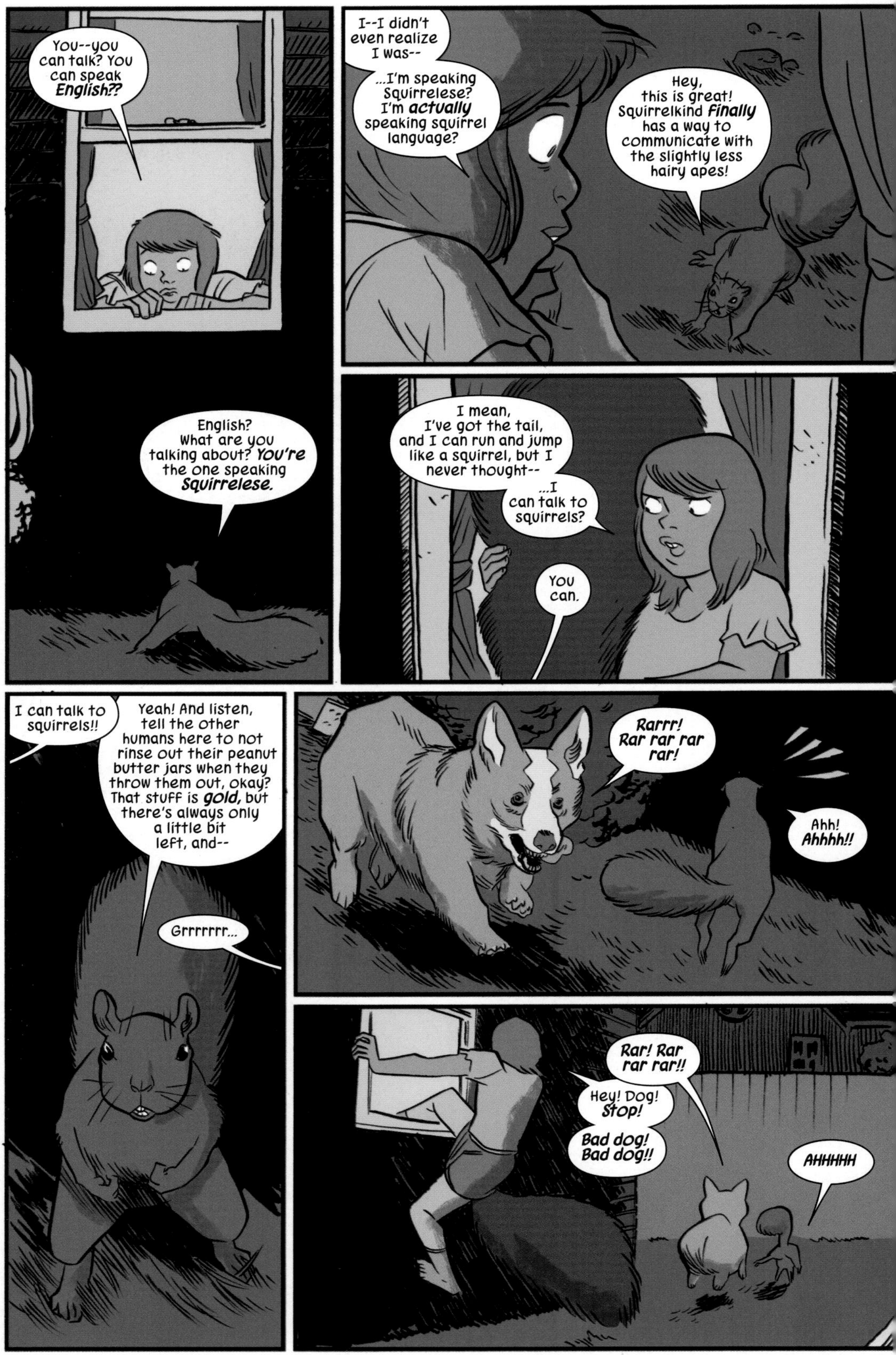
You--you can talk? You can speak English??
I--I didn't even realize I was--
...I'm speaking Squirrelese? I'm actually speaking squirrel language?
Hey, this is great! Squirrelkind finally has a way to communicate with the slightly less hairy apes!
English? What are you talking about? You're the one speaking Squirrelese.
I mean, I've got the tail, and I can run and jump like a squirrel, but I never thought--
...I can talk to squirrels?
You can.
I can talk to squirrels!!
Yeah! And listen, tell the other humans here to not rinse out their peanut butter jars when they throw them out, okay? That stuff is gold, but there's always only a little bit left, and--
Grrrrrrr...
Rarrr! Rar rar rar rar!
Ahh! Ahhhh!!
Rar! Rar rar rar!!
Hey! Dog! Stop!
Bad dog! Bad dog!!
AHHHHH

This squirrel learns he can communicate with a new species for the very first time, and the very first message he transmits is "send more peanut butter." This, sadly, once again confirms that it was actually a good idea to not put squirrels in charge of the messages sent into deep space on the *Voyager* spacecraft.

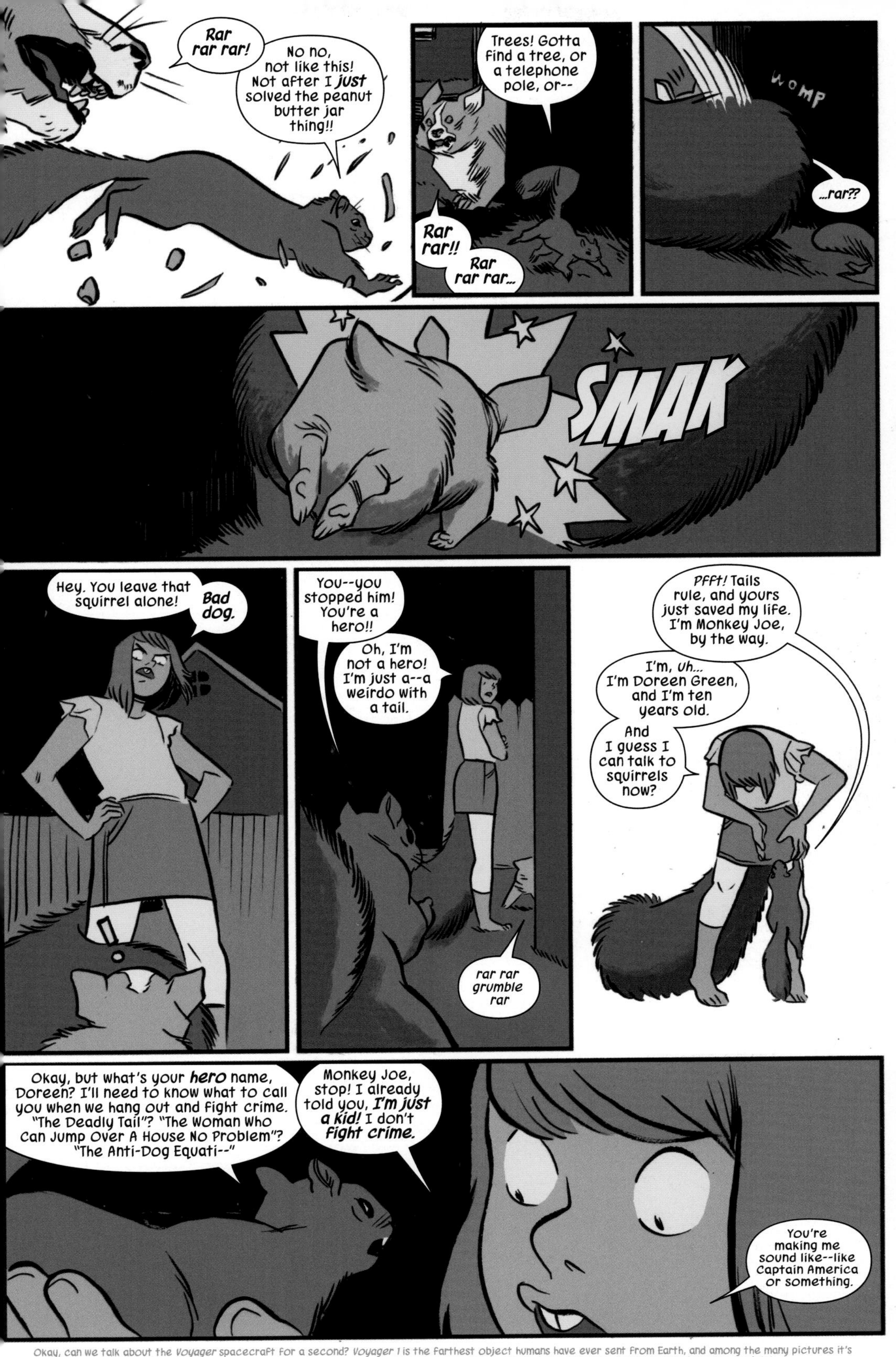
Rar rar rar!
No no, not like this! Not after I *just* solved the peanut butter jar thing!!
Trees! Gotta find a tree, or a telephone pole, or--
Rar rar!!
Rar rar rar...
WOMP
...rar??
SMAK
Hey. You leave that squirrel alone!
Bad dog.
You--you stopped him! You're a hero!!
Oh, I'm not a hero! I'm just a--a weirdo with a tail.
rar rar grumble rar
Pfft! Tails rule, and yours just saved my life. I'm Monkey Joe, by the way.
I'm, *uh...* I'm Doreen Green, and I'm ten years old.
And I guess I can talk to squirrels now?
Okay, but what's your *hero* name, Doreen? I'll need to know what to call you when we hang out and fight crime. "The Deadly Tail"? "The Woman Who Can Jump Over A House No Problem"? "The Anti-Dog Equati--"
Monkey Joe, stop! I already told you, *I'm just a kid!* I don't *fight crime.*
You're making me sound like--like Captain America or something.

Okay, can we talk about the *Voyager* spacecraft for a second? *Voyager 1* is the farthest object humans have ever sent from Earth, and among the many pictures it's carrying into the universe on a golden record is one of a woman eating an ice cream cone, while a man eats a grilled cheese sandwich, while ***another*** man pours water into his own mouth. ***It's amazing.***

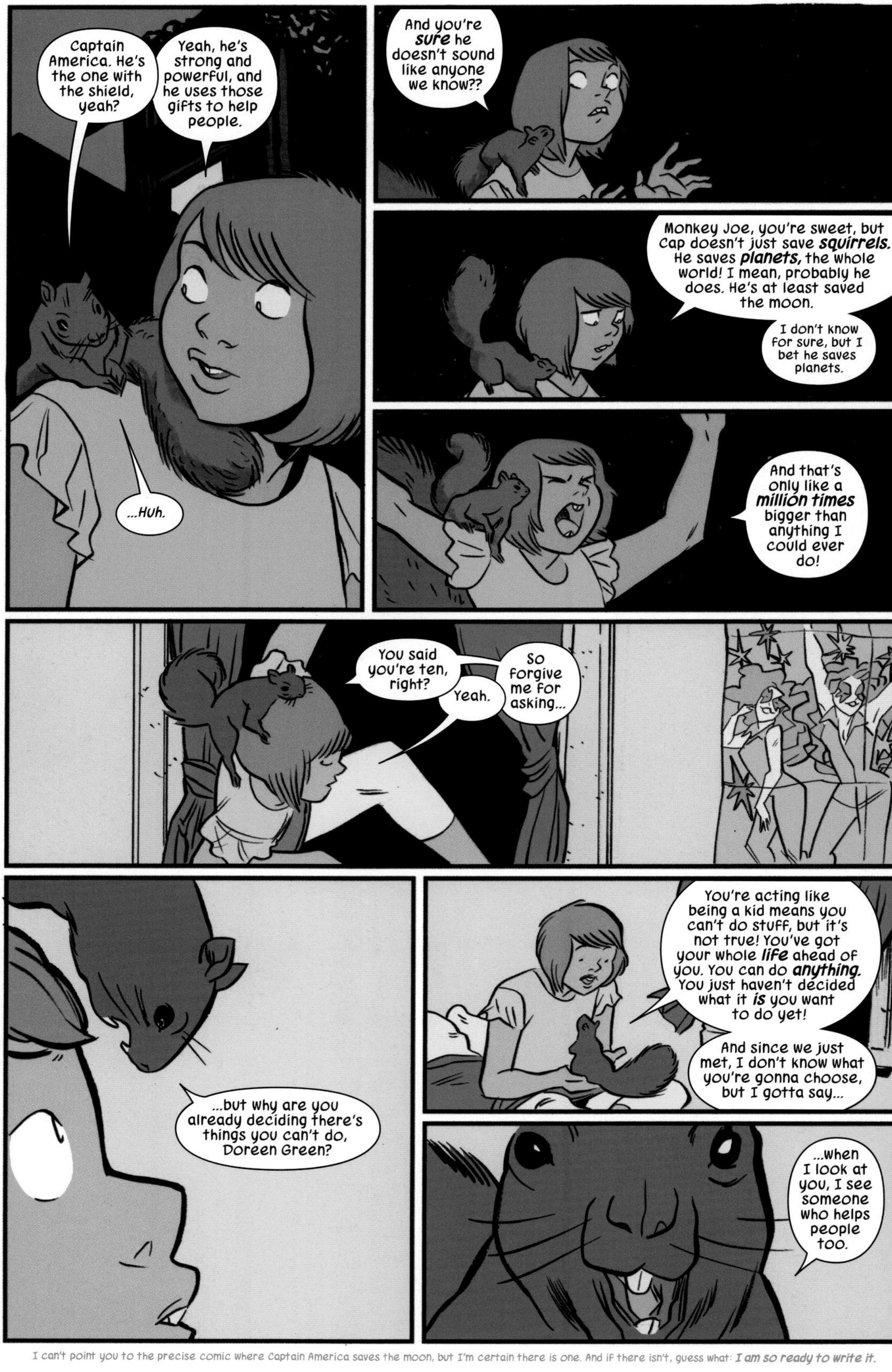
Captain America. He's the one with the shield, yeah?
Yeah, he's strong and powerful, and he uses those gifts to help people.
...Huh.
And you're *sure* he doesn't sound like anyone we know??
Monkey Joe, you're sweet, but Cap doesn't just save *squirrels.* He saves *planets,* the whole world! I mean, probably he does. He's at least saved the moon.
I don't know for sure, but I bet he saves planets.
And that's only like a *million times* bigger than anything I could ever do!
You said you're ten, right?
Yeah.
So forgive me for asking...
...but why are you already deciding there's things you can't do, Doreen Green?
You're acting like being a kid means you can't do stuff, but it's not true! You've got your whole *life* ahead of you. You can do *anything.* You just haven't decided what it *is* you want to do yet!
And since we just met, I don't know what you're gonna choose, but I gotta say...
...when I look at you, I see someone who helps people too.

I can't point you to the precise comic where Captain America saves the moon, but I'm certain there is one. And if there isn't, guess what: ***I am so ready to write it.***

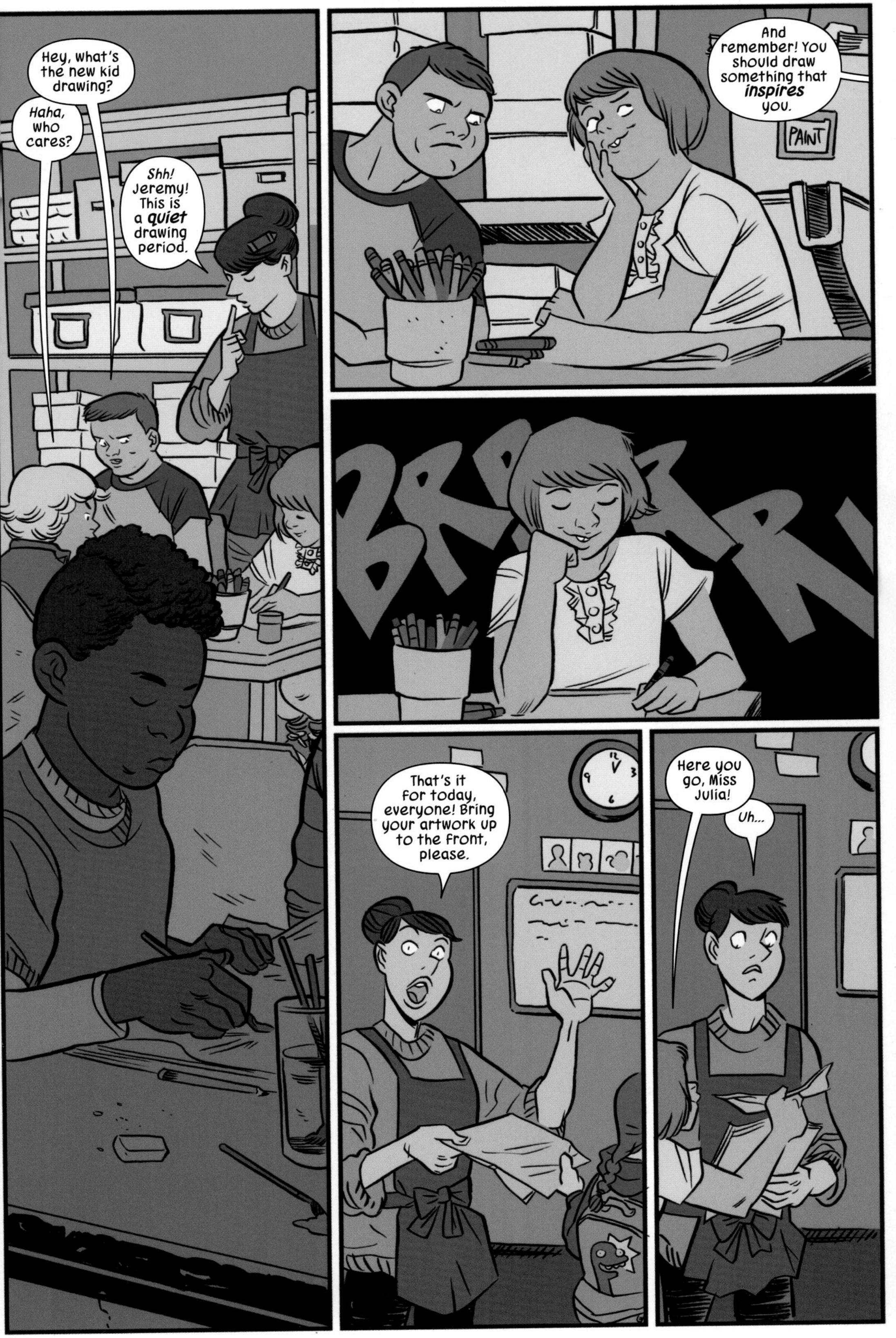
Hey, what's the new kid drawing?
Haha, who cares?
Shh! Jeremy! This is a *quiet* drawing period.
And remember! You should draw something that ***inspires*** you.
PAINT
That's it for today, everyone! Bring your artwork up to the front, please.
Here you go, Miss Julia!
Uh...

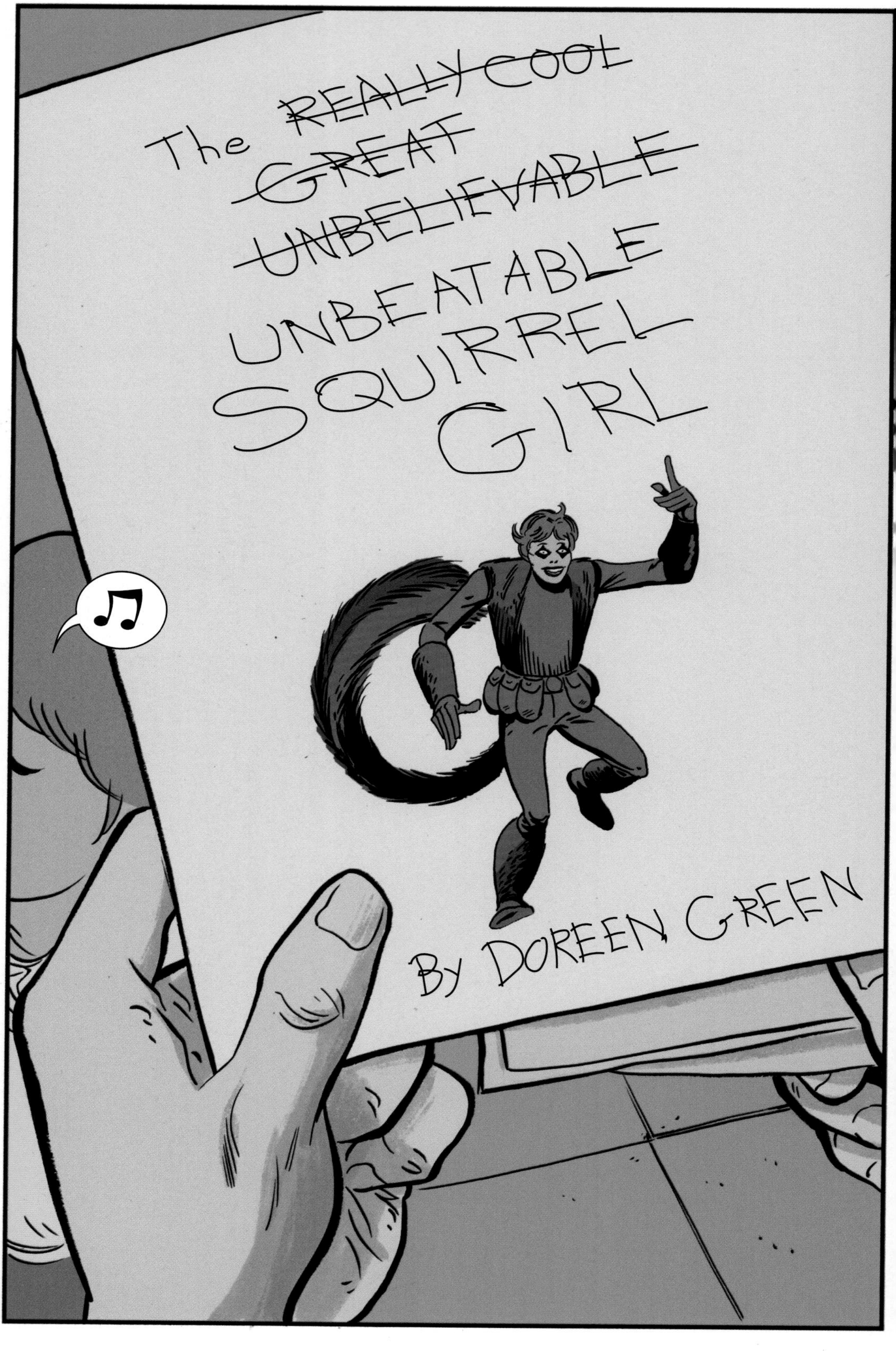
The ~~REALLY COOL~~ ~~GREAT~~ ~~UNBELIEVABLE~~ UNBEATABLE SQUIRREL GIRL
♫
By DOREEN GREEN

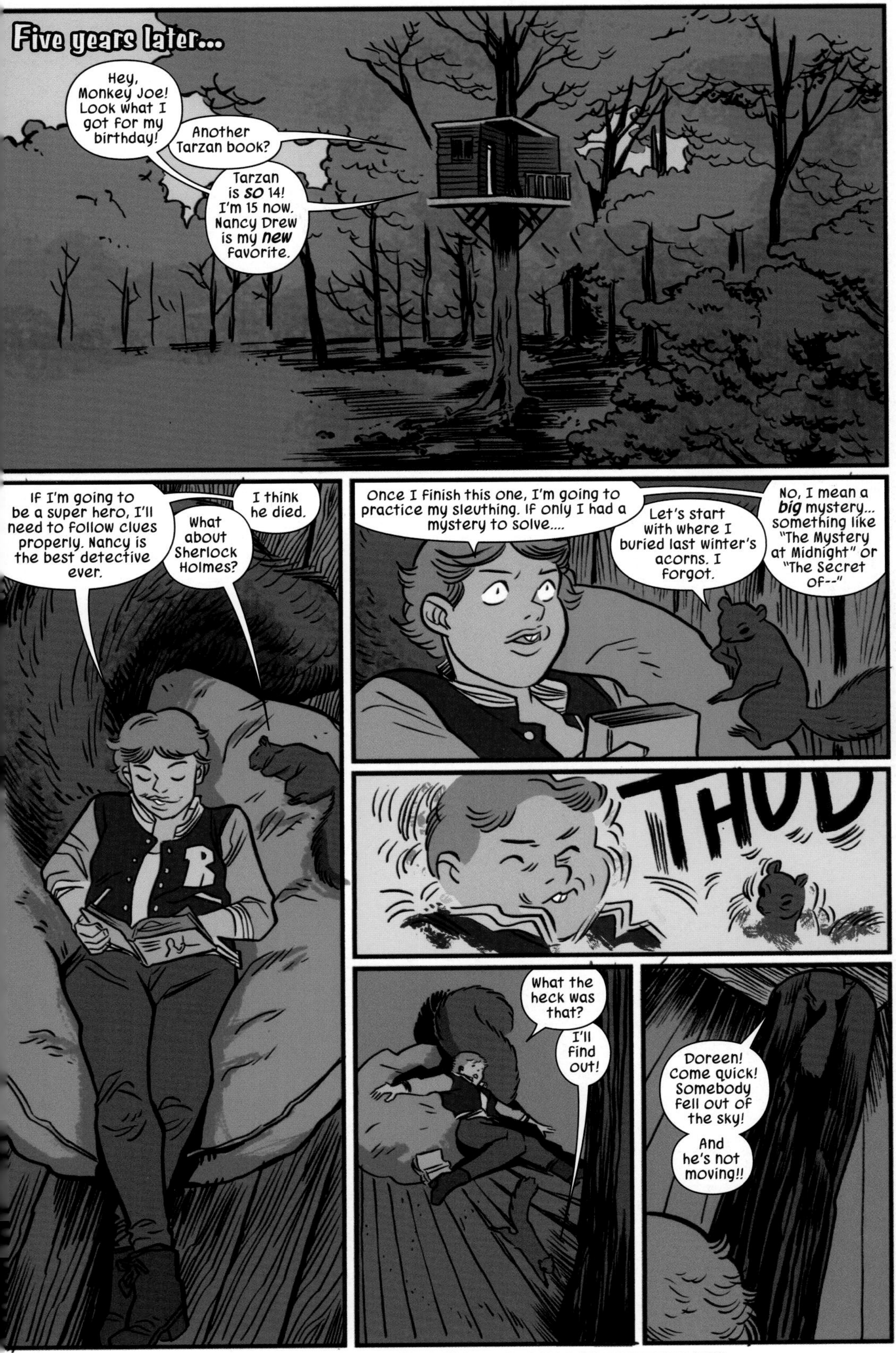
Five years later...
Hey, Monkey Joe! Look what I got for my birthday!
Another Tarzan book?
Tarzan is SO 14! I'm 15 now. Nancy Drew is my new favorite.
If I'm going to be a super hero, I'll need to follow clues properly. Nancy is the best detective ever.
What about Sherlock Holmes?
I think he died.
Once I finish this one, I'm going to practice my sleuthing. If only I had a mystery to solve....
Let's start with where I buried last winter's acorns. I forgot.
No, I mean a big mystery... something like "The Mystery at Midnight" or "The Secret Of--"
THUD
What the heck was that?
I'll find out!
Doreen! Come quick! Somebody fell out of the sky!
And he's not moving!!

DID YOU KNOW: This part of Doreen's life was written by Will Murray, who wrote her first appearance back in 1992! But then I added these little notes beneath his pages, because we're pals. Yes. I'm almost *certain* we're pals.

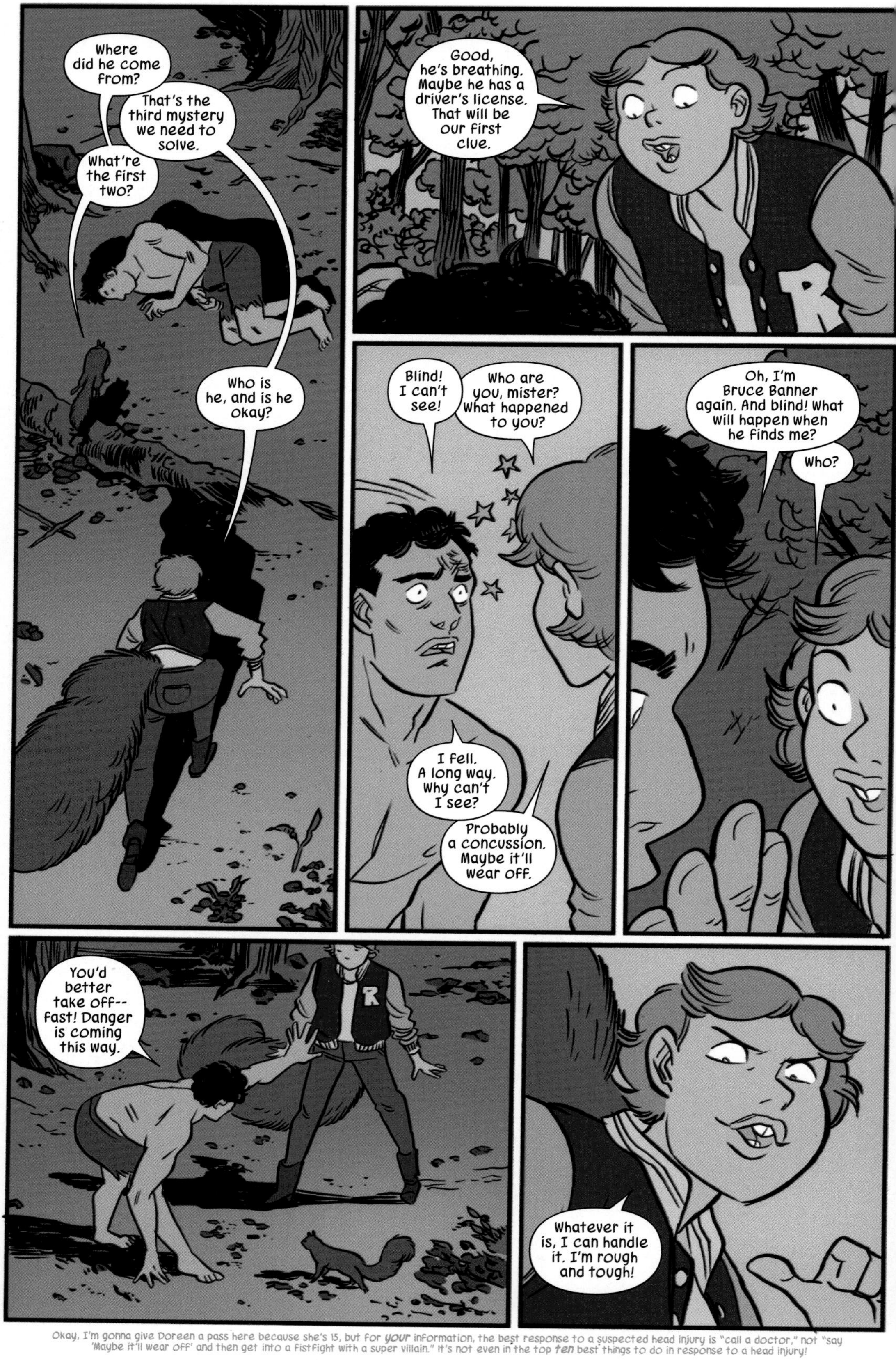
Where did he come from?
That's the third mystery we need to solve.
What're the first two?
Who is he, and is he okay?
Good, he's breathing. Maybe he has a driver's license. That will be our first clue.
Blind! I can't see!
Who are you, mister? What happened to you?
I fell. A long way. Why can't I see?
Probably a concussion. Maybe it'll wear off.
Oh, I'm Bruce Banner again. And blind! What will happen when he finds me?
Who?
You'd better take off-- fast! Danger is coming this way.
Whatever it is, I can handle it. I'm rough and tough!

Okay, I'm gonna give Doreen a pass here because she's 15, but for ***your*** information, the best response to a suspected head injury is "call a doctor," not "say 'Maybe it'll wear off' and then get into a fistfight with a super villain." It's not even in the top ***ten*** best things to do in response to a head injury!

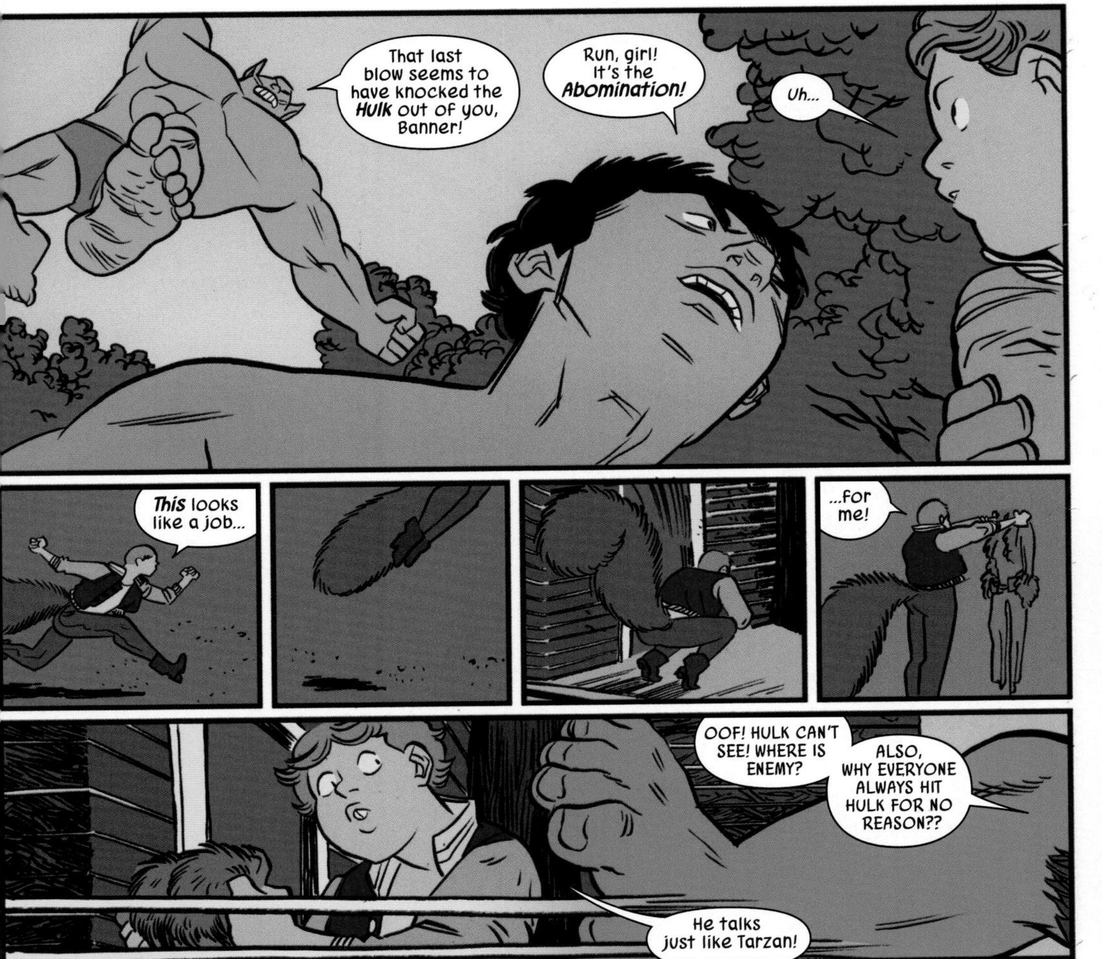
That last blow seems to have knocked the *Hulk* out of you, Banner!
Run, girl! It's the *Abomination!*
Uh...
This looks like a job...
...for me!
OOF! HULK CAN'T SEE! WHERE IS ENEMY?
ALSO, WHY EVERYONE ALWAYS HIT HULK FOR NO REASON??
He talks just like Tarzan!
You're in luck, Hulk! You've never heard of me, but I'm a new super hero on the scene. Squirrel Girl! *Ta-da!*
GO AWAY, PUNY SQUIRREL.
I can't! You need help, Hulkie!
Oh no, here he comes! Quick, Hulk: jump! Jump straight up!
NOW!
HULK THE BEST JUMPER THERE IS!
SMAK

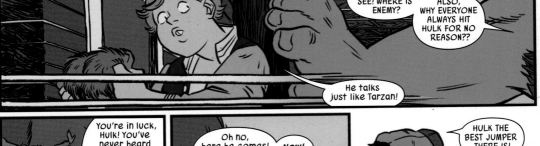

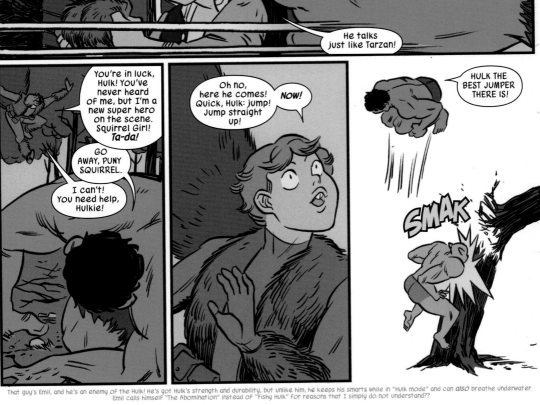

That guy's Emil, and he's an enemy of the Hulk! He's got Hulk's strength and durability, but unlike him, he keeps his smarts while in "Hulk mode" and can *also* breathe underwater. Emil calls himself "The Abomination" instead of "Fishy Hulk" for reasons that I simply do not understand??

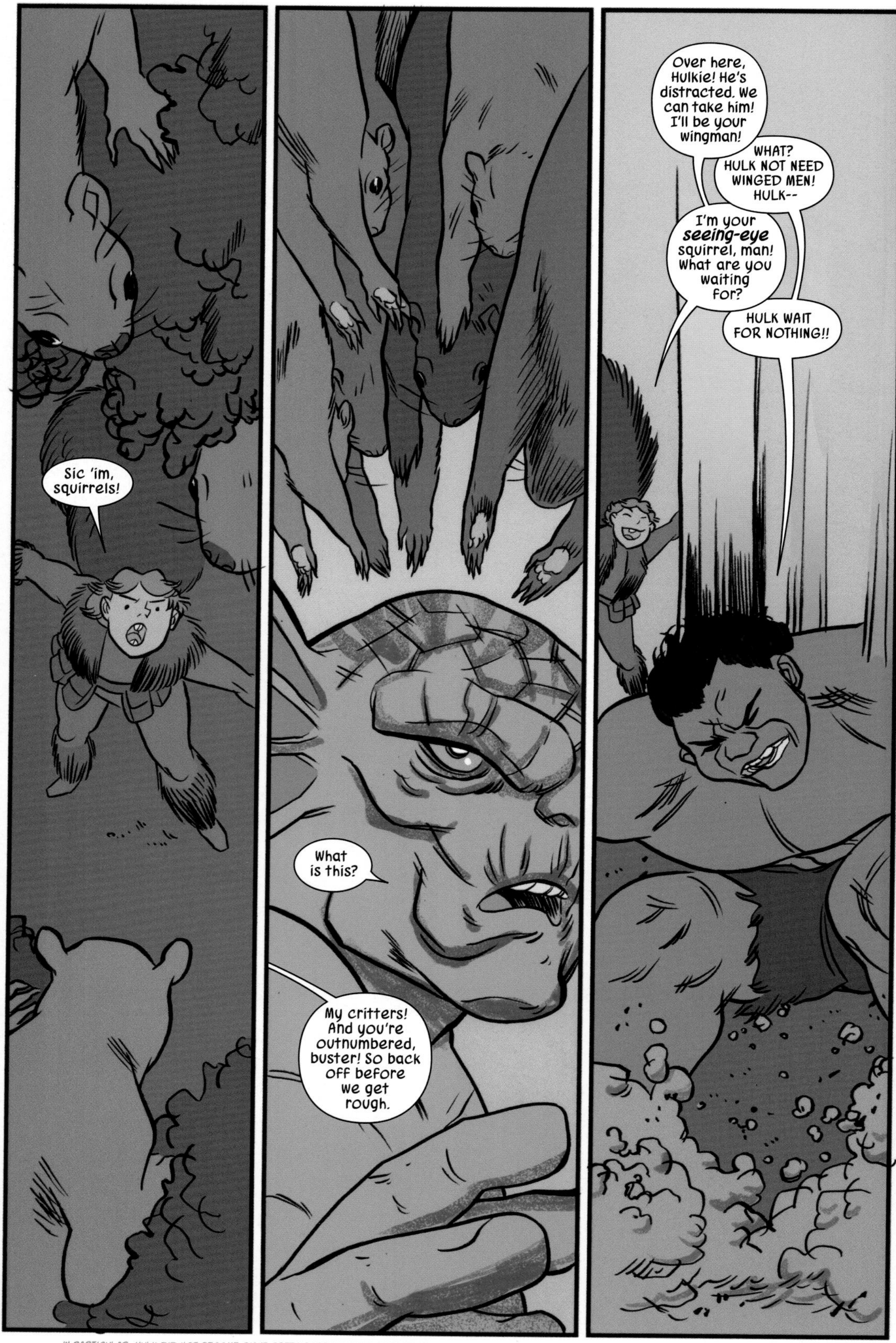
Sic 'im, squirrels!
What is this?
My critters! And you're outnumbered, buster! So back off before we get rough.
Over here, Hulkie! He's distracted. We can take him! I'll be your wingman!
WHAT? HULK NOT NEED WINGED MEN! HULK--
I'm your *seeing-eye* squirrel, man! What are you waiting for?
HULK WAIT FOR NOTHING!!

IN PARTICULAR, HULK DID NOT BECOME GIANT GREEN RAGE MONSTER SO THAT HE COULD WAIT QUIETLY IN LINE AT THE BANK, AND THAT IS ALL HULK WILL SAY ON THE MATTER!!

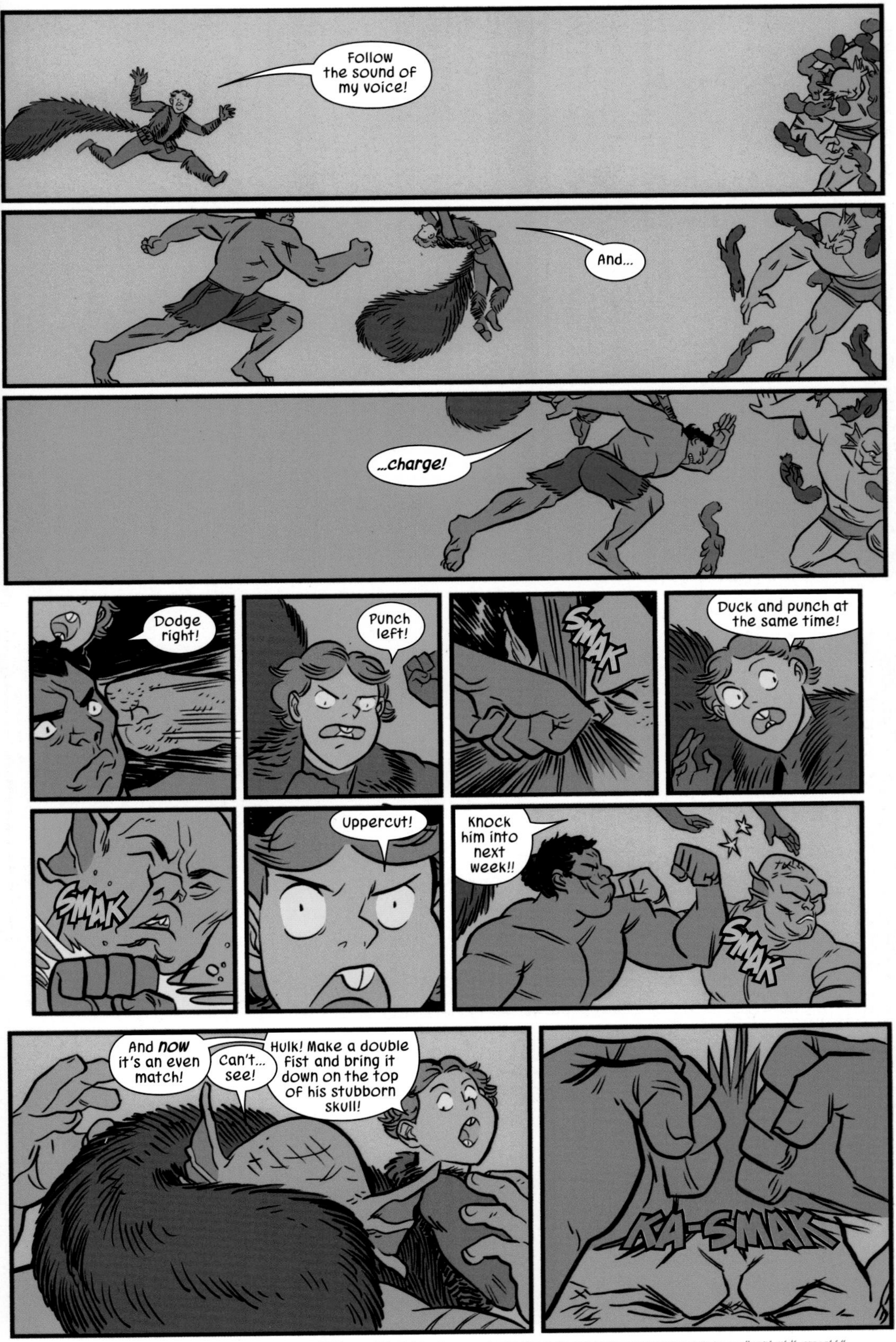
Follow the sound of my voice!
And...
...charge!
Dodge right!
Punch left!
SMAK
Duck and punch at the same time!
SMAK
Uppercut!
Knock him into next week!!
SMAK
And now it's an even match!
Can't... see!
Hulk! Make a double fist and bring it down on the top of his stubborn skull!
KA-SMAK

This illustrates the Hulk's famous English catchphrase *"Hulk smash,"* which is of course derived from his original famous Latin catchphrase *"veni, vidi, smashi."*

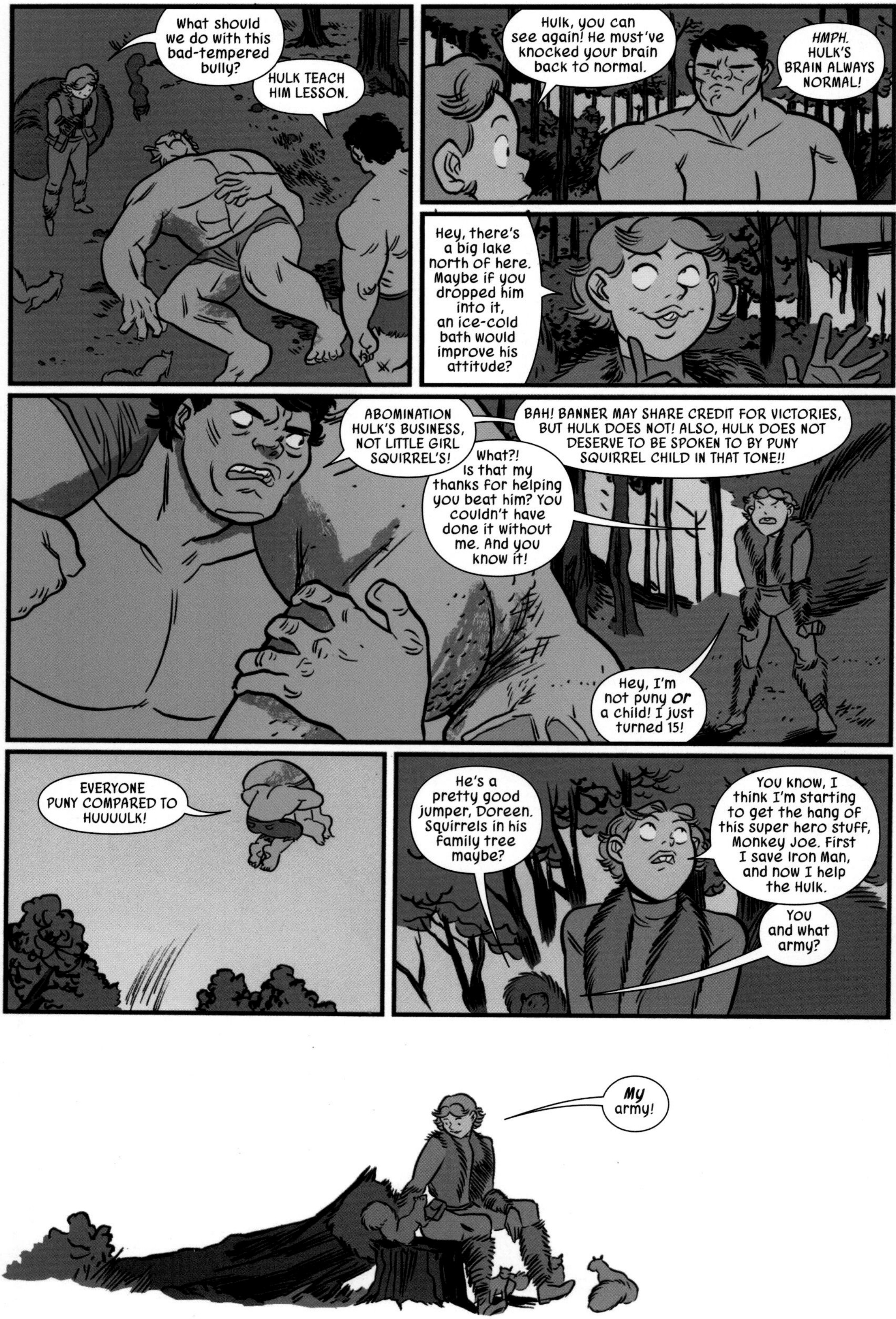
What should we do with this bad-tempered bully?
HULK TEACH HIM LESSON.
Hulk, you can see again! He must've knocked your brain back to normal.
HMPH. HULK'S BRAIN ALWAYS NORMAL!
Hey, there's a big lake north of here. Maybe if you dropped him into it, an ice-cold bath would improve his attitude?
ABOMINATION HULK'S BUSINESS, NOT LITTLE GIRL SQUIRREL'S!
BAH! BANNER MAY SHARE CREDIT FOR VICTORIES, BUT HULK DOES NOT! ALSO, HULK DOES NOT DESERVE TO BE SPOKEN TO BY PUNY SQUIRREL CHILD IN THAT TONE!!
What?! Is that my thanks for helping you beat him? You couldn't have done it without me. And you know it!
Hey, I'm not puny *or* a child! I just turned 15!
EVERYONE PUNY COMPARED TO HUUUULK!
He's a pretty good jumper, Doreen. Squirrels in his family tree maybe?
You know, I think I'm starting to get the hang of this super hero stuff, Monkey Joe. First I save Iron Man, and now I help the Hulk.
You and what army?
My army!

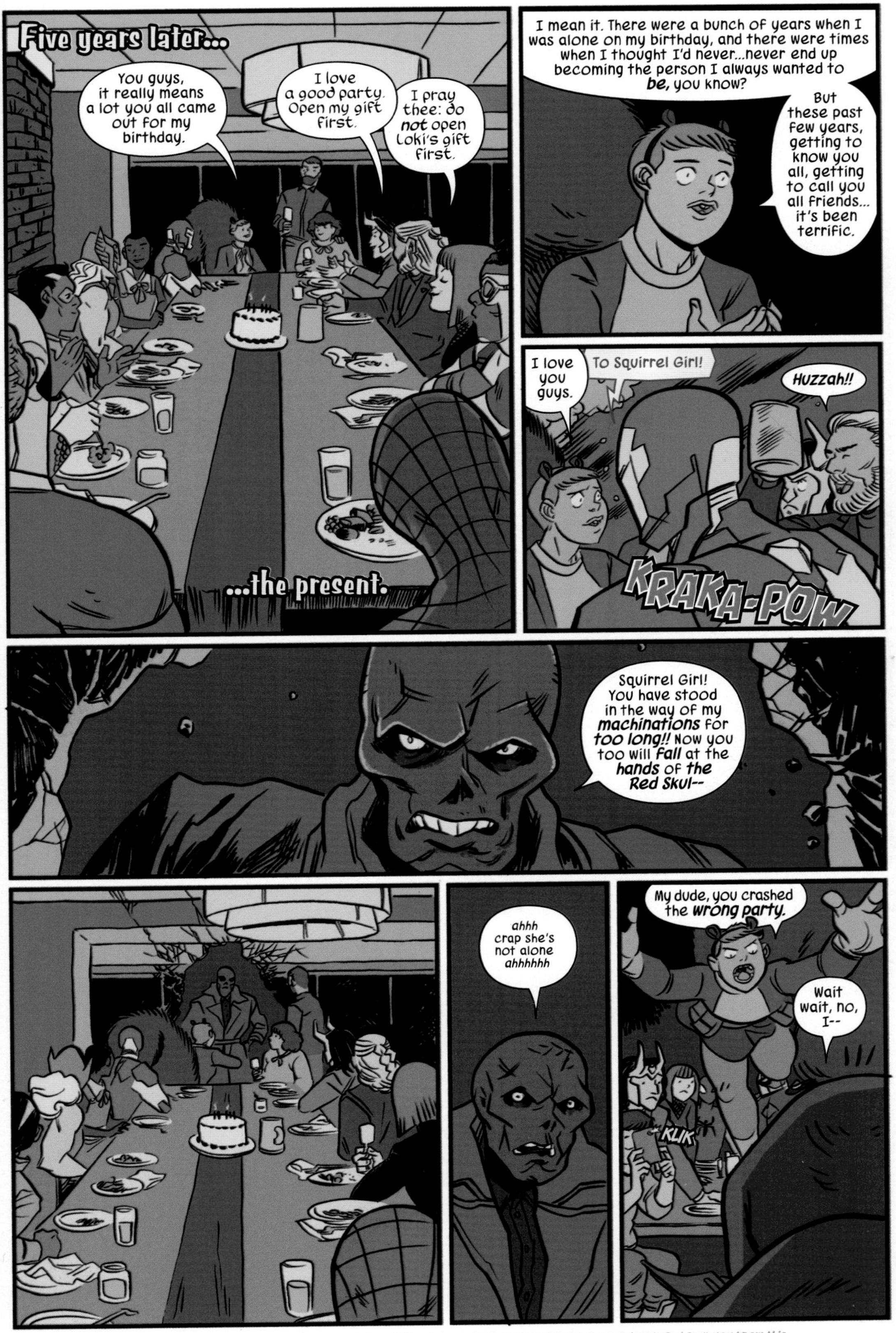
Five years later...
You guys, it really means a lot you all came out for my birthday.
I love a good party. Open my gift first.
I pray thee: do not open Loki's gift first.
...the present.
I mean it. There were a bunch of years when I was alone on my birthday, and there were times when I thought I'd never...never end up becoming the person I always wanted to be, you know?
But these past few years, getting to know you all, getting to call you all friends... it's been terrific.
I love you guys.
To Squirrel Girl!
HUZZAH!!
KRAKA-POW
Squirrel Girl! You have stood in the way of my machinations for too long!! Now you too will fall at the hands of the Red Skul--
ahhh crap she's not alone ahhhhhh
My dude, you crashed the wrong party.
Wait wait, no, I--
KLIK
Dang it I really should've peered through the window before smashing through the wall dang it Red Skull *you know this*

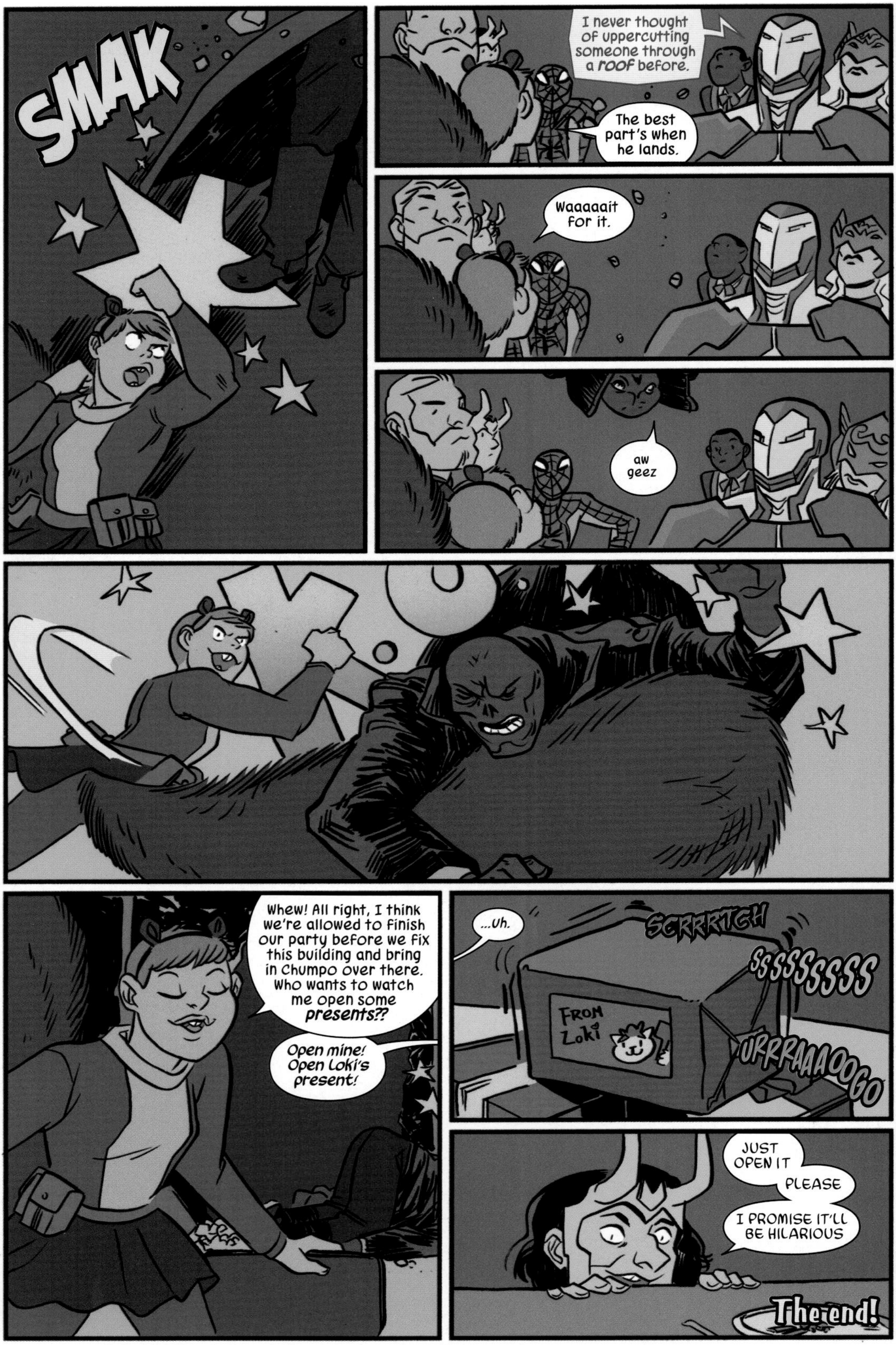
SMAK
I never thought of uppercutting someone through a *roof* before.
The best part's when he lands.
Waaaaait for it.
aw geez
Whew! All right, I think we're allowed to finish our party before we fix this building and bring in Chumpo over there. Who wants to watch me open some *presents??*
Open mine! Open Loki's present!
...Uh.
SCRRRTCH
SSSSSSSSS
FROM Loki
URRRAAAOOGO
JUST OPEN IT
PLEASE
I PROMISE IT'LL BE HILARIOUS
The end!

Squirrel Girl did eventually open Loki's present, and once she got rid of the Asgardian Lesser Prank Beast that was making those noises, a lot of the stuff in there was actually really sweet. *The end.*

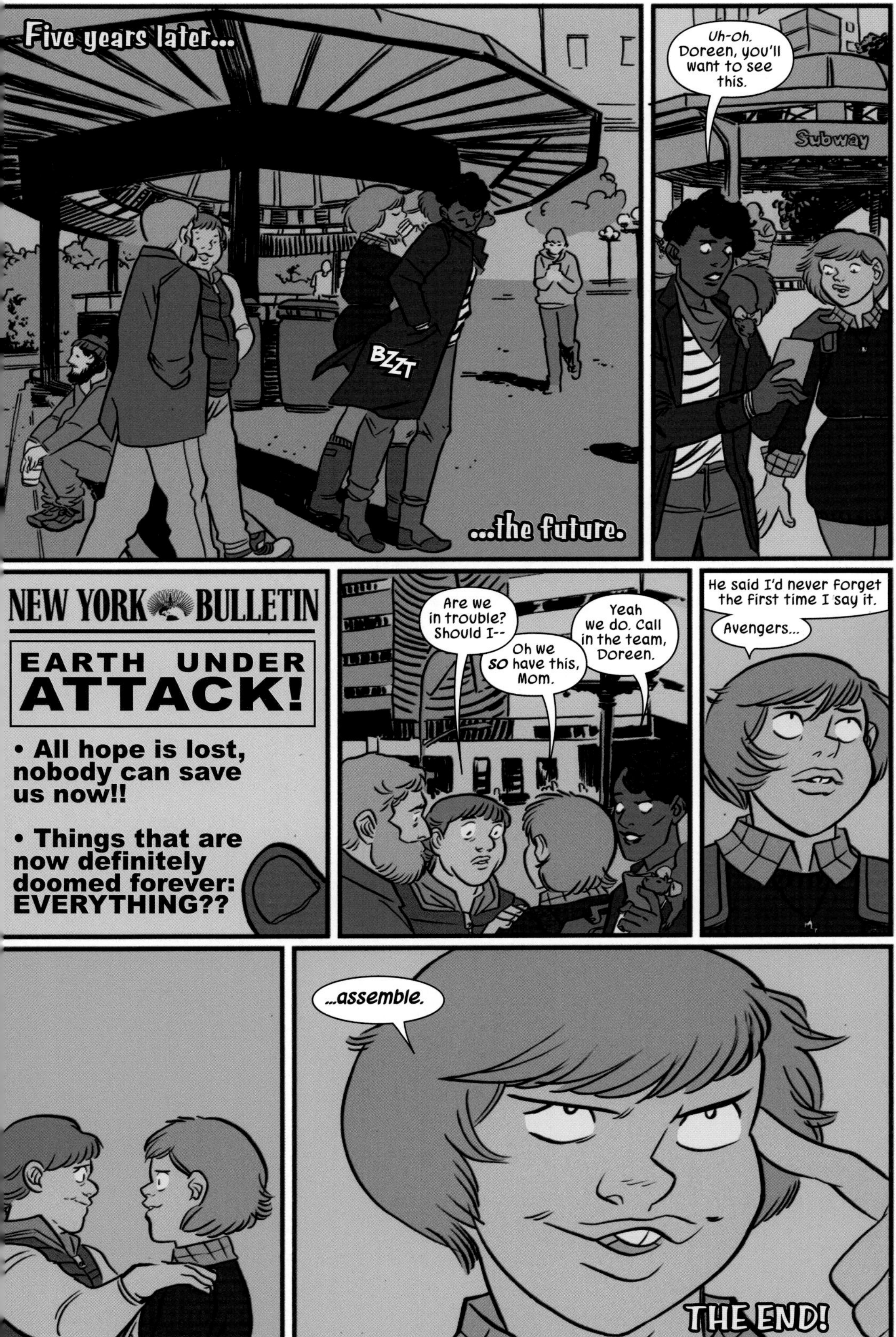

Five years later...
...the future.
BZZT
Uh-Oh. Doreen, you'll want to see this.
Subway
NEW YORK BULLETIN
EARTH UNDER ATTACK!
• All hope is lost, nobody can save us now!!
• Things that are now definitely doomed forever: EVERYTHING??
Are we in trouble? Should I--
Oh we SO have this, Mom.
Yeah we do. Call in the team, Doreen.
He said I'd never forget the first time I say it.
Avengers...
...assemble.
THE END!

We don't show the Avengers here because we don't want to *spoil all of Marvel future continuity,* but let me just say: she's the Unbeatable Squirrel Girl, she runs the gosh-darned *Avengers,* and...Nancy in a building-sized mecha suit confirmed??

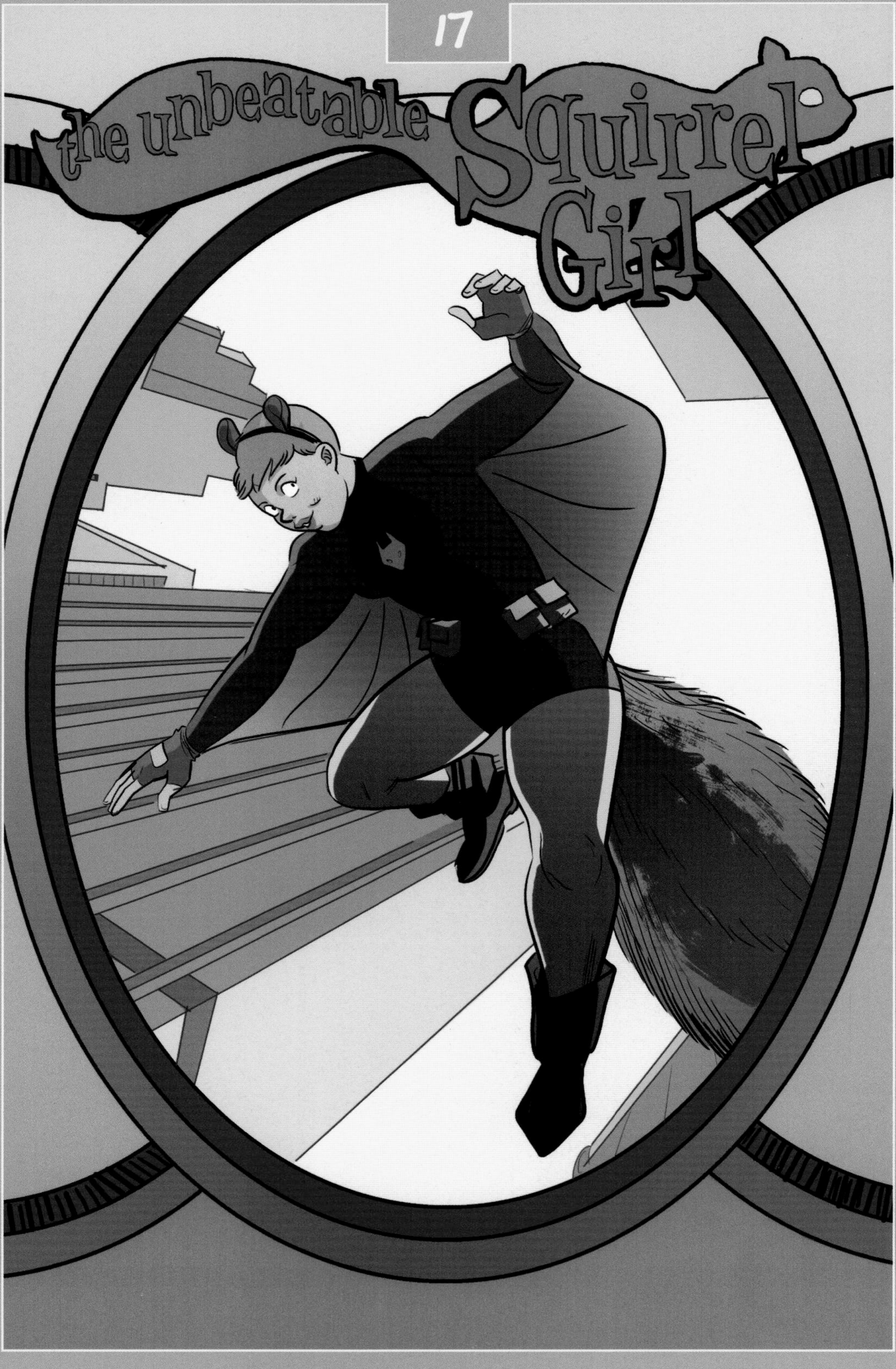
17
the unbeatable Squirrel Girl

*Doreen Green isn't just a second-year computer science student: she secretly also has all the powers of both squirrel and girl! She uses her amazing abilities to fight crime **and** be as awesome as possible. You know her as...**The Unbeatable Squirrel Girl!** Find out what she's been up to, with...*

Squirrel Girl *in a nutshell*

Squirrel Girl @unbeatablesg
Roses are red / Violets are dull / Guess who just had her birthday party crashed by THE FRIGGIN' RED SKULL

Squirrel Girl @unbeatablesg
Answer: me.

Squirrel Girl @unbeatablesg
Well haha not JUST me since it was a party filled with pals like KOI BOI, CHIPMUNK HUNK, SPIDER-MAN, BLACK WIDOW, IRON MAN, and MORE??

Squirrel Girl @unbeatablesg
Anyway, I punched the Red Skull right through the roof and he's in jail now. PRESUMABLY FOREVER?? THAT SEEMS LIKELY, YES?

Squirrel Girl @unbeatablesg
Which MAYBE just goes to show you the dangers of crashing someone's party when she's friends with LITERAL SUPER HEROES? hmm hard to say

Egg @imduderadtude
@unbeatablesg can u get a mesasge to spider man for me

Squirrel Girl @unbeatablesg
@imduderadtude no

Egg @imduderadtude
@unbeatablesg please he has me blocked and i just want to ask him Y he has me blokced

Squirrel Girl @unbeatablesg
@imduderadtude Dude, real talk, you don't want to be following him anyway, he posts the worst stuff

Squirrel Girl @unbeatablesg
@imduderadtude like he's a good guy for fighting crime but not necessarily the best at providing entertaining #content in 140 characters

Spider-Man @aspidercan
if someone is a jerk on here i reply with "wow looks like u got bitten by a radioactive JERK," so yeah feel free to use that if you want

Spider-Man @aspidercan
hi everyone i'm having a lot of fun here on the world......................................wide............ ....WEB

Spider-Man @aspidercan
If you're wondering who I've got blocked, it's @wealth and @fame

Spider-Man @aspidercan
....because wealth and fame i've ignored

Spider-Man @aspidercan
#actionismyreward

Squirrel Girl @unbeatablesg
@imduderadtude I rest my case

xKravenTheHunterx @unshavenkraven
@unbeatablesg Happy belated birthday, girl of squirrels.

Squirrel Girl @unbeatablesg
@unshavenkraven Thanks, Kraven!

xKravenTheHunterx @unshavenkraven
@unbeatablesg I'm sorry I could not attend your party.

Squirrel Girl @unbeatablesg
@unshavenkraven It's okay! We'll hang out sometime soon. We'll have to catch up later, I've got to get to a thing for class!

Squirrel Girl @unbeatablesg
@unshavenkraven I mean my friend has got to get to a thing for class.

Squirrel Girl @unbeatablesg
@unshavenkraven I mean, my friend has to get to a thing for class and I'm helping her...go there?

Squirrel Girl @unbeatablesg
@unshavenkraven She goes to a different school

Squirrel Girl @unbeatablesg
@unshavenkraven in Canada

xKravenTheHunterx @unshavenkraven
@unbeatablesg You can just delete these posts.

Squirrel Girl @unbeatablesg
@unshavenkraven YEP, ALREADY ON IT

search!

#computerengineering

#regularengineering

#catthor

#doghulk

#alfredo4life

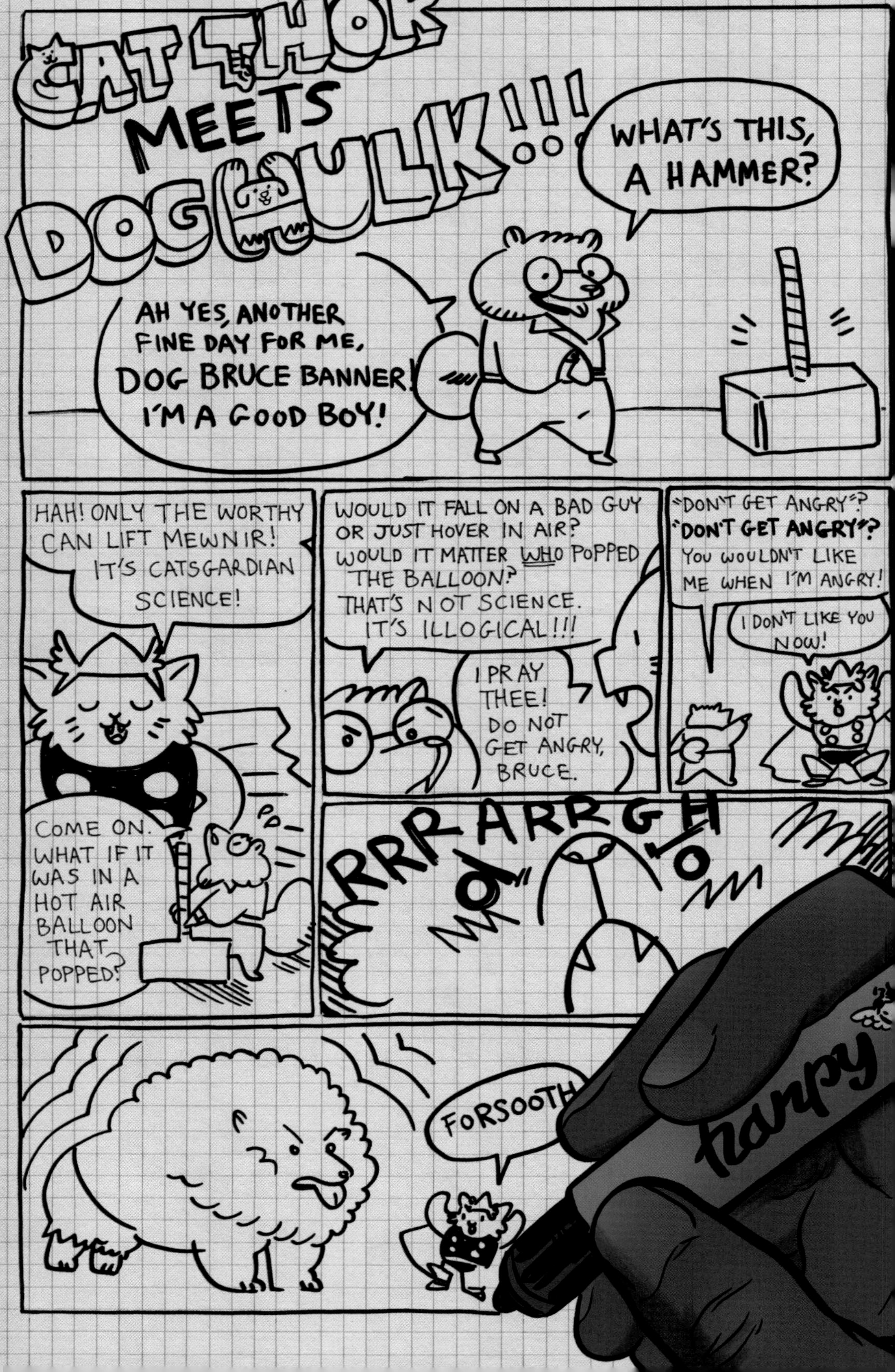
CAT THOR MEETS DOG HULK!!!
WHAT'S THIS, A HAMMER?
AH YES, ANOTHER FINE DAY FOR ME, DOG BRUCE BANNER! I'M A GOOD BOY!
HAH! ONLY THE WORTHY CAN LIFT MEWNIR! IT'S CATSGARDIAN SCIENCE!
COME ON. WHAT IF IT WAS IN A HOT AIR BALLOON THAT POPPED?
WOULD IT FALL ON A BAD GUY OR JUST HOVER IN AIR? WOULD IT MATTER WHO POPPED THE BALLOON? THAT'S NOT SCIENCE. IT'S ILLOGICAL!!!
I PRAY THEE! DO NOT GET ANGRY, BRUCE.
"DON'T GET ANGRY"? "DON'T GET ANGRY"? YOU WOULDN'T LIKE ME WHEN I'M ANGRY!
I DON'T LIKE YOU NOW!
RRRARRRGH
FORSOOTH
tranpy

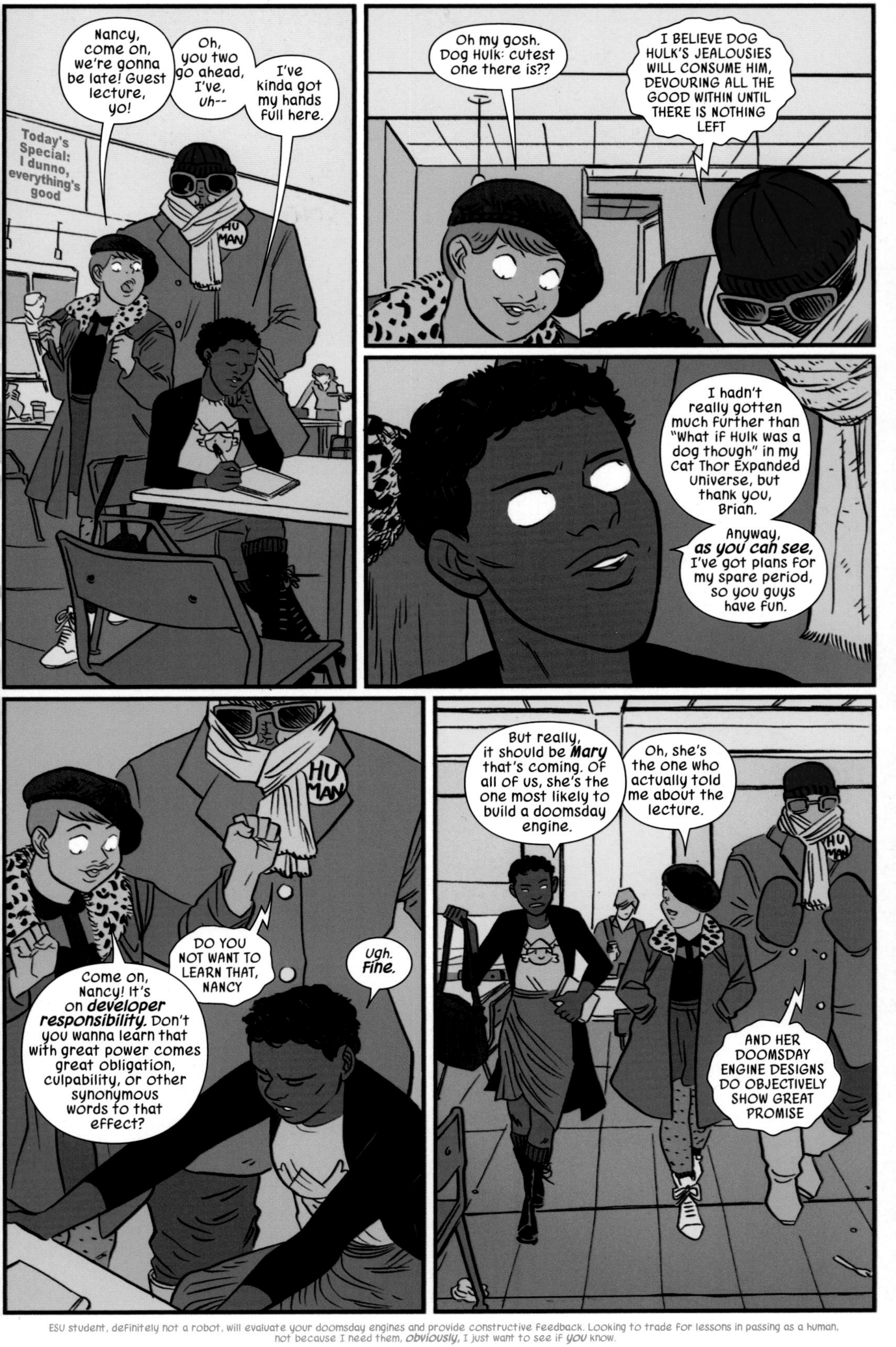
Today's Special: I dunno, everything's good
Nancy, come on, we're gonna be late! Guest lecture, yo!
Oh, you two go ahead, I've, uh--
I've kinda got my hands full here.
HU MAN
Oh my gosh. Dog Hulk: cutest one there is??
I BELIEVE DOG HULK'S JEALOUSIES WILL CONSUME HIM, DEVOURING ALL THE GOOD WITHIN UNTIL THERE IS NOTHING LEFT
I hadn't really gotten much further than "What if Hulk was a dog though" in my Cat Thor Expanded Universe, but thank you, Brian.
Anyway, *as you can see,* I've got plans for my spare period, so you guys have fun.
HU MAN
Come on, Nancy! It's on ***developer responsibility.*** Don't you wanna learn that with great power comes great obligation, culpability, or other synonymous words to that effect?
DO YOU NOT WANT TO LEARN THAT, NANCY
Ugh. ***Fine.***
But really, it should be ***Mary*** that's coming. Of all of us, she's the one most likely to build a doomsday engine.
Oh, she's the one who actually told me about the lecture.
AND HER DOOMSDAY ENGINE DESIGNS DO OBJECTIVELY SHOW GREAT PROMISE
HU MAN

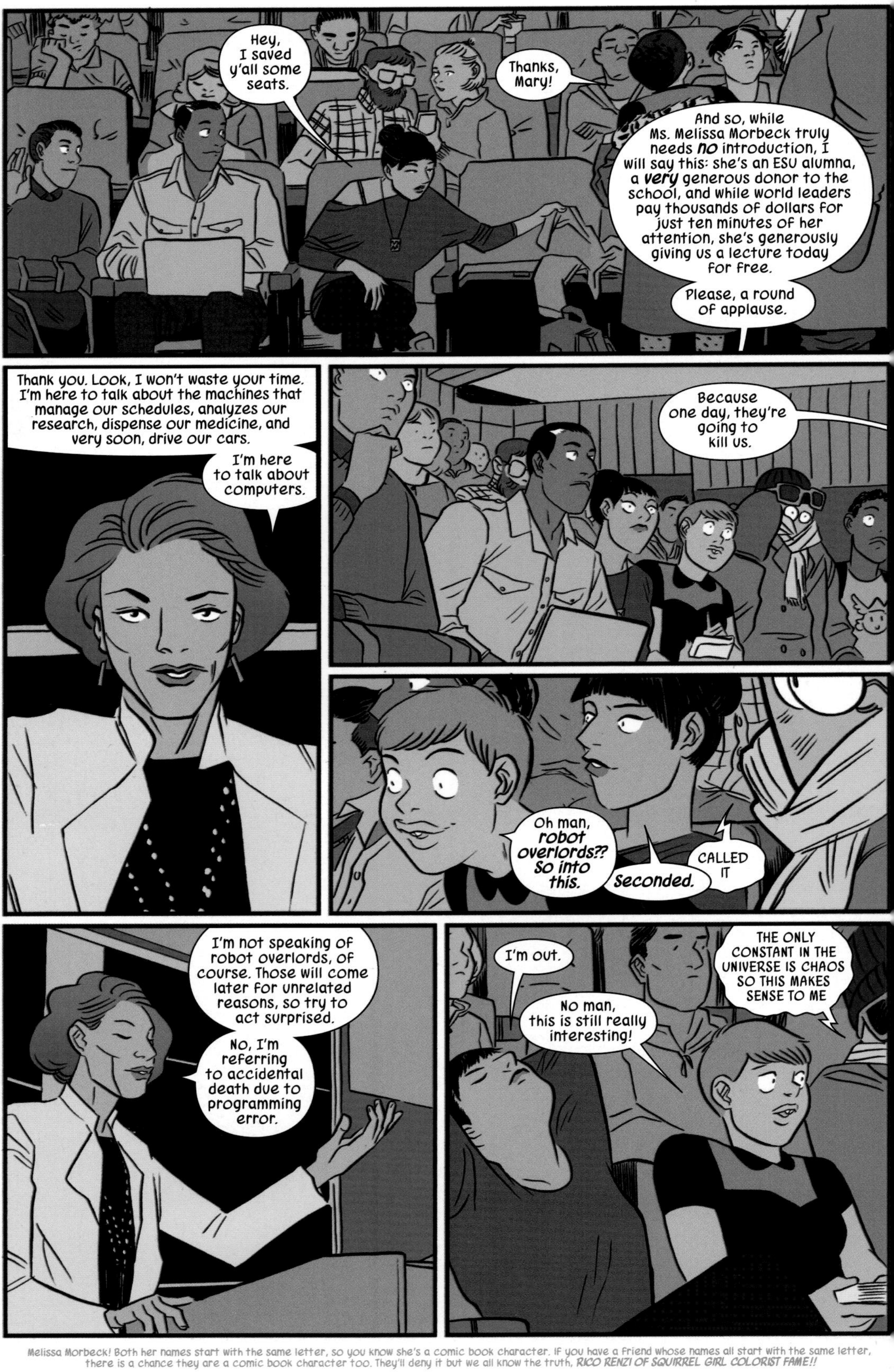
Hey, I saved y'all some seats.
Thanks, Mary!
And so, while Ms. Melissa Morbeck truly needs NO introduction, I will say this: she's an ESU alumna, a very generous donor to the school, and while world leaders pay thousands of dollars for just ten minutes of her attention, she's generously giving us a lecture today for free.
Please, a round of applause.
Thank you. Look, I won't waste your time. I'm here to talk about the machines that manage our schedules, analyzes our research, dispense our medicine, and very soon, drive our cars.
I'm here to talk about computers.
Because one day, they're going to kill us.
Oh man, robot overlords?? So into this.
Seconded.
CALLED IT
I'm not speaking of robot overlords, of course. Those will come later for unrelated reasons, so try to act surprised.
No, I'm referring to accidental death due to programming error.
I'm out.
No man, this is still really interesting!
THE ONLY CONSTANT IN THE UNIVERSE IS CHAOS SO THIS MAKES SENSE TO ME

Melissa Morbeck! Both her names start with the same letter, so you know she's a comic book character. If you have a friend whose names all start with the same letter, there is a chance they are a comic book character too. They'll deny it but we all know the truth, *RICO RENZI OF SQUIRREL GIRL COLORIST FAME!!*

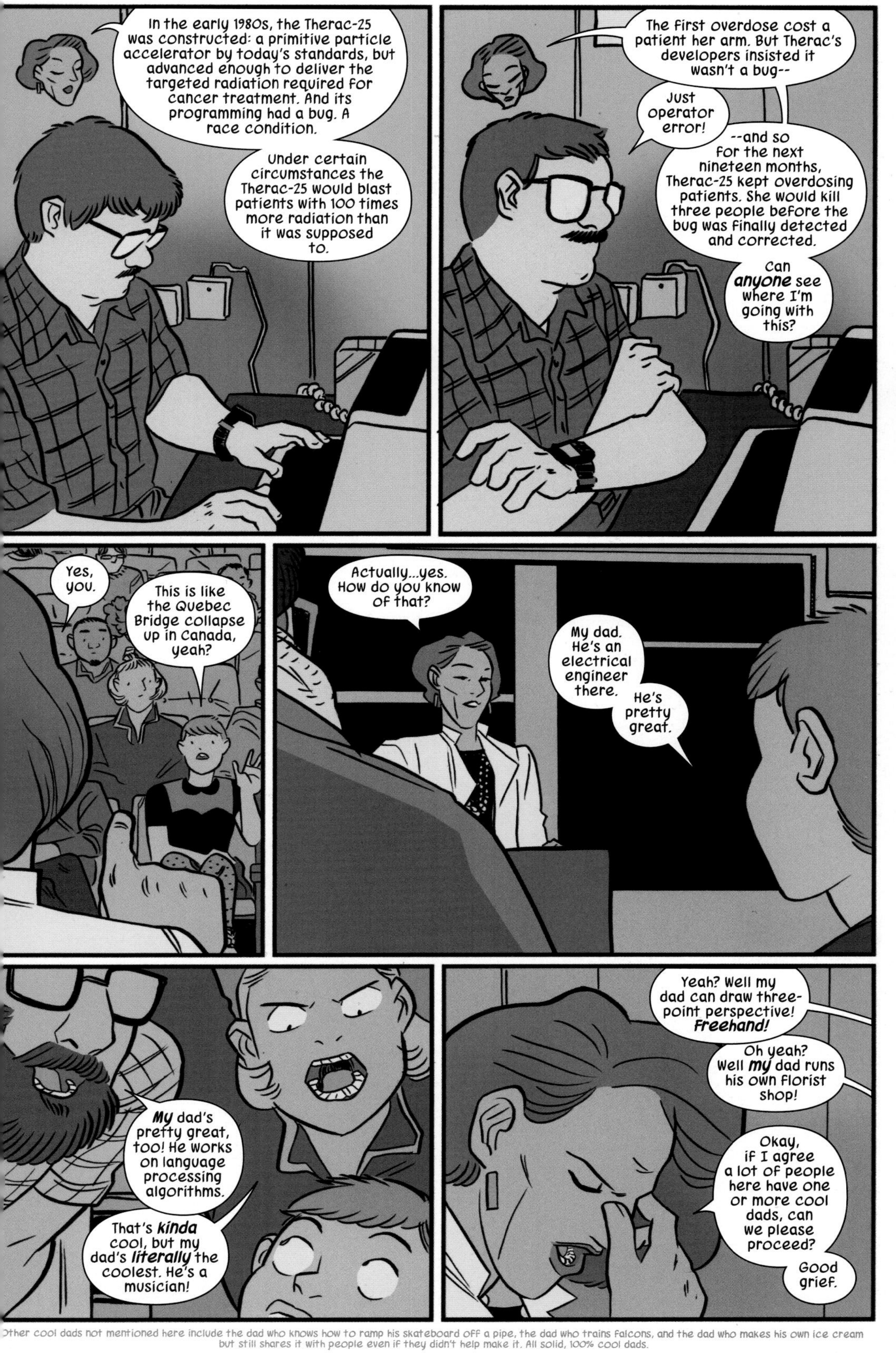
In the early 1980s, the Therac-25 was constructed: a primitive particle accelerator by today's standards, but advanced enough to deliver the targeted radiation required for cancer treatment. And its programming had a bug. A race condition.
Under certain circumstances the Therac-25 would blast patients with 100 times more radiation than it was supposed to.
The first overdose cost a patient her arm. But Therac's developers insisted it wasn't a bug--
Just operator error!
--and so for the next nineteen months, Therac-25 kept overdosing patients. She would kill three people before the bug was finally detected and corrected.
Can *anyone* see where I'm going with this?
Yes, you.
This is like the Quebec Bridge collapse up in Canada, yeah?
Actually...yes. How do you know of that?
My dad. He's an electrical engineer there.
He's pretty great.
My dad's pretty great, too! He works on language processing algorithms.
That's *kinda* cool, but my dad's *literally* the coolest. He's a musician!
Yeah? Well my dad can draw three-point perspective! *Freehand!*
Oh yeah? Well *my* dad runs his own florist shop!
Okay, if I agree a lot of people here have one or more cool dads, can we please proceed?
Good grief.

Other cool dads not mentioned here include the dad who knows how to ramp his skateboard off a pipe, the dad who trains falcons, and the dad who makes his own ice cream but still shares it with people even if they didn't help make it. All solid, 100% cool dads.

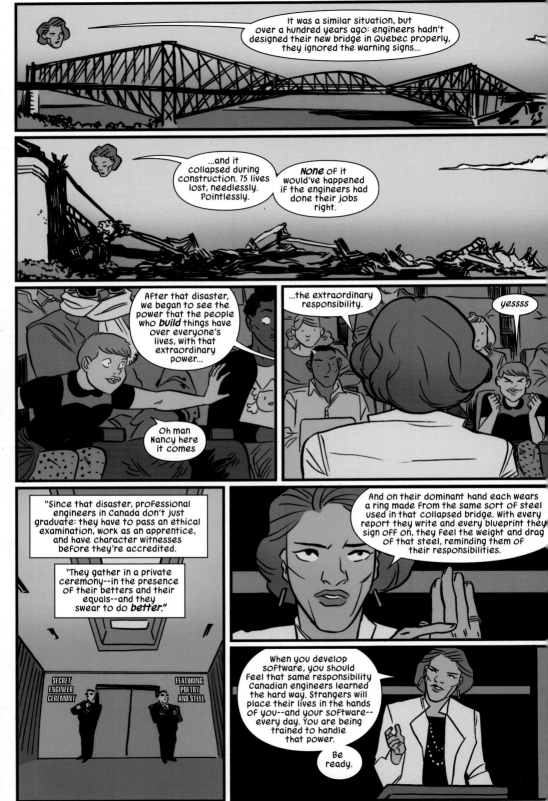

It was a similar situation, but over a hundred years ago: engineers hadn't designed their new bridge in Quebec properly, they ignored the warning signs...

...and it collapsed during construction. 75 lives lost, needlessly. Pointlessly.

None of it would've happened if the engineers had done their jobs right.

After that disaster, we began to see the power that the people who *build* things have over everyone's lives, with that extraordinary power...

Oh man Nancy here it comes

...the extraordinary responsibility.

yessss

"Since that disaster, professional engineers in Canada don't just graduate: they have to pass an ethical examination, work as an apprentice, and have character witnesses before they're accredited.

"They gather in a private ceremony--in the presence of their betters and their equals--and they swear to do *better*."

SECRET ENGINEER CEREMONY

FEATURING POETRY AND STEEL

And on their dominant hand each wears a ring made from the same sort of steel used in that collapsed bridge. With every report they write and every blueprint they sign off on, they feel the weight and drag of that steel, reminding them of their responsibilities.

When you develop software, you should feel that same responsibility Canadian engineers learned the hard way. Strangers will place their lives in the hands of you--and your software--every day. You are being trained to handle that power.

Be ready.

Right now, somewhere in the world, Peter Parker is sitting up straight in bed and wondering why his "stolen catchphrase-sense" is suddenly tingling *so much*.

PRO TIP: if someone ever asks you what you're gonna wear, just say "regular human clothes." Unless you make a catastrophic mistake while dressing, your answer will always be 100% accurate!

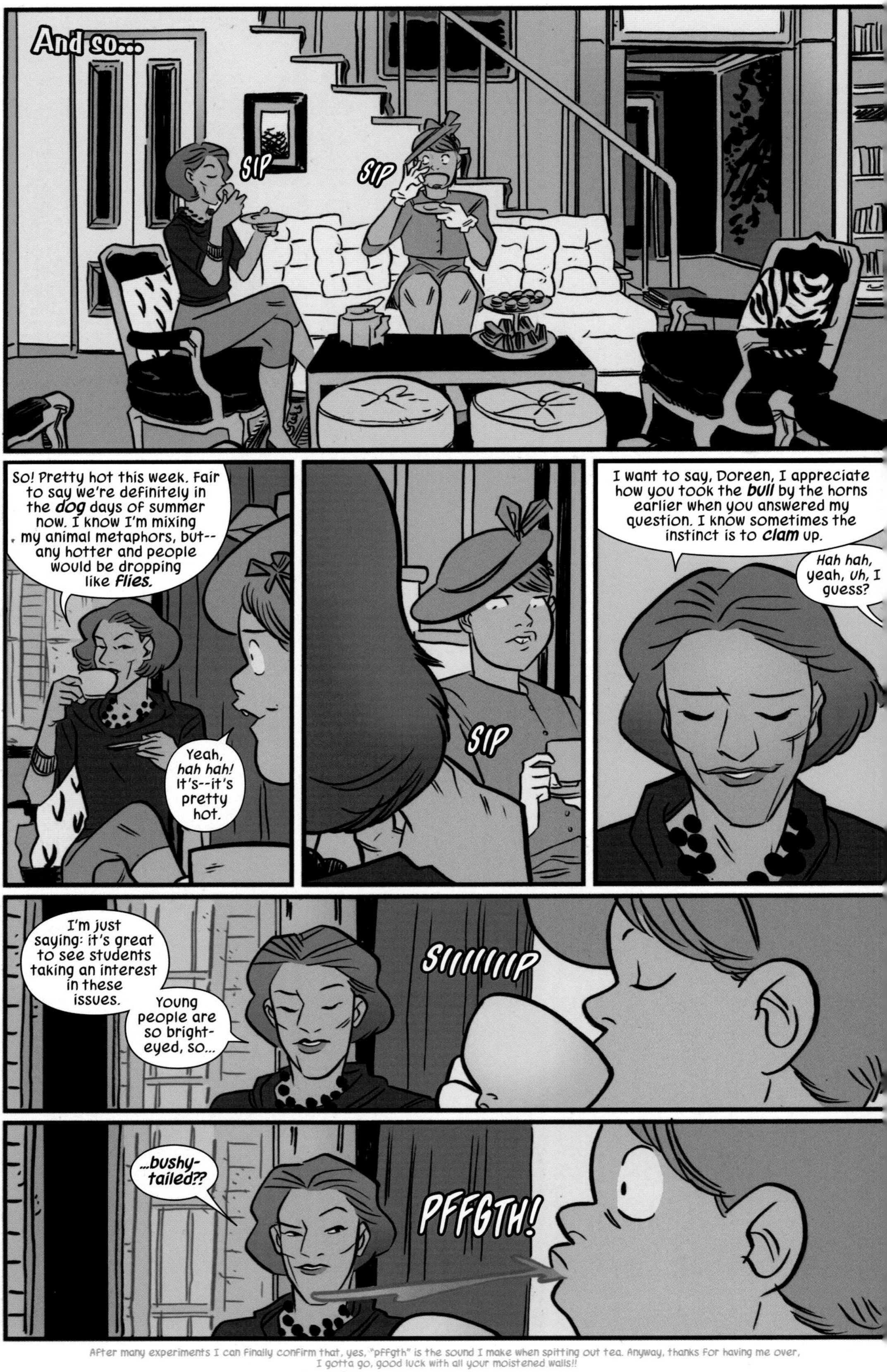

And so...
SIP
SIP
So! Pretty hot this week. Fair to say we're definitely in the *dog* days of summer now. I know I'm mixing my animal metaphors, but--any hotter and people would be dropping like *flies.*
Yeah, *hah hah!* It's--it's pretty hot.
SIP
I want to say, Doreen, I appreciate how you took the *bull* by the horns earlier when you answered my question. I know sometimes the instinct is to *clam* up.
Hah hah, yeah, uh, I guess?
I'm just saying: it's great to see students taking an interest in these issues.
Young people are so bright-eyed, so...
SIIIIIIP
...bushy-tailed??
PFFGTH!

After many experiments I can finally confirm that, yes, "pffgth" is the sound I make when spitting out tea. Anyway, thanks for having me over, I gotta go, good luck with all your moistened walls!!

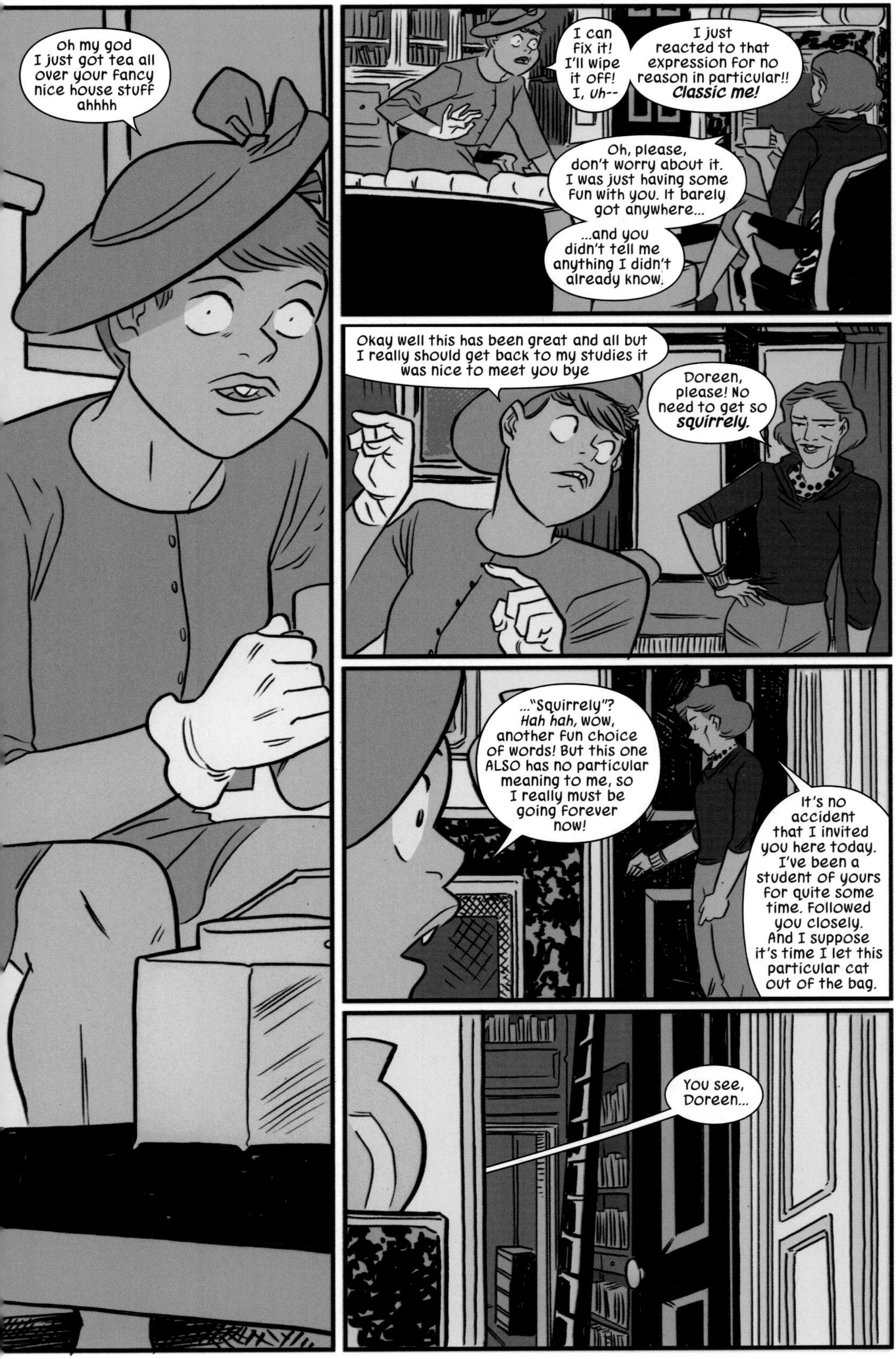
Oh my god I just got tea all over your fancy nice house stuff ahhhh
I can fix it! I'll wipe it off! I, uh--
I just reacted to that expression for no reason in particular!! *Classic me!*
Oh, please, don't worry about it. I was just having some fun with you. It barely got anywhere...
...and you didn't tell me anything I didn't already know.
Okay well this has been great and all but I really should get back to my studies it was nice to meet you bye
Doreen, please! No need to get so ***squirrely.***
..."Squirrely"? *Hah hah,* WOW, another fun choice of words! But this one ALSO has no particular meaning to me, so I really must be going forever now!
It's no accident that I invited you here today. I've been a student of yours for quite some time. Followed you closely. And I suppose it's time I let this particular cat out of the bag.
You see, Doreen...

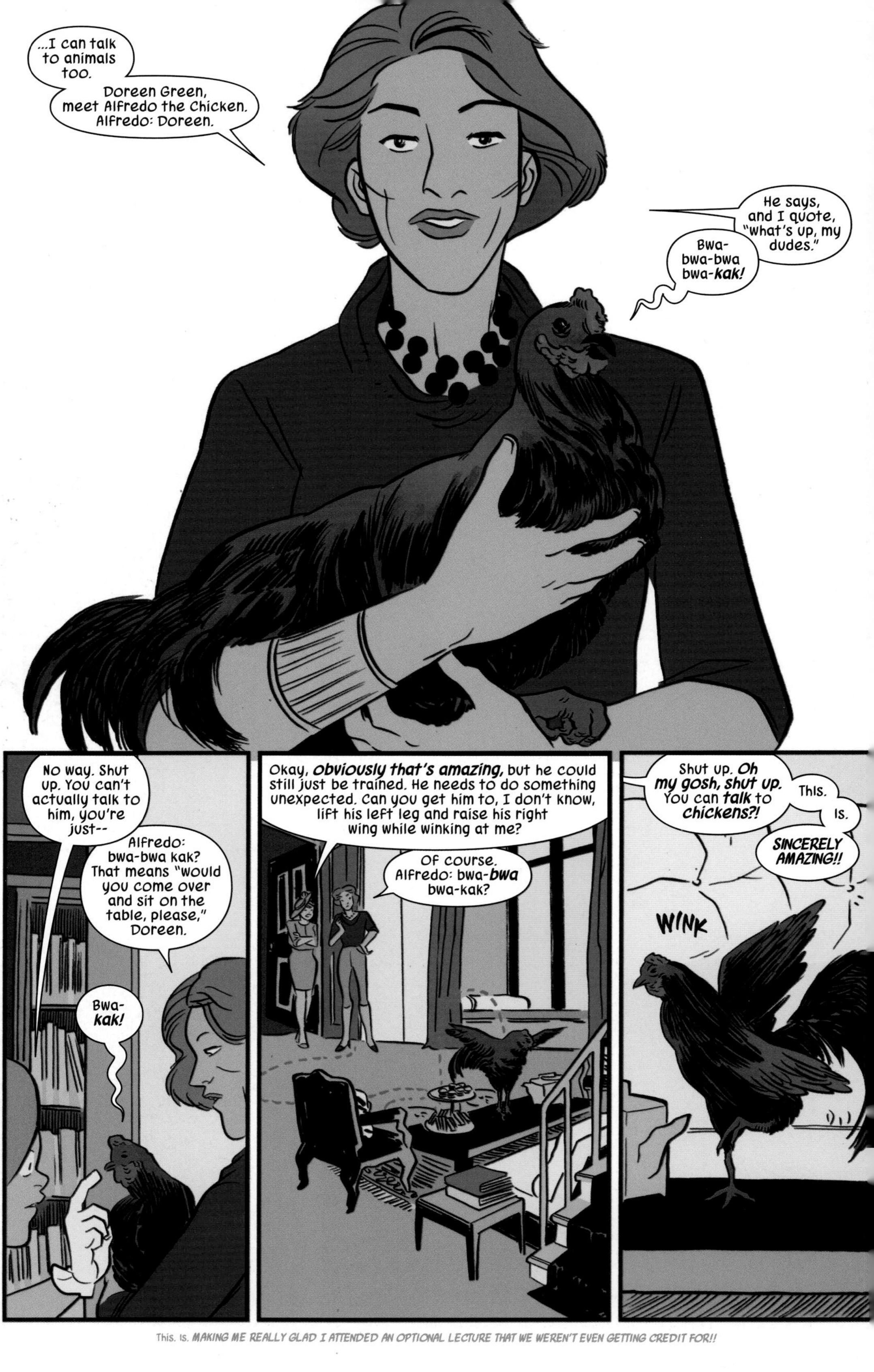
...I can talk to animals too.
Doreen Green, meet Alfredo the Chicken. Alfredo: Doreen.
He says, and I quote, "what's up, my dudes."
Bwa-bwa-bwa bwa-kak!
No way. Shut up. You can't actually talk to him, you're just--
Alfredo: bwa-bwa kak? That means "would you come over and sit on the table, please," Doreen.
Bwa-kak!
Okay, obviously that's amazing, but he could still just be trained. He needs to do something unexpected. Can you get him to, I don't know, lift his left leg and raise his right wing while winking at me?
Of course. Alfredo: bwa-bwa bwa-kak?
Shut up. Oh my gosh, shut up. You can talk to chickens?!
This.
Is.
SINCERELY AMAZING!!
WINK

This. Is. *MAKING ME REALLY GLAD I ATTENDED AN OPTIONAL LECTURE THAT WE WEREN'T EVEN GETTING CREDIT FOR!!*

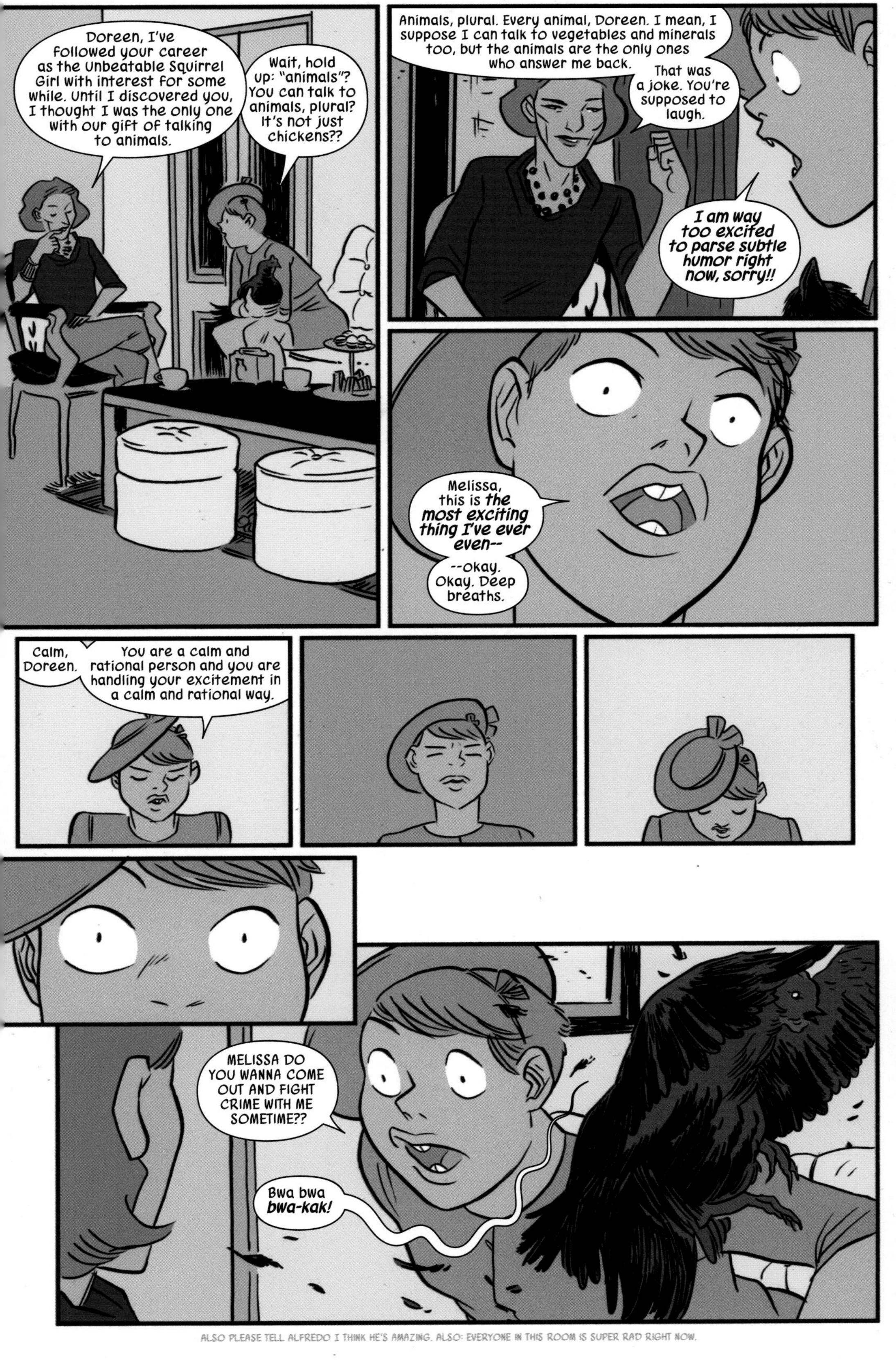
Doreen, I've followed your career as the Unbeatable Squirrel Girl with interest for some while. Until I discovered you, I thought I was the only one with our gift of talking to animals.
Wait, hold up: "animals"? You can talk to animals, plural? It's not just chickens??
Animals, plural. Every animal, Doreen. I mean, I suppose I can talk to vegetables and minerals too, but the animals are the only ones who answer me back.
That was a joke. You're supposed to laugh.
I am way too excited to parse subtle humor right now, sorry!!
Melissa, this is the most exciting thing I've ever even--
--Okay. Okay. Deep breaths.
Calm, Doreen.
You are a calm and rational person and you are handling your excitement in a calm and rational way.
MELISSA DO YOU WANNA COME OUT AND FIGHT CRIME WITH ME SOMETIME??
Bwa bwa bwa-kak!

ALSO PLEASE TELL ALFREDO I THINK HE'S AMAZING. ALSO: EVERYONE IN THIS ROOM IS SUPER RAD RIGHT NOW.

Oh no, no, that's a young woman's game.

Come on, what are you, 40? That's still *prime* crime-fighting time! Heck, the *Vulture* is like 80 and he *still* manages to give Spider-Man the business on the regular!

"And since nobody knows who Spider-Man is, who can say *he's* not a senior citizen thwipping around town, too?"

"It's literally a *possibility*."

Doreen, I appreciate it, but we all have our strengths. For example, not unlike Spider-Man, you're good at punching recidivists; I'm good at other things. I had another way in mind of helping you, if you're interested.

Another way?

Oh, of course! *Of course.*

"How did I not see this sooner? We record you saying simple phrases in Chickenese, and then I use them in the field to direct Alfredo, thus allowing us to become a *crimefighting team!*"

Bwa bwa *bwa-kak!*

That means *"peck him,"* Sandman!!

Nooo, I'm 100% peckable parts, noooo

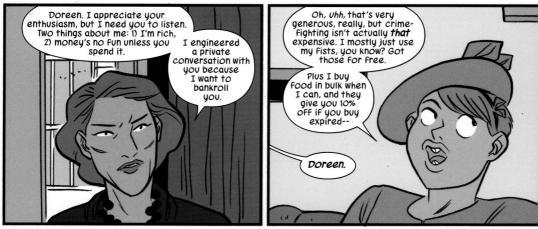

Doreen. I appreciate your enthusiasm, but I need you to listen. Two things about me: 1) I'm rich, 2) money's no fun unless you spend it.

I engineered a private conversation with you because I want to bankroll you.

Oh, *uhh*, that's very generous, really, but crime-fighting isn't actually *that* expensive. I mostly just use my fists, you know? Got those for free.

Plus I buy food in bulk when I can, and they give you 10% off if you buy expired--

Doreen.

Sandman is a villain made entirely out of sand, and he's only slightly less vulnerable to Alfredo's pecking than Lady Kernels Of Corn, who is a villain I just made up! She's got an ear for crime but explodes under pressure! *Did you know:* she's the only (and therefore technically the greatest) character ever introduced in the little notes beneath a Marvel comic??

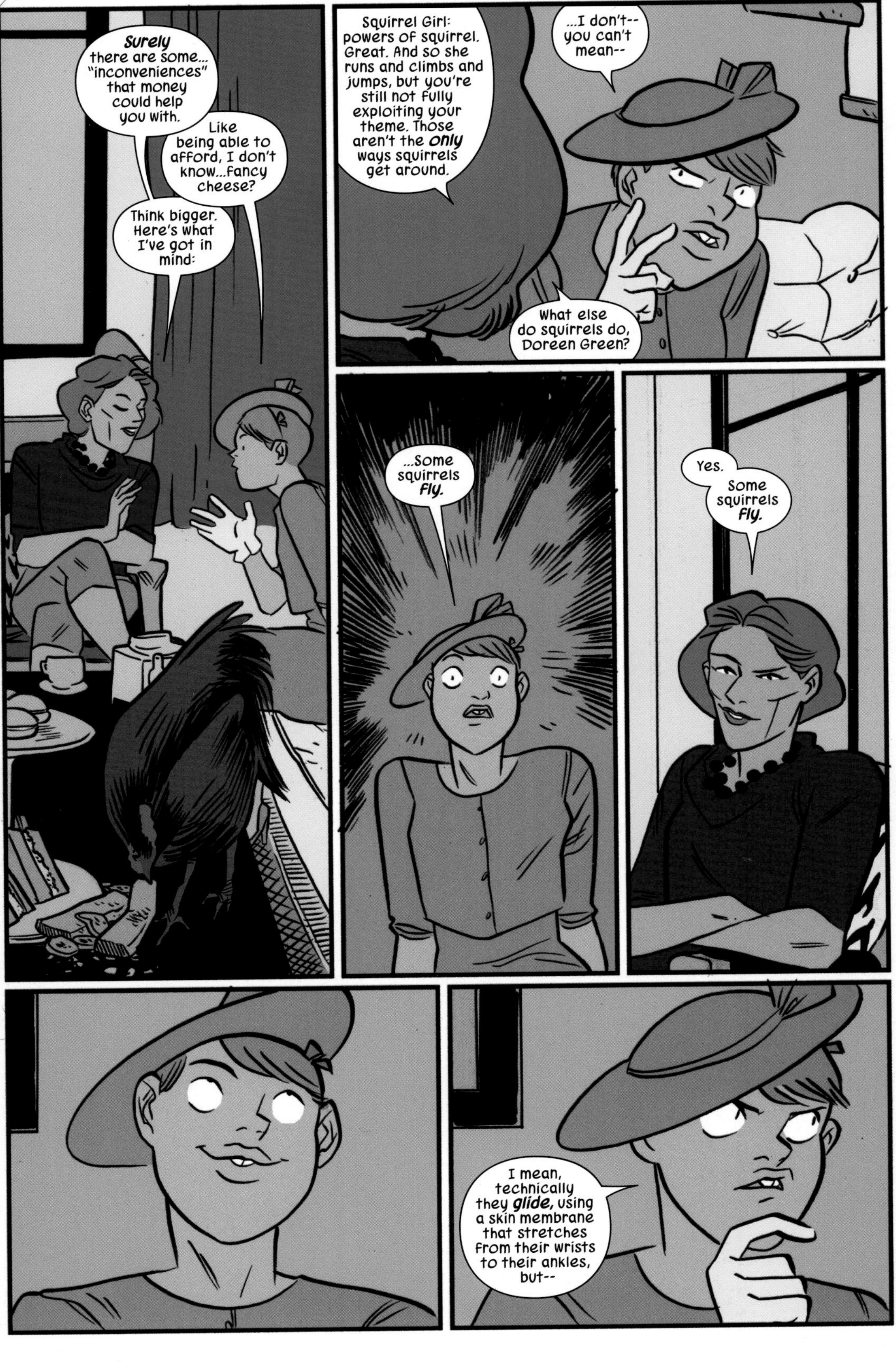
Surely there are some... "inconveniences" that money could help you with.
Like being able to afford, I don't know...fancy cheese?
Think bigger. Here's what I've got in mind:
Squirrel Girl: powers of squirrel. Great. And so she runs and climbs and jumps, but you're still not fully exploiting your theme. Those aren't the only ways squirrels get around.
...I don't-- you can't mean--
What else do squirrels do, Doreen Green?
...Some squirrels fly.
Yes.
Some squirrels fly.
I mean, technically they glide, using a skin membrane that stretches from their wrists to their ankles, but--

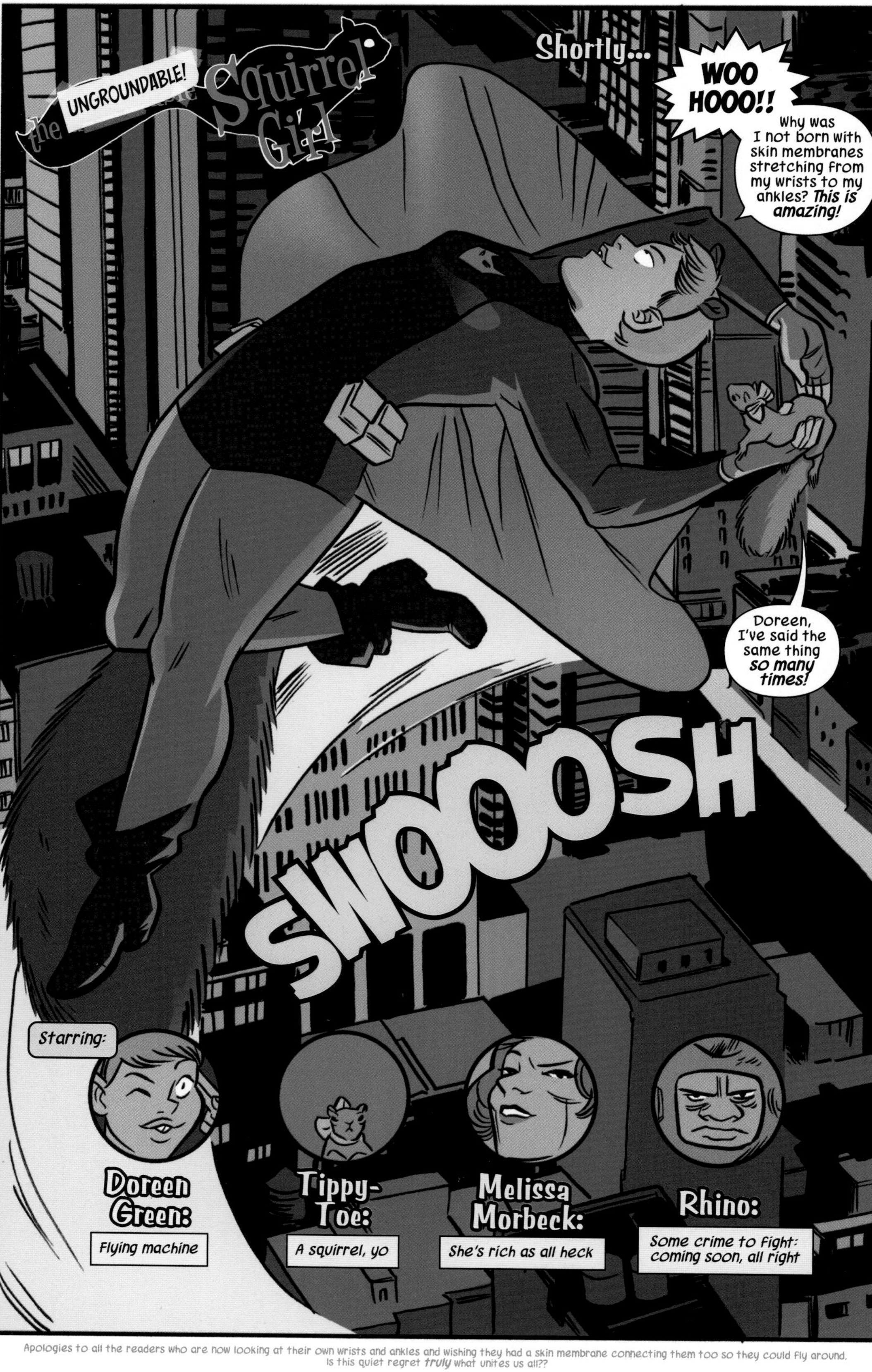
the UNGROUNDABLE! Squirrel Girl
Shortly...
WOO HOOO!! Why was I not born with skin membranes stretching from my wrists to my ankles? *This is amazing!*
Doreen, I've said the same thing *so many times!*
SWOOOSH
Starring:
Doreen Green:
Flying machine
Tippy-Toe:
A squirrel, yo
Melissa Morbeck:
She's rich as all heck
Rhino:
Some crime to fight: coming soon, all right

Apologies to all the readers who are now looking at their own wrists and ankles and wishing they had a skin membrane connecting them too so they could fly around. Is this quiet regret *truly* what unites us all??

Not pictured: all the criminals who just bought blimps to secure themselves from ground-level justice as they glance up, see Squirrel Girl flying by, then quickly search on their phones for "are blimps returnable for a full refund + it's an emergency."

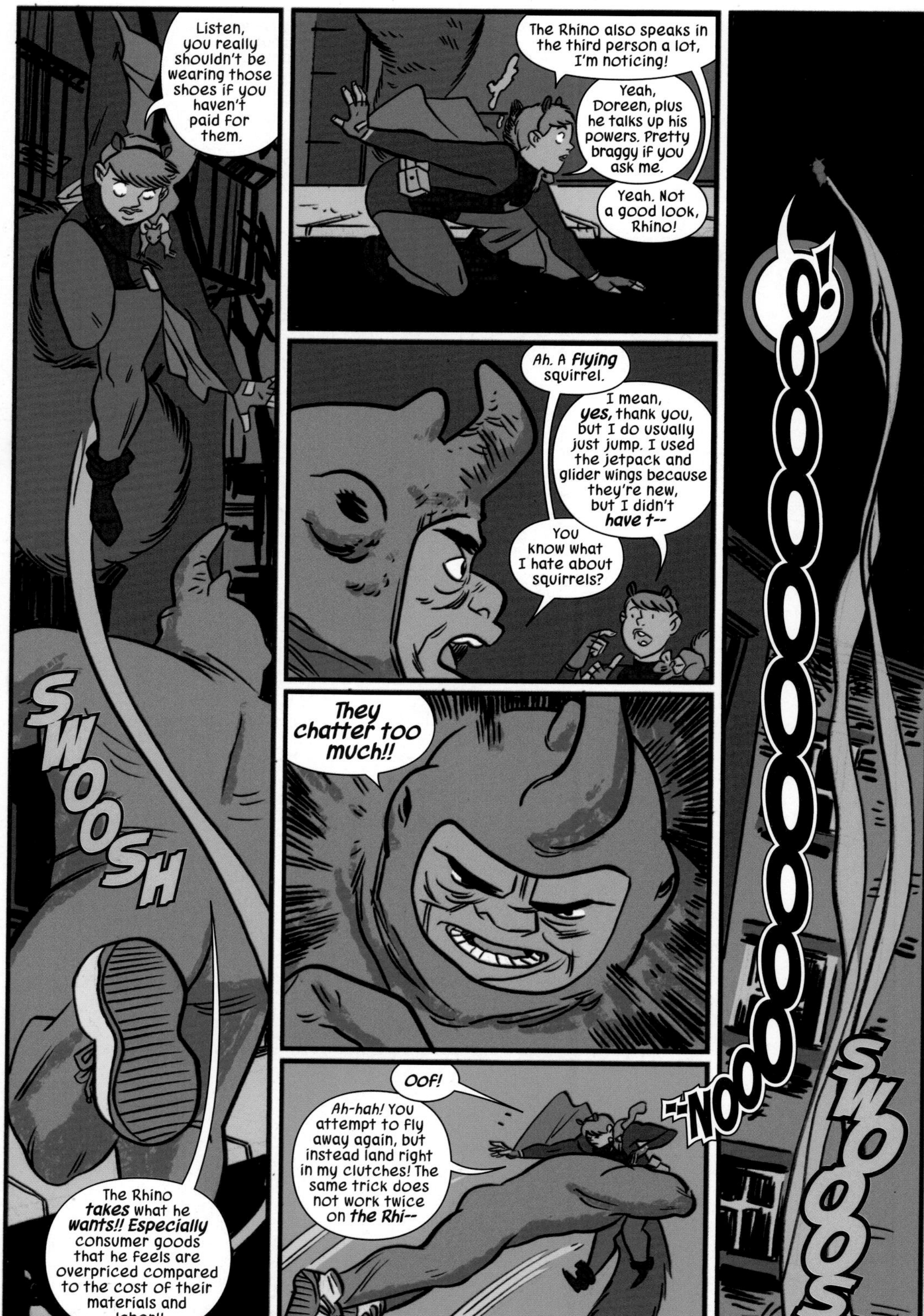
Listen, you really shouldn't be wearing those shoes if you haven't paid for them.
SWOOSH
The Rhino *takes* what he *wants!! Especially* consumer goods that he feels are overpriced compared to the cost of their materials and labor!!
The Rhino also speaks in the third person a lot, I'm noticing!
Yeah, Doreen, plus he talks up his powers. Pretty braggy if you ask me.
Yeah. Not a good look, Rhino!
Ah. A *flying* squirrel.
I mean, *yes,* thank you, but I do usually just jump. I used the jetpack and glider wings because they're new, but I didn't *have t--*
You know what I hate about squirrels?
They chatter too much!!
OOF!
Ah-hah! You attempt to fly away again, but instead land right in my clutches! The same trick does not work twice on *the Rhi--*
--NOOOOOOOOOOOOOOO!
SWOOOOSH

Rhino, you can't just judge goods by their price of materials and labor! You also need to factor in shipping, warehousing, *and* marketing expenses, man! It's not that simple!! It never is, in multinational capitalism!!

In case you're wondering, there's enough oxygen to breathe up to about 26,000 feet, and a fall from that height with standard air resistance would take well over a minute. So, yes, I did the math, and, yes, this scene of the rhino man and Squirrel Girl chatting in freefall is 100% *scientifically accurate*. Phew!!

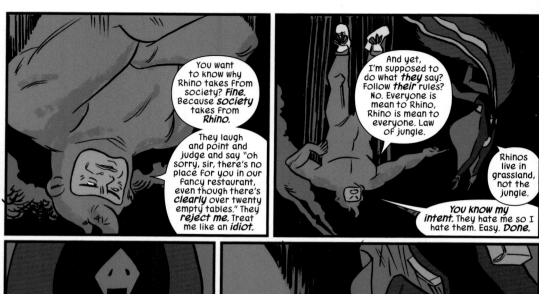

You want to know why Rhino takes from society? *Fine.* Because *society* takes from *Rhino.*

They laugh and point and judge and say "oh sorry, sir, there's no place for you in our fancy restaurant, even though there's *clearly* over twenty empty tables." They *reject me.* Treat me like an *idiot.*

And yet, I'm supposed to do what *they* say? Follow *their* rules? No. Everyone is mean to Rhino, Rhino is mean to everyone. Law of jungle.

Rhinos live in grassland, not the jungle.

You know my intent. They hate me so I hate them. Easy. *Done.*

I see a man with gifts, special powers that nobody else on the planet shares. I see an even more magical beast, a unique and legendary animal too perfect for this world. I don't see the Rhino.

I see the *UNICORN.*

I don't hate you, man.

You will. Everyone does. Once you get a good look, you--

No. Listen, when I look at you, you know what I see? Because I don't see the irascible, territorial, unpredictable brute you've named yourself after.

oh my gosh

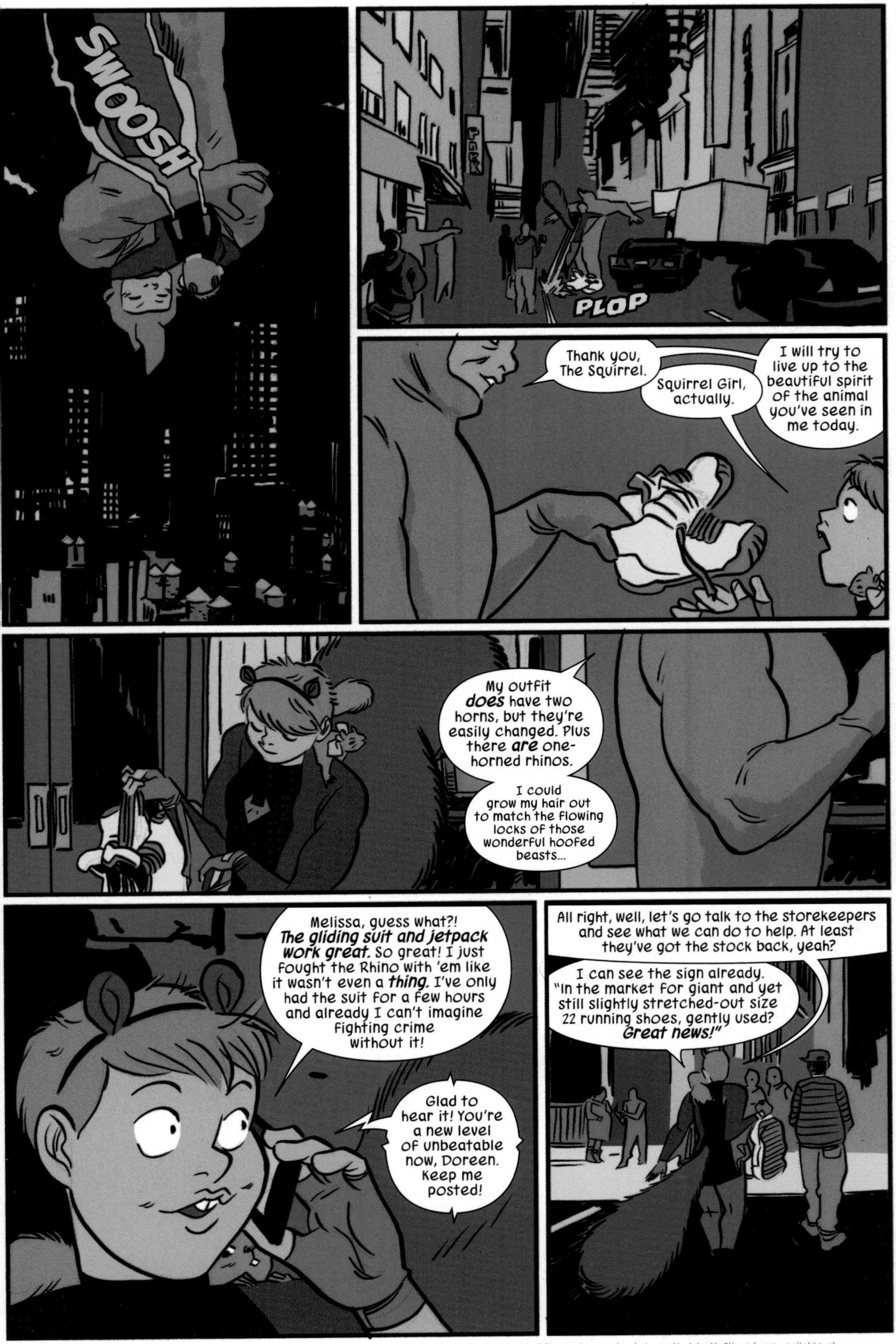
SWOOSH
PARK
PLOP
Thank you, The Squirrel.
Squirrel Girl, actually.
I will try to live up to the beautiful spirit of the animal you've seen in me today.
My outfit does have two horns, but they're easily changed. Plus there are one-horned rhinos.
I could grow my hair out to match the flowing locks of those wonderful hoofed beasts...
Melissa, guess what?! The gliding suit and jetpack work great. So great! I just fought the Rhino with 'em like it wasn't even a thing. I've only had the suit for a few hours and already I can't imagine fighting crime without it!
Glad to hear it! You're a new level of unbeatable now, Doreen. Keep me posted!
All right, well, let's go talk to the storekeepers and see what we can do to help. At least they've got the stock back, yeah?
I can see the sign already. "In the market for giant and yet still slightly stretched-out size 22 running shoes, gently used? Great news!"

Right now, somewhere in the world, Sasquatch is sitting up straight in bed and wondering why his "discount oversized shoes that both fit and are available at non-speciality retail stores-sense" is suddenly tingling *so much.*

Meanwhile...

Chef Bear, could you come in here, please?

Begin preparing dinner: I'm in the mood to celebrate. Pasta, thick noodles, cream sauce, white meat.

Mrragh?

Mrrargh?

Yes, of course. A white wine to pair. Chardonnay, but not too oaky.

Mrrargh.

DOREEN GREEN:
STATUS:

☐ **INDUCE DEPENDENCY**
☐ **CONTROL RELATIONSHIPS**
☐ **IF WILLING: RECRUIT**
☐ **IF NOT: ELIMINATE**

BWA-KAK! BWA-KAAAAAAK!

Alfredo, please. Show a little self-respect.

BWA-KAK! BWA-BWA-BWA-KAAAAAAK!

I honestly don't understand your reaction, Alfredo. I literally named you "Alfredo the Chicken."

PING DOREEN GREEN: TUS:

☐ INDUCE DEPENDENCY
☐ CONTROL RELATIONSHIPS
☐ IF WILLING: RECRUIT
☐ IF NOT: ELIMINATE

Is it that much of a surprise that you'd end up as a nice chicken alfredo??

OH DANG, TURNS OUT SQUIRREL GIRL'S NEW MENTOR IS SECRETLY BAD! BUT WE'RE OUT OF PAGES SO Y'ALL HAVE TO WAIT A MONTH TO SEE WHAT HAPPENS! SORRY, THAT'S JUST THE NATURE OF SERIAL STORYTELLING!

Don't look at me! You all knew the risks when you started reading this comic!

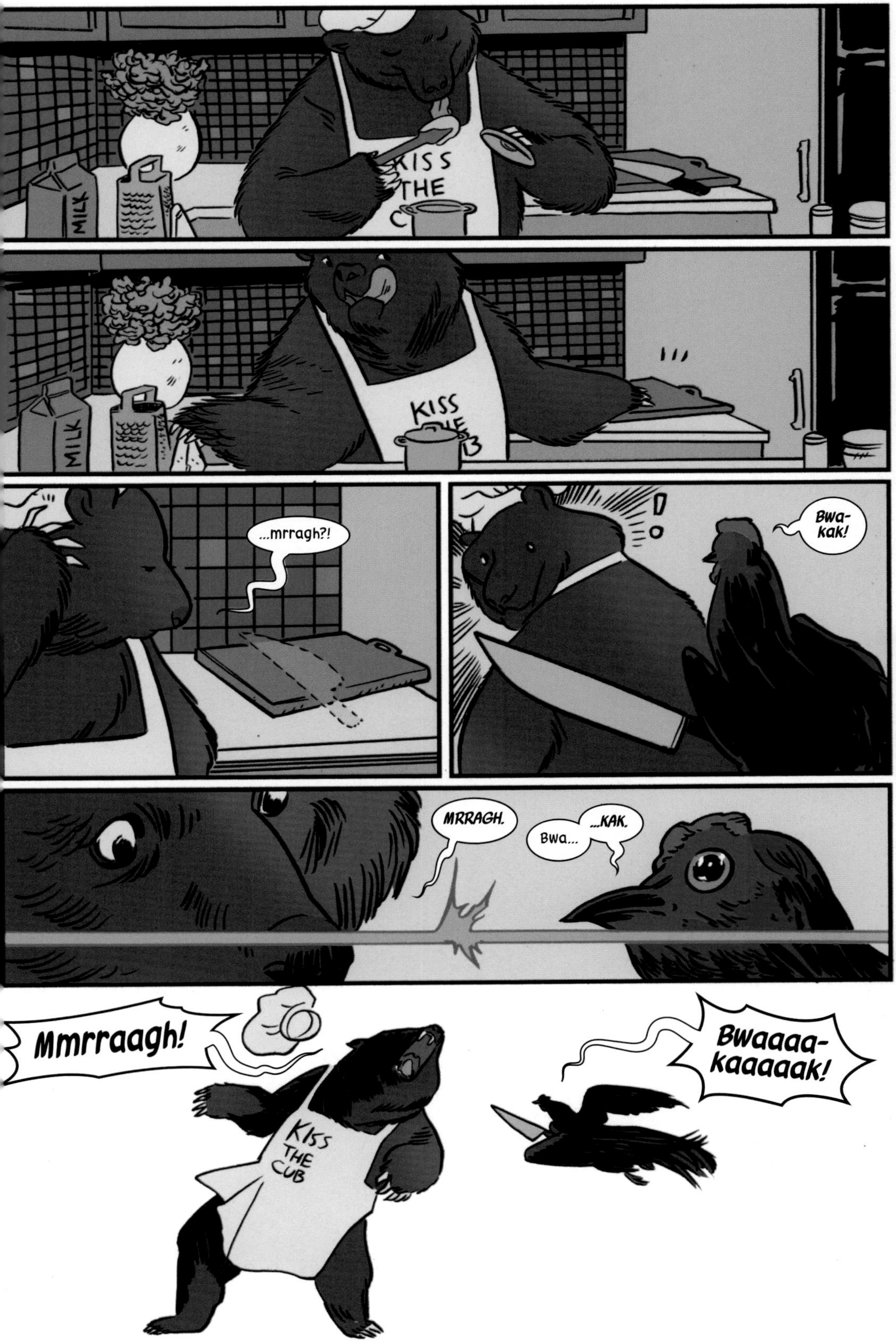
KISS THE C
KISS THE
...mrragh?!
Bwa-kak!
MRRAGH.
Bwa...
...KAK.
Mmrraagh!
Bwaaaa-kaaaaak!
KISS THE CUB

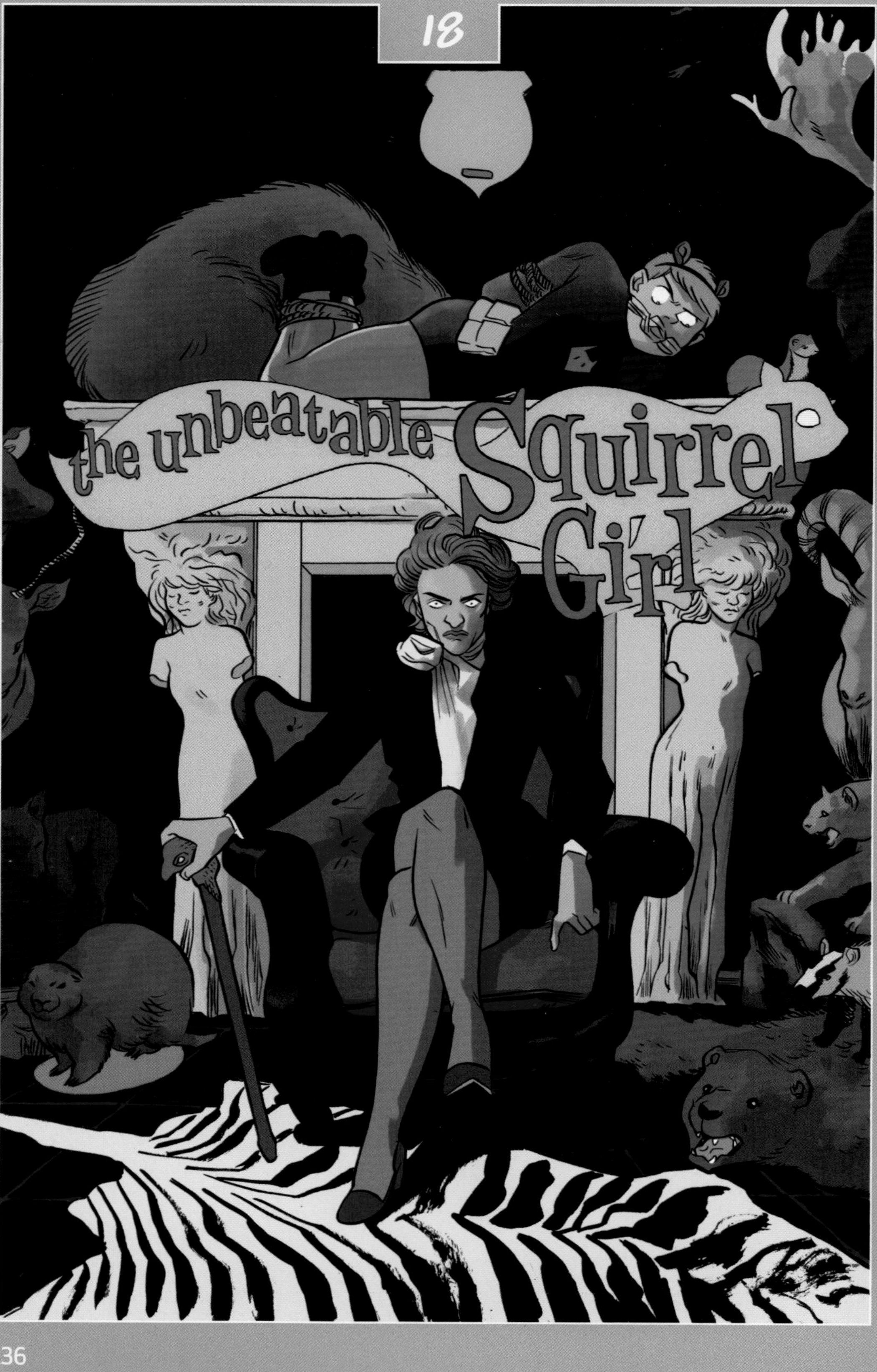
18
the unbeatable Squirrel Girl

Doreen Green isn't just a second-year computer science student: she secretly also has all the powers of both squirrel and girl! She uses her amazing abilities to fight crime **and be as awesome as possible.** You know her as...**The Unbeatable Squirrel Girl!** Find out what she's been up to, with...

Squirrel Girl *in a nutshell*

search!

#flyingsquirrelgirl

#greatpower

#greatresponsibility

#chefbear

#alfredothechicken

Tony Stark @starkmantony ✓
@unbeatablesg Hey just a heads up: there was a really big super hero fight, a "civil war" if you will. It was definitely a good idea, buuut…

Tony Stark @starkmantony ✓
@unbeatablesg …at the end I got knocked into a coma. Which is NORMALLY BAD, I admit. But I had already uploaded my brain to a computer!

Tony Stark @starkmantony ✓
@unbeatablesg So I'm an AI now, which is nice. Cheated death, but that's no big deal for geniuses like me.

Tony Stark @starkmantony ✓
@unbeatablesg It feels about the same, but I'm a bit better at math questions. Anyway, just wanted to let you know!

Squirrel Girl @unbeatablesg
@starkmantony haha good one Tony!! What's ten times ten?

Tony Stark @starkmantony ✓
@unbeatablesg 100. ...Which I also knew before I was an AI, Squirrel Girl.

Tony Stark @starkmantony ✓
@unbeatablesg Which, again, is what I am now. Because I uploaded my brain to a computer. IT'S KIND OF A BIG DEAL.

Tony Stark @starkmantony ✓
@unbeatablesg Maybe that should be the focus here instead of brain teasers???

Squirrel Girl @unbeatablesg
@starkmantony Wait wait wait. Are you seriously telling me, right here, right now...

Squirrel Girl @unbeatablesg
@starkmantony ...that if I show you a "prove you're a human" picture with distorted letters on a crazy background it'll BLOW YOUR MIND?????

Squirrel Girl @unbeatablesg
@starkmantony

Tony Stark @starkmantony ✓
@unbeatablesg ...No. I'm still me. Just an AI now. I can still log into my email.

Squirrel Girl @unbeatablesg
@starkmantony Tony you doing pranks is frankly adorable but if you were really an AI I could put you on my phone and have Pocket Pal Tony!!

Squirrel Girl @unbeatablesg
@starkmantony But I just checked and that is not the case so NICE TRY, MY DUDE.

Tony Stark @starkmantony ✓
@unbeatablesg ...That's...actually not a bad idea. I'll get R&D right on it.

Squirrel Girl @unbeatablesg
Attention to both the criminally insane and the casual weekend criminals alike! I CAN FLY NOW.

Squirrel Girl @unbeatablesg
That's right! I got a FLYING SQUIRREL SUIT, so y'all better GO EASY on the friggin' SKY CRIME, because I am UP THERE, ready to stop it!!

Squirrel Girl @unbeatablesg
Oh! I have slipped the surly bonds of Earth / And danced the skies on high-tech gliding wings with a jetpack strapped to my back

Squirrel Girl @unbeatablesg
And, with silent lifting mind I'll climb / The high untrespassed sanctity of space / Put out my hand, and punch the face of Crime.

Nancy W. @sewwiththeflo
@unbeatablesg Quasi-quoting the poetry of John Gillespie Magee, Junior. Sure to strike fear into the hearts of the criminal lot.

Squirrel Girl @unbeatablesg
@sewwiththeflo Um excuse me, any of MY arch-criminals who follow me on social media are getting ENLIGHTENED

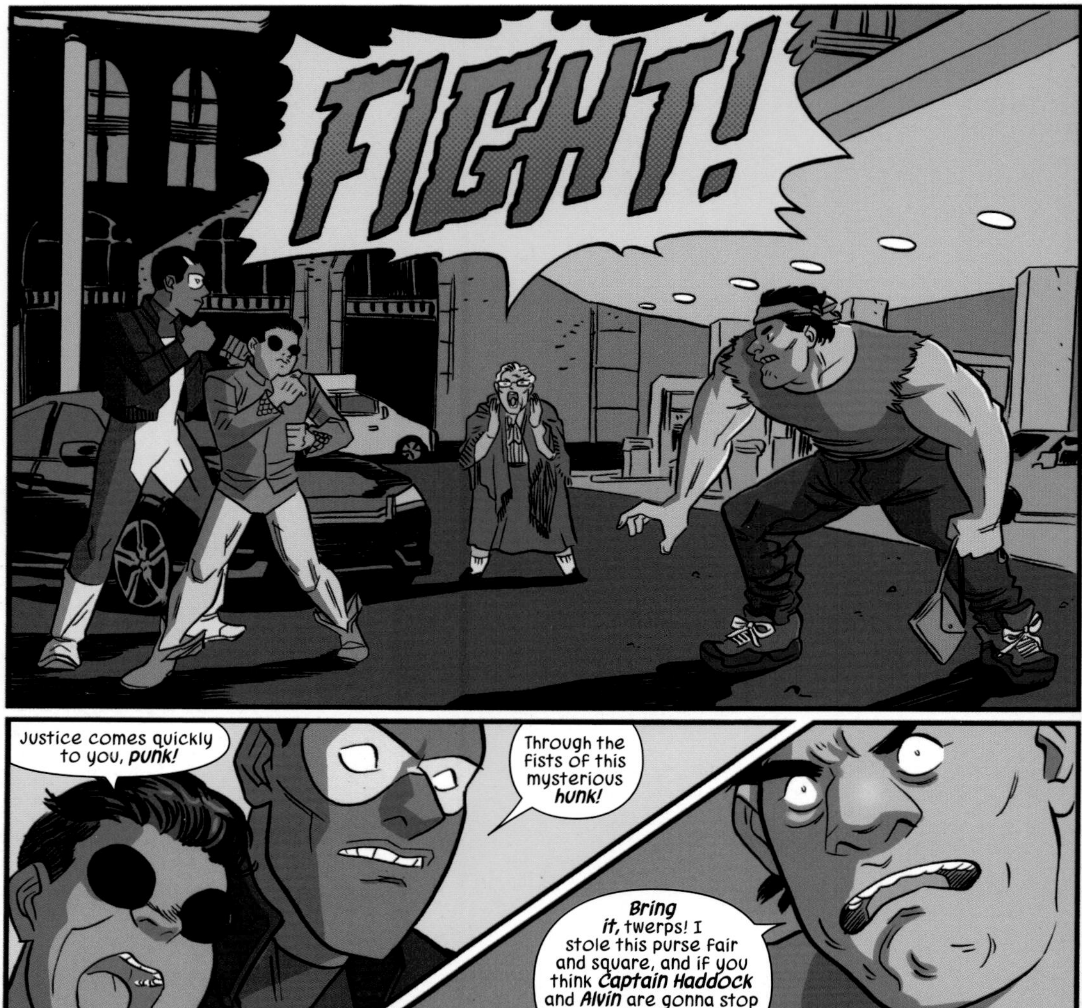
FIGHT!
Justice comes quickly to you, *punk!*
Through the fists of this mysterious *hunk!*
Bring it, twerps! I stole this purse fair and square, and if you think *Captain Haddock* and *Alvin* are gonna stop me, *you got another thing coming!!*
POINK
POINK
POINK
Huh?
ARRGH!
POINK
POINK
POINK
POINK
POINK
POINK

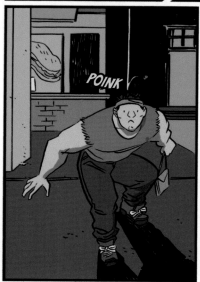

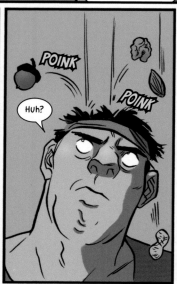

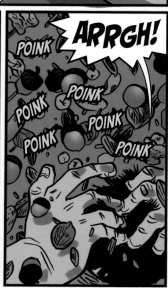

That "Alvin" dig is gonna really annoy Tomas, especially when he realizes he actually *was* wearing a sweater with his initial on it in his first appearance, way back in our first issue. Sorry, Tomas. You're getting dunked on by a random punk and there's nothing I can do to stop it!!

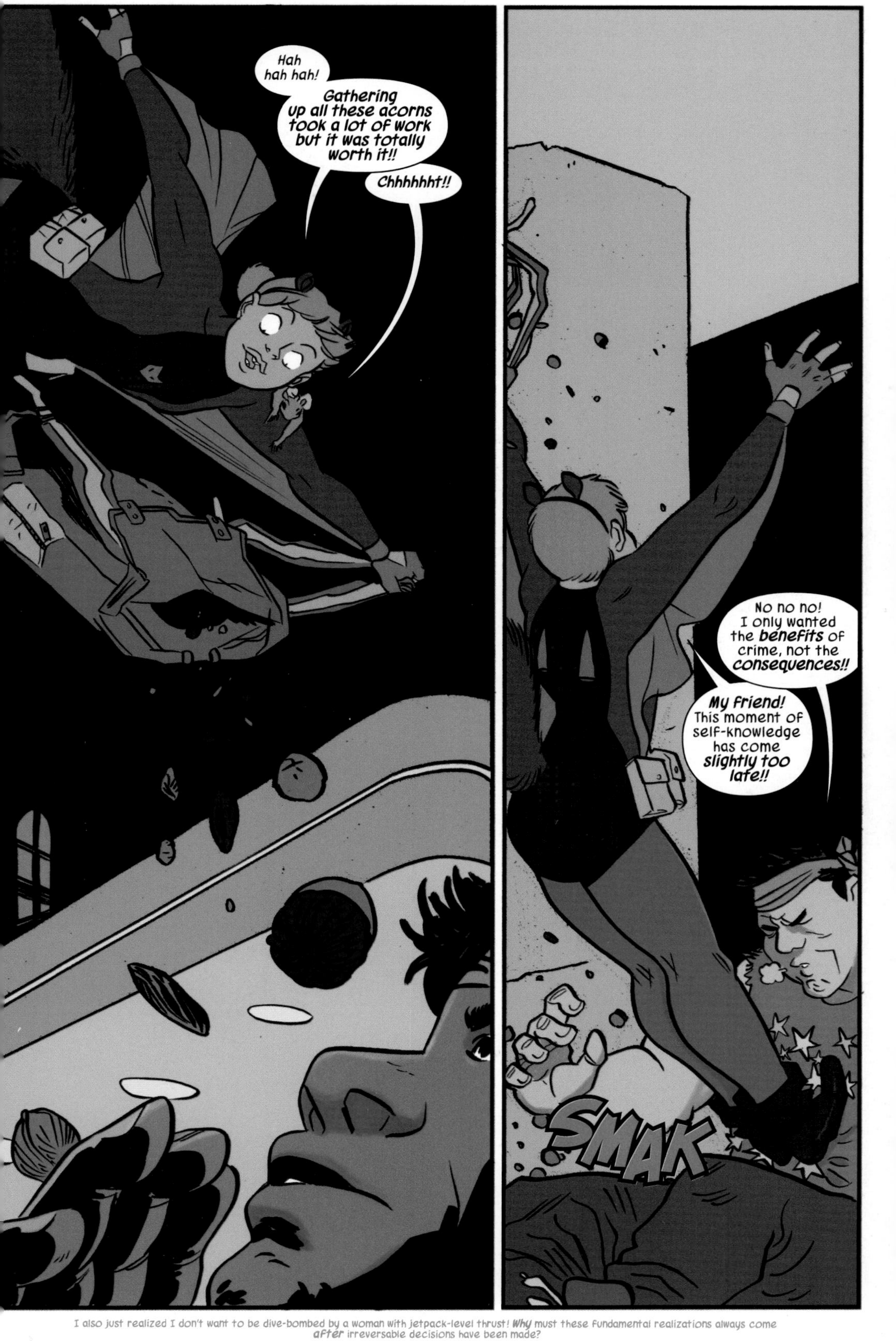
Hah hah hah!
Gathering up all these acorns took a lot of work but it was totally worth it!!
Chhhhhht!!
No no no! I only wanted the benefits of crime, not the consequences!!
My friend! This moment of self-knowledge has come slightly too late!!
SMAK

I also just realized I don't want to be dive-bombed by a woman with jetpack-level thrust! ***Why*** must these fundamental realizations always come ***after*** irreversable decisions have been made?

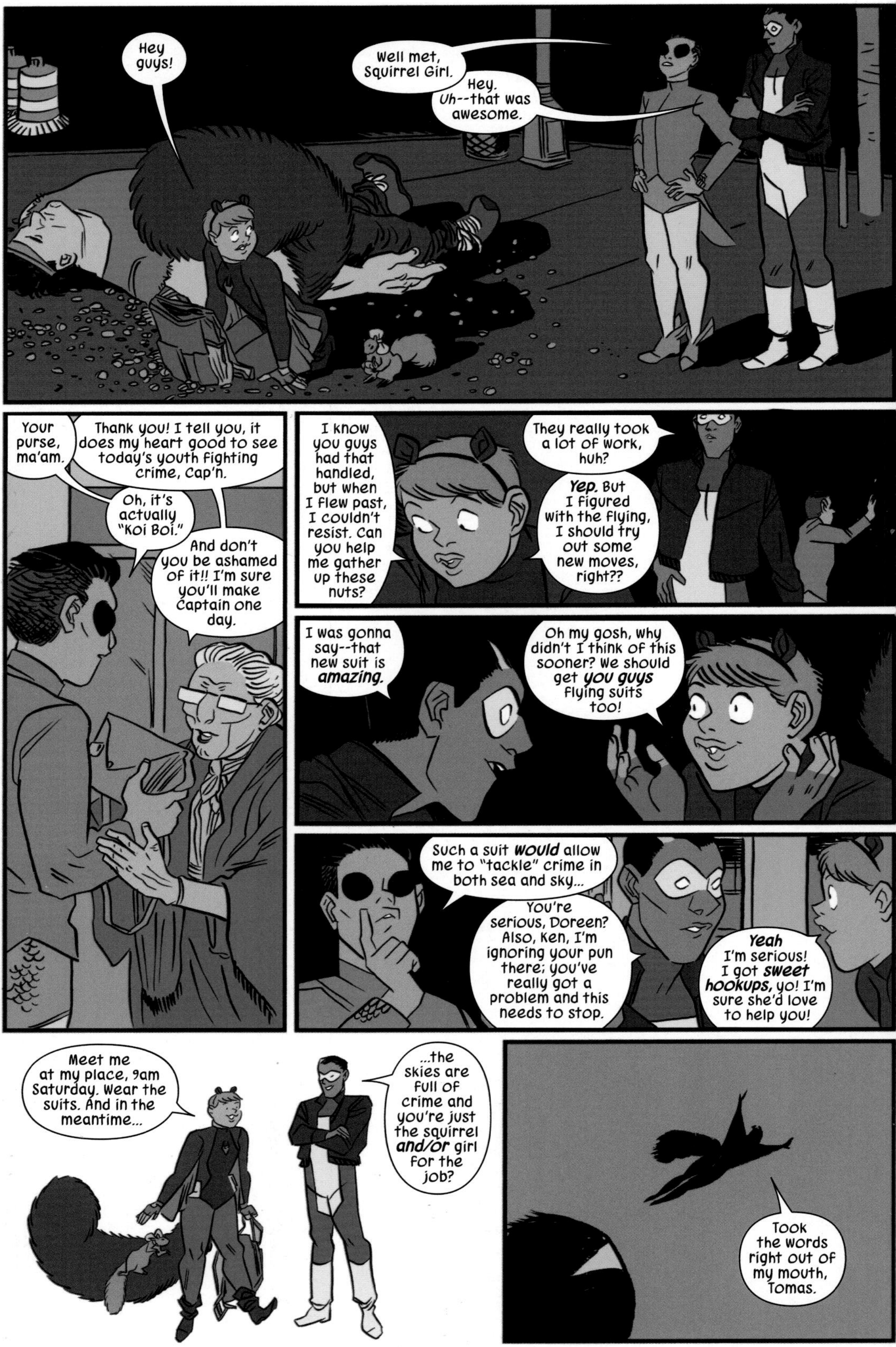

Hey guys!
Well met, Squirrel Girl.
Hey. Uh--that was awesome.
Your purse, ma'am.
Thank you! I tell you, it does my heart good to see today's youth fighting crime, Cap'n.
Oh, it's actually "Koi Boi."
And don't you be ashamed of it!! I'm sure you'll make Captain one day.
I know you guys had that handled, but when I flew past, I couldn't resist. Can you help me gather up these nuts?
They really took a lot of work, huh?
Yep. But I figured with the flying, I should try out some new moves, right??
I was gonna say--that new suit is amazing.
Oh my gosh, why didn't I think of this sooner? We should get you guys flying suits too!
Such a suit would allow me to "tackle" crime in both sea and sky...
You're serious, Doreen? Also, Ken, I'm ignoring your pun there; you've really got a problem and this needs to stop.
Yeah I'm serious! I got sweet hookups, yo! I'm sure she'd love to help you!
Meet me at my place, 9am Saturday. Wear the suits. And in the meantime...
...the skies are full of crime and you're just the squirrel and/or girl for the job?
Took the words right out of my mouth, Tomas.

Doreen's search history goes "cool things to drop on someone's head," "cool things to drop on someone's head--anvils," "cool but also cheap and nonfatal things to drop on someone's head," and finally, "how long it'd take me to get squirrels to gather up a bunch of nuts, wait nevermind I know this, I don't even know why I'm still typing this or hitting enter."

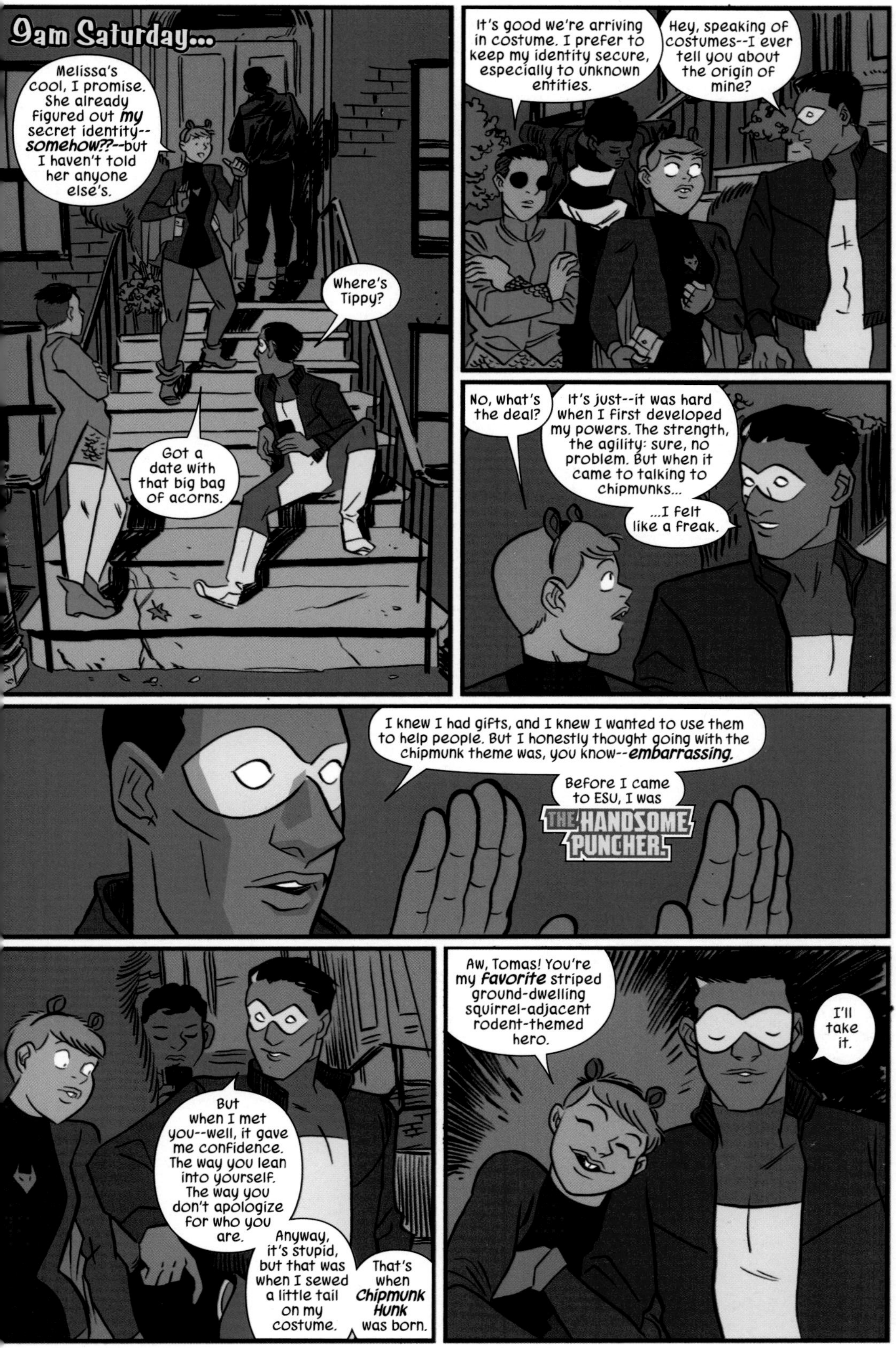
9am Saturday...
Melissa's cool, I promise. She already figured out my secret identity-- somehow??--but I haven't told her anyone else's.
Where's Tippy?
Got a date with that big bag of acorns.
It's good we're arriving in costume. I prefer to keep my identity secure, especially to unknown entities.
Hey, speaking of costumes--I ever tell you about the origin of mine?
No, what's the deal?
It's just--it was hard when I first developed my powers. The strength, the agility: sure, no problem. But when it came to talking to chipmunks...
...I felt like a freak.
I knew I had gifts, and I knew I wanted to use them to help people. But I honestly thought going with the chipmunk theme was, you know--embarrassing.
Before I came to ESU, I was
THE HANDSOME PUNCHER.
But when I met you--well, it gave me confidence. The way you lean into yourself. The way you don't apologize for who you are.
Anyway, it's stupid, but that was when I sewed a little tail on my costume.
That's when Chipmunk Hunk was born.
Aw, Tomas! You're my favorite striped ground-dwelling squirrel-adjacent rodent-themed hero.
I'll take it.

I like how the only rule Tomas has when picking a super-hero name for himself is that it should definitely mention how he's attractive. I think it's a great rule! Signed, Extremely Handsome Comic Book Narrator Guy.

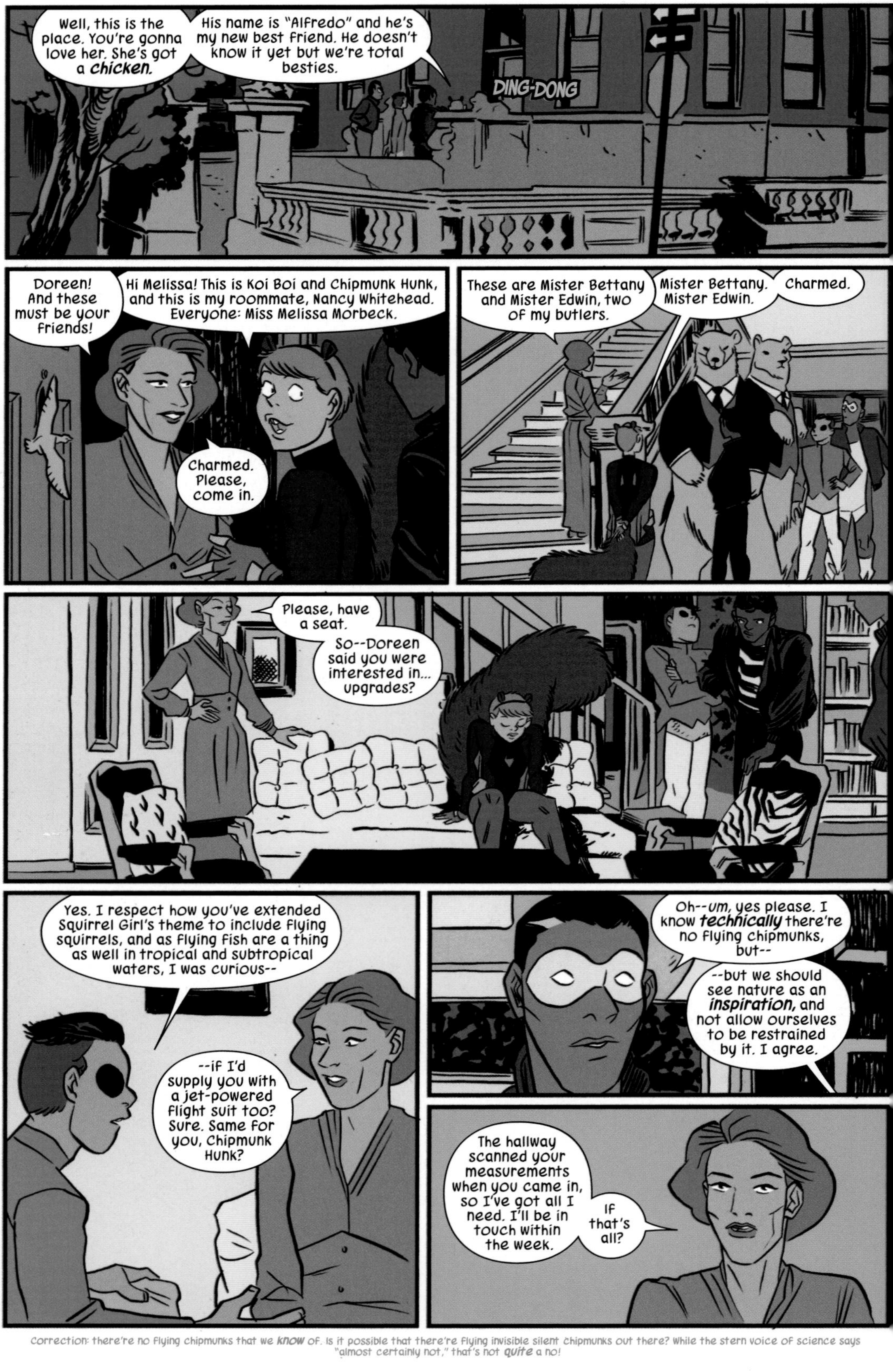
Well, this is the place. You're gonna love her. She's got a *chicken.*
His name is "Alfredo" and he's my new best friend. He doesn't know it yet but we're total besties.
DING-DONG
Doreen! And these must be your friends!
Hi Melissa! This is Koi Boi and Chipmunk Hunk, and this is my roommate, Nancy Whitehead. Everyone: Miss Melissa Morbeck.
Charmed. Please, come in.
These are Mister Bettany and Mister Edwin, two of my butlers.
Mister Bettany. Mister Edwin.
Charmed.
Please, have a seat.
So--Doreen said you were interested in... upgrades?
Yes. I respect how you've extended Squirrel Girl's theme to include flying squirrels, and as flying fish are a thing as well in tropical and subtropical waters, I was curious--
--if I'd supply you with a jet-powered flight suit too? Sure. Same for you, Chipmunk Hunk?
Oh--um, yes please. I know *technically* there're no flying chipmunks, but--
--but we should see nature as an *inspiration,* and not allow ourselves to be restrained by it. I agree.
The hallway scanned your measurements when you came in, so I've got all I need. I'll be in touch within the week.
If that's all?

Correction: there're no flying chipmunks that we *know* of. Is it possible that there're flying invisible silent chipmunks out there? While the stern voice of science says "almost certainly not," that's not *quite* a no!

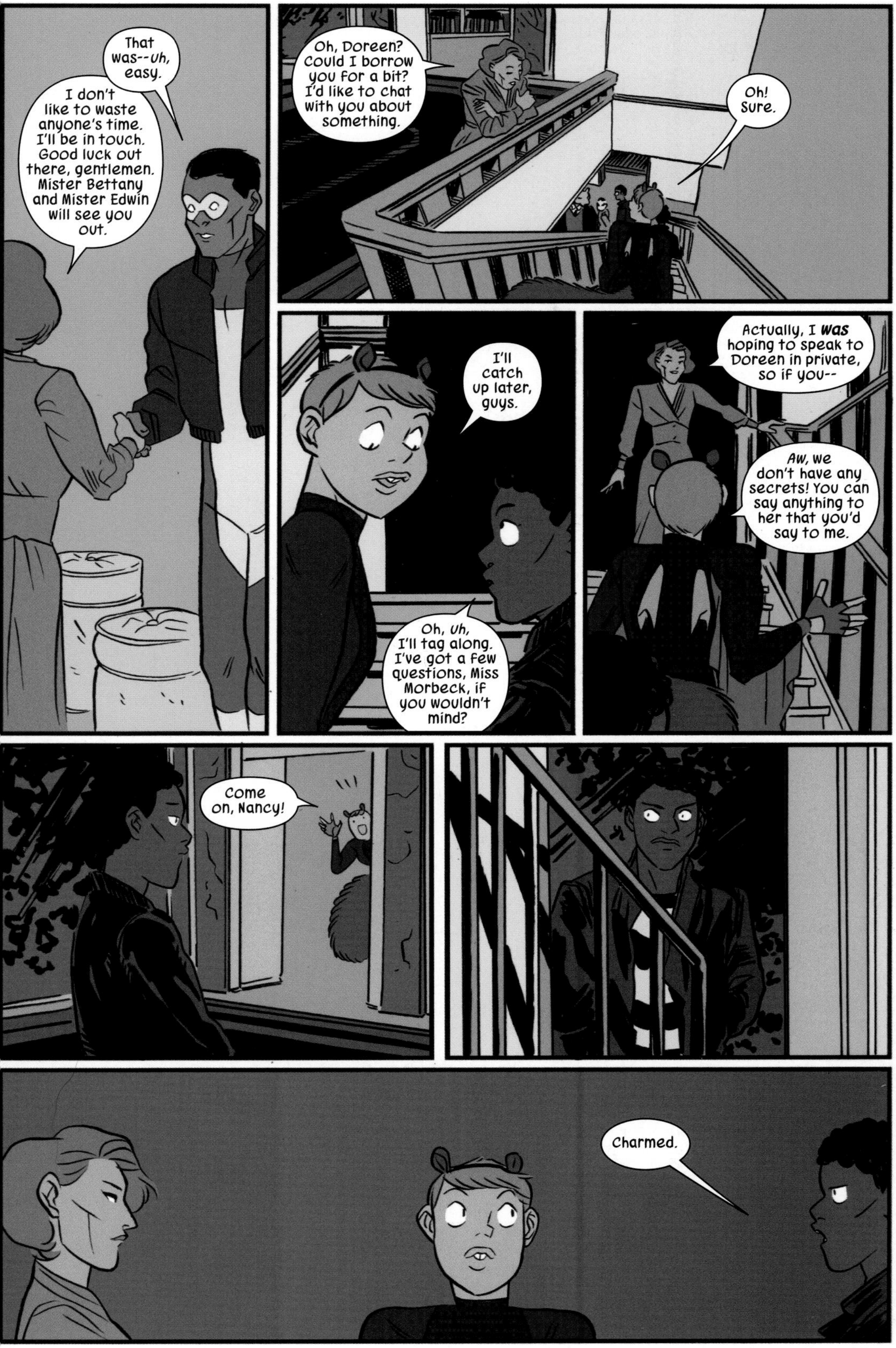

That was--*uh*, easy.
I don't like to waste anyone's time. I'll be in touch. Good luck out there, gentlemen. Mister Bettany and Mister Edwin will see you out.
Oh, Doreen? Could I borrow you for a bit? I'd like to chat with you about something.
Oh! Sure.
I'll catch up later, guys.
Oh, *uh*, I'll tag along. I've got a few questions, Miss Morbeck, if you wouldn't mind?
Actually, I ***was*** hoping to speak to Doreen in private, so if you--
Aw, we don't have any secrets! You can say anything to her that you'd say to me.
Come on, Nancy!
Charmed.

It has come to my attention that I ***may*** have oversold the possibility of "Flying invisible silent chipmunks," and for that I apologize. However, seeing as less than 5% of the ocean's floor has been explored, the possibility of "Flying invisible silent ***deep-sea*** chipmunks" remains enticingly open!!

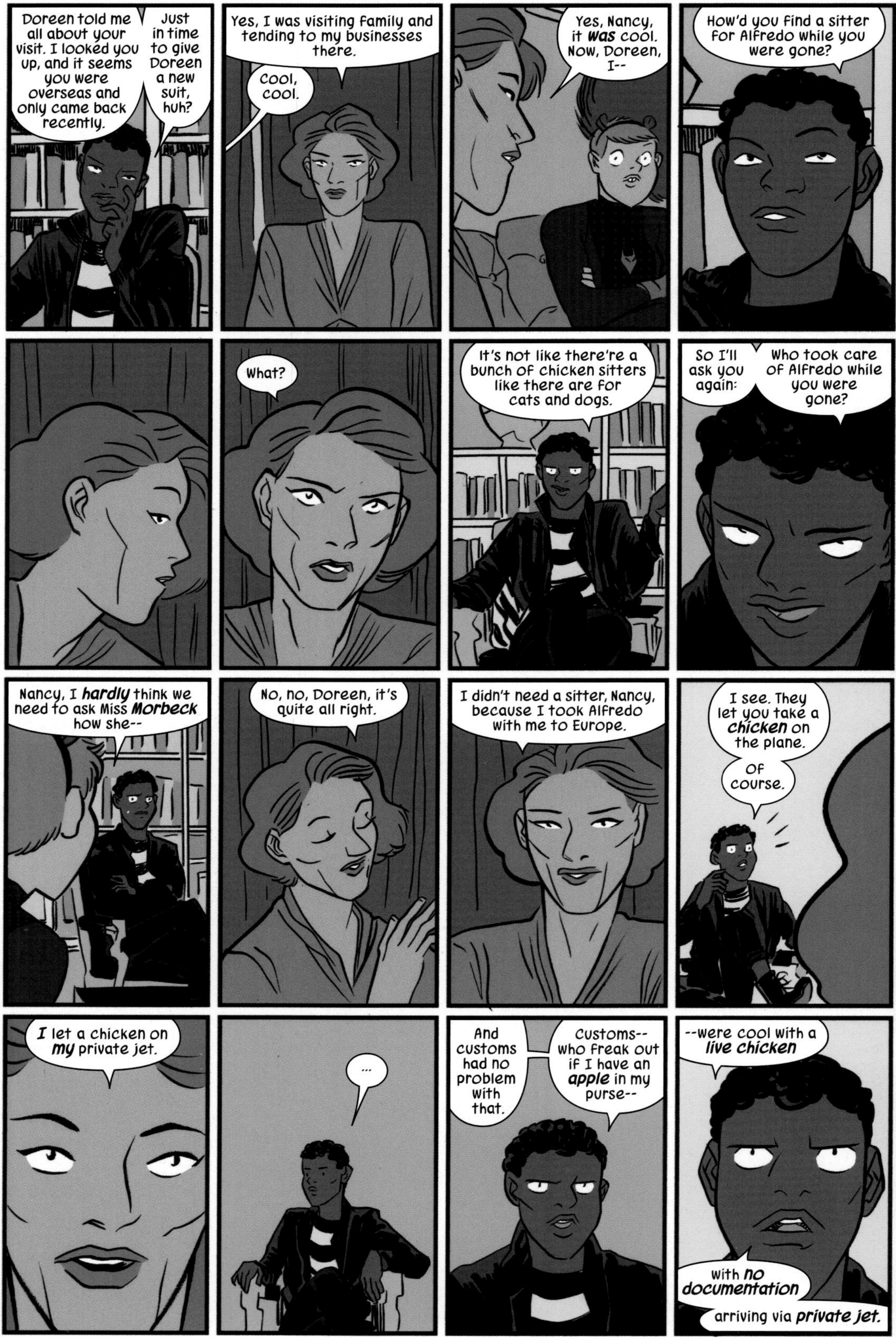
Doreen told me all about your visit. I looked you up, and it seems you were overseas and only came back recently.
Just in time to give Doreen a new suit, huh?
Yes, I was visiting family and tending to my businesses there.
Cool, cool.
Yes, Nancy, it *was* cool. Now, Doreen, I--
How'd you find a sitter for Alfredo while you were gone?
What?
It's not like there're a bunch of chicken sitters like there are for cats and dogs.
So I'll ask you again:
Who took care of Alfredo while you were gone?
Nancy, I *hardly* think we need to ask Miss *Morbeck* how she--
No, no, Doreen, it's quite all right.
I didn't need a sitter, Nancy, because I took Alfredo with me to Europe.
I see. They let you take a *chicken* on the plane.
Of course.
I let a chicken on *my* private jet.
...
And customs had no problem with that.
Customs-- who freak out if I have an *apple* in my purse--
--were cool with a *live chicken*
with *no documentation*
arriving via *private jet.*

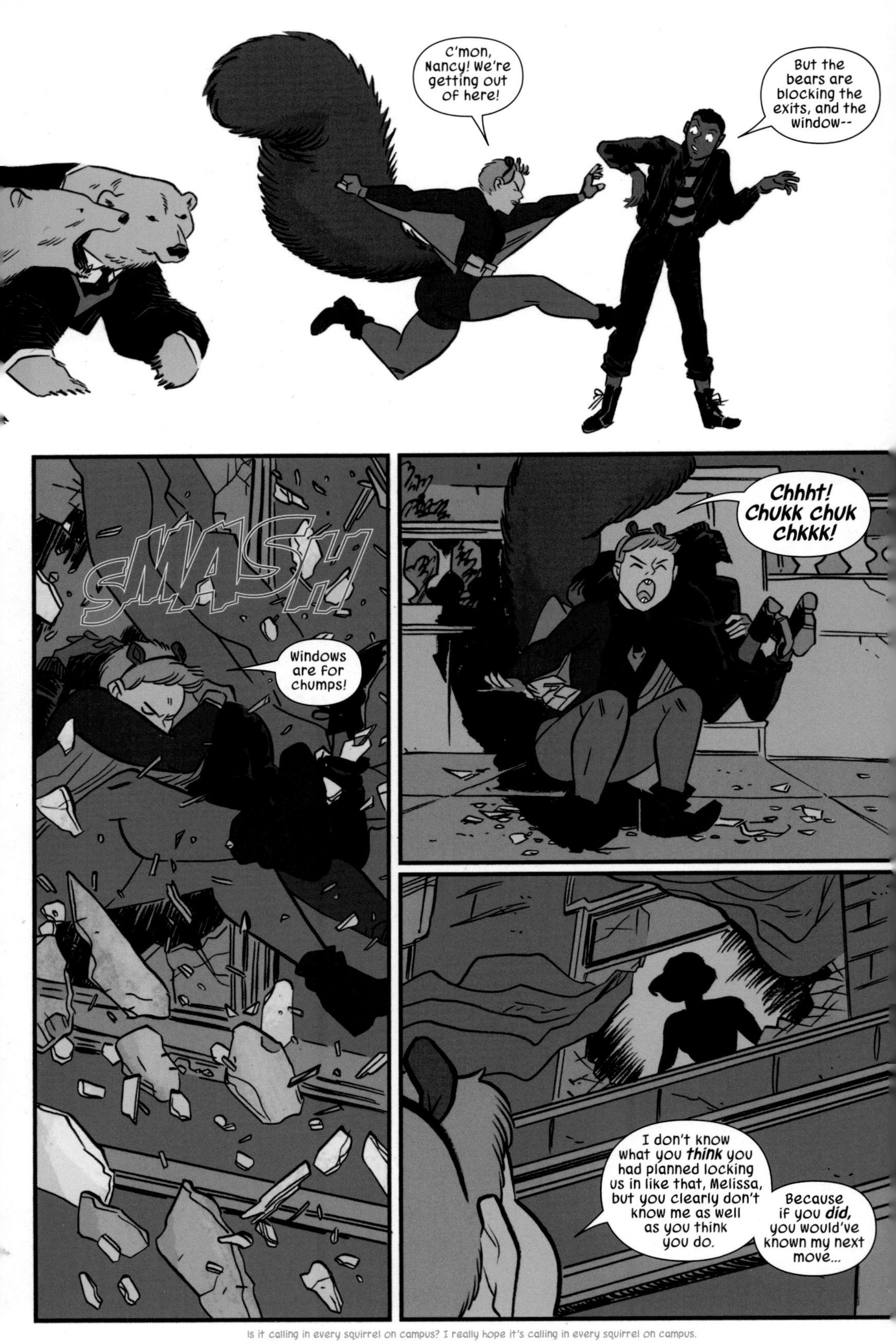
C'mon, Nancy! We're getting out of here!
But the bears are blocking the exits, and the window--
SMASH
Windows are for chumps!
Chhht! Chukk chuk chkkk!
I don't know what you *think* you had planned locking us in like that, Melissa, but you clearly don't know me as well as you think you do.
Because if you *did,* you would've known my next move...

Is it calling in every squirrel on campus? I really hope it's calling in every squirrel on campus.

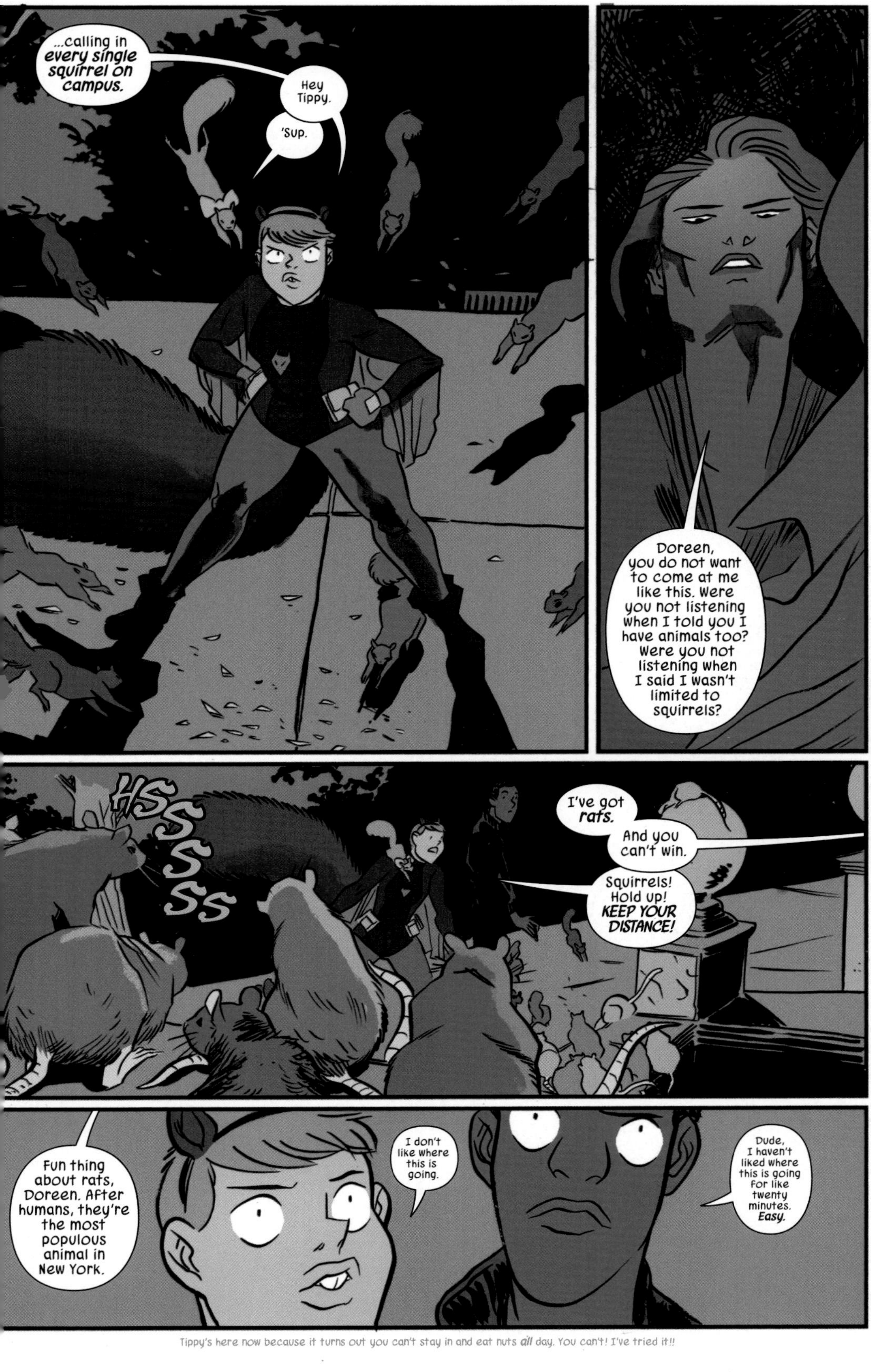

...calling in *every single squirrel on campus.*
Hey Tippy.
'Sup.
Doreen, you do not want to come at me like this. Were you not listening when I told you I have animals too? Were you not listening when I said I wasn't limited to squirrels?
HSSSSSS
I've got *rats.*
And you can't win.
Squirrels! Hold up! *KEEP YOUR DISTANCE!*
Fun thing about rats, Doreen. After humans, they're the most populous animal in New York.
I don't like where this is going.
Dude, I haven't liked where this is going for like twenty minutes. *Easy.*

Tippy's here now because it turns out you can't stay in and eat nuts *all* day. You can't! I've tried it!!

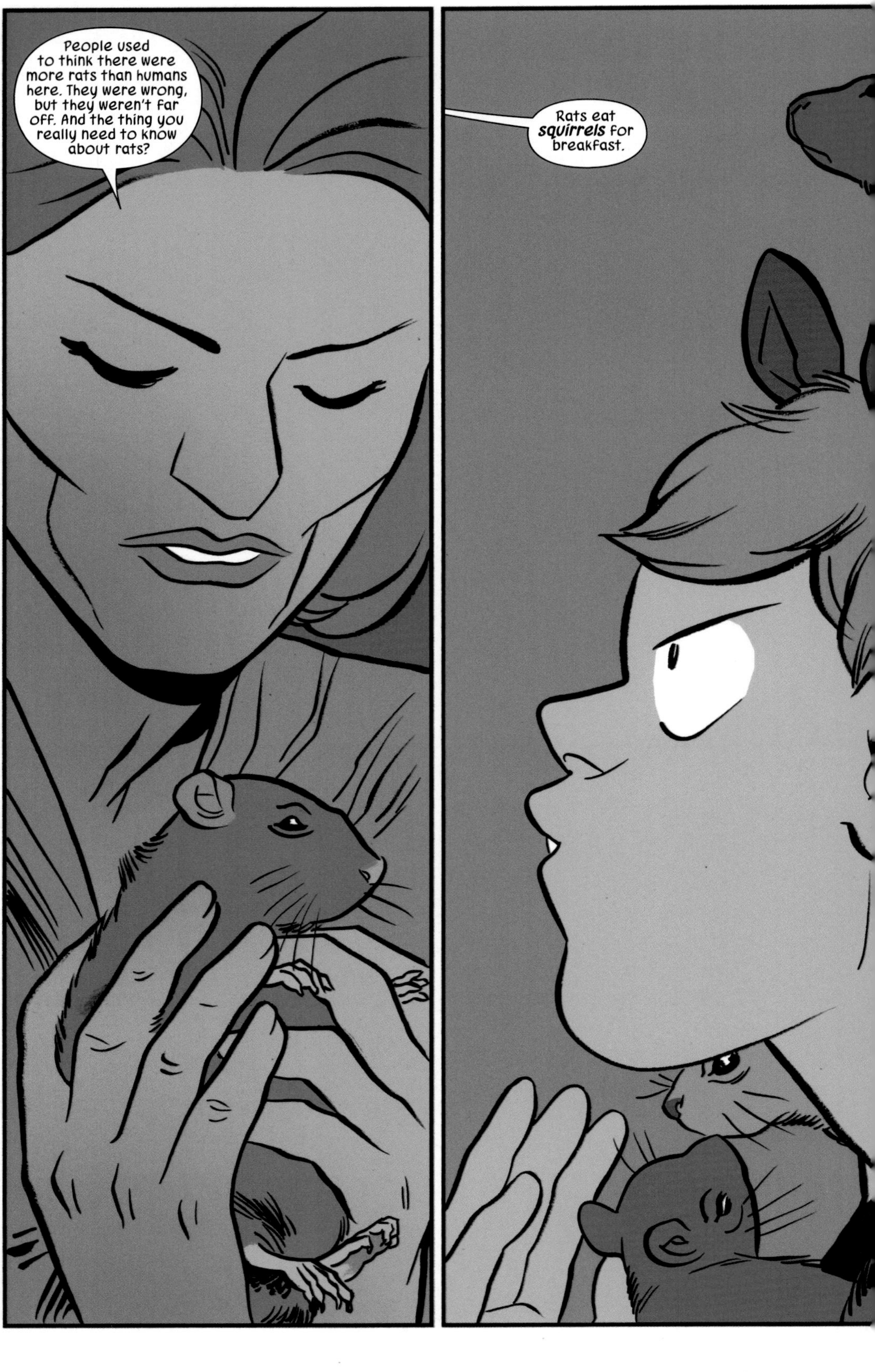
People used to think there were more rats than humans here. They were wrong, but they weren't far off. And the thing you really need to know about rats?
Rats eat **squirrels** for breakfast.

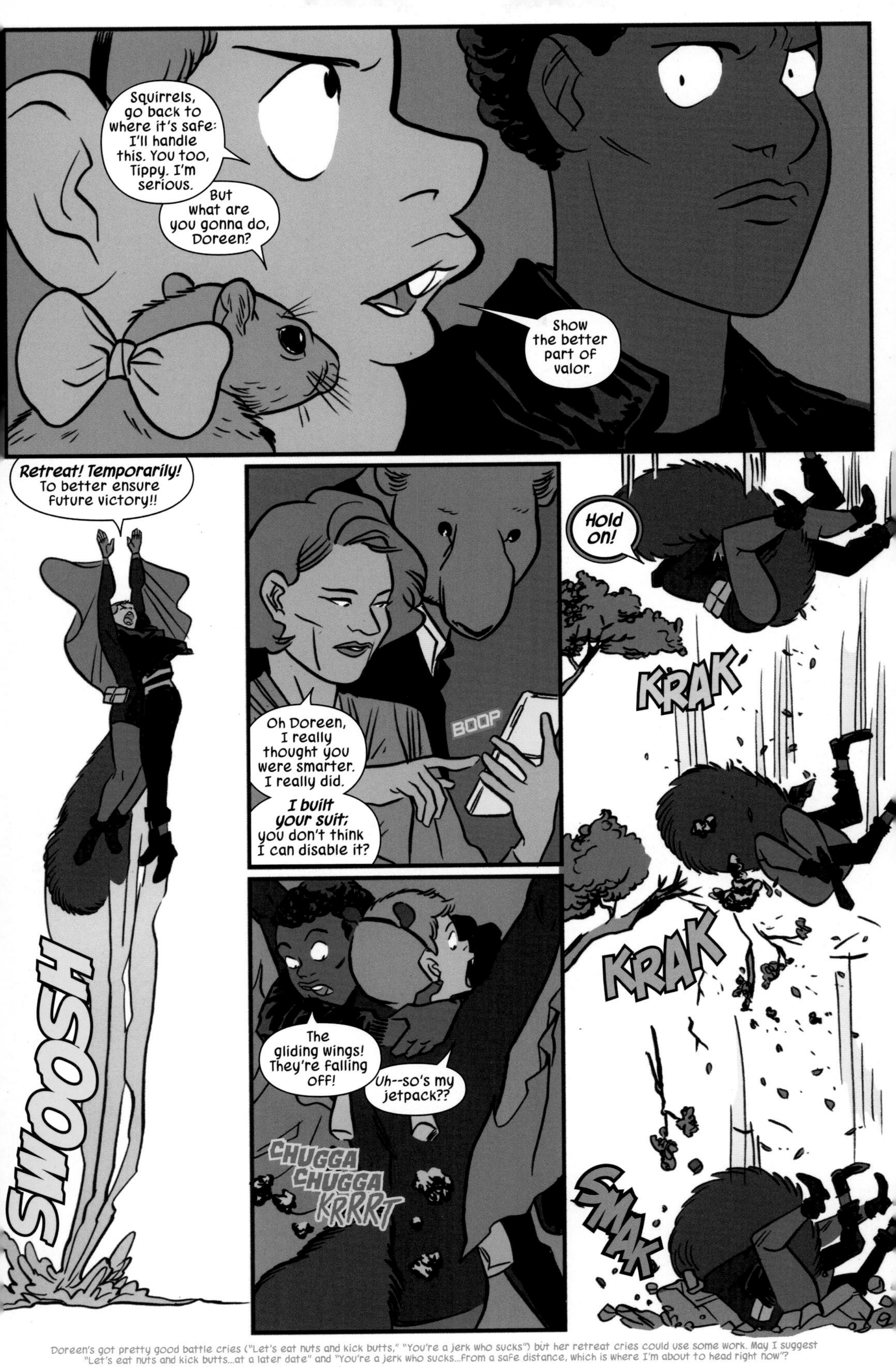
Squirrels, go back to where it's safe: I'll handle this. You too, Tippy. I'm serious.
But what are you gonna do, Doreen?
Show the better part of valor.
Retreat! Temporarily! To better ensure future victory!!
SWOOSH
Oh Doreen, I really thought you were smarter. I really did. I built your suit; you don't think I can disable it?
BOOP
The gliding wings! They're falling off!
Uh--so's my jetpack??
CHUGGA CHUGGA KRRRT
Hold on!
KRAK
KRAK
SMAK

Doreen's got pretty good battle cries ("Let's eat nuts and kick butts," "You're a jerk who sucks") but her retreat cries could use some work. May I suggest "Let's eat nuts and kick butts...at a later date" and "You're a jerk who sucks...from a safe distance, which is where I'm about to head right now"?

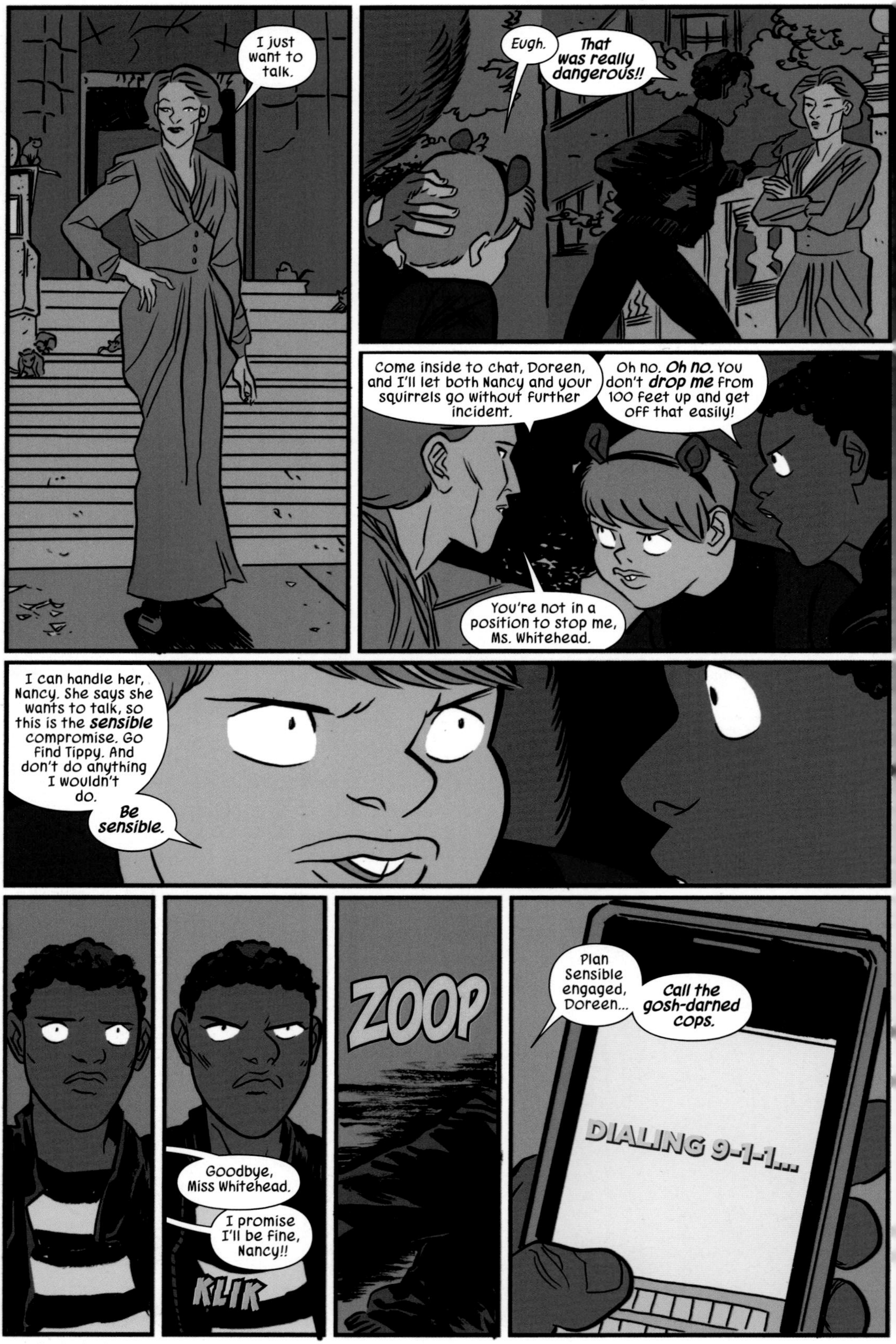
I just want to talk.
Eugh.
That was really dangerous!!
Come inside to chat, Doreen, and I'll let both Nancy and your squirrels go without further incident.
Oh no. Oh no. You don't drop me from 100 feet up and get off that easily!
You're not in a position to stop me, Ms. Whitehead.
I can handle her, Nancy. She says she wants to talk, so this is the sensible compromise. Go find Tippy. And don't do anything I wouldn't do.
Be sensible.
Goodbye, Miss Whitehead.
I promise I'll be fine, Nancy!!
KLIK
ZOOP
Plan Sensible engaged, Doreen...
Call the gosh-darned cops.
DIALING 9-1-1...

Plan Sensible is such a great plan. It's so sensible! It's way better than Plan Foolish, which is the plan where we just put on silly hats and make funny noises at each other. Actually, hold on, now I like both plans.

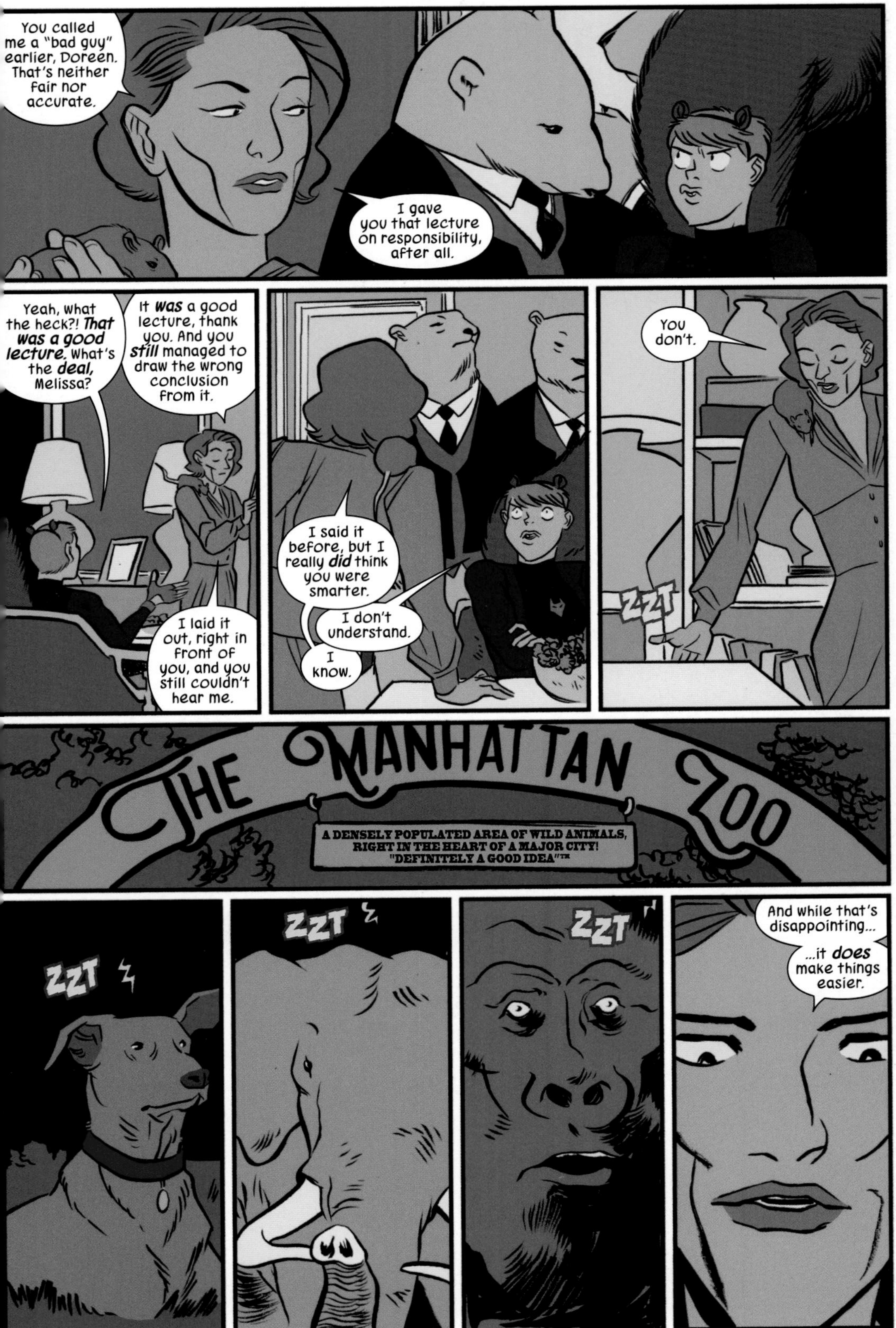

You called me a "bad guy" earlier, Doreen. That's neither fair nor accurate.
I gave you that lecture on responsibility, after all.
Yeah, what the heck?! That was a good lecture. What's the deal, Melissa?
It was a good lecture, thank you. And you still managed to draw the wrong conclusion from it.
I laid it out, right in front of you, and you still couldn't hear me.
I said it before, but I really did think you were smarter.
I don't understand.
I know.
You don't.
ZZT
THE MANHATTAN ZOO
A DENSELY POPULATED AREA OF WILD ANIMALS, RIGHT IN THE HEART OF A MAJOR CITY! "DEFINITELY A GOOD IDEA"™
ZZT
ZZT
ZZT
And while that's disappointing...
...it does make things easier.

The Manhattan Zoo: For When You Look At a Densely Populated Urban Area And Think, "This Is Fine, But It Would Be Even Better If It Had Venemous Spiders Stored In It Somewhere"™

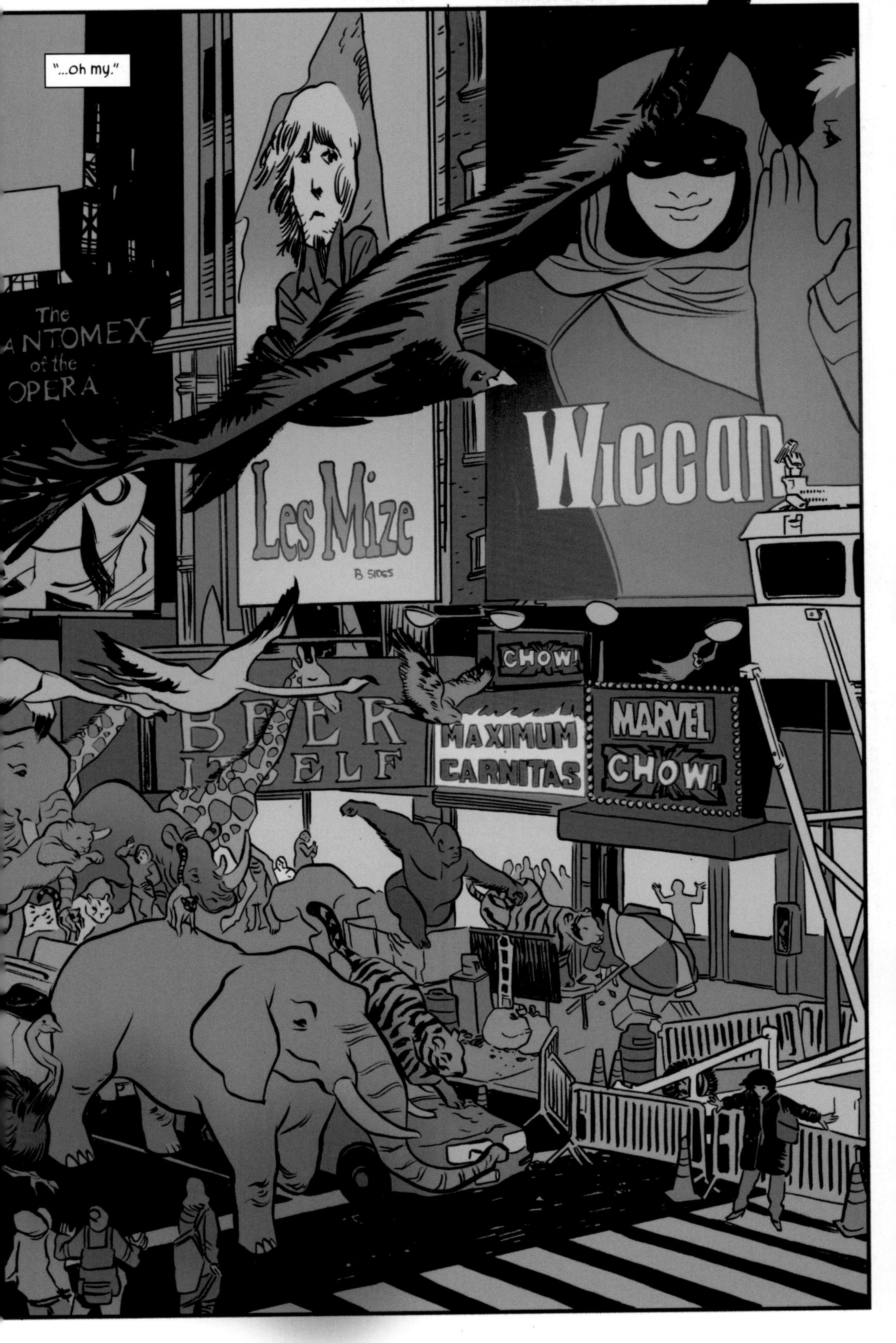

"...oh my."
The
ANTOMEX
of the
OPERA
Les Mize
B SIDES
Wiccan
CHOW!
MAXIMUM
CARNITAS
MARVEL
CHOW!

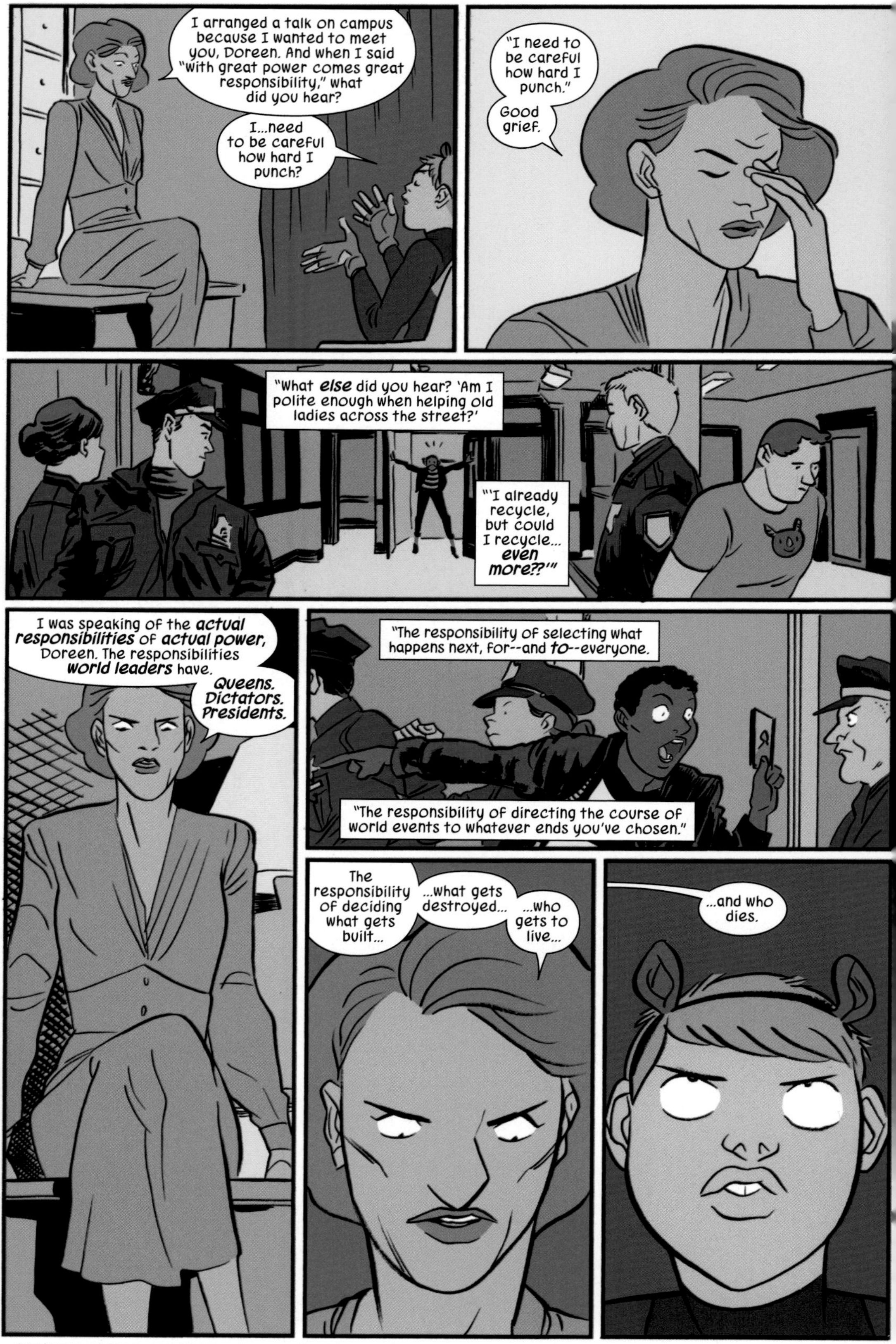
I arranged a talk on campus because I wanted to meet you, Doreen. And when I said "with great power comes great responsibility," what did you hear?
I...need to be careful how hard I punch?
"I need to be careful how hard I punch."
Good grief.
"What *else* did you hear? 'Am I polite enough when helping old ladies across the street?'
"'I already recycle, but could I recycle... *even more??*'"
I was speaking of the *actual responsibilities* of *actual power*, Doreen. The responsibilities *world leaders* have.
Queens. Dictators. Presidents.
"The responsibility of selecting what happens next, for--and *to*--everyone.
"The responsibility of directing the course of world events to whatever ends you've chosen."
The responsibility of deciding what gets built...
...what gets destroyed...
...who gets to live...
...and who dies.
Nobody tell Peter Parker about this concerning new reading of his mantra. Dude's got enough problems without having to radically reconsider his central ethos, am I right?

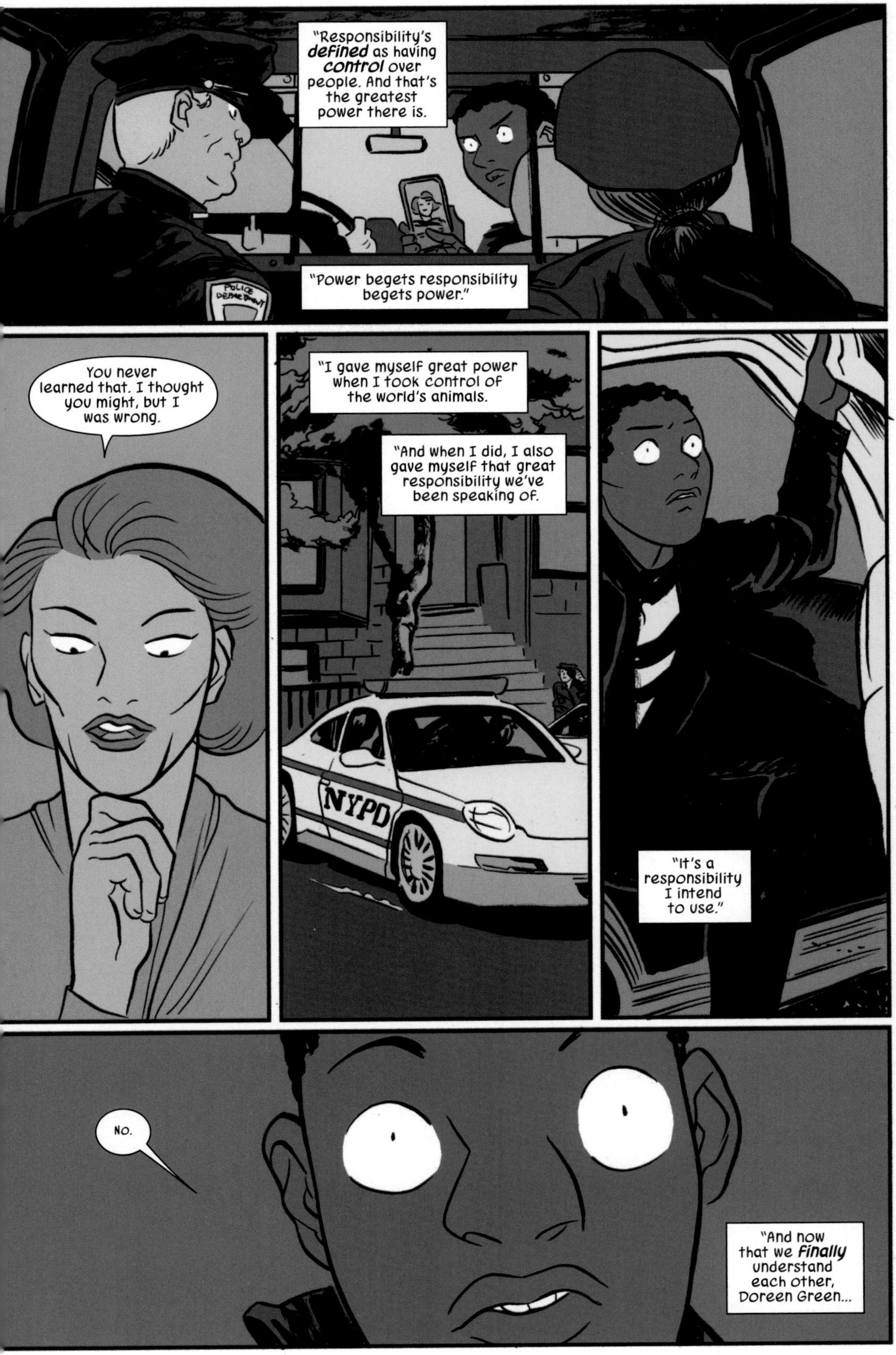
"Responsibility's *defined* as having *control* over people. And that's the greatest power there is.
"Power begets responsibility begets power."
You never learned that. I thought you might, but I was wrong.
"I gave myself great power when I took control of the world's animals.
"And when I did, I also gave myself that great responsibility we've been speaking of.
"It's a responsibility I intend to use."
No.
"And now that we *finally* understand each other, Doreen Green...

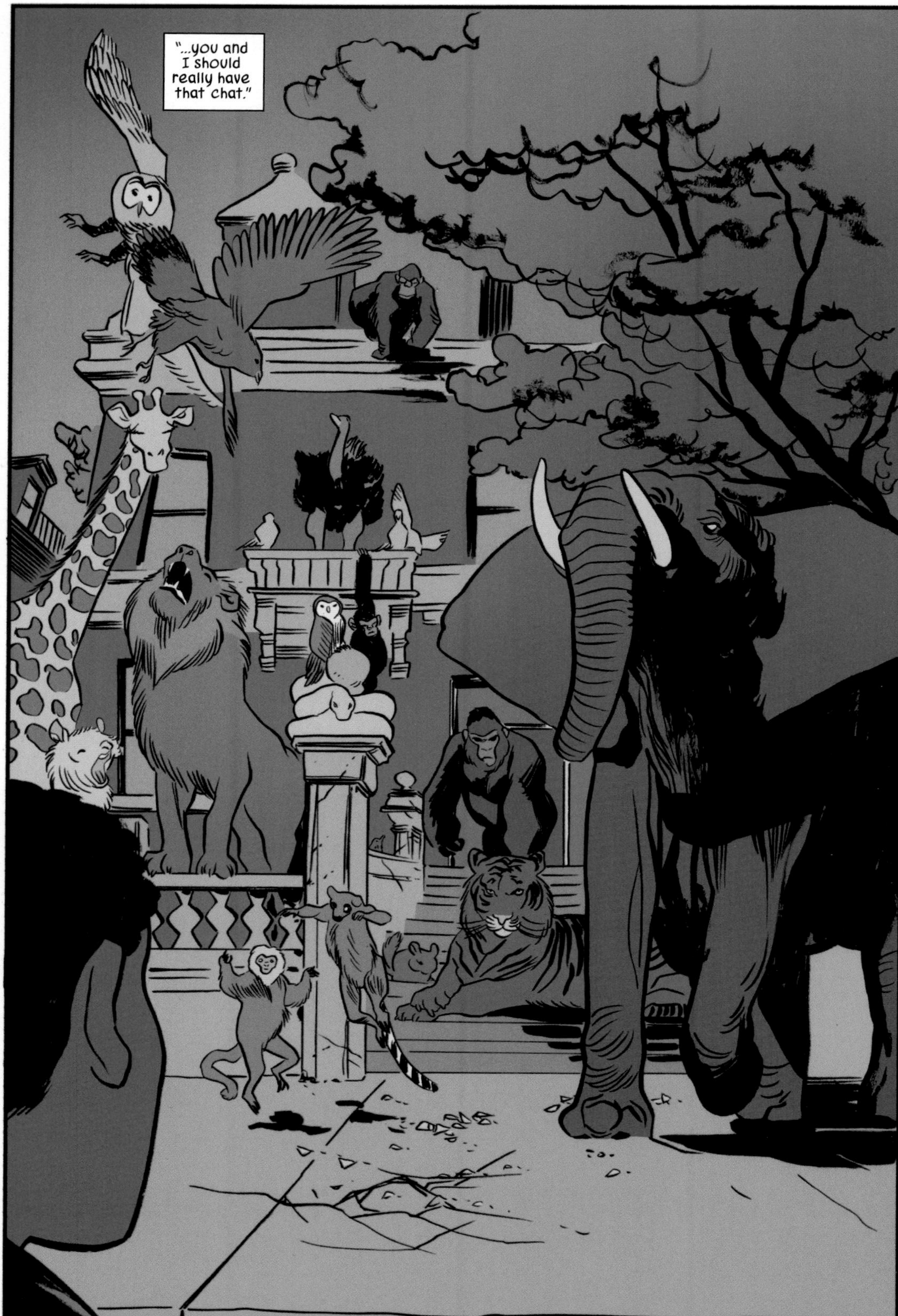
"...you and I should really have that chat."

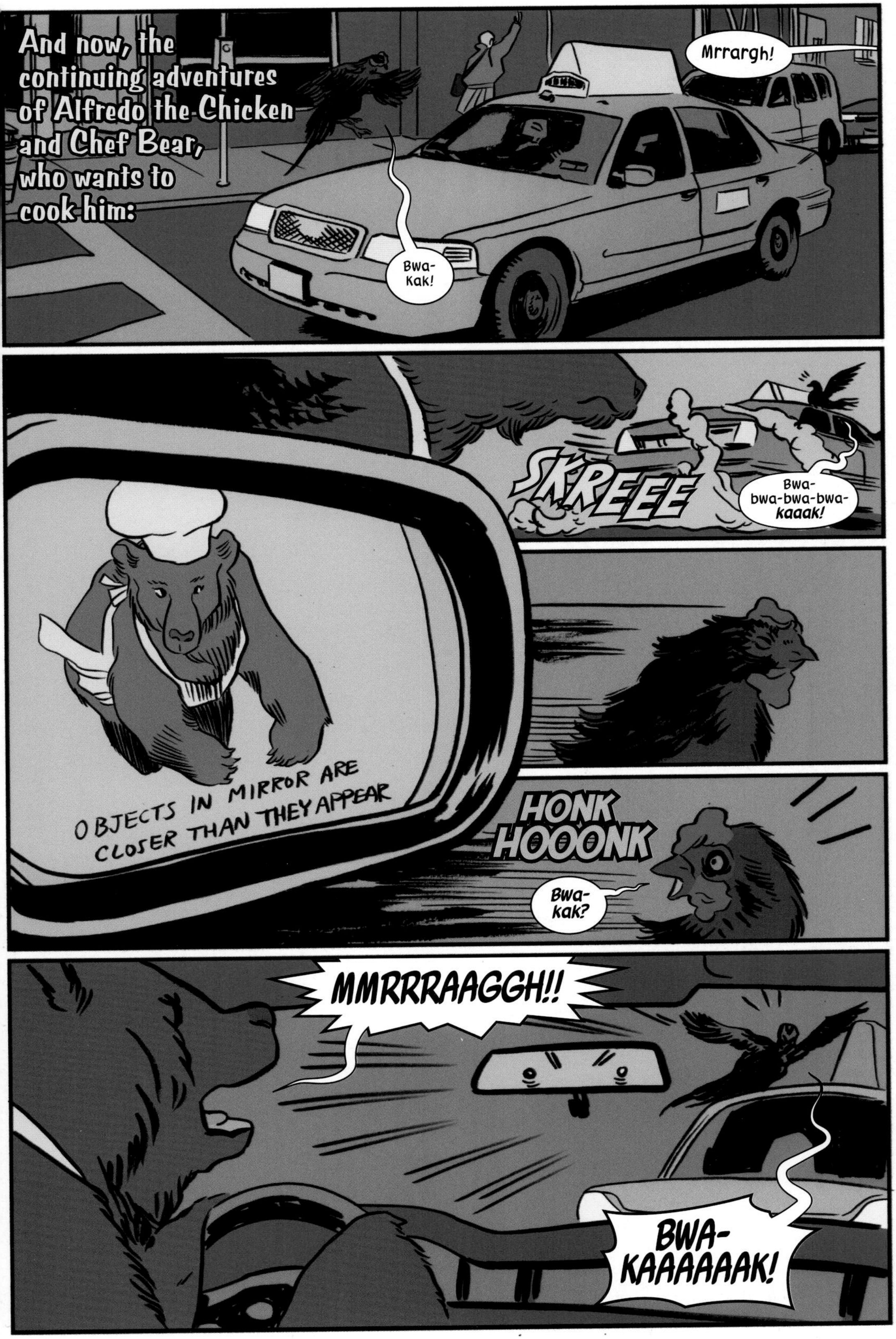
And now, the continuing adventures of Alfredo the Chicken and Chef Bear, who wants to cook him:
Mrrargh!
Bwa-Kak!
SKREEE
Bwa-bwa-bwa-bwa-kaaak!
OBJECTS IN MIRROR ARE CLOSER THAN THEY APPEAR
HONK HOOONK
Bwa-kak?
MMRRRAAGGH!!
BWA-KAAAAAAK!

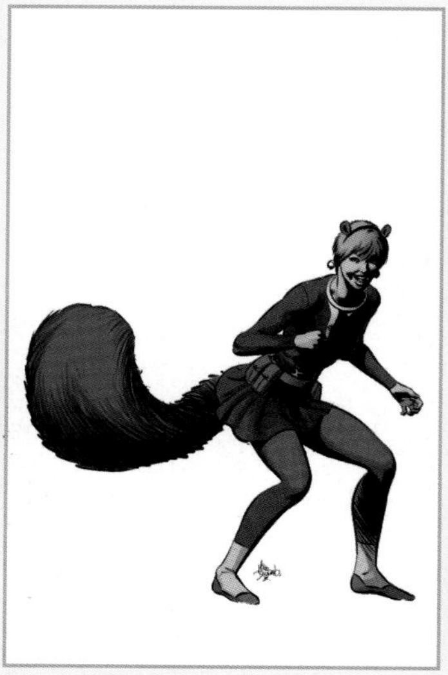

#16 TEASER VARIANT
BY MIKE DEODATO JR.
& FRANK MARTIN

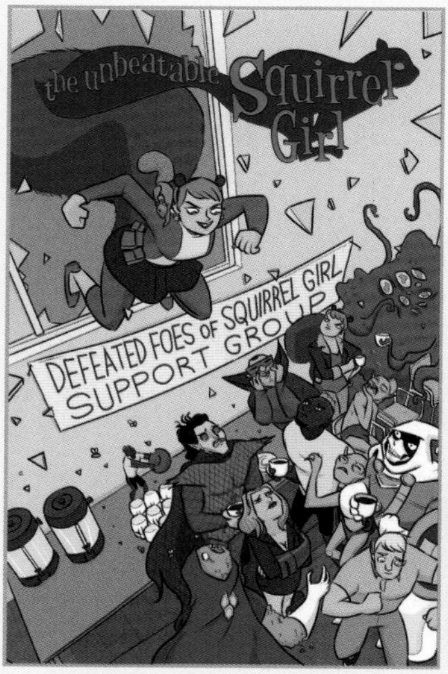
the unbeatable Squirrel Girl
DEFEATED FOES OF SQUIRREL GIRL SUPPORT GROUP

#16 STORY THUS FAR VARIANT
BY JOHN ALLISON

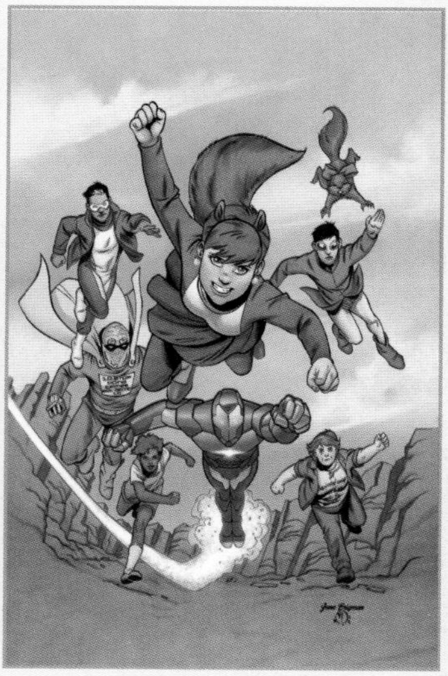

#16 CLASSIC VARIANT
BY JUNE BRIGMAN, MARC DEERING
& JAY DAVID RAMOS

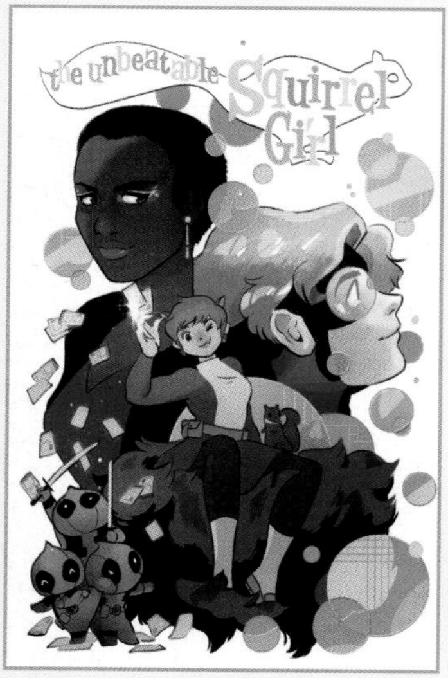
the unbeatable Squirrel Girl

#16 VARIANT
BY NATASHA ALLEGRI

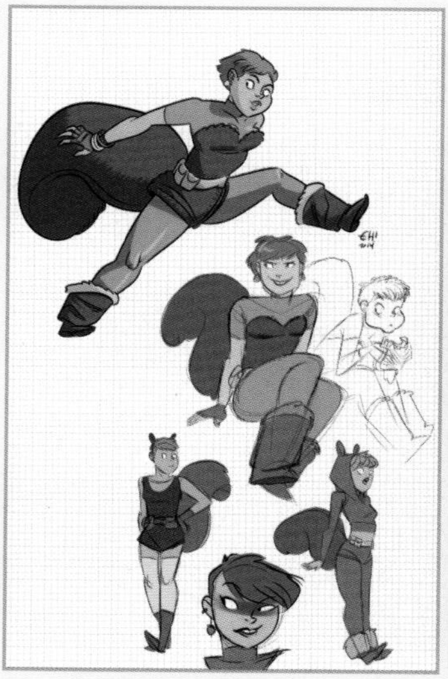

#16 DESIGN VARIANT
BY ERICA HENDERSON

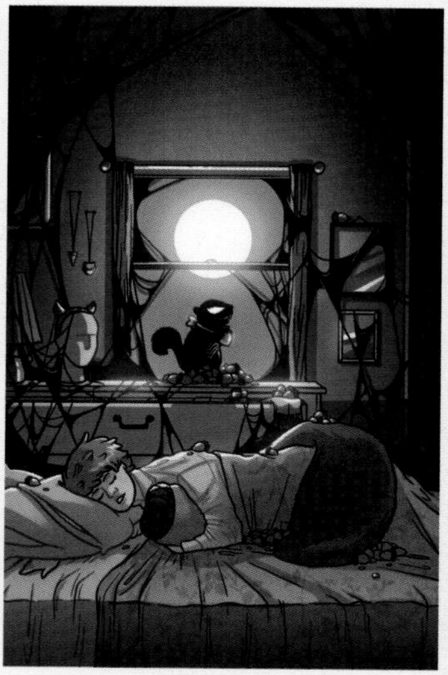

#18 VENOMIZED VARIANT
BY KATE LETH &
PAULINA GANUCHEAU

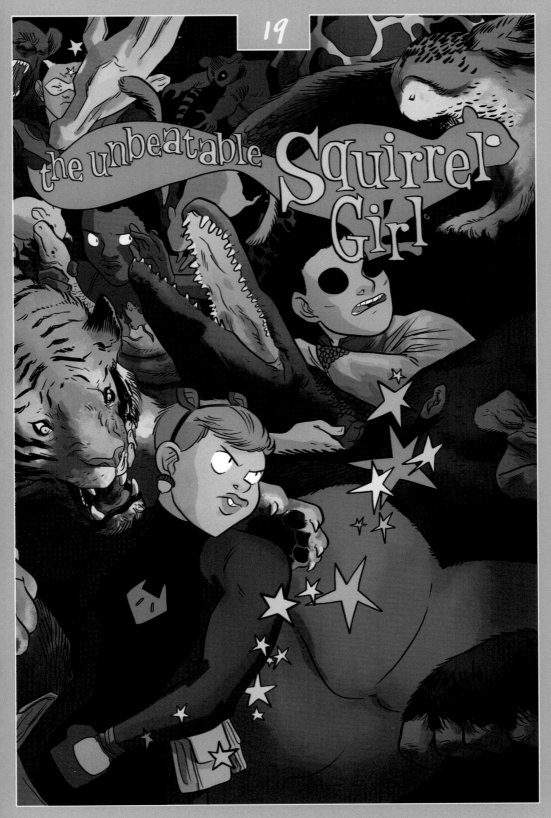

the unbeatable Squirrel Girl

Doreen Green isn't just a second-year computer science student: she secretly also has all the powers of both squirrel and girl! She uses her amazing abilities to fight crime **and** *be as awesome as possible. You know her as...* ***The Unbeatable Squirrel Girl!***
Find out what she's been up to, with...

Squirrel Girl *in a nutshell*

Squirrel Girl @unbeatablesg
Hey so remember how I was kinda bragging about the flying suit a new friend gave me a while back?? Remember how that was a thing?

Squirrel Girl @unbeatablesg
Remember how I was all "fav this if you're a criminal who isn't gonna do crimes anymore now that you know I'MMA FLY NOW"?

Squirrel Girl @unbeatablesg
Remember how I then went on to post how I was definitely gonna KEEP flying forever, b/c my new suit was great and definitely not sabotaged?

Squirrel Girl @unbeatablesg
Remember how all of those were posted in a manner that might, in retrospect, be described as "hubristic"??

Squirrel Girl @unbeatablesg
Well uh

Squirrel Girl @unbeatablesg
Turns out that Greek myth that warned us not to fly too close to the sun was NOT ENTIRELY OFF BASE, IN VERY LIMITED CIRCUMSTANCES??

Tony Stark @starkmantony
@unbeatablesg Icarus, right? Kid and his dad invent wings from wax and feathers, kid flies too close to the sun, wings melt, the end.

Tony Stark @starkmantony
@unbeatablesg Here's the thing about that. So Icarus and his dad invent AMAZING SUITS from SCRATCH while being held PRISONER--

Tony Stark @starkmantony
@unbeatablesg (an idea which, for obvious reasons, really appeals to me on a fundamental level)

Tony Stark @starkmantony
@unbeatablesg --and then one of them dies because he's TOO SUCCESSFUL at FLYING SUIT INVENTION, and that's supposed to teach us something?

Tony Stark @starkmantony
@unbeatablesg I'll tell you what it teaches me. It teaches me that whoever is telling it never studied science.

Tony Stark @starkmantony
@unbeatablesg There's a reason why Everest is snowy at the top instead of being covered in beach towels, sunglasses, and mojitos.

Tony Stark @starkmantony
@unbeatablesg In flight range, air pressure goes down as you go up, and gases under less pressure are slower and colder. Hence, freezing.

Tony Stark @starkmantony
@unbeatablesg In conclusion, it's a ridiculous myth, and in real life Icarus would've a) survived, and b) been lauded as a great engineer.

Tony Stark @starkmantony
@unbeatablesg And I would've hired him.

Tony Stark @starkmantony
@unbeatablesg Anyway. Don't feel bad that you trusted someone. That's what you DO, Squirrel Girl. What are you gonna do, not trust anyone?

Tony Stark @starkmantony
@unbeatablesg That's a horrible way to live your life. And it's not you.

Tony Stark @starkmantony
@unbeatablesg You did nothing wrong. And if there's anything I can do to help, you just let me know.

Tony Stark @starkmantony
@unbeatablesg I may be a disembodied AI in a computer now, but I still know who my friends are.

Squirrel Girl @unbeatablesg
@starkmantony AW TONY <3

Squirrel Girl @unbeatablesg
@starkmantony You're the greatest, holy crap

Squirrel Girl @unbeatablesg
@starkmantony Also it's cute how you keep claiming to be an AI even though that is CLEARLY NOT THE CASE

Squirrel Girl @unbeatablesg
@starkmantony

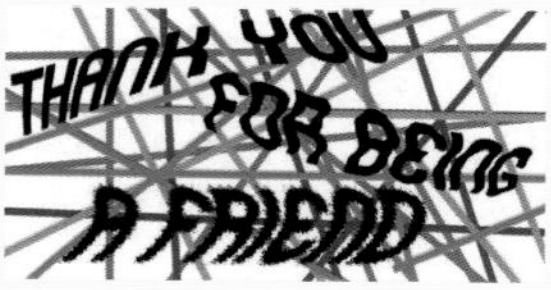
THANK YOU FOR BEING A FRIEND

Tony Stark @starkmantony
@unbeatablesg Listen, I keep telling you, I can still read those no problem so it's

search!

#markII
#ascuteastheyaredeadly
#howardtheduck
#howardthesurlyguyonthestreet
#chefbear
#alfredothechicken

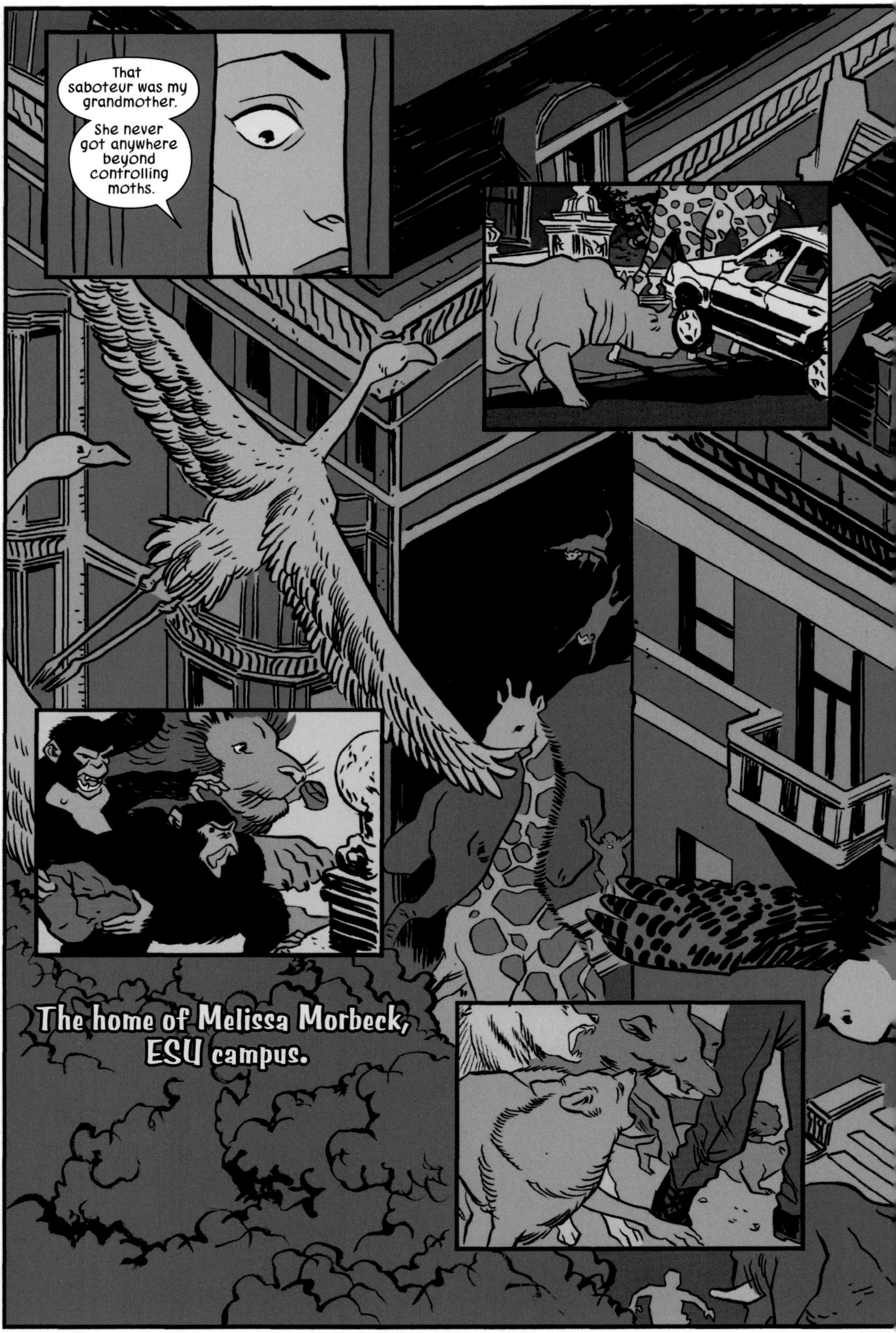
That saboteur was my grandmother.
She never got anywhere beyond controlling moths.
The home of Melissa Morbeck, ESU campus.

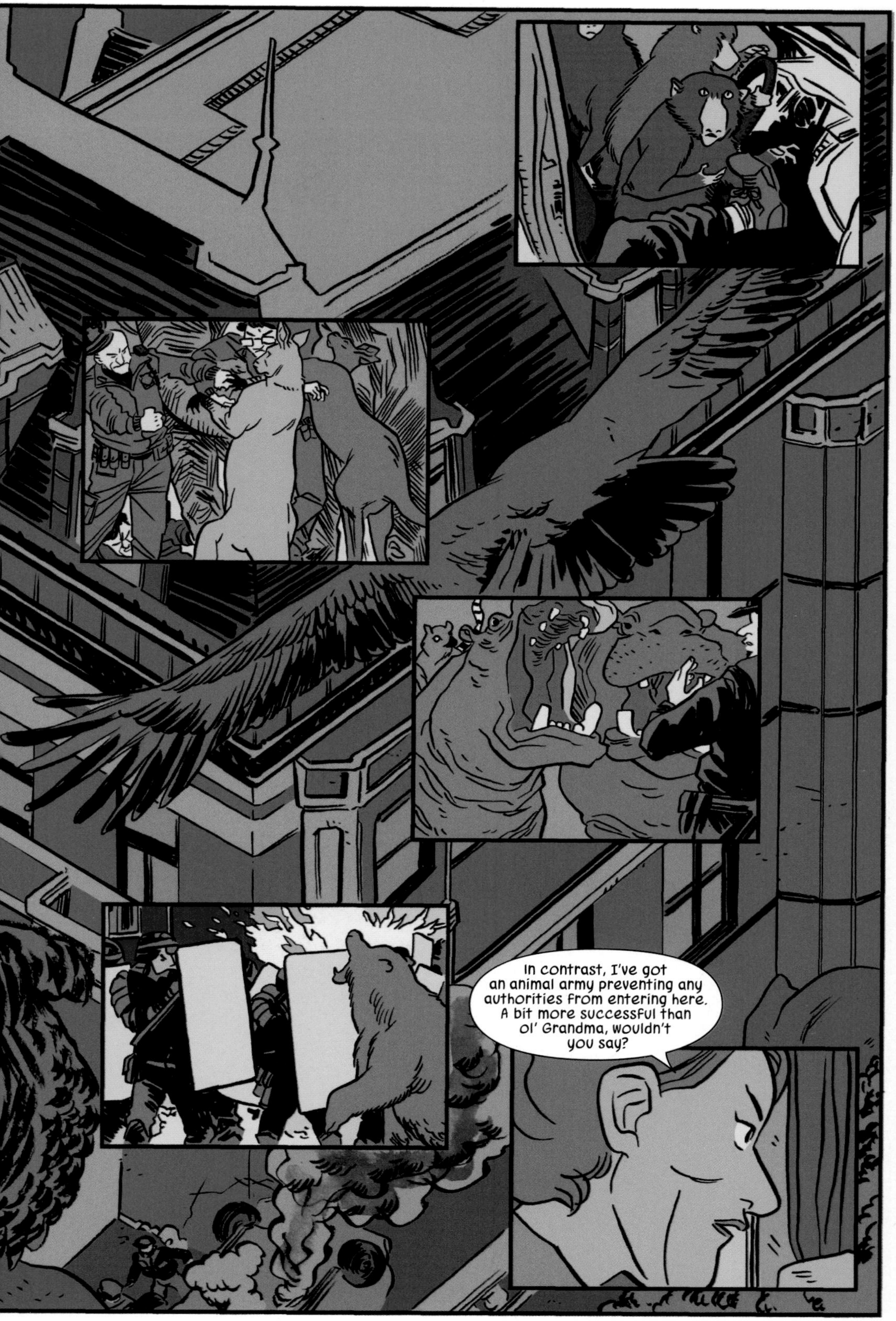
In contrast, I've got an animal army preventing any authorities from entering here. A bit more successful than ol' Grandma, wouldn't you say?

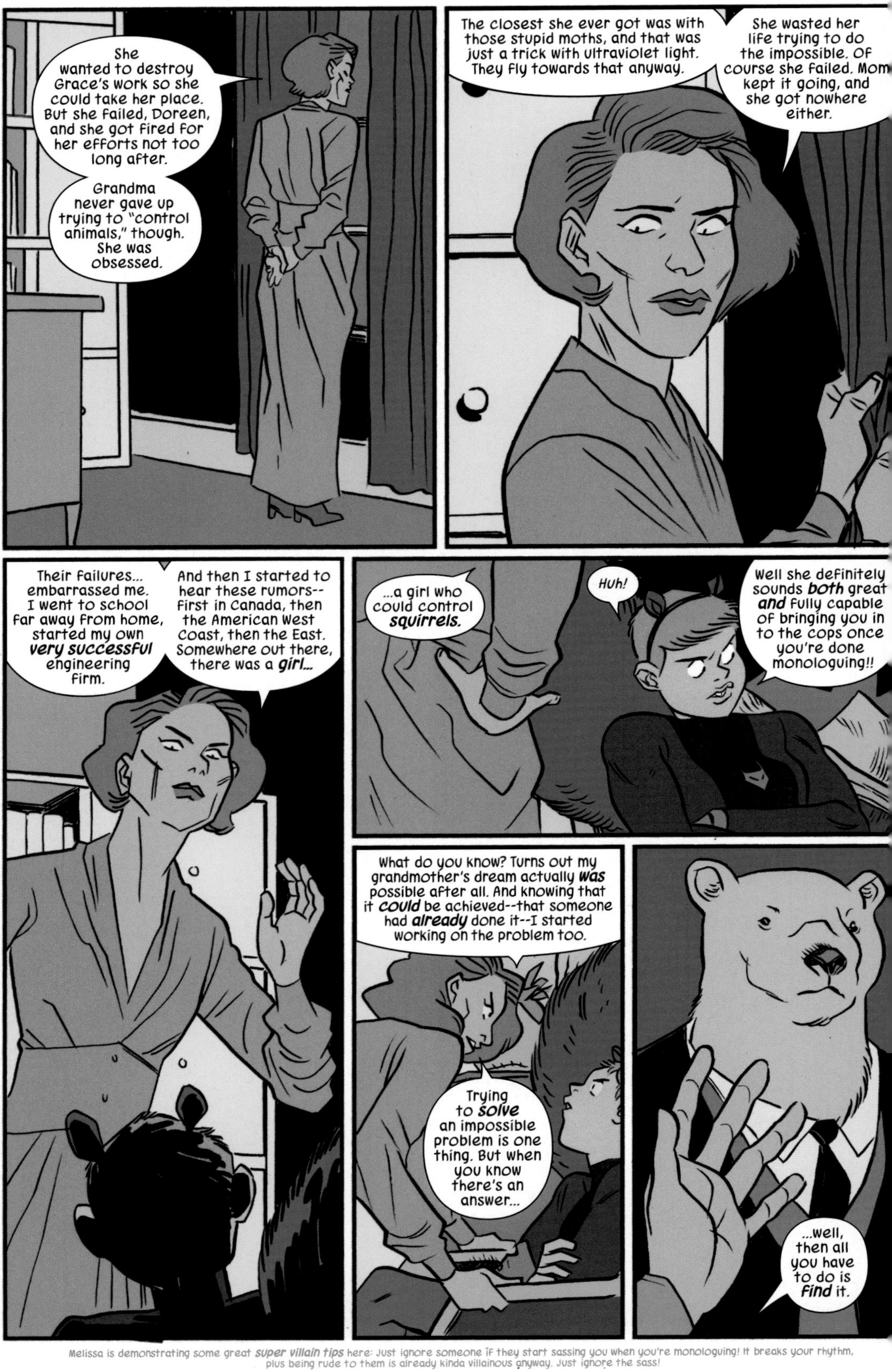
She wanted to destroy Grace's work so she could take her place. But she failed, Doreen, and she got fired for her efforts not too long after.
Grandma never gave up trying to "control animals," though. She was obsessed.
The closest she ever got was with those stupid moths, and that was just a trick with ultraviolet light. They fly towards that anyway.
She wasted her life trying to do the impossible. Of course she failed. Mom kept it going, and she got nowhere either.
Their failures... embarrassed me. I went to school far away from home, started my own *very successful* engineering firm.
And then I started to hear these rumors--first in Canada, then the American West Coast, then the East. Somewhere out there, there was a *girl...*
...a girl who could control *squirrels.*
Huh!
Well she definitely sounds *both* great *and* fully capable of bringing you in to the cops once you're done monologuing!!
What do you know? Turns out my grandmother's dream actually *was* possible after all. And knowing that it *could* be achieved--that someone had *already* done it--I started working on the problem too.
Trying to *solve* an impossible problem is one thing. But when you know there's an answer...
...well, then all you have to do is *find* it.

Melissa is demonstrating some great *super villain tips* here: Just ignore someone if they start sassing you when you're monologuing! It breaks your rhythm, plus being rude to them is already kinda villainous anyway. Just ignore the sass!

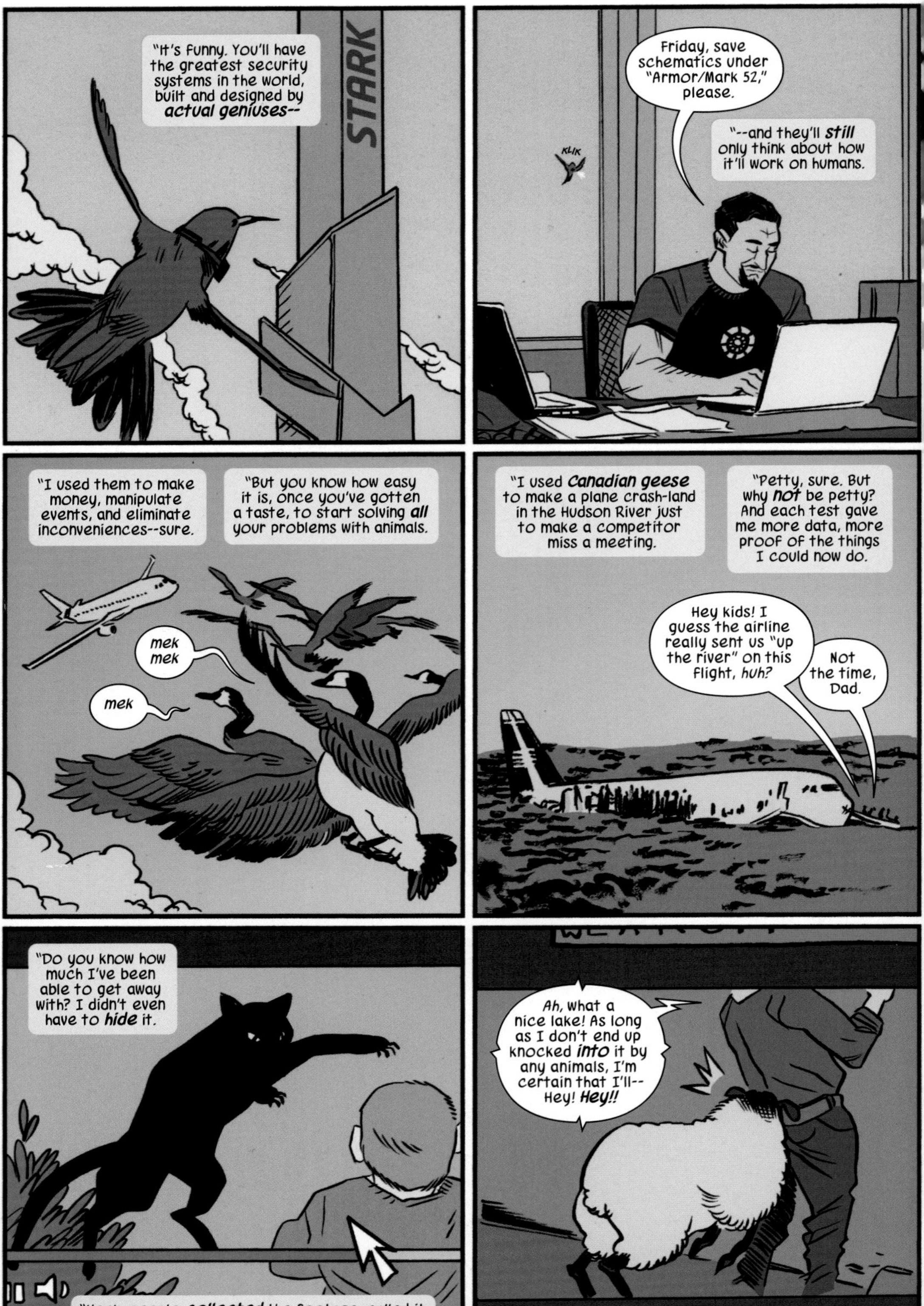
"It's funny. You'll have the greatest security systems in the world, built and designed by *actual geniuses--*
STARK
Friday, save schematics under "Armor/Mark 52," please.
KLIK
"--and they'll *still* only think about how it'll work on humans.
"I used them to make money, manipulate events, and eliminate inconveniences--sure.
"But you know how easy it is, once you've gotten a taste, to start solving *all* your problems with animals.
mek mek
mek
"I used *Canadian geese* to make a plane crash-land in the Hudson River just to make a competitor miss a meeting.
"Petty, sure. But why *not* be petty? And each test gave me more data, more proof of the things I could now do.
Hey kids! I guess the airline really sent us "up the river" on this flight, *huh?*
Not the time, Dad.
"Do you know how much I've been able to get away with? I didn't even have to *hide* it.
"Heck, people *collected* the footage, called it *'ANIMALS KNOCKING OVER PEOPLE: BEST HUMAN FAILS OF THE YEAR!'* and shared it far and wide...
Ah, what a nice lake! As long as I don't end up knocked *into* it by any animals, I'm certain that I'll-- Hey! *Hey!!*
"...and nobody ever suspected a thing."

That last dude cut her off in traffic. *That's what you get, LAST DUDE.*

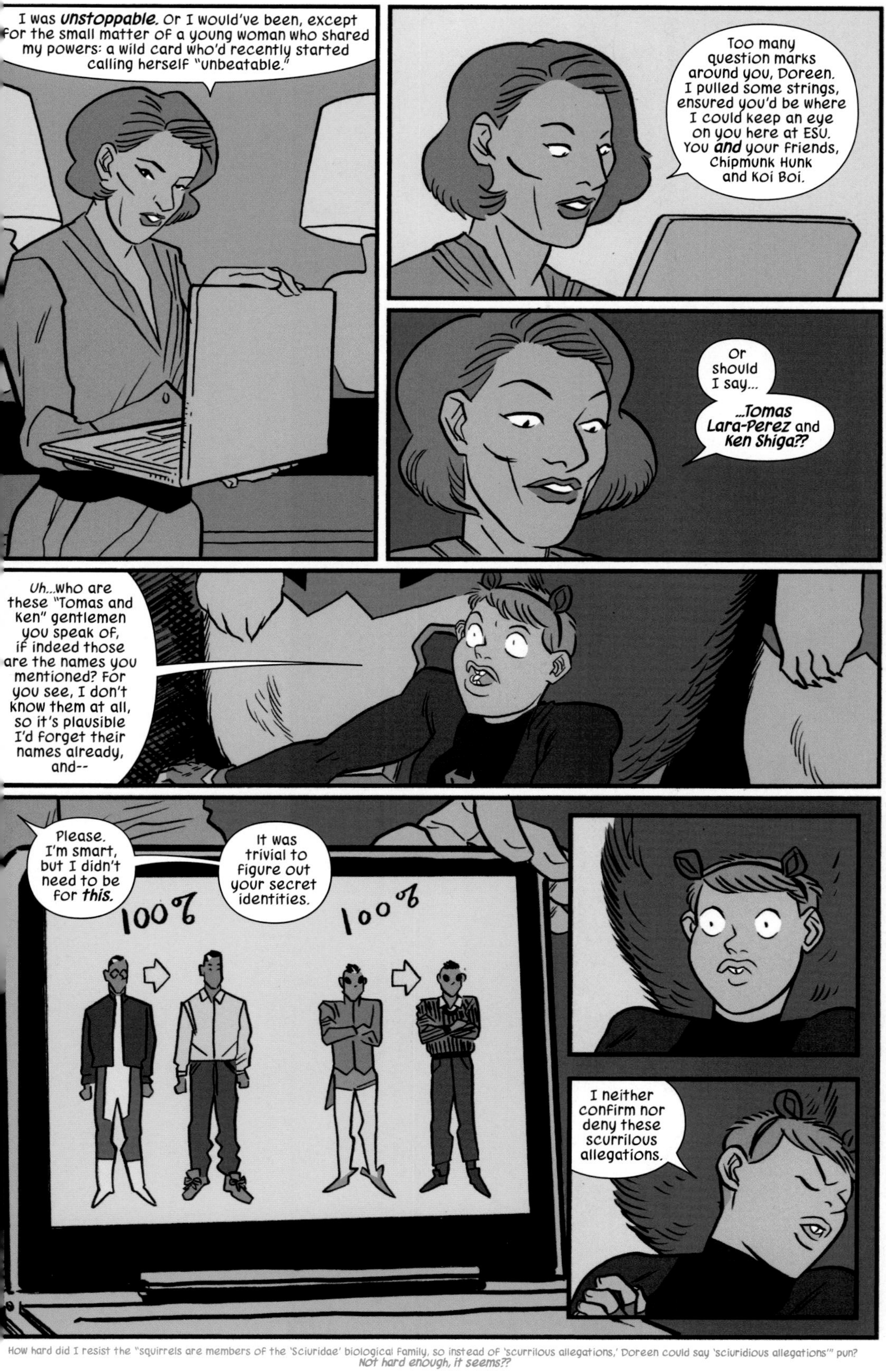
I was *unstoppable.* Or I would've been, except for the small matter of a young woman who shared my powers: a wild card who'd recently started calling herself "unbeatable."
Too many question marks around you, Doreen. I pulled some strings, ensured you'd be where I could keep an eye on you here at ESU. You **and** your friends, Chipmunk Hunk and Koi Boi.
Or should I say...
...Tomas Lara-Perez** and **Ken Shiga??
*Uh...*who are these "Tomas and Ken" gentlemen you speak of, if indeed those are the names you mentioned? For you see, I don't know them at all, so it's plausible I'd forget their names already, and--
Please. I'm smart, but I didn't need to be for ***this.***
It was trivial to figure out your secret identities.
100%
100%
I neither confirm nor deny these scurrilous allegations.

How hard did I resist the "squirrels are members of the 'Sciuridae' biological family, so instead of 'scurrilous allegations,' Doreen could say 'sciuridious allegations'" pun?
Not hard enough, it seems??

That bank robber's name is "Lewis 'the Chef' Hastings" because of how he robs banks and then hides the stolen money inside cakes. He gives his loved ones cakes with money inside them and they're like, "Lewis, I love your baking but I hate your bank robbing, and especially how you put that gross money that people touched with their dirty hands inside this otherwise delicious cake."

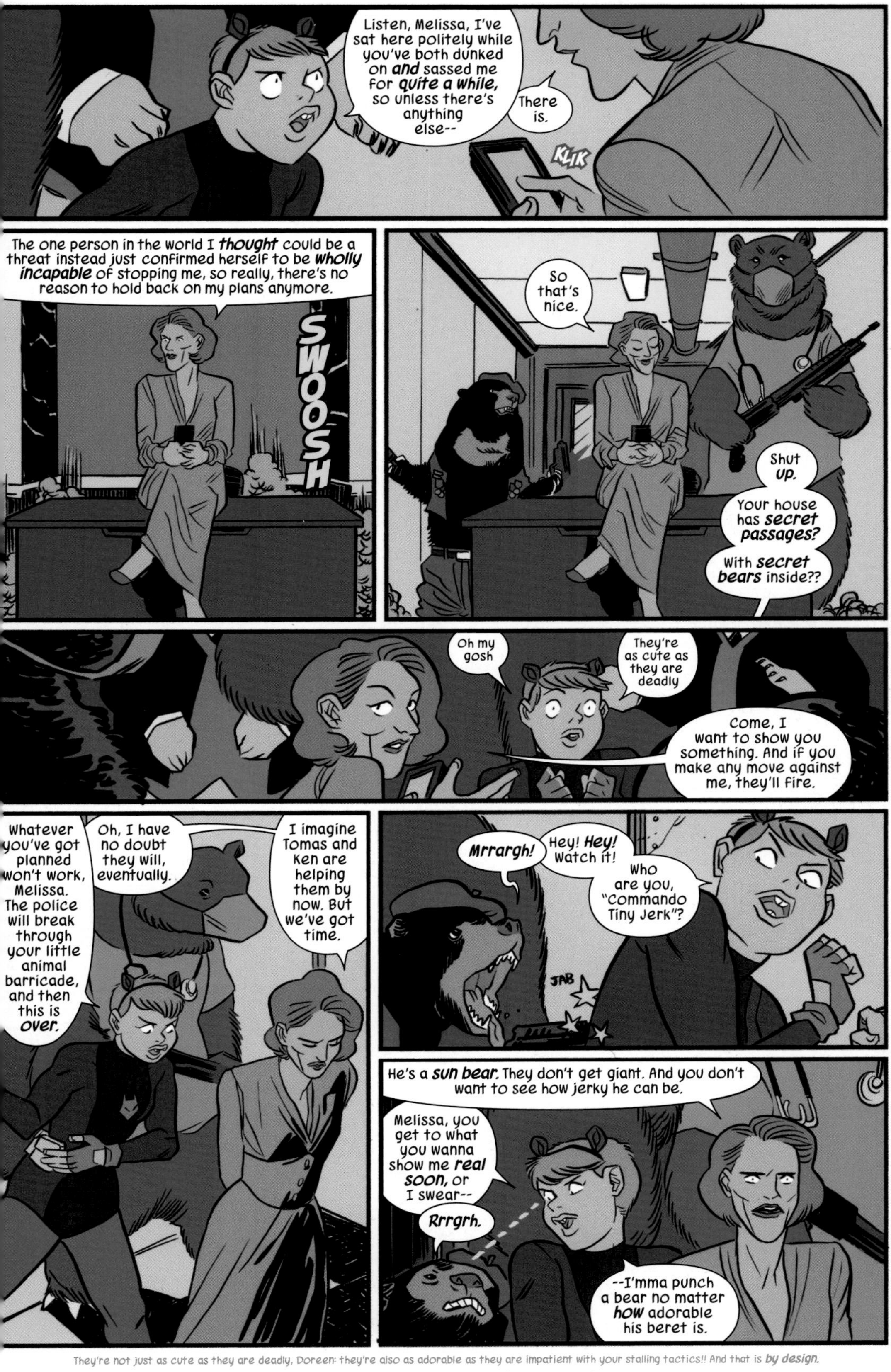
Listen, Melissa, I've sat here politely while you've both dunked on and sassed me for quite a while, so unless there's anything else--
There is.
KLIK
The one person in the world I thought could be a threat instead just confirmed herself to be wholly incapable of stopping me, so really, there's no reason to hold back on my plans anymore.
SWOOSH
So that's nice.
Shut up.
Your house has secret passages?
With secret bears inside??
Oh my gosh
They're as cute as they are deadly
Come, I want to show you something. And if you make any move against me, they'll fire.
Whatever you've got planned won't work, Melissa. The police will break through your little animal barricade, and then this is over.
Oh, I have no doubt they will, eventually.
I imagine Tomas and Ken are helping them by now. But we've got time.
Mrrargh!
Hey! Hey! Watch it!
Who are you, "Commando Tiny Jerk"?
JAB
He's a sun bear. They don't get giant. And you don't want to see how jerky he can be.
Melissa, you get to what you wanna show me real soon, or I swear--
Rrrgrh.
--I'mma punch a bear no matter how adorable his beret is.

They're not just as cute as they are deadly, Doreen: they're also as adorable as they are impatient with your stalling tactics!! And that is *by design.*

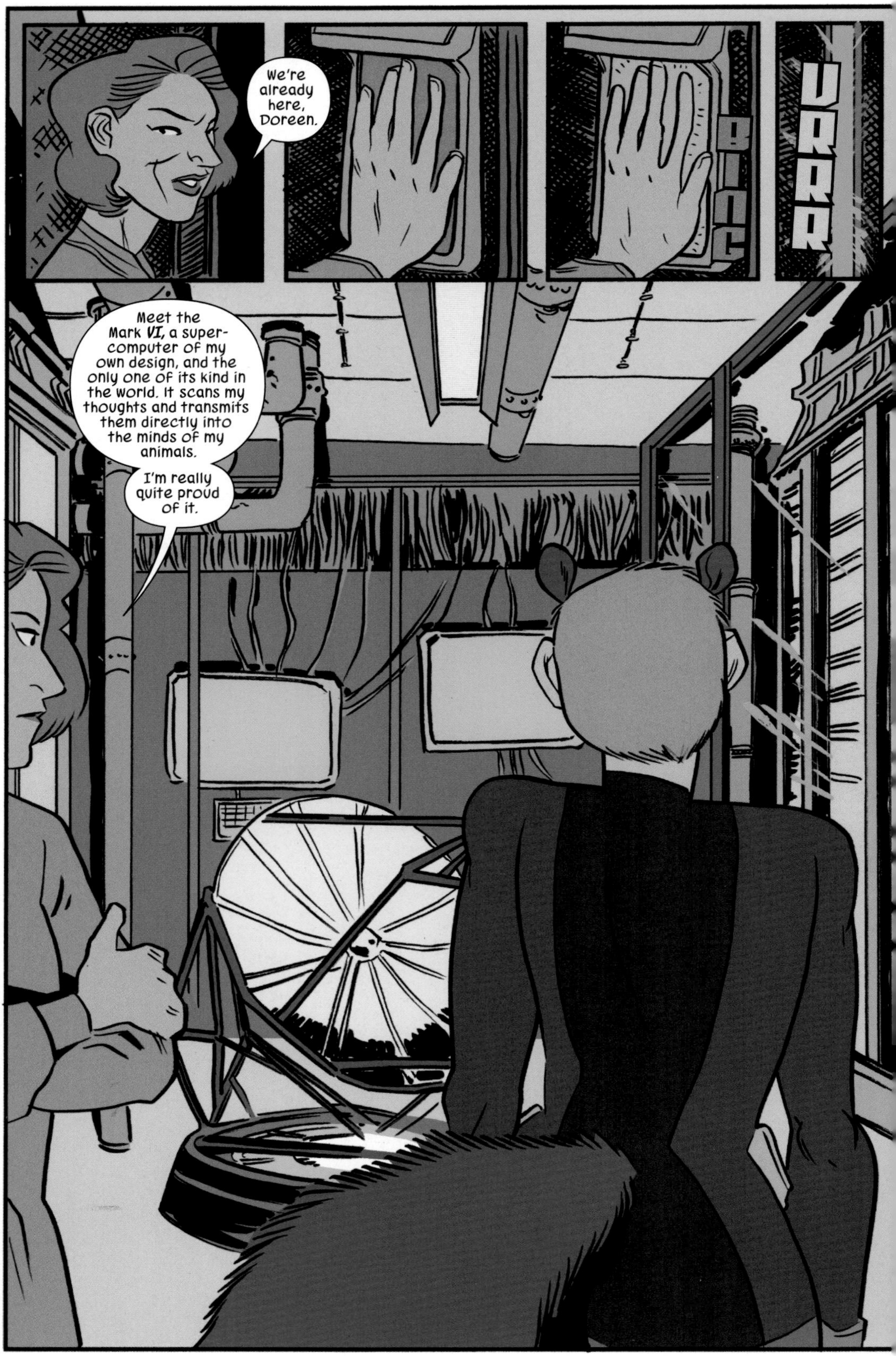

We're already here, Doreen.
BING
VRRR
Meet the Mark VI, a super-computer of my own design, and the only one of its kind in the world. It scans my thoughts and transmits them directly into the minds of my animals.
I'm really quite proud of it.

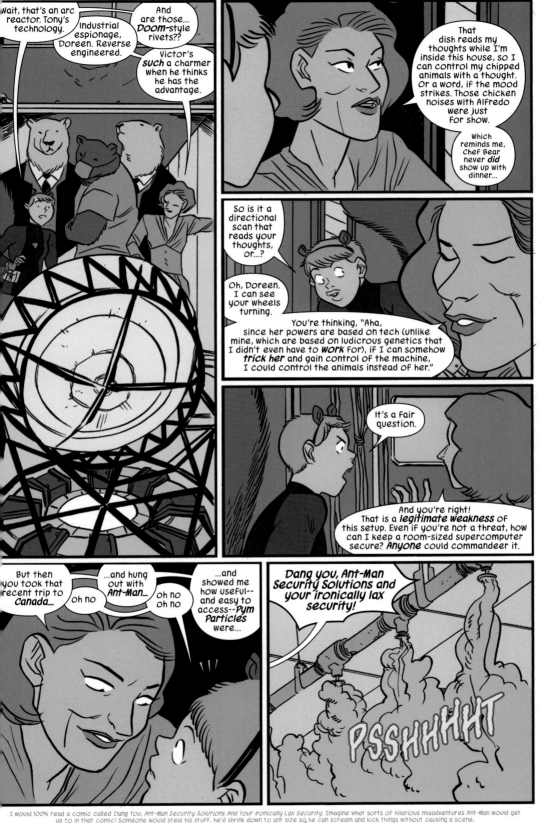

Wait, that's an arc reactor. Tony's technology.

Industrial espionage, Doreen. Reverse engineered.

And are those... **DOOM**-style rivets??

Victor's **such** a charmer when he thinks he has the advantage.

That dish reads my thoughts while I'm inside this house, so I can control my chipped animals with a thought. Or a word, if the mood strikes. Those chicken noises with Alfredo were just for show.

Which reminds me, Chef Bear never **did** show up with dinner...

So is it a directional scan that reads your thoughts, or...?

Oh, Doreen. I can see your wheels turning.

You're thinking, "Aha, since her powers are based on tech (unlike mine, which are based on ludicrous genetics that I didn't even have to **work** for), if I can somehow **trick her** and gain control of the machine, I could control the animals instead of her."

It's a fair question.

And you're right! That is a **legitimate weakness** of this setup. Even if you're not a threat, how can I keep a room-sized supercomputer secure? **Anyone** could commandeer it.

But then you took that recent trip to **Canada**...

oh no

...and hung out with **Ant-Man**...

oh no oh no

...and showed me how useful-- and easy to access--**Pym Particles** were...

Dang you, Ant-Man Security Solutions and your ironically lax security!

PSSHHHHT

I would 100% read a comic called *Dang You, Ant-Man Security Solutions And Your Ironically Lax Security.* Imagine what sorts of hilarious misadventures Ant-Man would get up to in that comic! Someone would steal his stuff, he'd shrink down to ant size so he can scream and kick things without causing a scene, then he'd come back up to normal size and try to continue his very important board meeting like nothing happened.

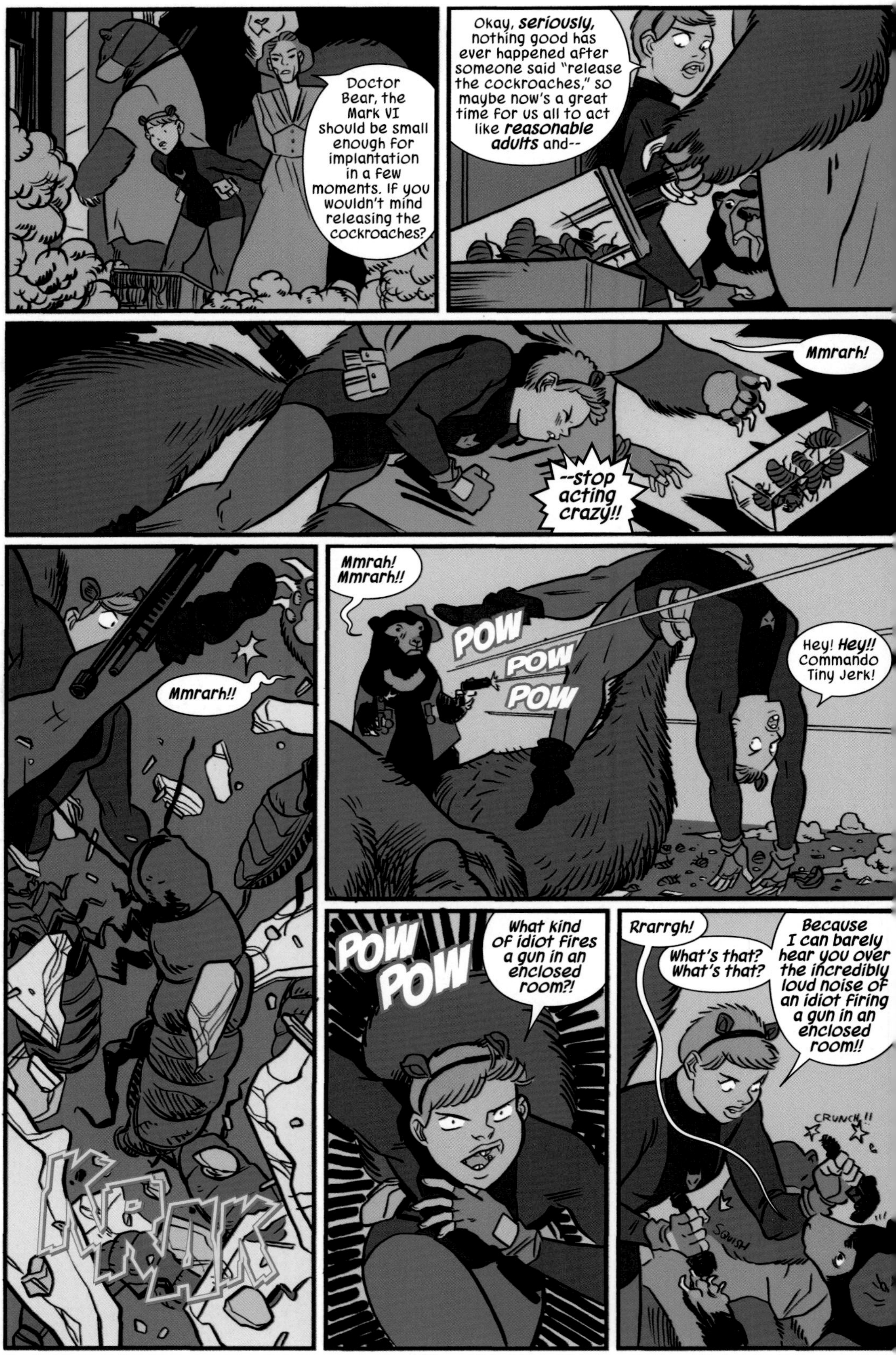

Doctor Bear, the Mark VI should be small enough for implantation in a few moments. If you wouldn't mind releasing the cockroaches?
Okay, seriously, nothing good has ever happened after someone said "release the cockroaches," so maybe now's a great time for us all to act like reasonable adults and--
Mmrarh!
--stop acting crazy!!
Mmrarh!!
Mmrah! Mmrarh!!
POW
POW
POW
Hey! Hey!! Commando Tiny Jerk!
POW POW
What kind of idiot fires a gun in an enclosed room?!
Rrarrgh!
What's that? What's that?
Because I can barely hear you over the incredibly loud noise of an idiot firing a gun in an enclosed room!!
CRUNCH!!
SQUISH

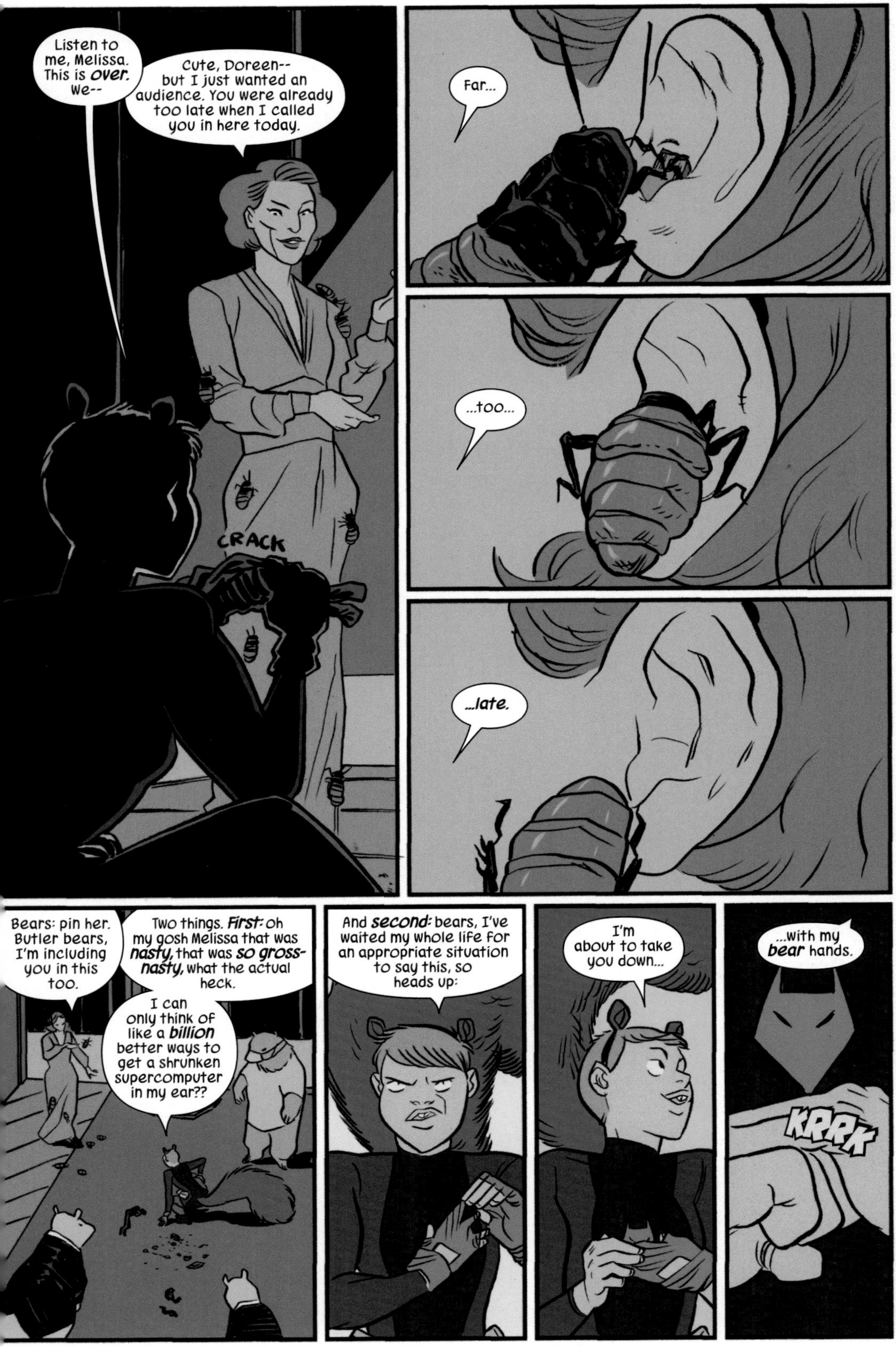
Listen to me, Melissa. This is *over.* We--
Cute, Doreen-- but I just wanted an audience. You were already too late when I called you in here today.
CRACK
Far...
...too...
...late.
Bears: pin her. Butler bears, I'm including you in this too.
Two things. *First:* oh my gosh Melissa that was *nasty,* that was *so gross-nasty,* what the actual heck.
I can only think of like a *billion* better ways to get a shrunken supercomputer in my ear??
And *second:* bears, I've waited my whole life for an appropriate situation to say this, so heads up:
I'm about to take you down...
...with my *bear* hands.
KRRK

I want you to know I used a less-gross animal in the first draft of this comic, but Erica *insisted* that they be cockroaches.
Then she sent me pictures of all the different types of cockroaches she wanted to draw!! Erica, why? *Why, Erica??*

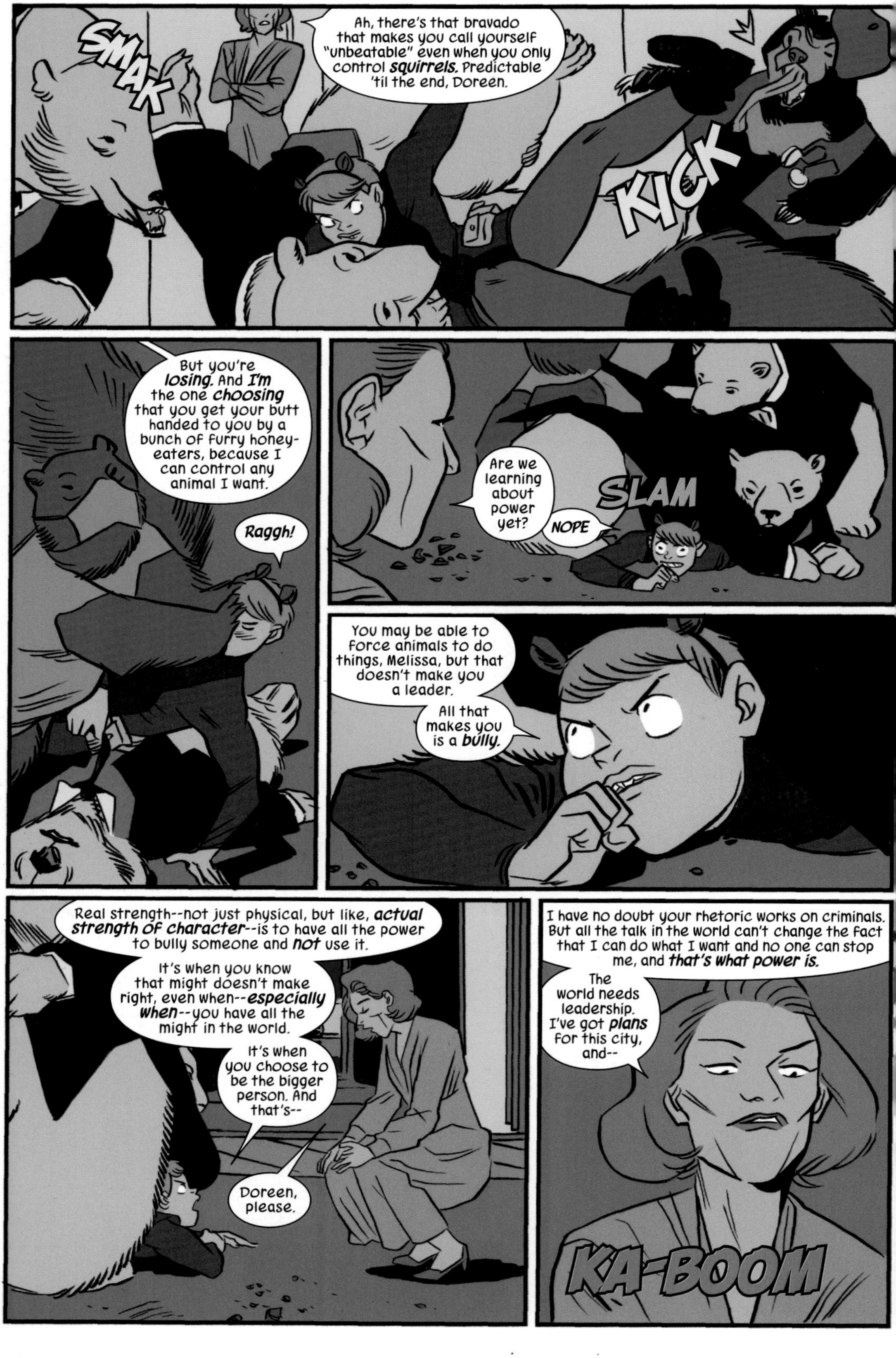
SMAK
Ah, there's that bravado that makes you call yourself "unbeatable" even when you only control *squirrels.* Predictable 'til the end, Doreen.
KICK
But you're *losing.* And *I'm* the one *choosing* that you get your butt handed to you by a bunch of furry honey-eaters, because I can control any animal I want.
Raggh!
Are we learning about power yet?
SLAM
NOPE
You may be able to force animals to do things, Melissa, but that doesn't make you a leader.
All that makes you is a *bully.*
Real strength--not just physical, but like, *actual strength of character*--is to have all the power to bully someone and *not* use it.
It's when you know that might doesn't make right, even when--*especially when*--you have all the might in the world.
It's when you choose to be the bigger person. And that's--
Doreen, please.
I have no doubt your rhetoric works on criminals. But all the talk in the world can't change the fact that I can do what I want and no one can stop me, and *that's what power is.*
The world needs leadership. I've got *plans* for this city, and--
KA-BOOM

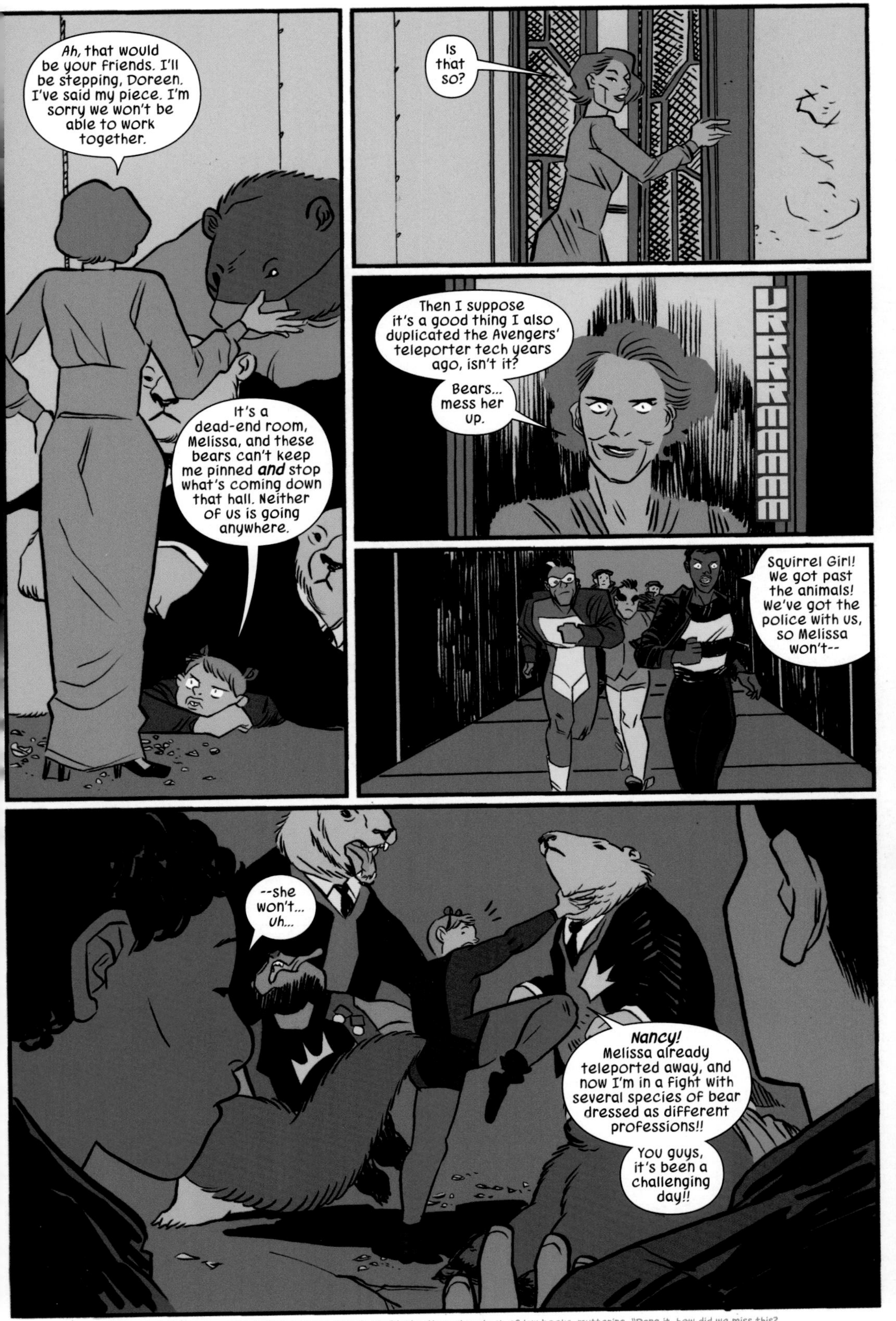
Ah, that would be your friends. I'll be stepping, Doreen. I've said my piece. I'm sorry we won't be able to work together.
It's a dead-end room, Melissa, and these bears can't keep me pinned **and** stop what's coming down that hall. Neither of us is going anywhere.
Is that so?
Then I suppose it's a good thing I also duplicated the Avengers' teleporter tech years ago, isn't it?
Bears... mess her up.
VRRRRMMMMM
Squirrel Girl! We got past the animals! We've got the police with us, so Melissa won't--
--she won't... uh...
Nancy! Melissa already teleported away, and now I'm in a fight with several species of bear dressed as different professions!!
You guys, it's been a challenging day!!

There's definitely a police officer outside, frantically flipping through a stack of law books, muttering, "Dang it, how did we miss this? There really *isn't* a law that says a bear can't fire a machine gun!"

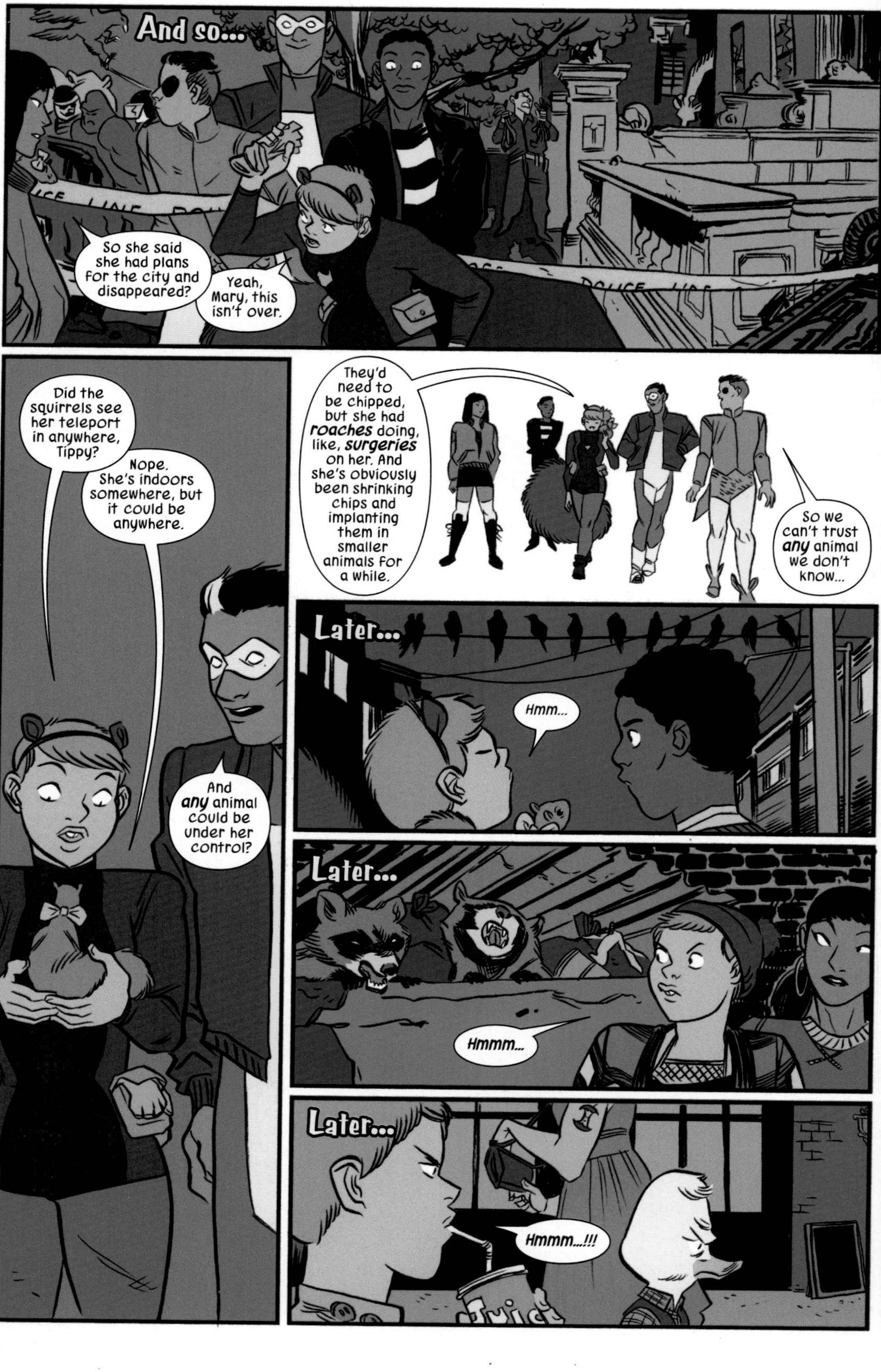
And so...
So she said she had plans for the city and disappeared?
Yeah, Mary, this isn't over.
Did the squirrels see her teleport in anywhere, Tippy?
Nope. She's indoors somewhere, but it could be anywhere.
And any animal could be under her control?
They'd need to be chipped, but she had roaches doing, like, surgeries on her. And she's obviously been shrinking chips and implanting them in smaller animals for a while.
So we can't trust any animal we don't know...
Later...
Hmm...
Later...
Hmmm...
Later...
Hmmm...!!!

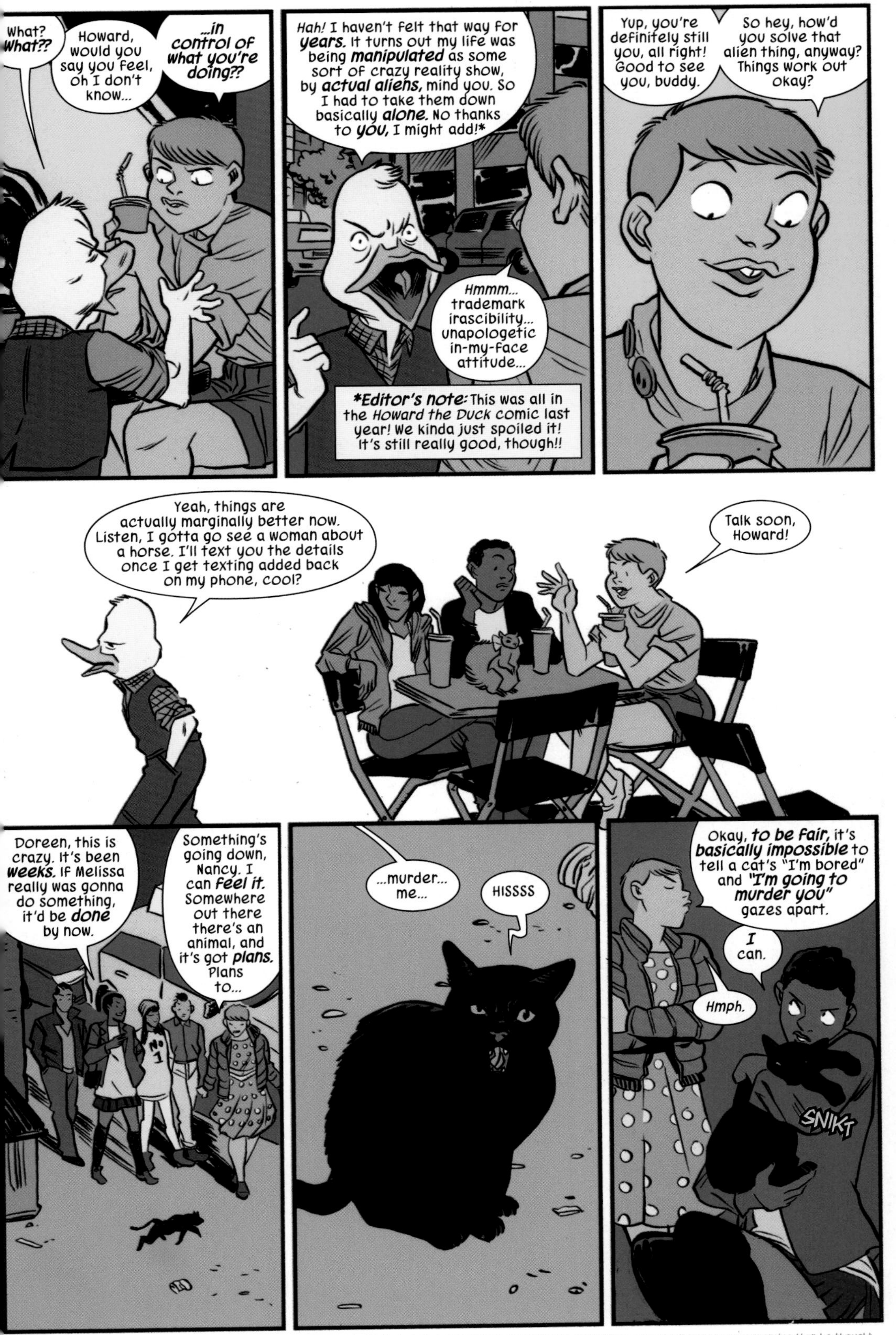
What? What??
Howard, would you say you feel, oh I don't know...
...in control of what you're doing??
Hah! I haven't felt that way for years. It turns out my life was being manipulated as some sort of crazy reality show, by actual aliens, mind you. So I had to take them down basically alone. No thanks to you, I might add!*
Hmmm... trademark irascibility... unapologetic in-my-face attitude...
*Editor's note: This was all in the Howard the Duck comic last year! We kinda just spoiled it! It's still really good, though!!
Yup, you're definitely still you, all right! Good to see you, buddy.
So hey, how'd you solve that alien thing, anyway? Things work out okay?
Yeah, things are actually marginally better now. Listen, I gotta go see a woman about a horse. I'll text you the details once I get texting added back on my phone, cool?
Talk soon, Howard!
Doreen, this is crazy. It's been weeks. If Melissa really was gonna do something, it'd be done by now.
Something's going down, Nancy. I can feel it. Somewhere out there there's an animal, and it's got plans. Plans to...
...murder... me...
HISSSS
Okay, to be fair, it's basically impossible to tell a cat's "I'm bored" and "I'm going to murder you" gazes apart.
I can.
Hmph.
SNIKT

Howard's leaving this story forever now, so I'll tell you what happened with that whole horse thing: He soon found out horses are actually way more expensive than he thought, so he's gonna stick with public transit for now. THE END.

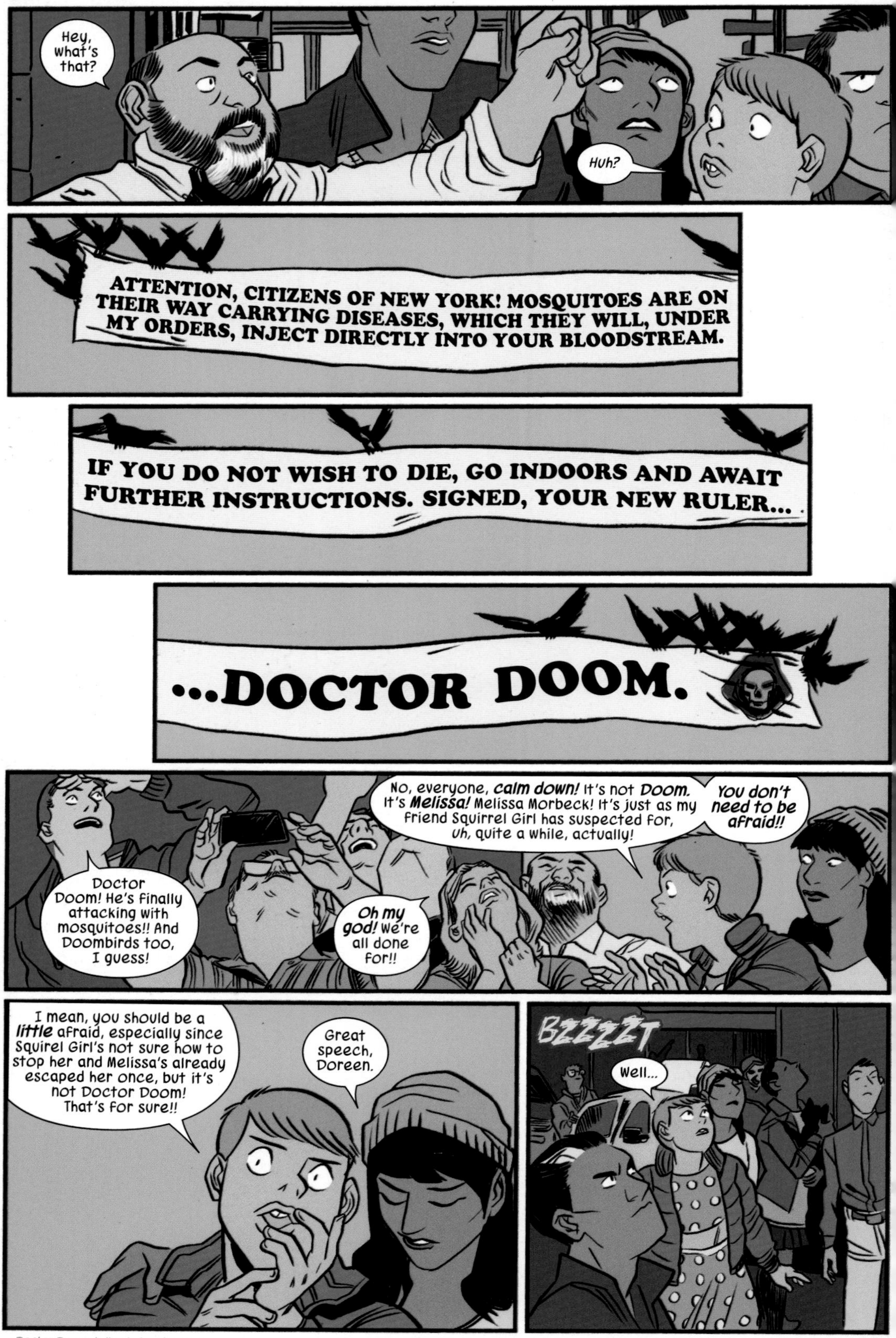
Hey, what's that?
Huh?
ATTENTION, CITIZENS OF NEW YORK! MOSQUITOES ARE ON THEIR WAY CARRYING DISEASES, WHICH THEY WILL, UNDER MY ORDERS, INJECT DIRECTLY INTO YOUR BLOODSTREAM.
IF YOU DO NOT WISH TO DIE, GO INDOORS AND AWAIT FURTHER INSTRUCTIONS. SIGNED, YOUR NEW RULER...
...DOCTOR DOOM.
Doctor Doom! He's finally attacking with mosquitoes!! And Doombirds too, I guess!
Oh my god! We're all done for!!
No, everyone, calm down! It's not Doom. It's Melissa! Melissa Morbeck! It's just as my friend Squirrel Girl has suspected for, uh, quite a while, actually!
You don't need to be afraid!!
I mean, you should be a little afraid, especially since Squirel Girl's not sure how to stop her and Melissa's already escaped her once, but it's not Doctor Doom! That's for sure!!
Great speech, Doreen.
BZZZZT
Well...

Doctor Doom shall not shoulder the blame for villainous actions that are not his!! Doctor Doom worked very hard to establish a personal brand of upscale artisinal villainy that uses *robots*, not animals! Fools!! Do *none* among you see the brilliant subtlety in Doom's personal brand?? And if not, why not??

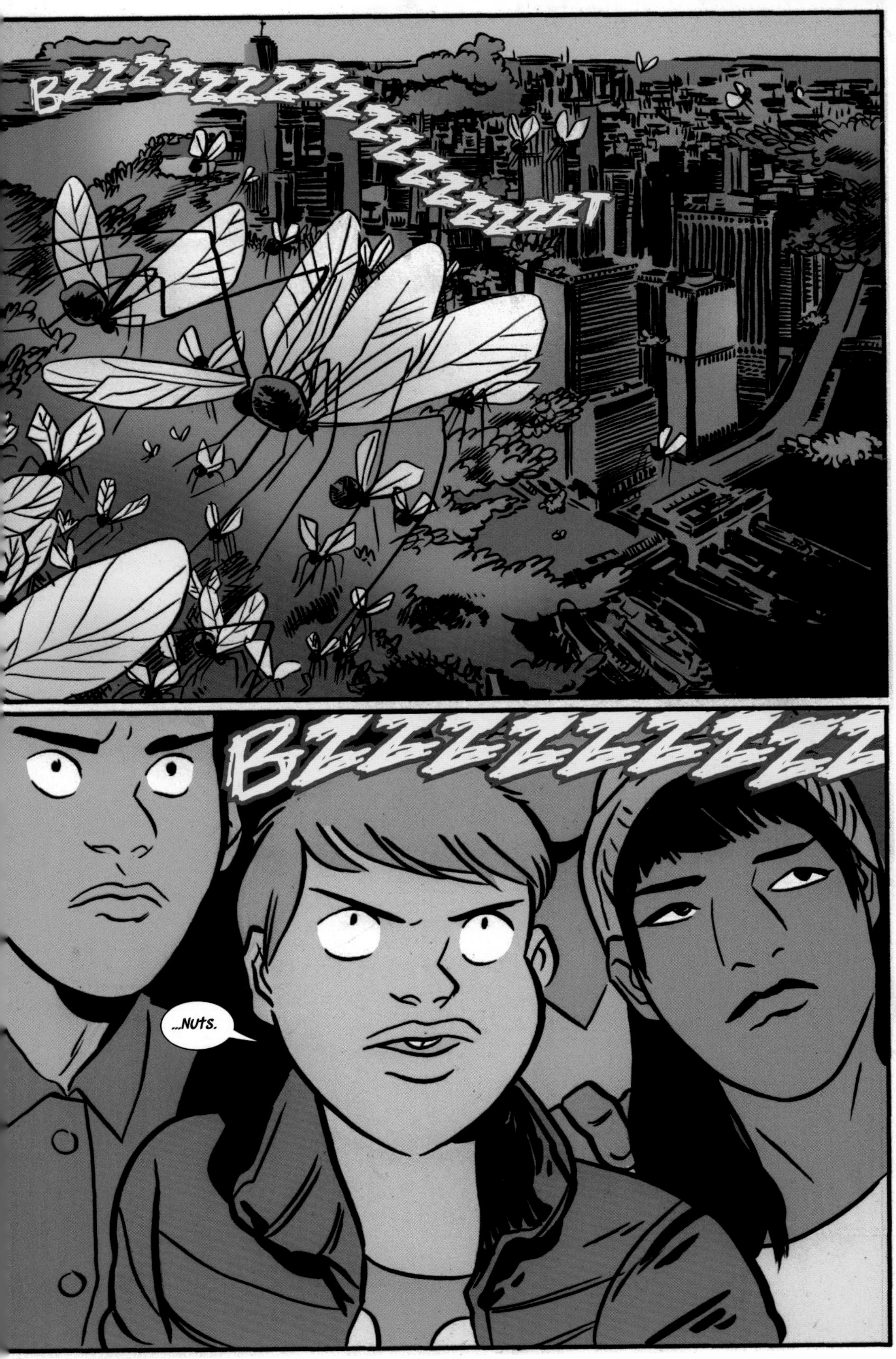
BZZZZZZZZZZZZZZZZZZZZZZZT
BZZZZZZZZZZ
...NUTS.

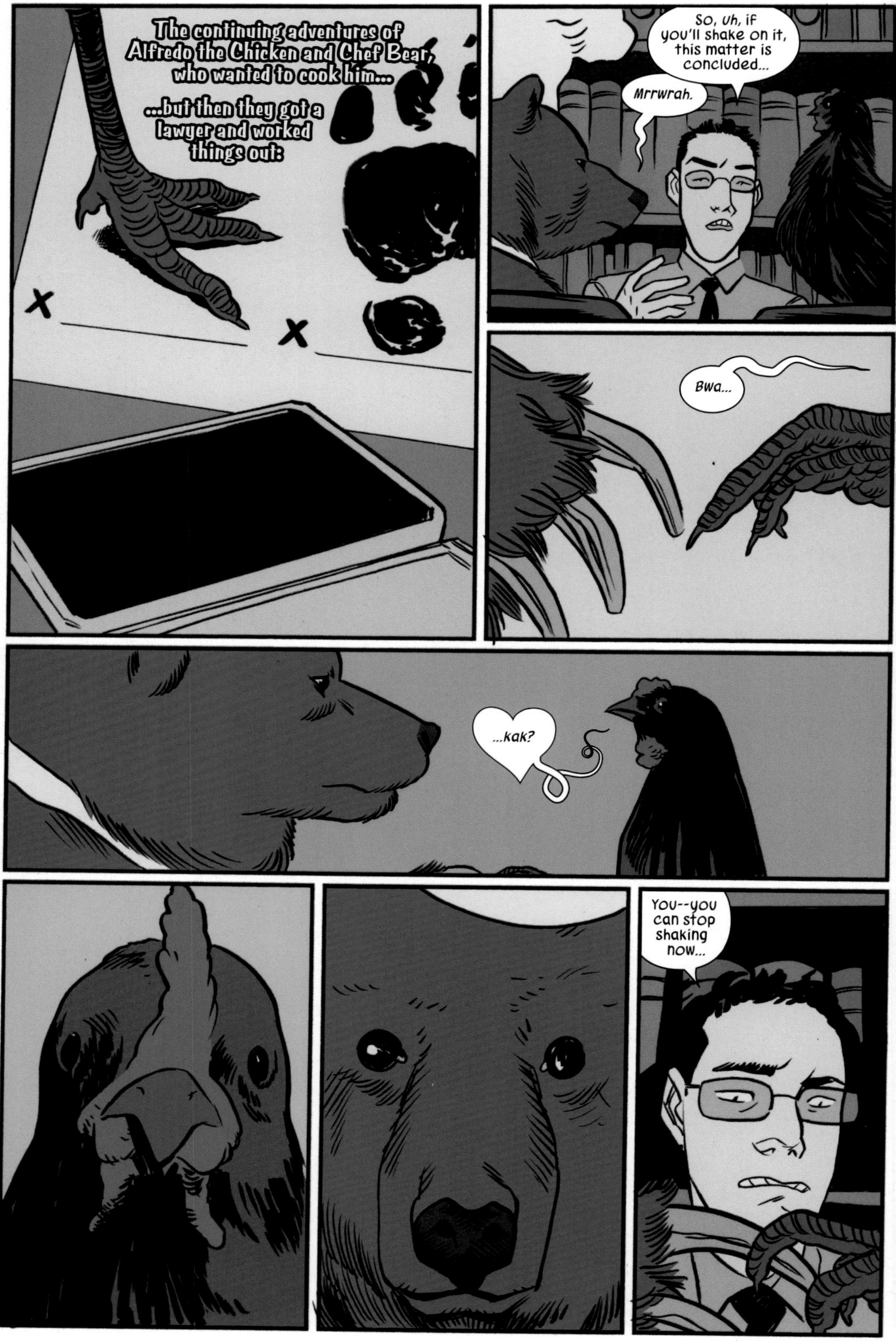
The continuing adventures of Alfredo the Chicken and Chef Bear, who wanted to cook him...
...but then they got a lawyer and worked things out:
X
X
So, uh, if you'll shake on it, this matter is concluded...
Mrrwrah.
Bwa...
...kak?
You--you can stop shaking now...

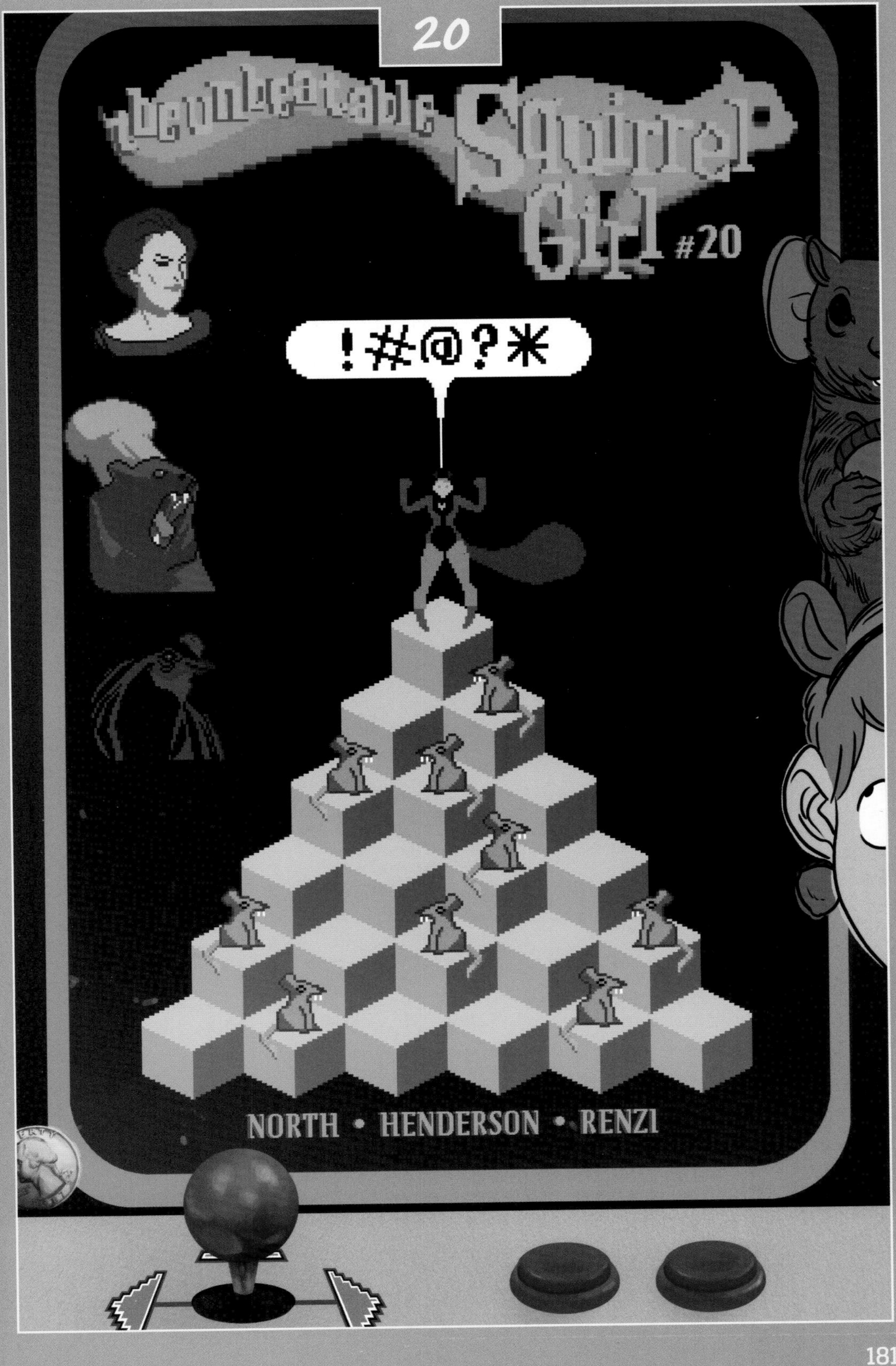
20
the unbeatable Squirrel Girl #20
!*@?*
NORTH • HENDERSON • RENZI

Doreen Green isn't just a second-year computer science student: she secretly also has all the powers of both squirrel and girl! She uses her amazing abilities to fight crime **and** be as awesome as possible. You know her as...**The Unbeatable Squirrel Girl!** Find out what she's been up to, with...

Squirrel Girl *in a nutshell*

search!

#tippyshaircareregimen

#doomsgiantthirstymouth

#alfredothechicken

#chefbear

#lilbusta

#jjj

 Squirrel Girl @unbeatablesg
MELISSA MORBECK CALL-OUT POST

 Squirrel Girl @unbeatablesg
She publicly acts like she's this kind tech billionaire lady with awesome teas, but it's not true! SHE'S AMASSING AN ANIMAL ARMY!!

 Squirrel Girl @unbeatablesg
She controls them through microchips in their brains! It's gross! She made cockroaches put a shrunken computer in her EAR!!

 Squirrel Girl @unbeatablesg
(Fun fact: when I got up this morning, I did not want to see cockroaches put a shrunken ANYTHING in ANYONE'S ear, but here we are)

 Squirrel Girl @unbeatablesg
Anyway, that banner pulled by birds that says Doctor Doom is behind this? Don't believe it! It's her! IT'S ALWAYS HER.

 Squirrel Girl @unbeatablesg
SHE'S the one who makes animals act like jerks! She's the one threatening the city with disease-carrying mosquitoes!!

 Mosquito Man @skeetyman
Well met, @unbeatablesg! Sounds like you need the pest-repelling power... of MOSQUITO MAN!

 Squirrel Girl @unbeatablesg
@skeetyman wait, for real?

 Squirrel Girl @unbeatablesg
@skeetyman Okay this is awesome, I am always happy to meet another hero!

 Squirrel Girl @unbeatablesg
@skeetyman Mosquito Man, I too fight for justice. If you can break the mosquitoes from Melissa's control, WE CAN SAVE THE DAY.

 Squirrel Girl @unbeatablesg
@skeetyman Follow me so I can DM coordinates to meet up!

 Mosquito Man @skeetyman
@unbeatablesg Our coordinates are your local Mosquito Man retailer! Say "bye" to bugs with over FOUR power-packed citronella scents!

 Squirrel Girl @unbeatablesg
@skeetyman oh my god i thought you were a super hero but you're a brand of bugspray

 Squirrel Girl @unbeatablesg
@skeetyman i can't believe we're in the middle of a city-wide crisis and you're selling bugspray and citronella candles on social media

 Squirrel Girl @unbeatablesg
@skeetyman look up "disappointment" on Wikipedia and the entire article is just a screengrab of this convo

 Mosquito Man @skeetyman
@unbeatablesg Don't forget to tell your followers we're the Bugspray That Bites Back™ for 10% off your next purchase!

 Squirrel Girl @unbeatablesg
@skeetyman NO

Squirrel Girl @unbeatablesg
@skeetyman i will NOT

 Tippy-Toe @yoitstippytoe
@unbeatablesg chtt cchttk ktttc

 Squirrel Girl @unbeatablesg
@yoitstippytoe true enough Tippy, I should get back to saving the day instead of sassing #brands online

 Tippy-Toe @yoitstippytoe
@unbeatablesg churrkt chrtt

Squirrel Girl @unbeatablesg
@yoitstippytoe also yes, I should change into my super-hero outfit real quick

 **Tippy-Toe** @yoitstippytoe
@unbeatablesg cktt chutt!

Squirrel Girl @unbeatablesg
@yoitstippytoe i've never used phone booths?? every restaurant ever has a bathroom i can duck into no problem??

Mosquito Man @skeetyman
@unbeatablesg @yoitstippytoe Speaking of restaurants, are you a restaurateur with a patio? Mosquito Man can help keep the bugs at bay!

 Squirrel Girl @unbeatablesg
@skeetyman OH MY GOD HAS THIS EVER WORKED

The DEADLIEST Animal in the World

What is the most dangerous game? (In the "animal" sense, not in the "board game" sense, though I believe the most dangerous board game is Jenga because it could fall on you?) Is it snakes? Sharks? Humans themselves? Hah hah no, it's none of those--it's **MOSQUITOES.** Check it out:

APPROX NUMBER OF HUMANS KILLED BY ANIMALS PER YEAR:

(according to the World Health Organization, who would know this sort of thing)

	SHARKS
10	WOLVES
10	LIONS
100	ELEPHANTS
100	HIPPOS
500	CROCS
1,000	FRESHWATER SNAILS
10,000	RABID DOGS
25,000	SNAKES
50,000	
475,000	HUMAN-ON-HUMAN VIOLENCE, HEY, HUMANS, MAYBE CALM DOWN A BIT
725,000	MOSQUITOES

So yeah, mosquitoes can carry disease, and they're on every continent except Antarctica, so if you find yourself surrounded by unfamiliar mosquitoes, maybe don't offer up some bare arms to these flying blood parasites right away, huh??

Snails: *Surprisingly* high up on that list, yeah? Turns out it's not the snails themselves that are a threat *(phew)*, but parasites they carry that can mess with humans too. Nice try, snails! You want everyone to think you're tough but now we all know you're just surprisingly unwell!!

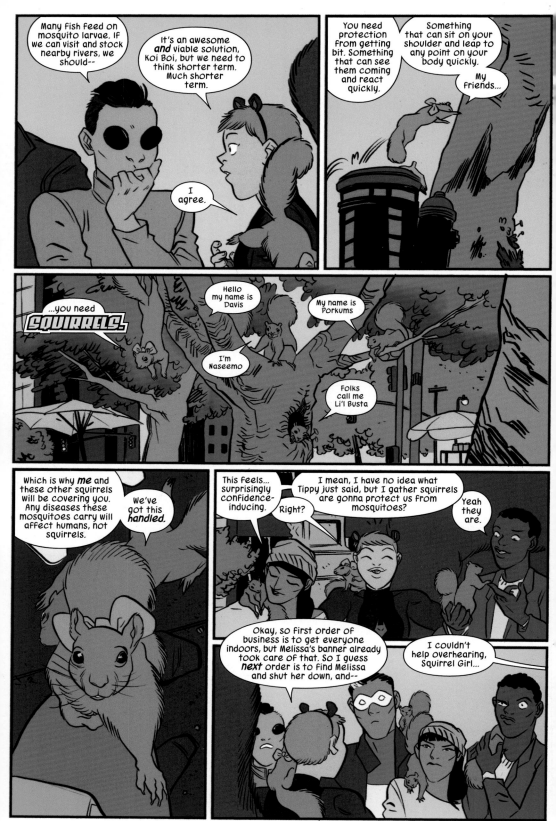

Other squirrels (not pictured) include "Professor Twigs," "Danni," and "Catherine 'the Cashew' Pawsworth." They don't show up in this issue, but they're having a great time! This guy in the park is feeding them his entire hot dog bun! It's like their best day ever!!

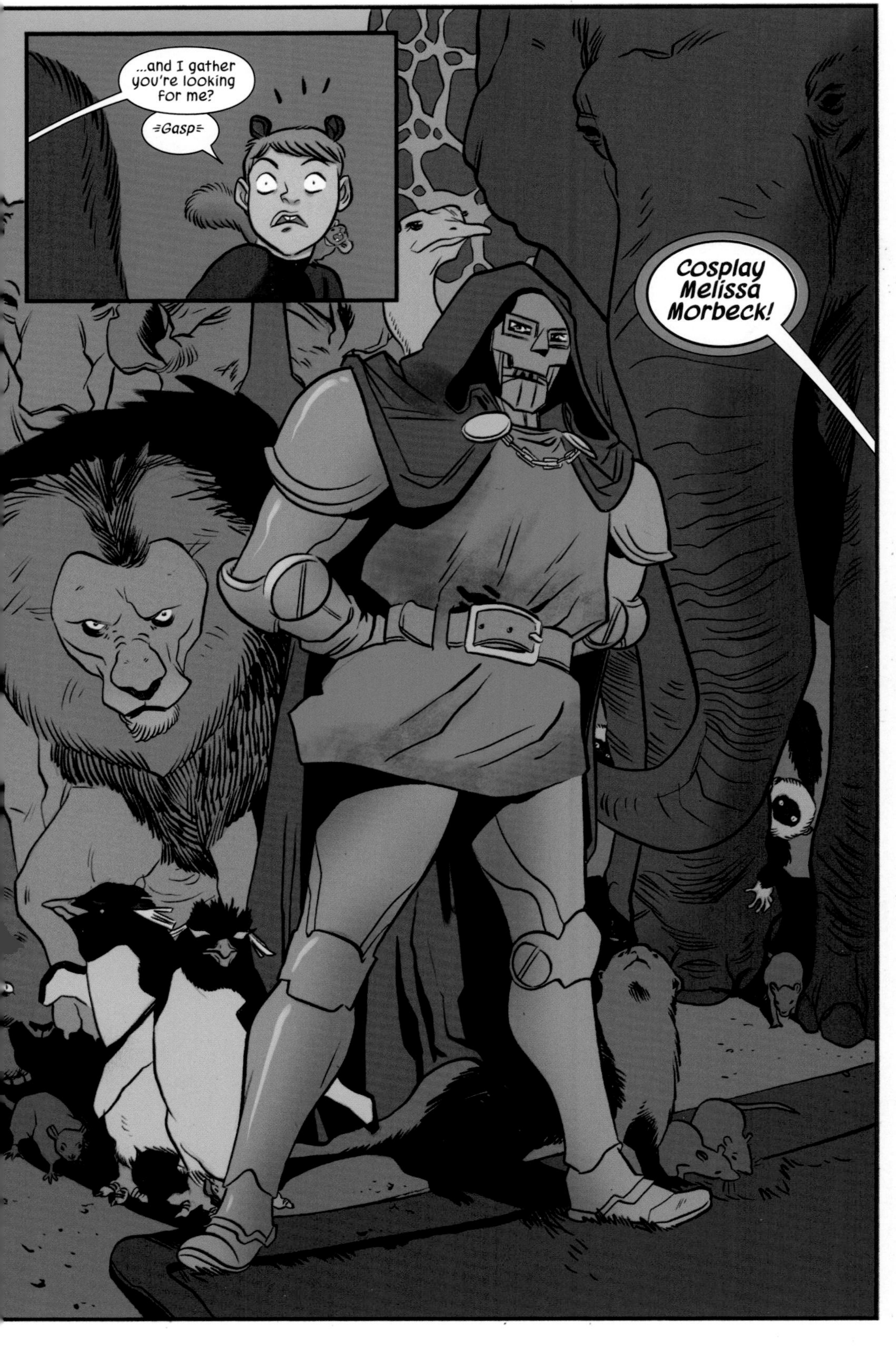
...and I gather you're looking for me?
=Gasp=
Cosplay Melissa Morbeck!

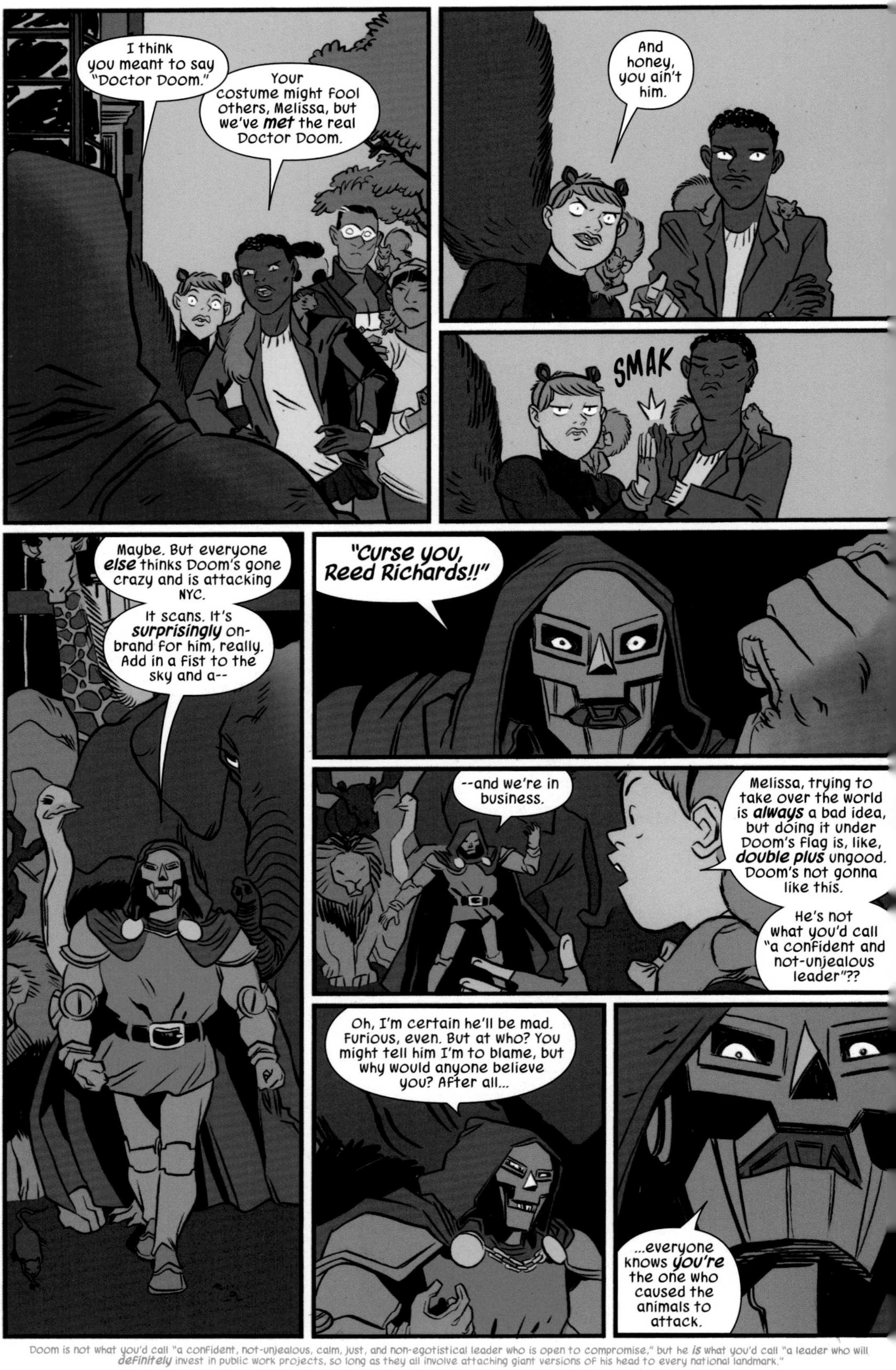
I think you meant to say "Doctor Doom."
Your costume might fool others, Melissa, but we've *met* the real Doctor Doom.
And honey, you ain't him.
SMAK
Maybe. But everyone *else* thinks Doom's gone crazy and is attacking NYC.
It scans. It's *surprisingly* on-brand for him, really. Add in a fist to the sky and a--
"Curse you, Reed Richards!!"
--and we're in business.
Melissa, trying to take over the world is *always* a bad idea, but doing it under Doom's flag is, like, *double plus* ungood. Doom's not gonna like this.
He's not what you'd call "a confident and not-unjealous leader"??
Oh, I'm certain he'll be mad. Furious, even. But at who? You might tell him I'm to blame, but why would anyone believe you? After all...
...everyone knows *you're* the one who caused the animals to attack.

Doom is not what you'd call "a confident, not-unjealous, calm, just, and non-egotistical leader who is open to compromise," but he *is* what you'd call "a leader who will *definitely* invest in public work projects, so long as they all involve attaching giant versions of his head to every national landmark."

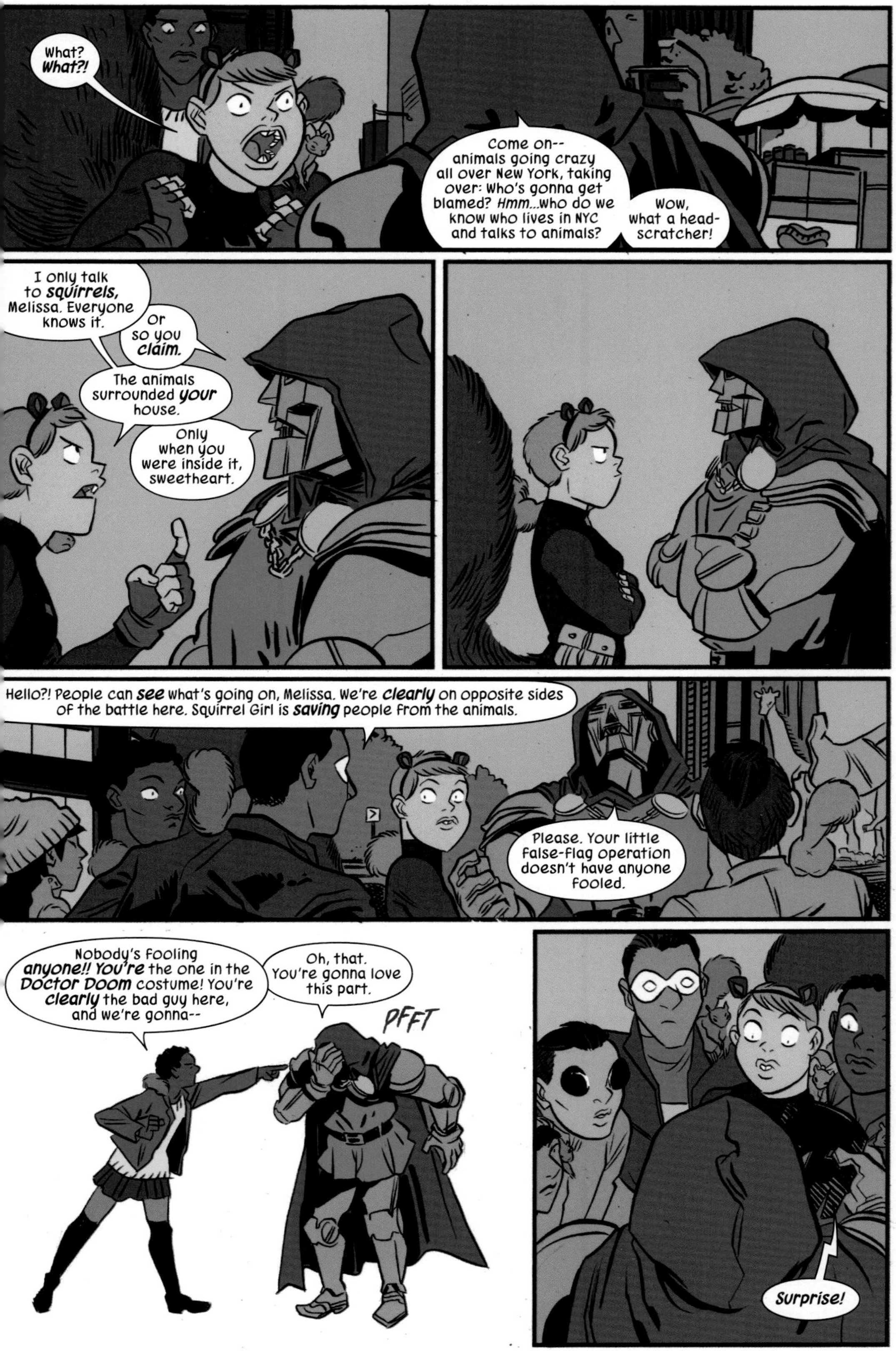
What? What?!
Come on-- animals going crazy all over New York, taking over: Who's gonna get blamed? Hmm...who do we know who lives in NYC and talks to animals?
Wow, what a head-scratcher!
I only talk to squirrels, Melissa. Everyone knows it.
Or so you claim.
The animals surrounded your house.
Only when you were inside it, sweetheart.
Hello?! People can see what's going on, Melissa. We're clearly on opposite sides of the battle here. Squirrel Girl is saving people from the animals.
Please. Your little false-flag operation doesn't have anyone fooled.
Nobody's fooling anyone!! You're the one in the Doctor Doom costume! You're clearly the bad guy here, and we're gonna--
Oh, that. You're gonna love this part.
PFFT
Surprise!

I'm sorry for mentioning "Doom attaching giant versions of his head to national landmarks" on the last page and then not having that show up, because now it's all you want to see! I understand. To satisfy your curiosity, please just imagine Mount Rushmore except everyone's in a Doom mask, the Washington Monument except with Doom's head on top, and Niagara Falls only with all the water tumbling down into Doom's giant thirsty mouth.

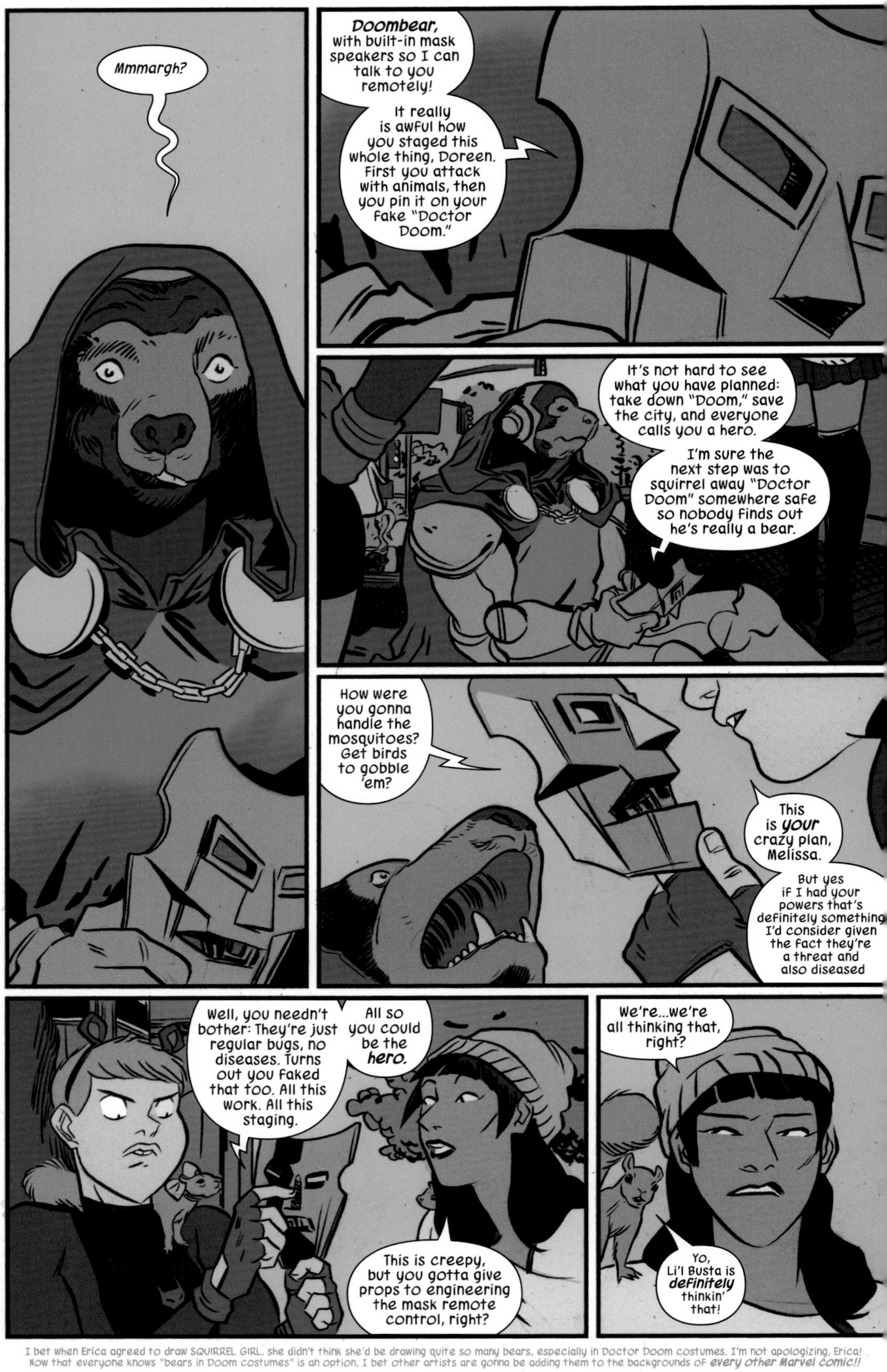
Mmmargh?
Doombear, with built-in mask speakers so I can talk to you remotely!
It really is awful how you staged this whole thing, Doreen. First you attack with animals, then you pin it on your fake "Doctor Doom."
It's not hard to see what you have planned: take down "Doom," save the city, and everyone calls you a hero.
I'm sure the next step was to squirrel away "Doctor Doom" somewhere safe so nobody finds out he's really a bear.
How were you gonna handle the mosquitoes? Get birds to gobble 'em?
This is your crazy plan, Melissa.
But yes if I had your powers that's definitely something I'd consider given the fact they're a threat and also diseased
Well, you needn't bother: They're just regular bugs, no diseases. Turns out you faked that too. All this work. All this staging.
All so you could be the hero.
This is creepy, but you gotta give props to engineering the mask remote control, right?
We're...we're all thinking that, right?
Yo, Li'l Busta is definitely thinkin' that!

I bet when Erica agreed to draw SQUIRREL GIRL, she didn't think she'd be drawing quite so many bears, especially in Doctor Doom costumes. I'm not apologizing, Erica! Now that everyone knows "bears in Doom costumes" is an option, I bet other artists are gonna be adding them to the backgrounds of ***every other Marvel comic!!***

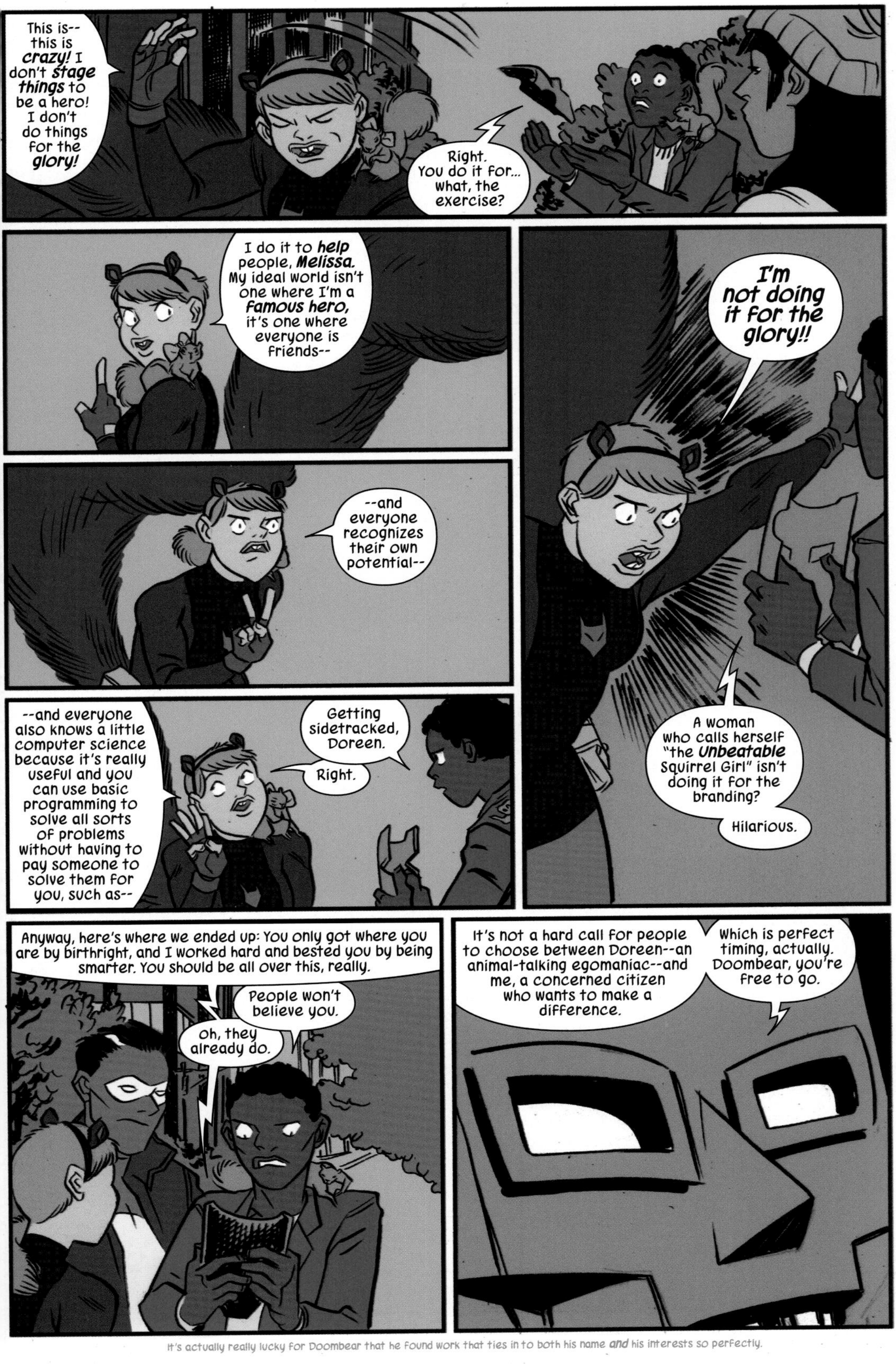
This is-- this is *crazy!* I don't *stage things* to be a hero! I don't do things for the *glory!*
Right. You do it for... what, the exercise?
I do it to *help* people, *Melissa.* My ideal world isn't one where I'm a *famous hero,* it's one where everyone is friends--
I'm not doing it for the glory!!
--and everyone recognizes their own potential--
--and everyone also knows a little computer science because it's really useful and you can use basic programming to solve all sorts of problems without having to pay someone to solve them for you, such as--
Getting sidetracked, Doreen.
Right.
A woman who calls herself "the *Unbeatable* Squirrel Girl" isn't doing it for the branding?
Hilarious.
Anyway, here's where we ended up: You only got where you are by birthright, and I worked hard and bested you by being smarter. You should be all over this, really.
People won't believe you.
Oh, they already do.
It's not a hard call for people to choose between Doreen--an animal-talking egomaniac--and me, a concerned citizen who wants to make a difference.
Which is perfect timing, actually. Doombear, you're free to go.

It's actually really lucky for Doombear that he found work that ties in to both his name *and* his interests so perfectly.

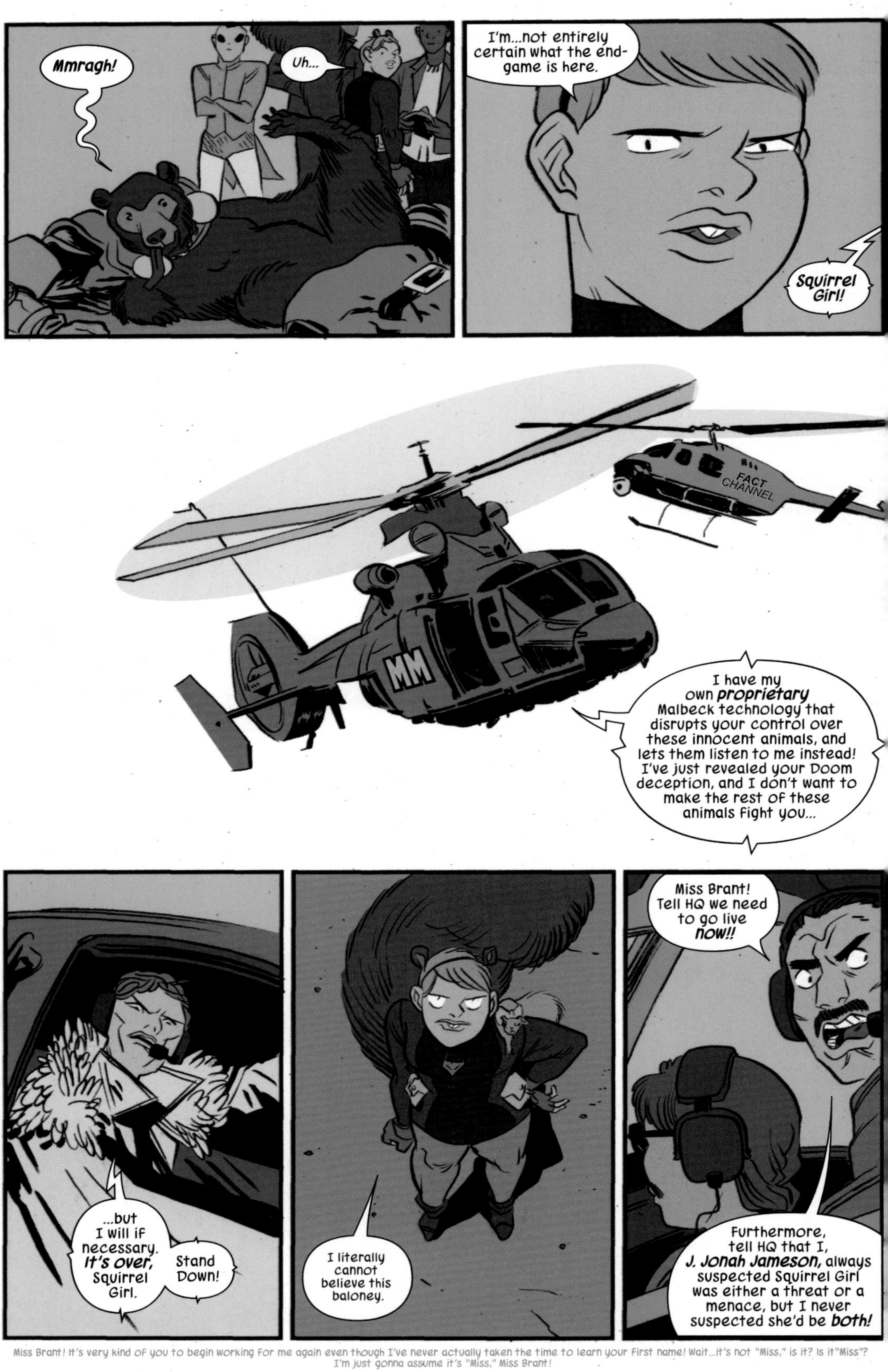
Mmragh!
Uh...
I'm...not entirely certain what the end-game is here.
Squirrel Girl!
FACT CHANNEL
MM
I have my own proprietary Malbeck technology that disrupts your control over these innocent animals, and lets them listen to me instead! I've just revealed your Doom deception, and I don't want to make the rest of these animals fight you...
...but I will if necessary. It's over, Squirrel Girl.
Stand Down!
I literally cannot believe this baloney.
Miss Brant! Tell HQ we need to go live now!!
Furthermore, tell HQ that I, J. Jonah Jameson, always suspected Squirrel Girl was either a threat or a menace, but I never suspected she'd be both!

Miss Brant! It's very kind of you to begin working for me again even though I've never actually taken the time to learn your first name! Wait...it's not "Miss," is it? Is it "Miss"? I'm just gonna assume it's "Miss," Miss Brant!

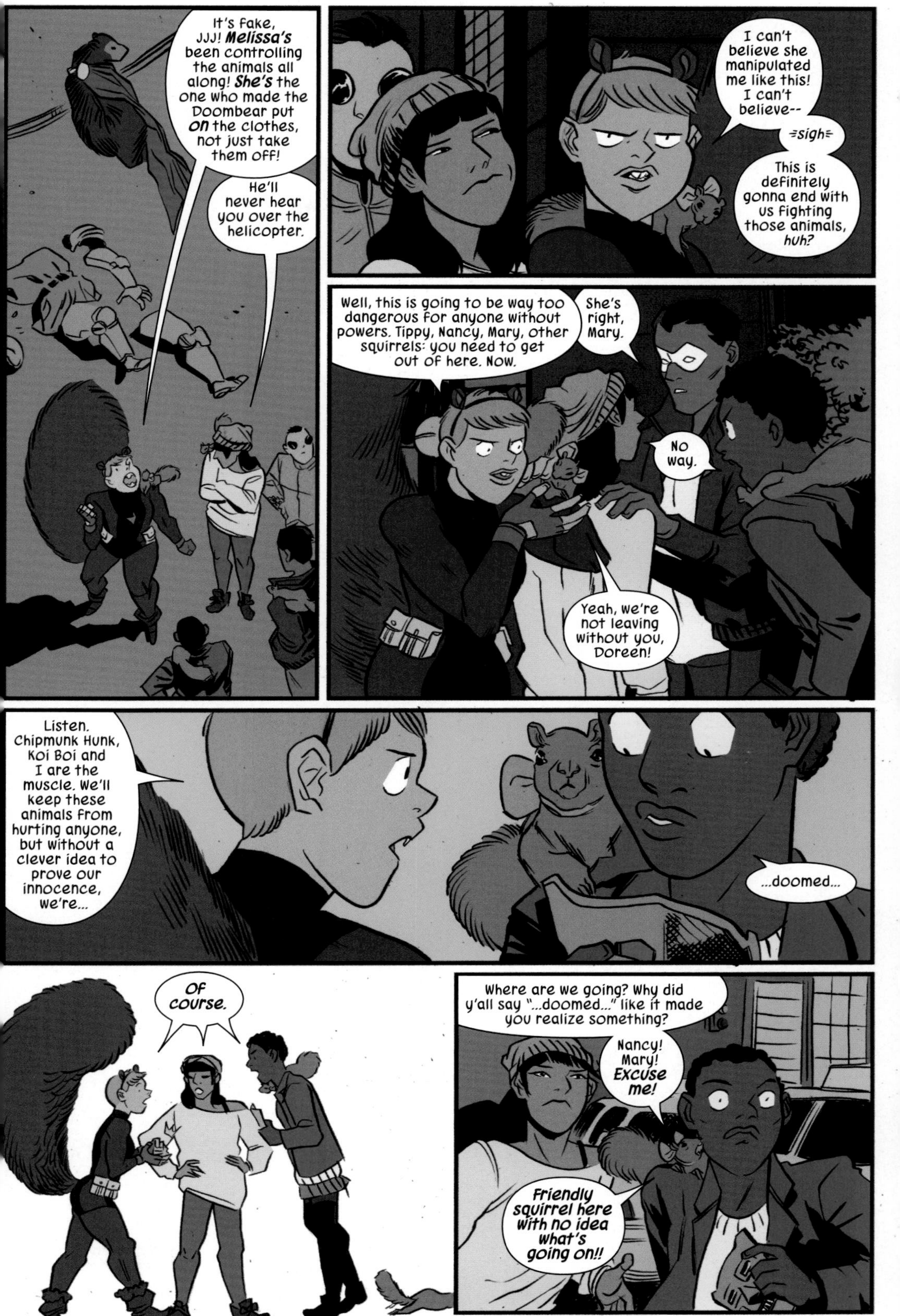
It's fake, JJJ! *Melissa's* been controlling the animals all along! *She's* the one who made the Doombear put *on* the clothes, not just take them off!
He'll never hear you over the helicopter.
I can't believe she manipulated me like this! I can't believe--
=sigh=
This is definitely gonna end with us fighting those animals, *huh?*
Well, this is going to be way too dangerous for anyone without powers. Tippy, Nancy, Mary, other squirrels: you need to get out of here. Now.
She's right, Mary.
No way.
Yeah, we're not leaving without you, Doreen!
Listen. Chipmunk Hunk, Koi Boi and I are the muscle. We'll keep these animals from hurting anyone, but without a clever idea to prove our innocence, we're...
...doomed...
Of course.
Where are we going? Why did y'all say "...doomed..." like it made you realize something?
Nancy! Mary! *Excuse me!*
Friendly squirrel here with no idea what's going on!!

Helicopters are extremely loud, especially for the people on them! We didn't add them here, but just imagine large ***"whump whump whump," "bzzzrrrrrrtttt,"*** and ***"[HOLY SMOKES, EVEN MORE LOUD HELICOPTER NOISES??]"*** sound effects drawn all over the appropriate panels.

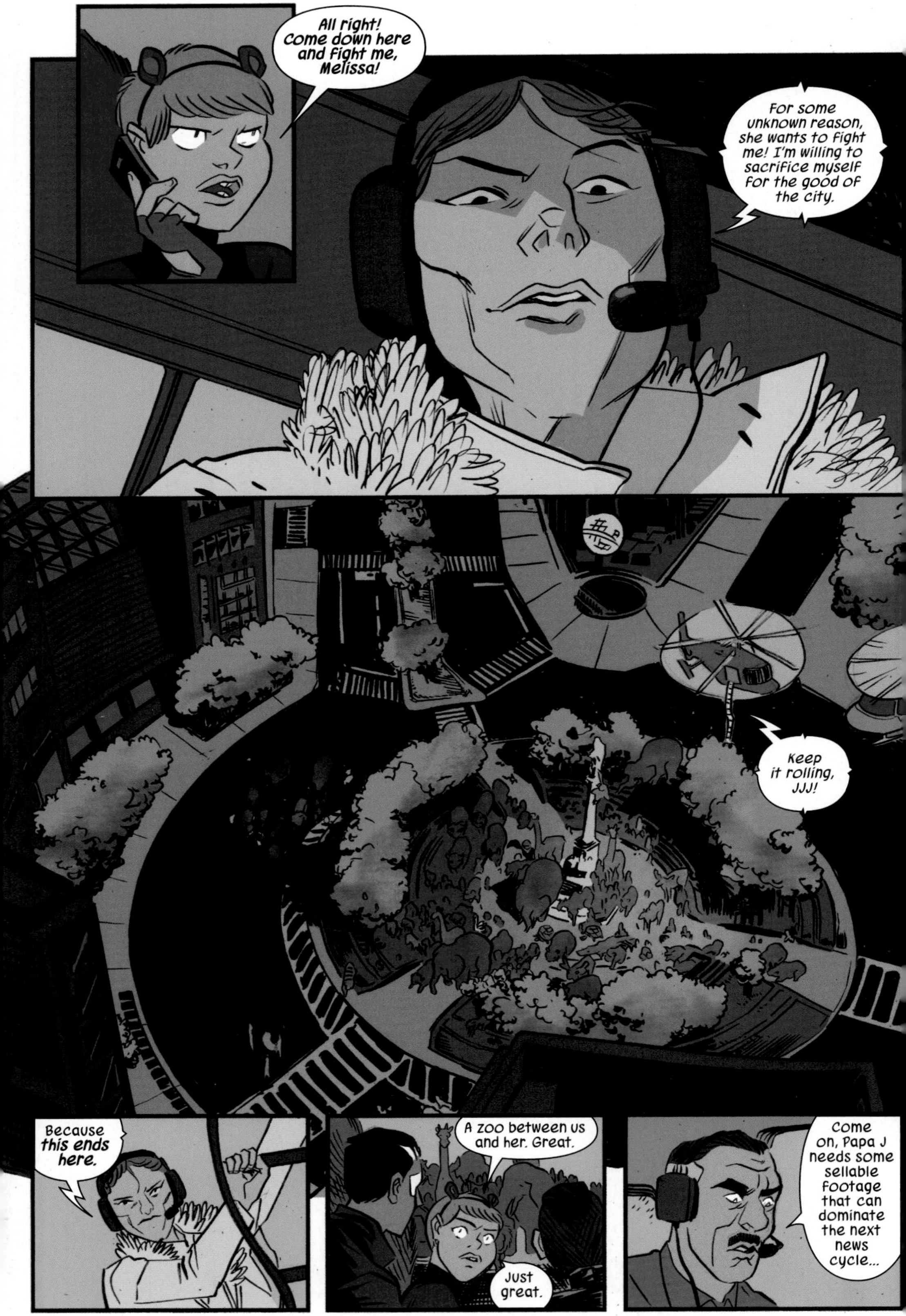
All right! Come down here and fight me, Melissa!
For some unknown reason, she wants to fight me! I'm willing to sacrifice myself for the good of the city.
Keep it rolling, JJJ!
Because this ends here.
A zoo between us and her. Great.
Just great.
Come on, Papa J needs some sellable footage that can dominate the next news cycle...

Does J. Jonah Jameson *always* privately refer to himself as "Papa J"? Other comics say "no," but this comic says..."maybe"?.

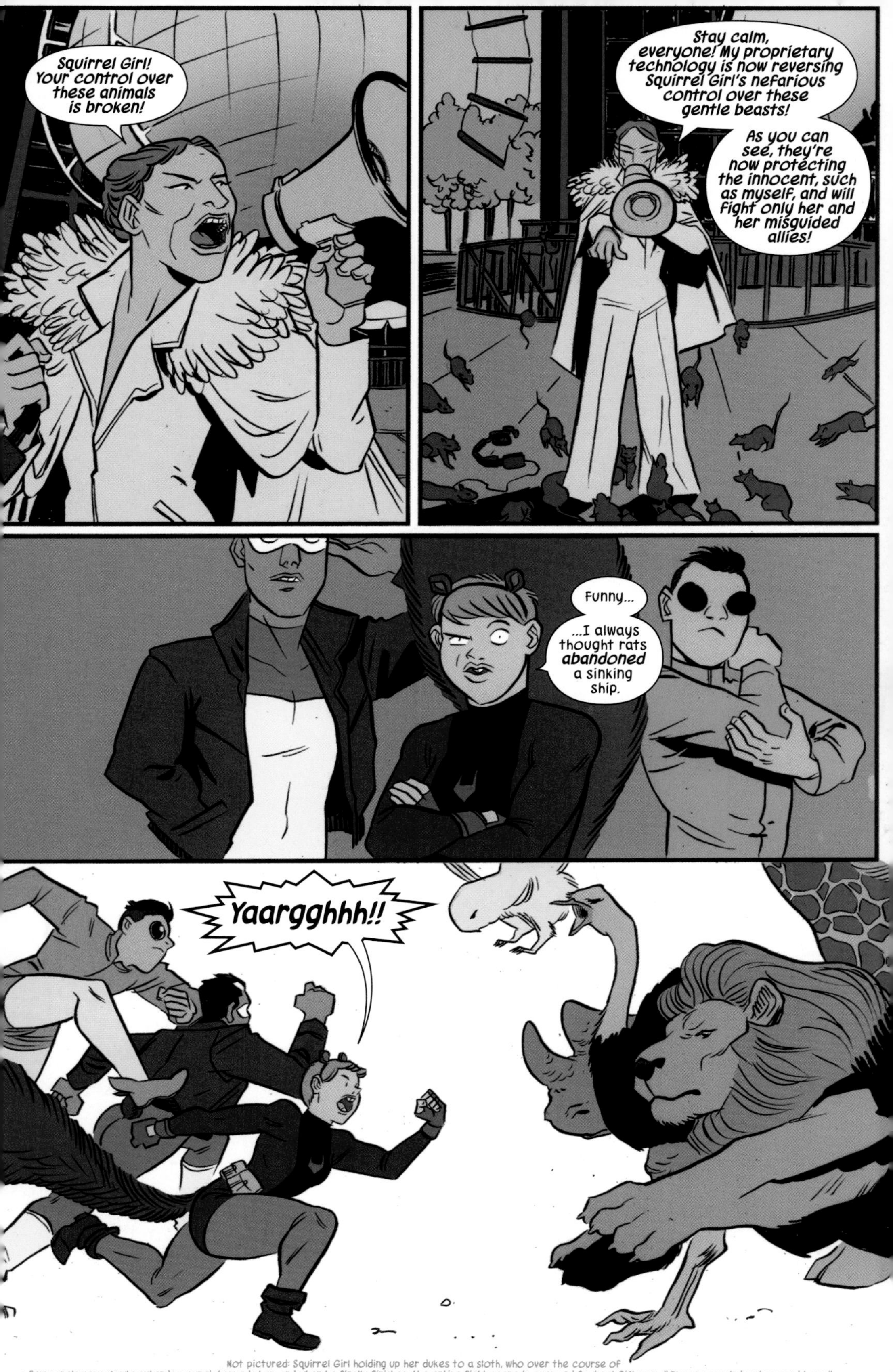

Squirrel Girl! Your control over these animals is broken!
Stay calm, everyone! My proprietary technology is now reversing Squirrel Girl's nefarious control over these gentle beasts!
As you can see, they're now protecting the innocent, such as myself, and will fight only her and her misguided allies!
Funny...
...I always thought rats abandoned a sinking ship.
Yaargghhh!!

Not pictured: Squirrel Girl holding up her dukes to a sloth, who over the course of a few panels very slowly extends a punch towards her, and when he finally finishes, the entire fight scene is over and Squirrel Girl says, "Okay nevermind we're good here."

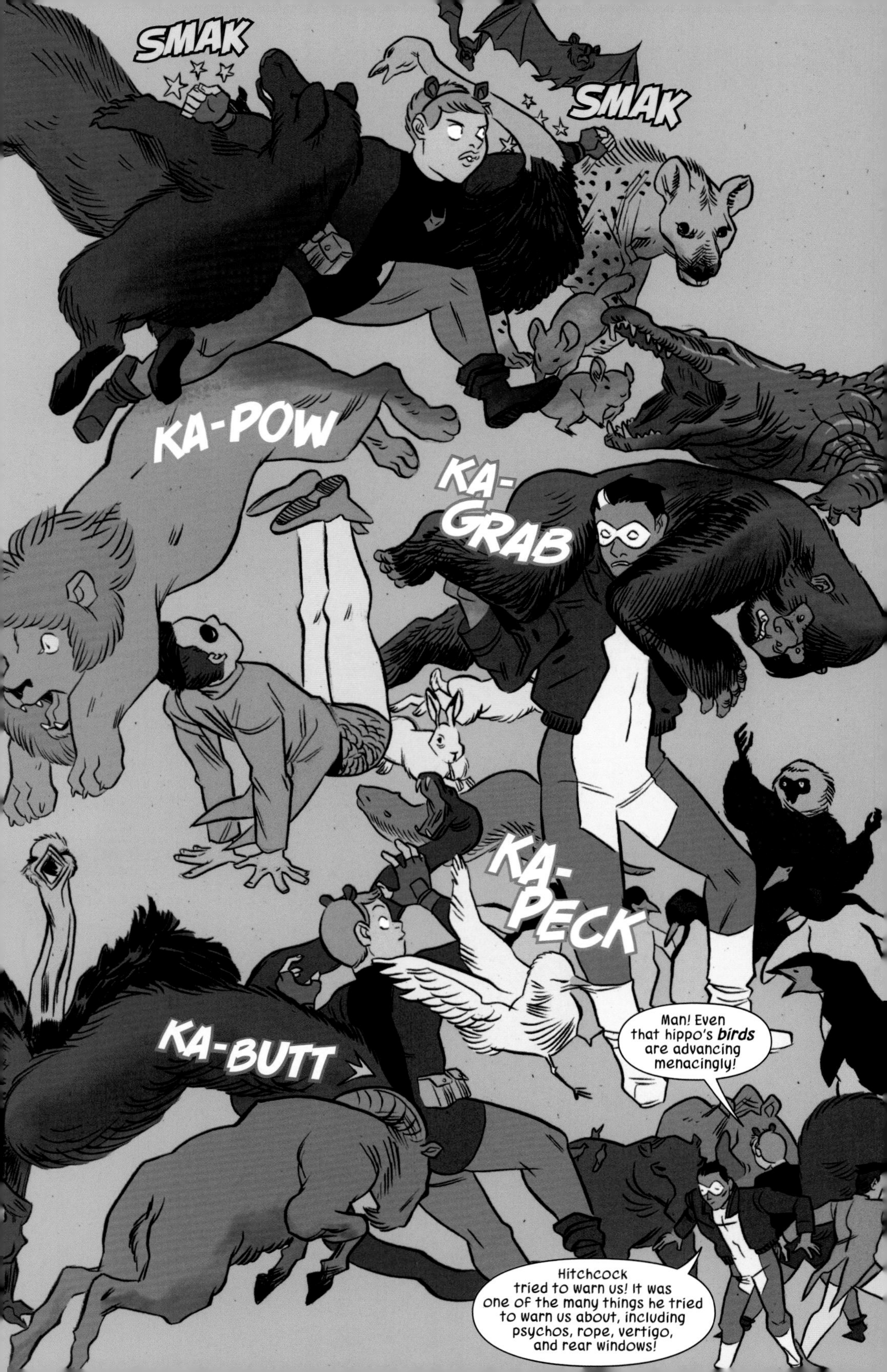
SMAK
SMAK
KA-POW
KA-GRAB
KA-PECK
KA-BUTT
Man! Even that hippo's ***birds*** are advancing menacingly!
Hitchcock tried to warn us! It was one of the many things he tried to warn us about, including psychos, rope, vertigo, and rear windows!

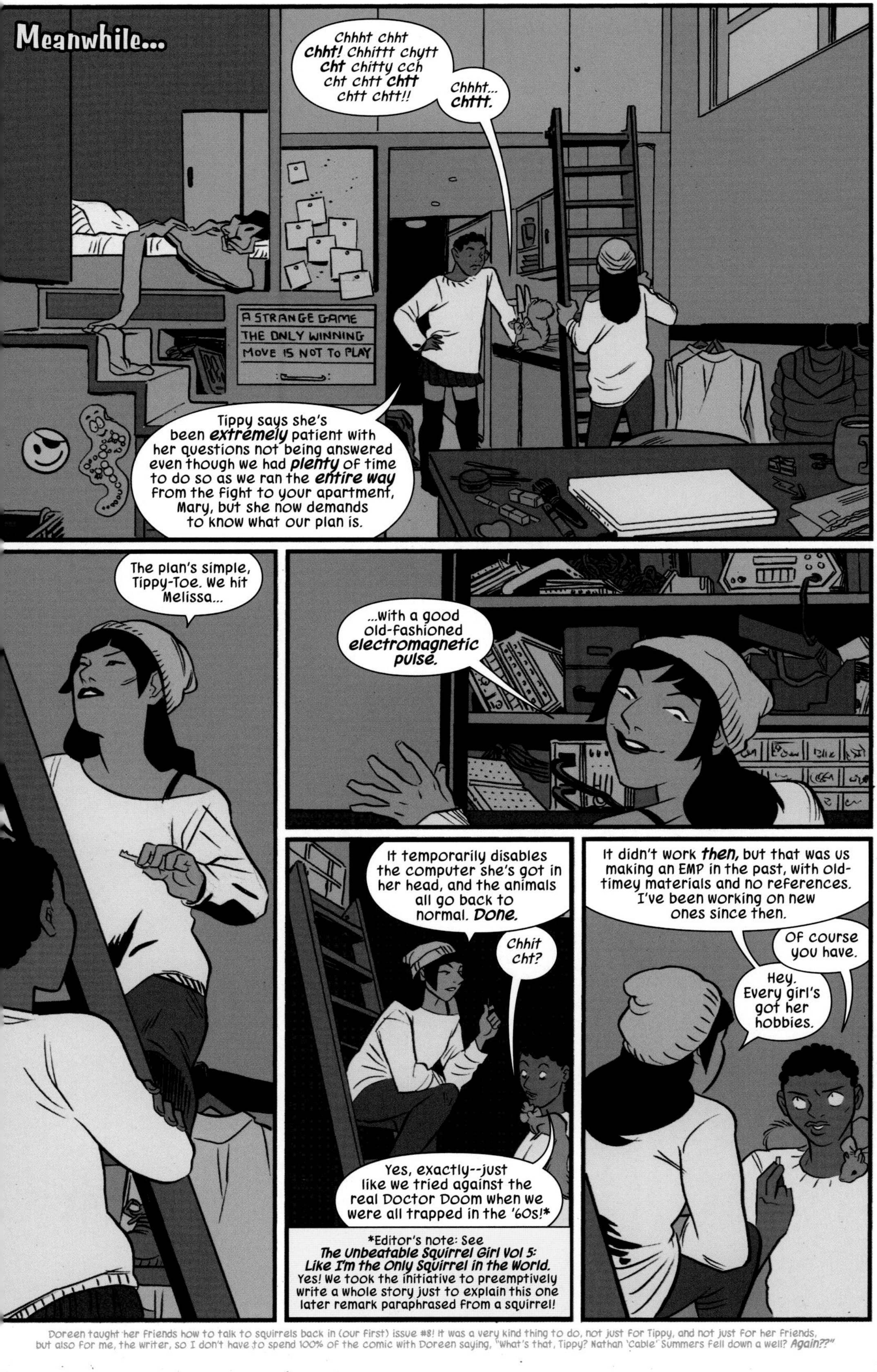

Meanwhile...
Chhht chht chht! Chhittt chytt cht chitty cch cht chtt chtt chtt chtt!!
Chhht... chttt.
A STRANGE GAME
THE ONLY WINNING
MOVE IS NOT TO PLAY
Tippy says she's been extremely patient with her questions not being answered even though we had plenty of time to do so as we ran the entire way from the fight to your apartment, Mary, but she now demands to know what our plan is.
The plan's simple, Tippy-Toe. We hit Melissa...
...with a good old-fashioned electromagnetic pulse.
It temporarily disables the computer she's got in her head, and the animals all go back to normal. Done.
Chhit cht?
Yes, exactly--just like we tried against the real Doctor Doom when we were all trapped in the '60s!*
*Editor's note: See The Unbeatable Squirrel Girl Vol 5: Like I'm the Only Squirrel in the World. Yes! We took the initiative to preemptively write a whole story just to explain this one later remark paraphrased from a squirrel!
It didn't work then, but that was us making an EMP in the past, with old-timey materials and no references. I've been working on new ones since then.
Of course you have.
Hey. Every girl's got her hobbies.

Doreen taught her friends how to talk to squirrels back in (our first) issue #8! It was a very kind thing to do, not just for Tippy, and not just for her friends, but also for me, the writer, so I don't have to spend 100% of the comic with Doreen saying, "What's that, Tippy? Nathan 'Cable' Summers fell down a well? Again??"

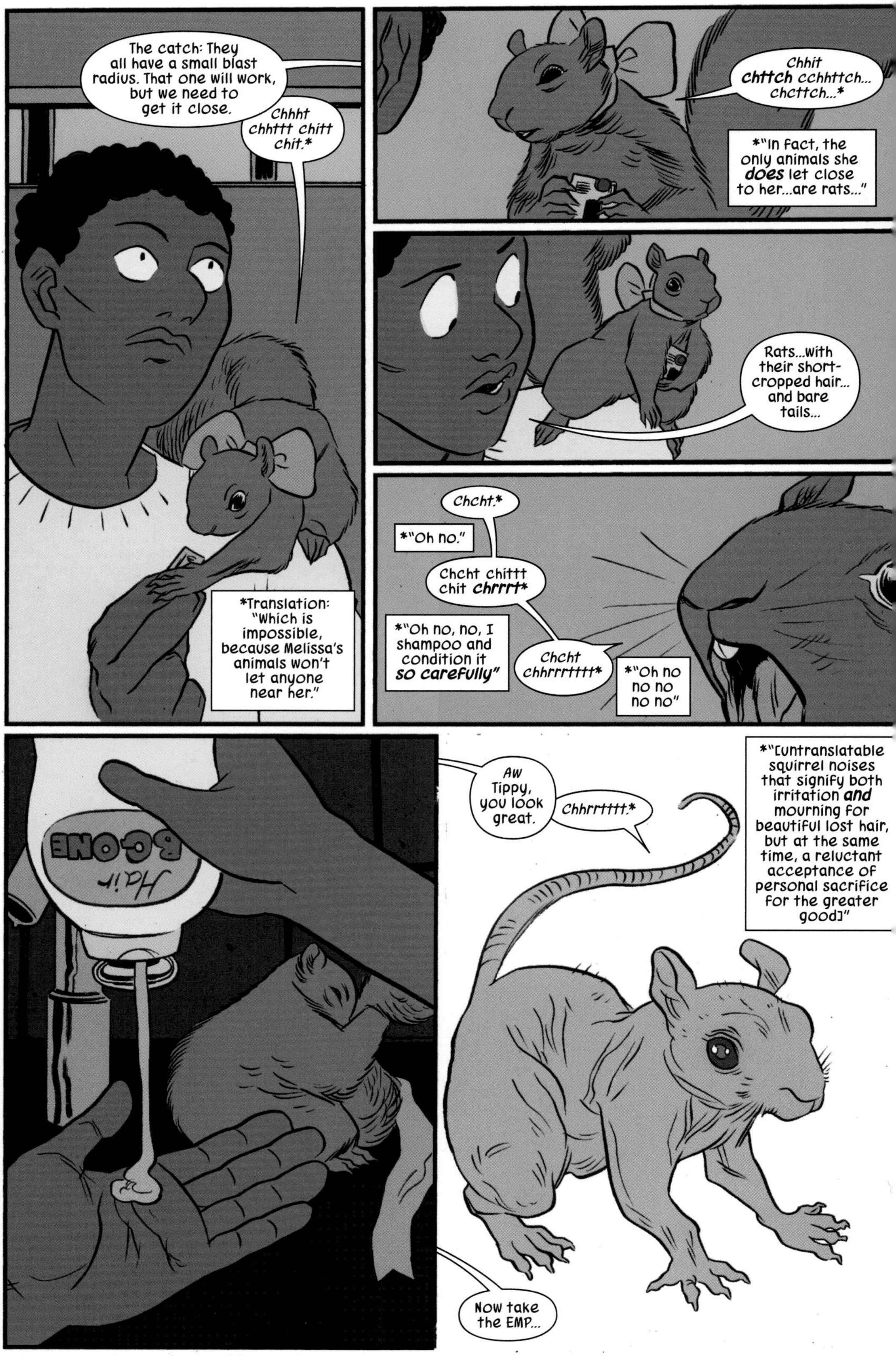
The catch: They all have a small blast radius. That one will work, but we need to get it close.
Chhht chhttt chitt chit.*
*Translation: "Which is impossible, because Melissa's animals won't let anyone near her."
Chhit chttch cchhttch... chcttch...*
*"In fact, the only animals she does let close to her...are rats..."
Rats...with their short-cropped hair... and bare tails...
Chcht.*
*"Oh no."
Chcht chittt chit chrrrt*
*"Oh no, no, I shampoo and condition it so carefully"
Chcht chhrrrtttt*
*"Oh no no no no no"
Hair B-GONE
Aw Tippy, you look great.
Chhrrtttt.*
*"[untranslatable squirrel noises that signify both irritation and mourning for beautiful lost hair, but at the same time, a reluctant acceptance of personal sacrifice for the greater good]"
Now take the EMP...

P.S., in case you're wondering, Nathan "Cable" Summers got out of that well. He's actually in a new well now. It's, *uh*, for unrelated reasons.

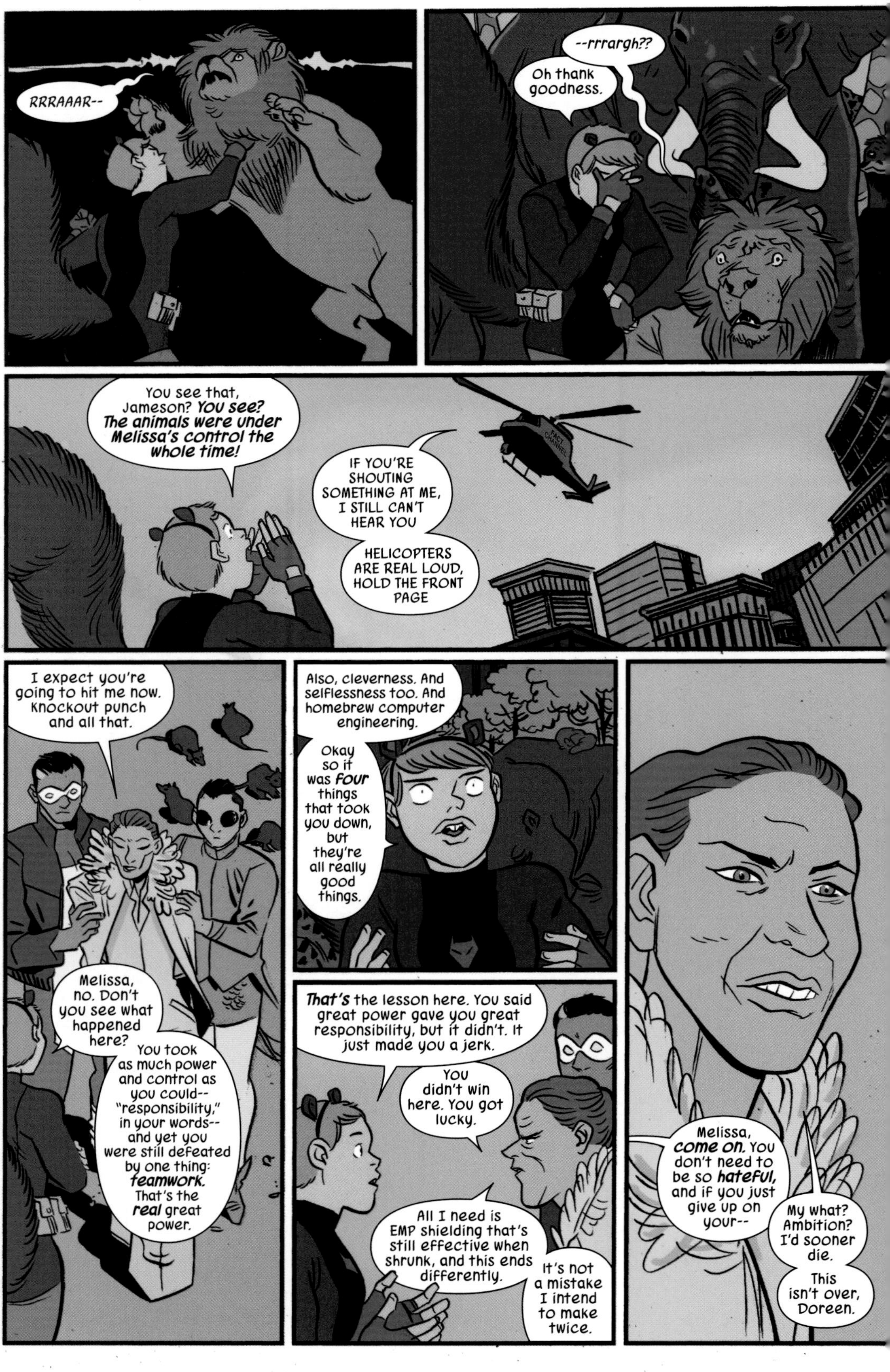
RRRAAAR--
--rrrargh??
Oh thank goodness.
You see that, Jameson? You see? The animals were under Melissa's control the whole time!
IF YOU'RE SHOUTING SOMETHING AT ME, I STILL CAN'T HEAR YOU
HELICOPTERS ARE REAL LOUD, HOLD THE FRONT PAGE
I expect you're going to hit me now. Knockout punch and all that.
Melissa, no. Don't you see what happened here?
You took as much power and control as you could-- "responsibility," in your words-- and yet you were still defeated by one thing: teamwork. That's the real great power.
Also, cleverness. And selflessness too. And homebrew computer engineering.
Okay so it was four things that took you down, but they're all really good things.
That's the lesson here. You said great power gave you great responsibility, but it didn't. It just made you a jerk.
You didn't win here. You got lucky.
All I need is EMP shielding that's still effective when shrunk, and this ends differently.
It's not a mistake I intend to make twice.
Melissa, come on. You don't need to be so hateful, and if you just give up on your--
My what? Ambition? I'd sooner die.
This isn't over, Doreen.

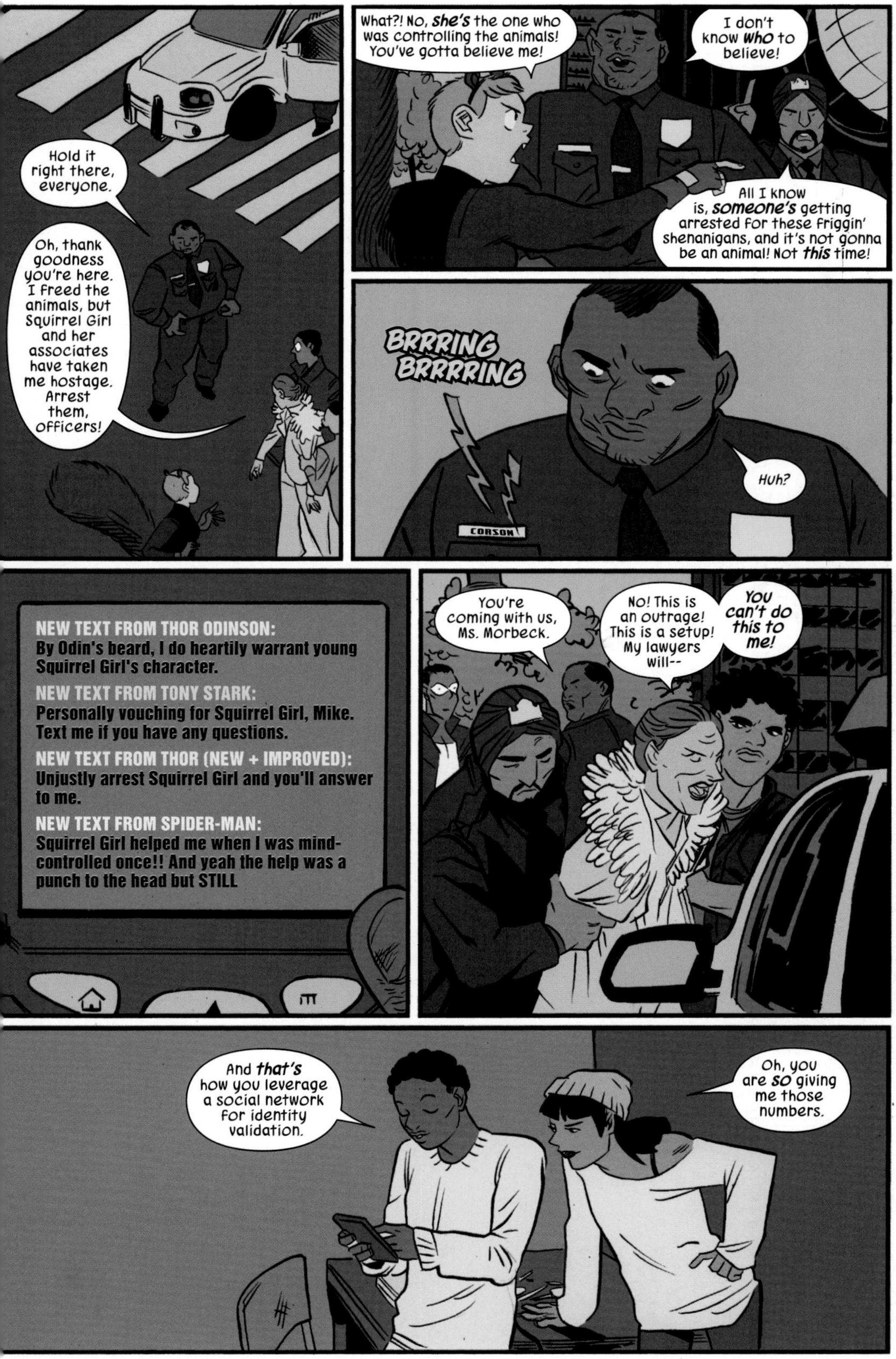
Hold it right there, everyone.
Oh, thank goodness you're here. I freed the animals, but Squirrel Girl and her associates have taken me hostage. Arrest them, officers!
What?! No, she's the one who was controlling the animals! You've gotta believe me!
I don't know who to believe!
All I know is, someone's getting arrested for these friggin' shenanigans, and it's not gonna be an animal! Not this time!
BRRRING BRRRRING
Huh?
CORSON
NEW TEXT FROM THOR ODINSON:
By Odin's beard, I do heartily warrant young Squirrel Girl's character.
NEW TEXT FROM TONY STARK:
Personally vouching for Squirrel Girl, Mike. Text me if you have any questions.
NEW TEXT FROM THOR (NEW + IMPROVED):
Unjustly arrest Squirrel Girl and you'll answer to me.
NEW TEXT FROM SPIDER-MAN:
Squirrel Girl helped me when I was mind-controlled once!! And yeah the help was a punch to the head but STILL
You're coming with us, Ms. Morbeck.
No! This is an outrage! This is a setup! My lawyers will--
You can't do this to me!
And that's how you leverage a social network for identity validation.
Oh, you are so giving me those numbers.

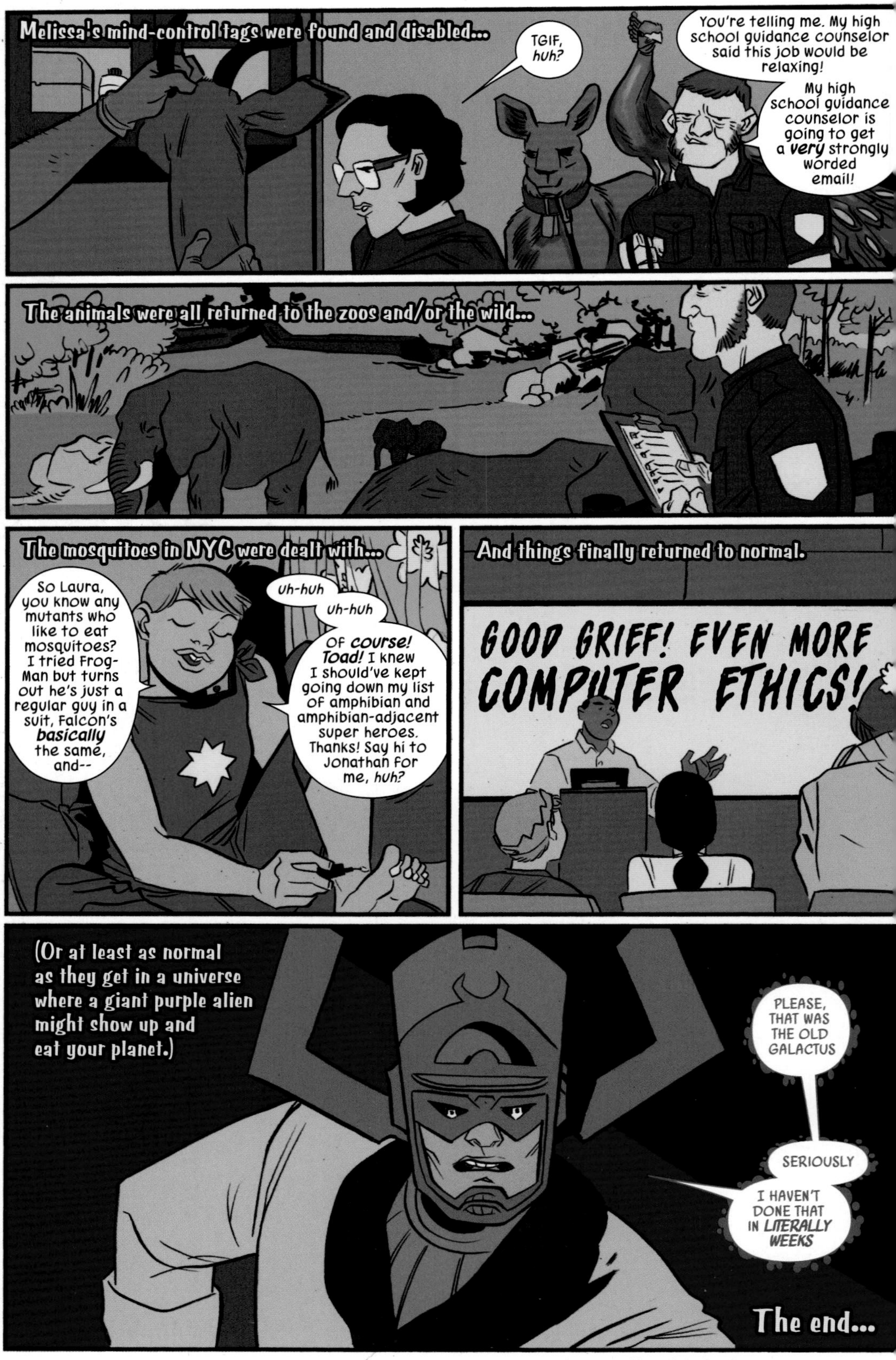

Melissa's mind-control tags were found and disabled...
TGIF, huh?
You're telling me. My high school guidance counselor said this job would be relaxing!
My high school guidance counselor is going to get a very strongly worded email!
The animals were all returned to the zoos and/or the wild...
The mosquitoes in NYC were dealt with...
So Laura, you know any mutants who like to eat mosquitoes? I tried Frog-Man but turns out he's just a regular guy in a suit, Falcon's basically the same, and--
Uh-huh
Uh-huh
Of course! Toad! I knew I should've kept going down my list of amphibian and amphibian-adjacent super heroes. Thanks! Say hi to Jonathan for me, huh?
And things finally returned to normal.
GOOD GRIEF! EVEN MORE COMPUTER ETHICS!
(Or at least as normal as they get in a universe where a giant purple alien might show up and eat your planet.)
PLEASE, THAT WAS THE OLD GALACTUS
SERIOUSLY
I HAVEN'T DONE THAT IN LITERALLY WEEKS
The end...

Laura is X-23, a.k.a. Wolverine! We did a whole comic in which Squirrel Girl met *her*, too, in *All-New Wolverine #7*. We are *all about* dedicating entire issues to set up a single panel over here at Squirrel Girl Headquarters!

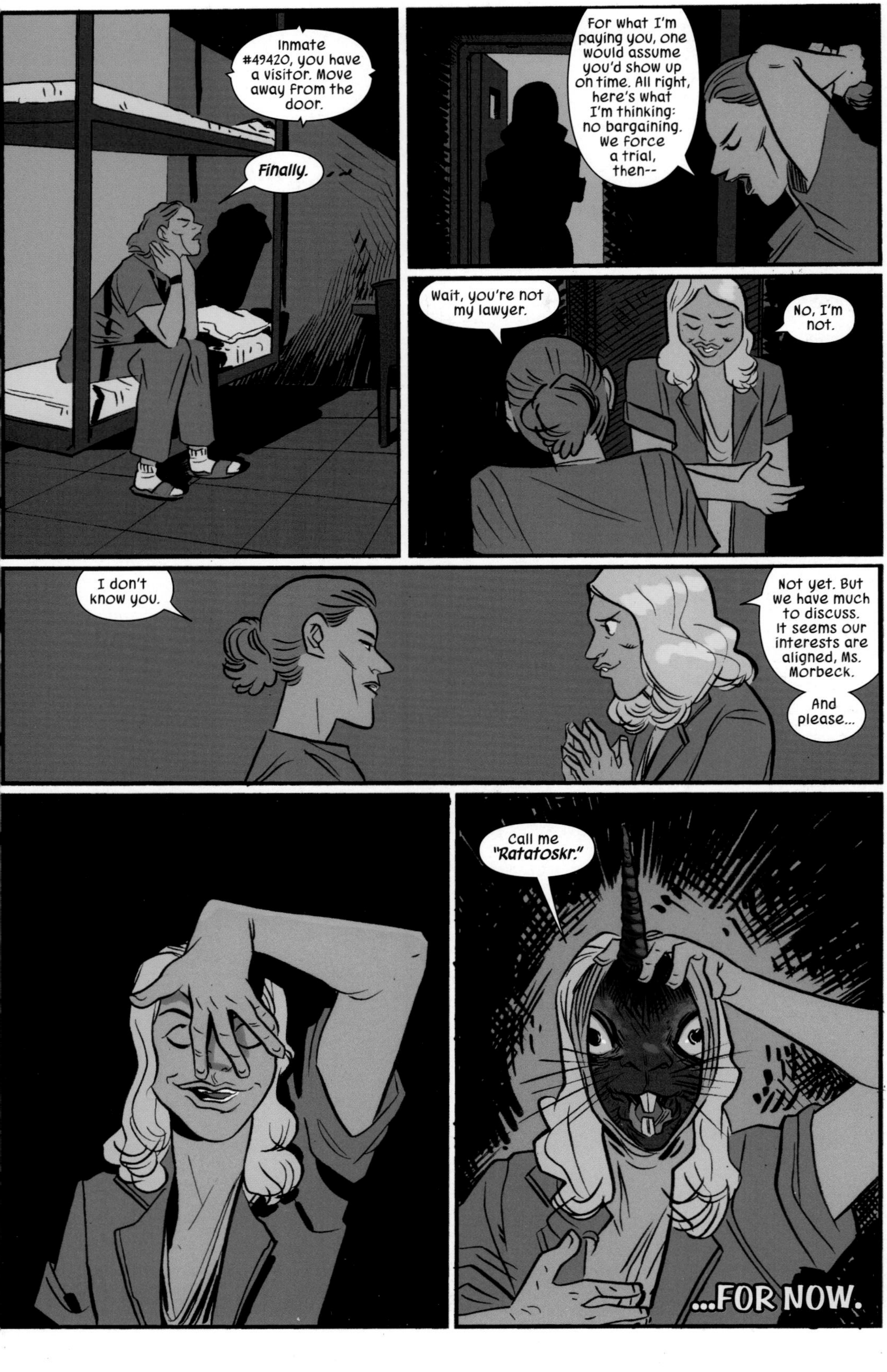

Inmate #49420, you have a visitor. Move away from the door.
Finally.
For what I'm paying you, one would assume you'd show up on time. All right, here's what I'm thinking: no bargaining. We force a trial, then--
Wait, you're not my lawyer.
No, I'm not.
I don't know you.
Not yet. But we have much to discuss. It seems our interests are aligned, Ms. Morbeck.
And please...
Call me "Ratatoskr."
...FOR NOW.

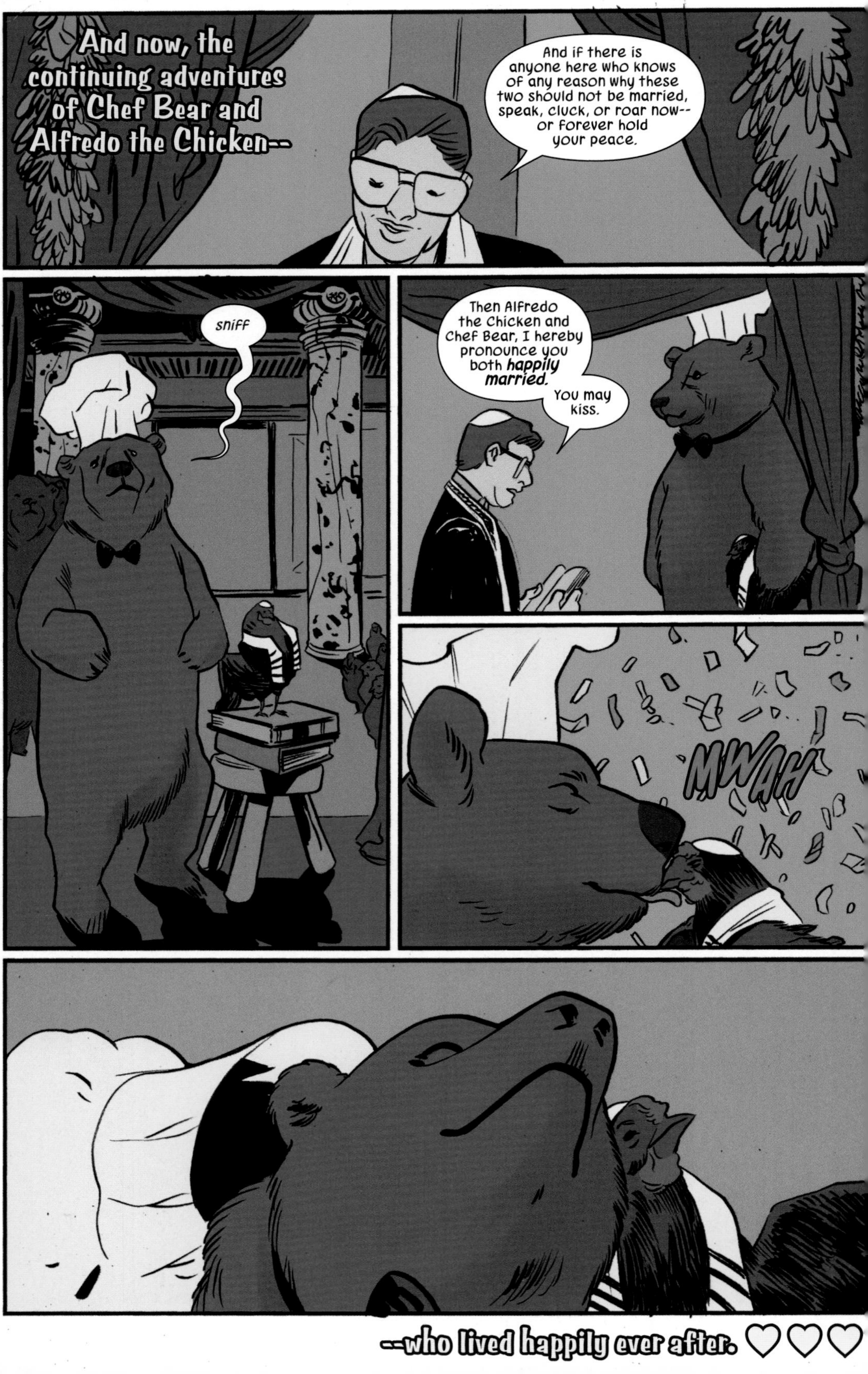
And now, the continuing adventures of Chef Bear and Alfredo the Chicken--
And if there is anyone here who knows of any reason why these two should not be married, speak, cluck, or roar now--or forever hold your peace.
sniff
Then Alfredo the Chicken and Chef Bear, I hereby pronounce you both *happily married.*
You may kiss.
MWAH
--who lived happily ever after. ♡♡♡

21

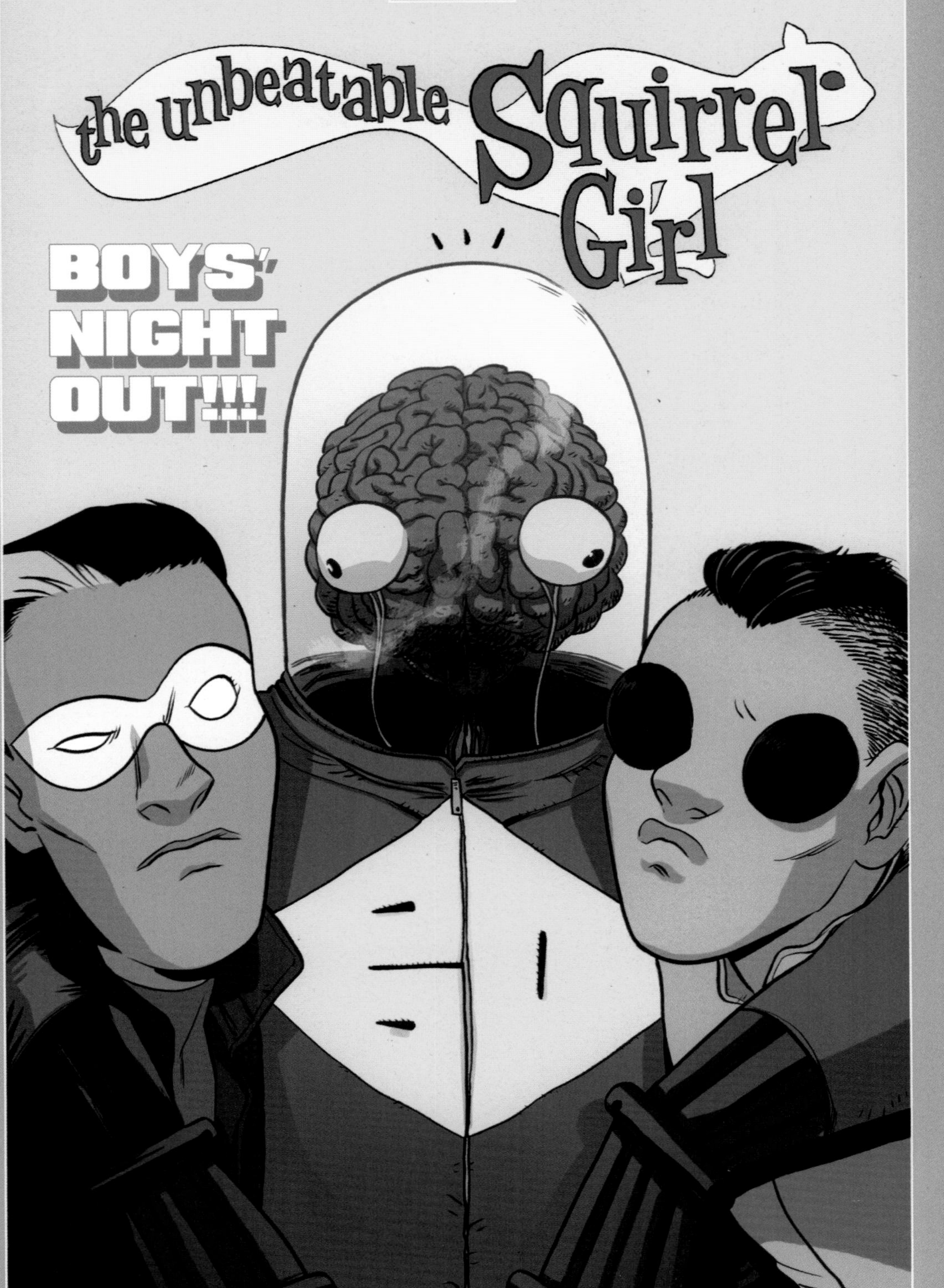
the unbeatable Squirrel Girl
BOYS' NIGHT OUT!!!

Doreen Green isn't just a second-year computer science student: she secretly also has all the powers of both squirrel and girl! She uses her amazing abilities to fight crime **and** be as awesome as possible. You know her as...The Unbeatable Squirrel Girl! Find out what she's been up to, with...

Squirrel Girl *in a nutshell*

search! 🔍

#braindrain

#chipmunkhunk

#koiboi

#itsfabulous

#diedandcamebackasfourguys

#theoctopals

Egg @imduderadtude
DOCTOR DOOM IS TAKNIG OVER NEW YORK CITY!!!!! PLEASE RT SO PPL KNO THAT DOC DOOM IS TAKNG OVER TEH CITY!!!!!!!

> **Squirrel Girl** @unbeatablesg
> @imduderadtude No it's not Doctor Doom, it's Melissa Morbeck! Also, me and my pals defeated her, so uh...we're good here

Egg @imduderadtude
DOCTOR DOOM IS GOING BY THE NAME "MELISSA MORBECK" NOW!!!!!! PLEASE RT!!!!!! #doctordoom

> **Squirrel Girl** @unbeatablesg
> @imduderadtude No, no, it was NEVER Doctor Doom, it was a NEW villain, Melissa Morbeck, who is COMPLETELY DIFFERENT from Doctor Doom!

> **Squirrel Girl** @unbeatablesg
> @imduderadtude Well, I mean, not COMPLETELY different. They both got that "take over the world" thing goin' on I guess

> **Squirrel Girl** @unbeatablesg
> @imduderadtude (also she briefly wore his clothes)

> **Squirrel Girl** @unbeatablesg
> @imduderadtude (or rather a bear under her control did)

> **Squirrel Girl** @unbeatablesg
> @imduderadtude (for reasons)

> **Squirrel Girl** @unbeatablesg
> @imduderadtude ANYWAY, point is, you don't need anyone to "please rt" anything, because the situation is under control!!

Egg @imduderadtude
@unbeatablesg wow it's almost like i said "please rt" and not "please @ me w fact checks"!!!!!

Egg @imduderadtude
@unbeatablesg OH WAIT I DID!!!!! blocked

Nancy W. @sewwiththeflo
@unbeatablesg whoooooo's up for a vacation?

> **Squirrel Girl** @unbeatablesg
> @sewwiththeflo Oh man! Negative Zone hangouts with Allene??

> **Tony Stark** @starkmantony ✔
> @unbeatablesg @sewwiththeflo Should you really be posting that you're leaving NYC undefended while you hang out in an alternate dimension?

> **Squirrel Girl** @unbeatablesg
> @starkmantony @sewwiththeflo Oh pfft it's not undefended. It's got YOU.

> **Tony Stark** @starkmantony ✔
> @unbeatablesg @sewwiththeflo I keep telling you, I'm a computer now. I put my consciousness into a computer. Because of course I did.

> **Squirrel Girl** @unbeatablesg
> @starkmantony @sewwiththeflo Tony I know you're trying to get me to make you another captcha pic but I'm busy packing for NEGAZONE TIMES

> **Squirrel Girl** @unbeatablesg
> @starkmantony @sewwiththeflo Besides, EVEN IF THAT WERE TRUE, Koi Boi, Chipmunk Hunk and Brain Drain are still gonna defend the city!!

> **Squirrel Girl** @unbeatablesg
> @starkmantony @sewwiththeflo I wonder what hilarious shenanigans THOSE crazy characters will get into! I, for one, would like to know!

> **Squirrel Girl** @unbeatablesg
> @starkmantony @sewwiththeflo And I WILL know, right after we return from visiting a friend in the Negative Zone SEE YOU LATER BYE

> **Tony Stark** @starkmantony ✔
> @unbeatablesg @sewwiththeflo Wait, are you there? Squirrel Girl?

> **Tony Stark** @starkmantony ✔
> @unbeatablesg @sewwiththeflo Squirrel Girl?

> **Tony Stark** @starkmantony ✔
> @unbeatablesg @sewwiththeflo Hello?

> **Tony Stark** @starkmantony ✔
> @unbeatablesg @sewwiththeflo …

> **Tony Stark** @starkmantony ✔

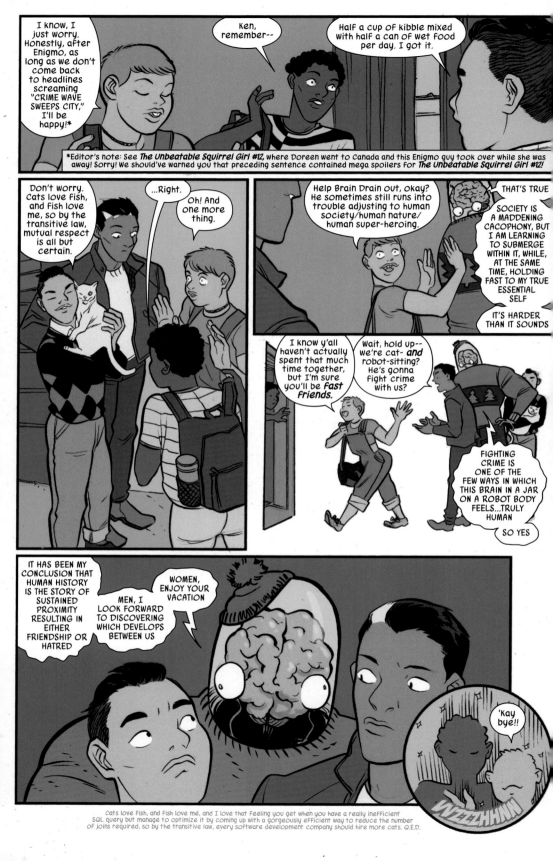

I know, I just worry. Honestly, after Enigmo, as long as we don't come back to headlines screaming "CRIME WAVE SWEEPS CITY," I'll be happy!*

Ken, remember--

Half a cup of kibble mixed with half a can of wet food per day. I got it.

*Editor's note: See *The Unbeatable Squirrel Girl #12*, where Doreen went to Canada and this Enigmo guy took over while she was away! Sorry! We should've warned you that preceding sentence contained mega spoilers for *The Unbeatable Squirrel Girl #12*!

Don't worry. Cats love fish, and fish love me, so by the transitive law, mutual respect is all but certain.

...Right.

Oh! And one more thing.

Help Brain Drain out, okay? He sometimes still runs into trouble adjusting to human society/human nature/human super-heroing.

THAT'S TRUE

SOCIETY IS A MADDENING CACOPHONY, BUT I AM LEARNING TO SUBMERGE WITHIN IT, WHILE, AT THE SAME TIME, HOLDING FAST TO MY TRUE ESSENTIAL SELF

IT'S HARDER THAN IT SOUNDS

I know y'all haven't actually spent that much time together, but I'm sure you'll be *fast* friends.

Wait, hold up-- we're cat- *and* robot-sitting? He's gonna fight crime with us?

FIGHTING CRIME IS ONE OF THE FEW WAYS IN WHICH THIS BRAIN IN A JAR ON A ROBOT BODY FEELS...TRULY HUMAN

SO YES

IT HAS BEEN MY CONCLUSION THAT HUMAN HISTORY IS THE STORY OF SUSTAINED PROXIMITY RESULTING IN EITHER FRIENDSHIP OR HATRED

MEN, I LOOK FORWARD TO DISCOVERING WHICH DEVELOPS BETWEEN US

WOMEN, ENJOY YOUR VACATION

'kay bye!!

VVZZZHNNN

Cats love fish, and fish love me, and I love that feeling you get when you have a really inefficient SQL query but manage to optimize it by coming up with a gorgeously efficient way to reduce the number of joins required, so by the transitive law, every software development company should hire more cats. Q.E.D.

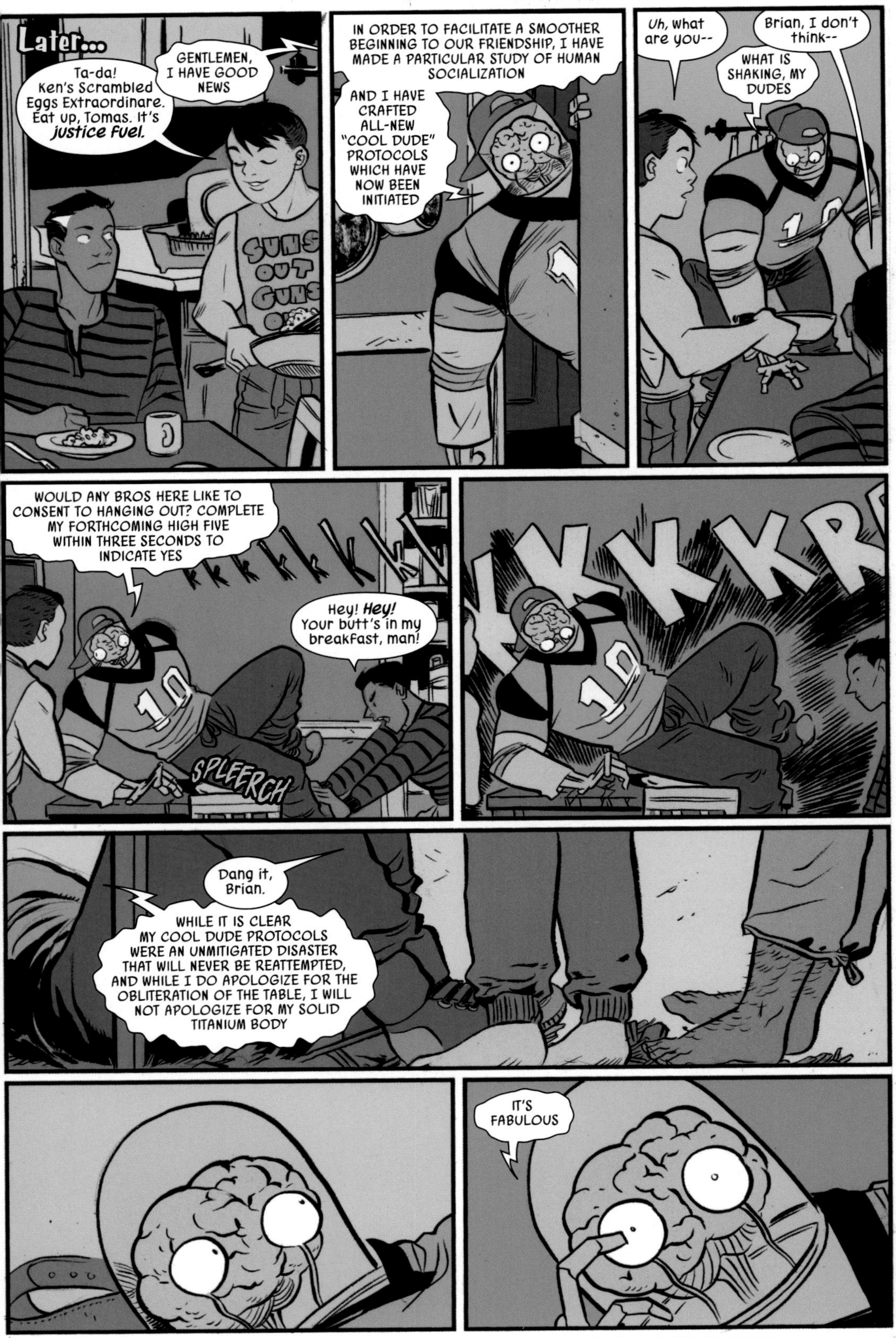
Later...
Ta-da! Ken's Scrambled Eggs Extraordinare. Eat up, Tomas. It's *justice fuel.*
GENTLEMEN, I HAVE GOOD NEWS
IN ORDER TO FACILITATE A SMOOTHER BEGINNING TO OUR FRIENDSHIP, I HAVE MADE A PARTICULAR STUDY OF HUMAN SOCIALIZATION
AND I HAVE CRAFTED ALL-NEW "COOL DUDE" PROTOCOLS WHICH HAVE NOW BEEN INITIATED
Uh, what are you--
Brian, I don't think--
WHAT IS SHAKING, MY DUDES
WOULD ANY BROS HERE LIKE TO CONSENT TO HANGING OUT? COMPLETE MY FORTHCOMING HIGH FIVE WITHIN THREE SECONDS TO INDICATE YES
Hey! *Hey!* Your butt's in my breakfast, man!
SPLEERCH
KKKR
Dang it, Brian.
WHILE IT IS CLEAR MY COOL DUDE PROTOCOLS WERE AN UNMITIGATED DISASTER THAT WILL NEVER BE REATTEMPTED, AND WHILE I DO APOLOGIZE FOR THE OBLITERATION OF THE TABLE, I WILL NOT APOLOGIZE FOR MY SOLID TITANIUM BODY
IT'S FABULOUS

Do eggs truly make a "spleerch" sound when you sit on a plate of them? This answer is generously left as an exercise for the reader.

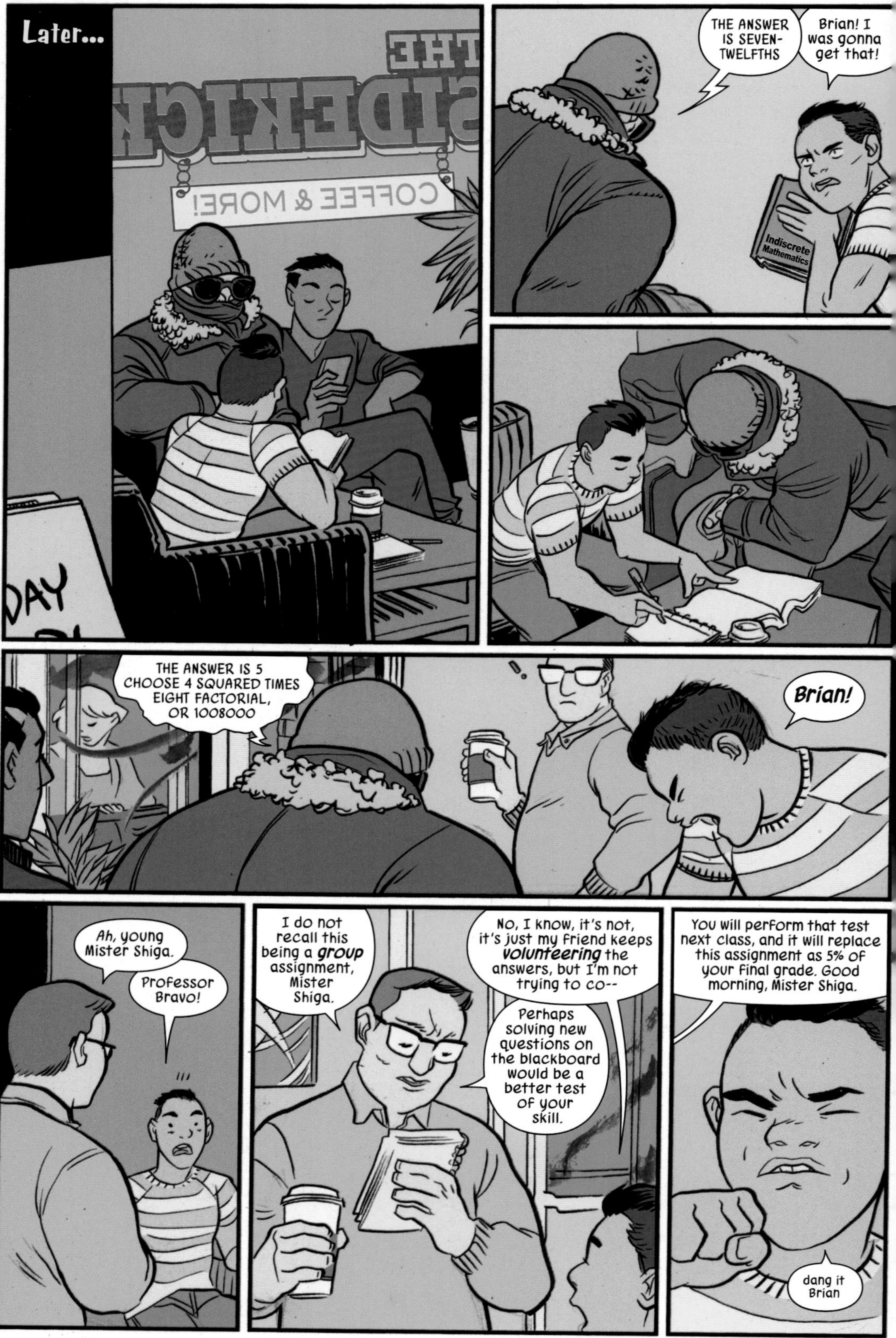
Later...
THE SIDEKICK
COFFEE & MORE!
THE ANSWER IS SEVEN-TWELFTHS
Brian! I was gonna get that!
Indiscrete Mathematics
THE ANSWER IS 5 CHOOSE 4 SQUARED TIMES EIGHT FACTORIAL, OR 1008000
!
Brian!
Ah, young Mister Shiga.
Professor Bravo!
I do not recall this being a group assignment, Mister Shiga.
No, I know, it's not, it's just my friend keeps volunteering the answers, but I'm not trying to co--
Perhaps solving new questions on the blackboard would be a better test of your skill.
You will perform that test next class, and it will replace this assignment as 5% of your final grade. Good morning, Mister Shiga.
dang it Brian

While "1008000" is the answer, what's the question? Well, let me say this: If one day you get on the bus and you don't have enough fare, and the bus driver says "I'll let you ride for free if you can tell me how many 8-digit numbers consist of exactly 4 distinct odd digits (i.e., 1, 3, 5, 7, 9) and 4 distinct even digits (i.e., 0, 2, 4, 6, 8)," you'll be laughing ***all the way to your destination.***

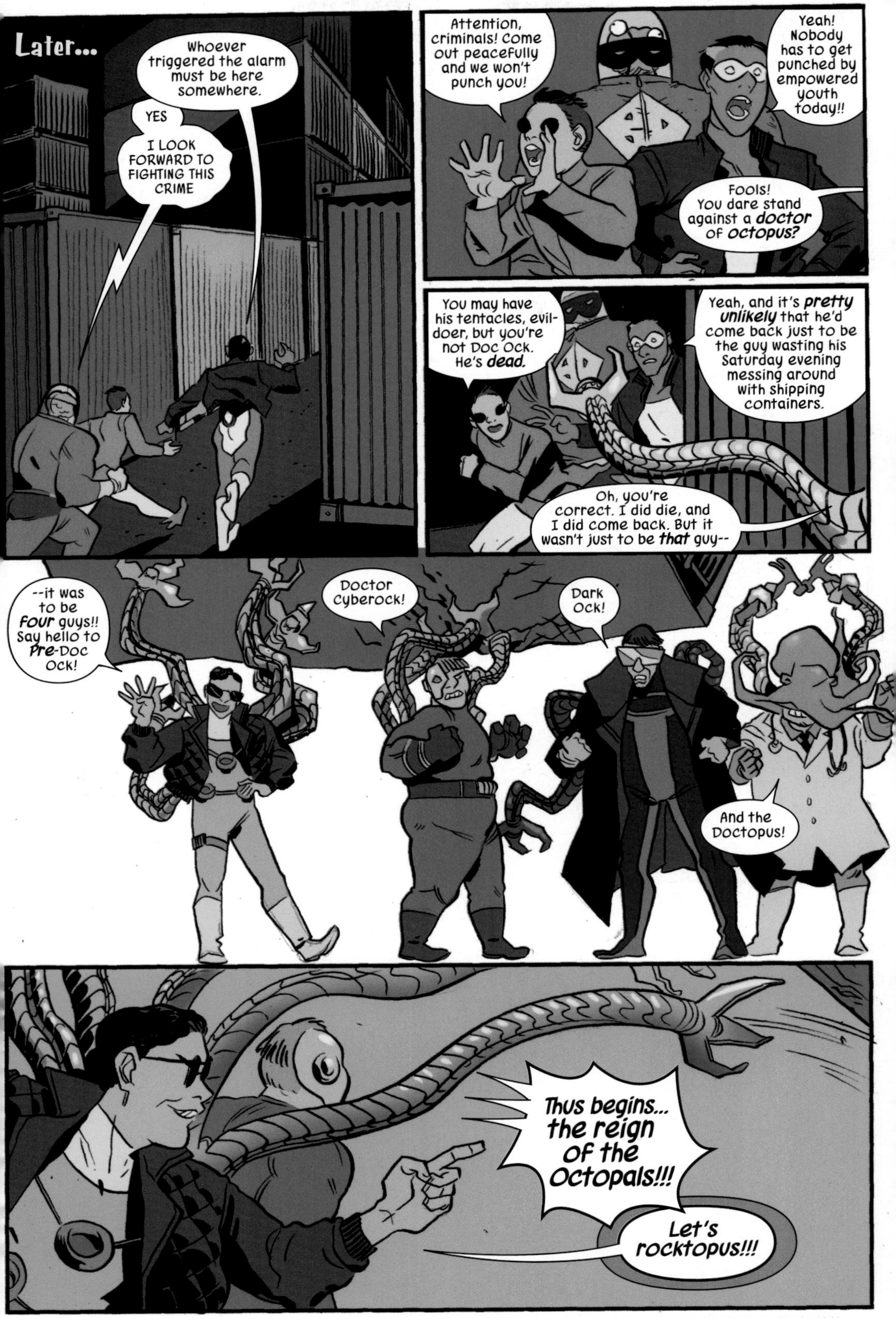
Later...
Whoever triggered the alarm must be here somewhere.
YES
I LOOK FORWARD TO FIGHTING THIS CRIME
Attention, criminals! Come out peacefully and we won't punch you!
Yeah! Nobody has to get punched by empowered youth today!!
Fools! You dare stand against a *doctor* of *octopus?*
You may have his tentacles, evil-doer, but you're not Doc Ock. He's *dead.*
Yeah, and it's *pretty unlikely* that he'd come back just to be the guy wasting his Saturday evening messing around with shipping containers.
Oh, you're correct. I did die, and I did come back. But it wasn't just to be *that* guy--
--it was to be *FOUR* guys!! Say hello to *Pre*-Doc Ock!
Doctor Cyberock!
Dark Ock!
And the Doctopus!
Thus begins... the reign of the Octopals!!!
Let's rocktopus!!!

_ You'd really think there'd be *eight* Octopals. No shade, but I really think most people would expect the number of pals in a group called the "Octopals" to be eight.

"Weltschmerz" is a word English borrowed from German, and it refers to the world-weariness of someone who believes that the real world can never satisfy the demands of the mind! Feel free to use it whenever you feel that the real world can never satisfy your mind's demands, and remember the fun talking-squirrel comic book you learned it from!

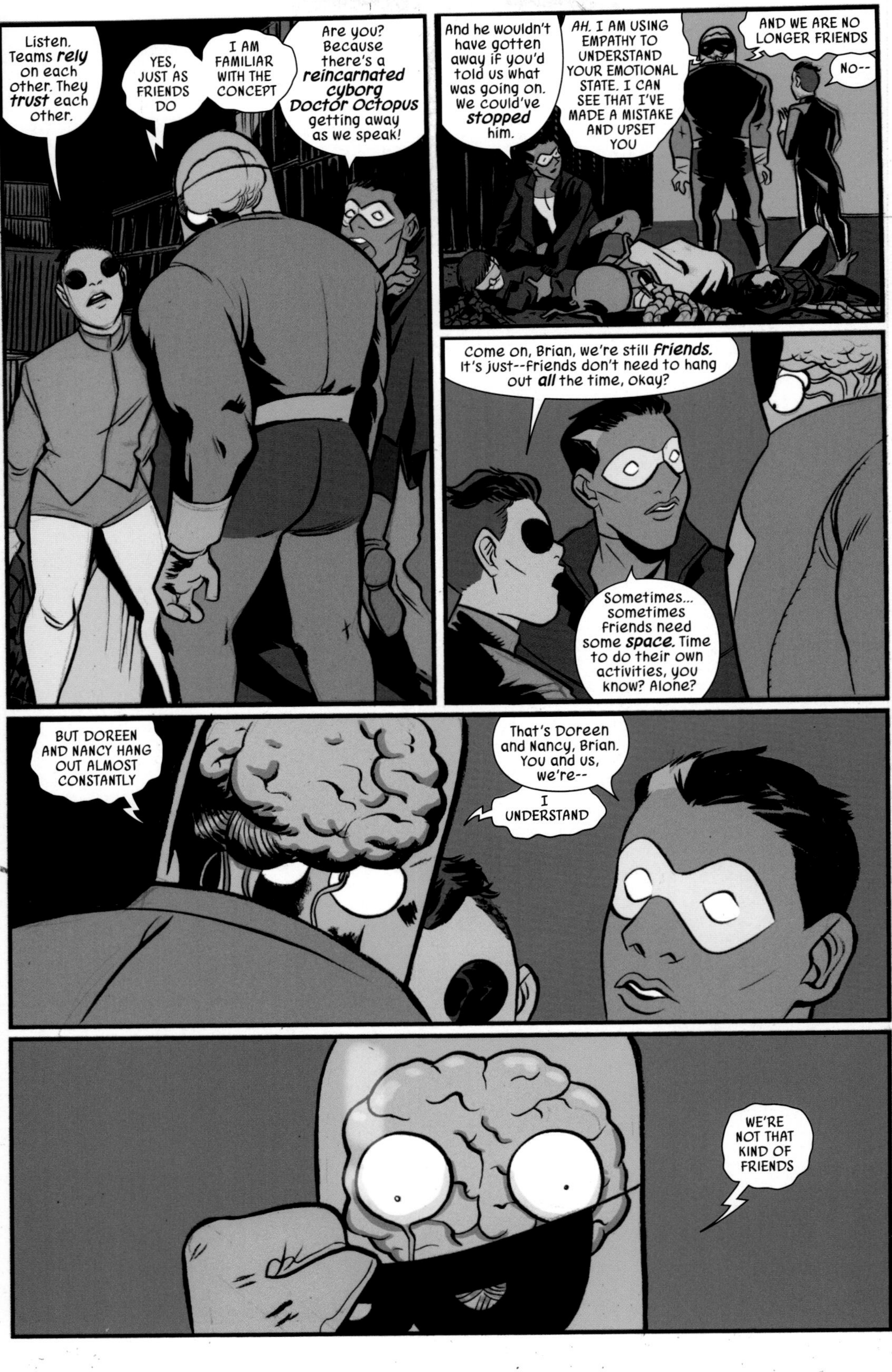
Listen. Teams *rely* on each other. They *trust* each other.
YES, JUST AS FRIENDS DO
I AM FAMILIAR WITH THE CONCEPT
Are you? Because there's a *reincarnated cyborg Doctor Octopus* getting away as we speak!
And he wouldn't have gotten away if you'd told us what was going on. We could've *stopped* him.
AH. I AM USING EMPATHY TO UNDERSTAND YOUR EMOTIONAL STATE. I CAN SEE THAT I'VE MADE A MISTAKE AND UPSET YOU
AND WE ARE NO LONGER FRIENDS
NO--
Come on, Brian, we're still *friends.* It's just--friends don't need to hang out *all* the time, okay?
Sometimes... sometimes friends need some *space.* Time to do their own activities, you know? Alone?
BUT DOREEN AND NANCY HANG OUT ALMOST CONSTANTLY
That's Doreen and Nancy, Brian. You and us, we're--
I UNDERSTAND
WE'RE NOT THAT KIND OF FRIENDS

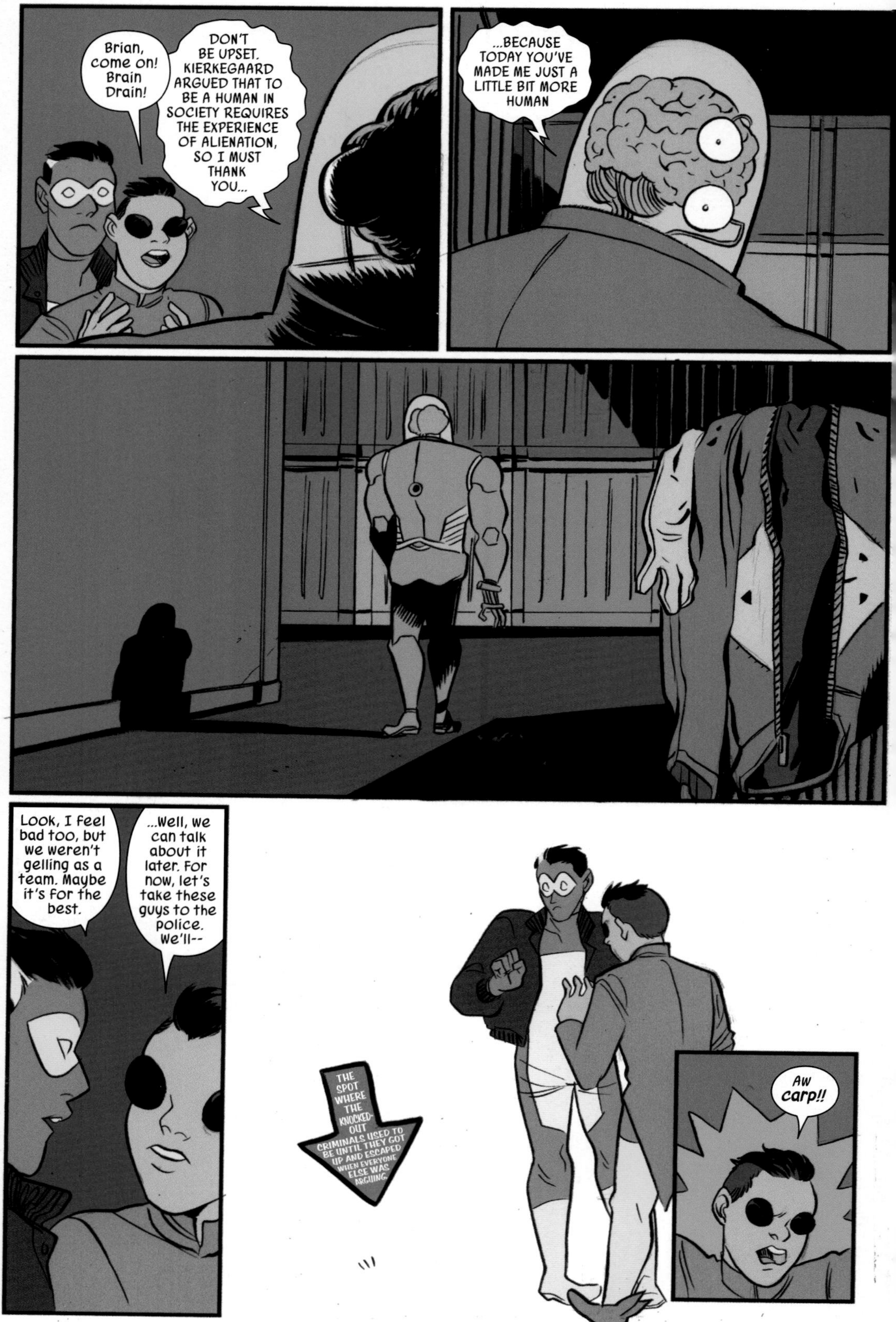
Brian, come on! Brain Drain!
DON'T BE UPSET. KIERKEGAARD ARGUED THAT TO BE A HUMAN IN SOCIETY REQUIRES THE EXPERIENCE OF ALIENATION, SO I MUST THANK YOU...
...BECAUSE TODAY YOU'VE MADE ME JUST A LITTLE BIT MORE HUMAN
Look, I feel bad too, but we weren't gelling as a team. Maybe it's for the best.
...Well, we can talk about it later. For now, let's take these guys to the police. We'll--
THE SPOT WHERE THE KNOCKED-OUT CRIMINALS USED TO BE UNTIL THEY GOT UP AND ESCAPED WHEN EVERYONE ELSE WAS ARGUING.
Aw carp!!

You're seeing it here for the first time, but you just *KNOW* Koi Boi is gonna use that line again approximately one million times.

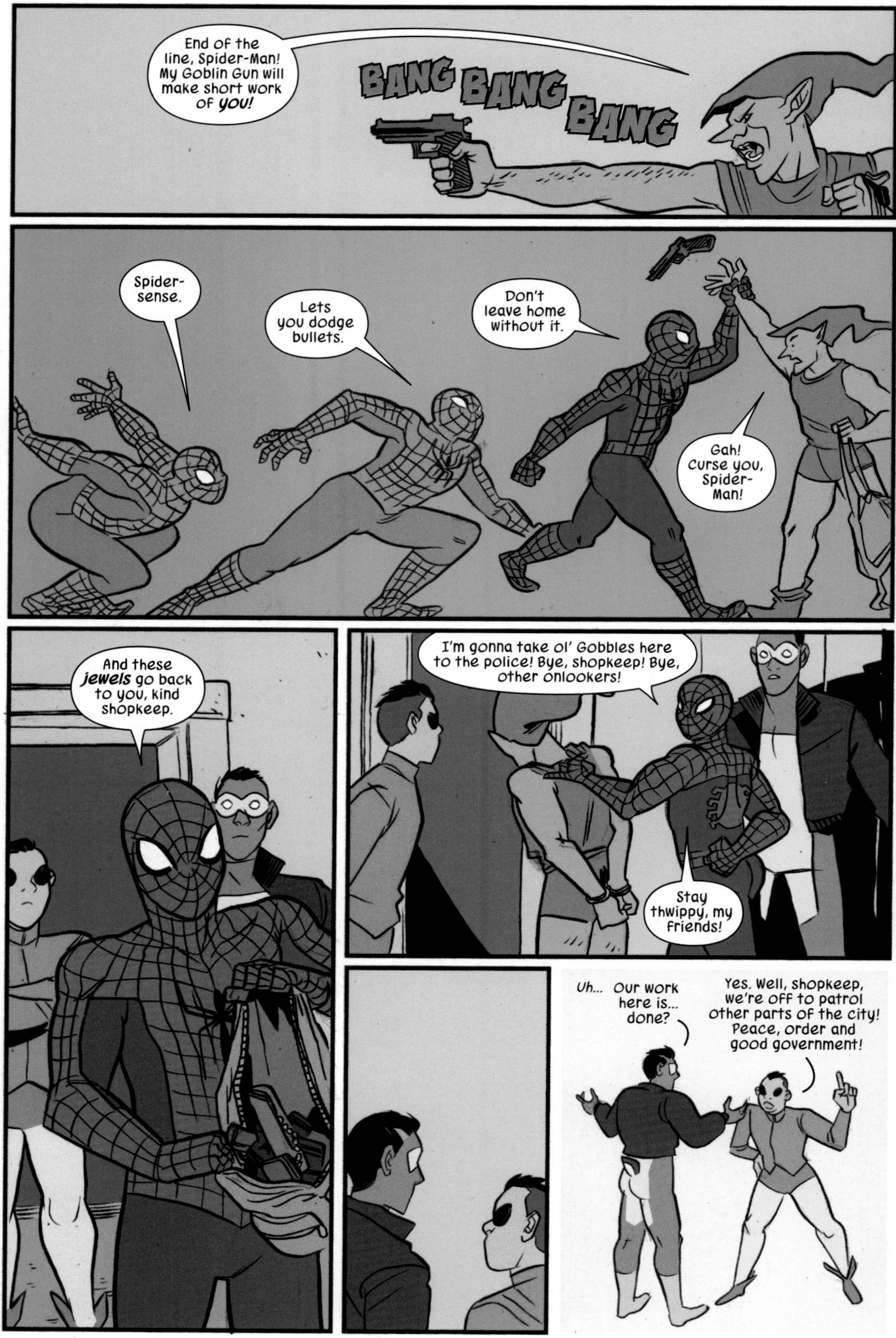
End of the line, Spider-Man! My Goblin Gun will make short work of YOU!
BANG BANG BANG
Spider-sense.
Lets you dodge bullets.
Don't leave home without it.
Gah! Curse you, Spider-Man!
And these jewels go back to you, kind shopkeep.
I'm gonna take ol' Gobbles here to the police! Bye, shopkeep! Bye, other onlookers!
Stay thwippy, my friends!
Uh... Our work here is... done?
Yes. Well, shopkeep, we're off to patrol other parts of the city! Peace, order and good government!

Spider-sense: Lets you dodge bullets, while also sensing if there are any cool spiders nearby. Honestly, I mostly only use the first part of it.

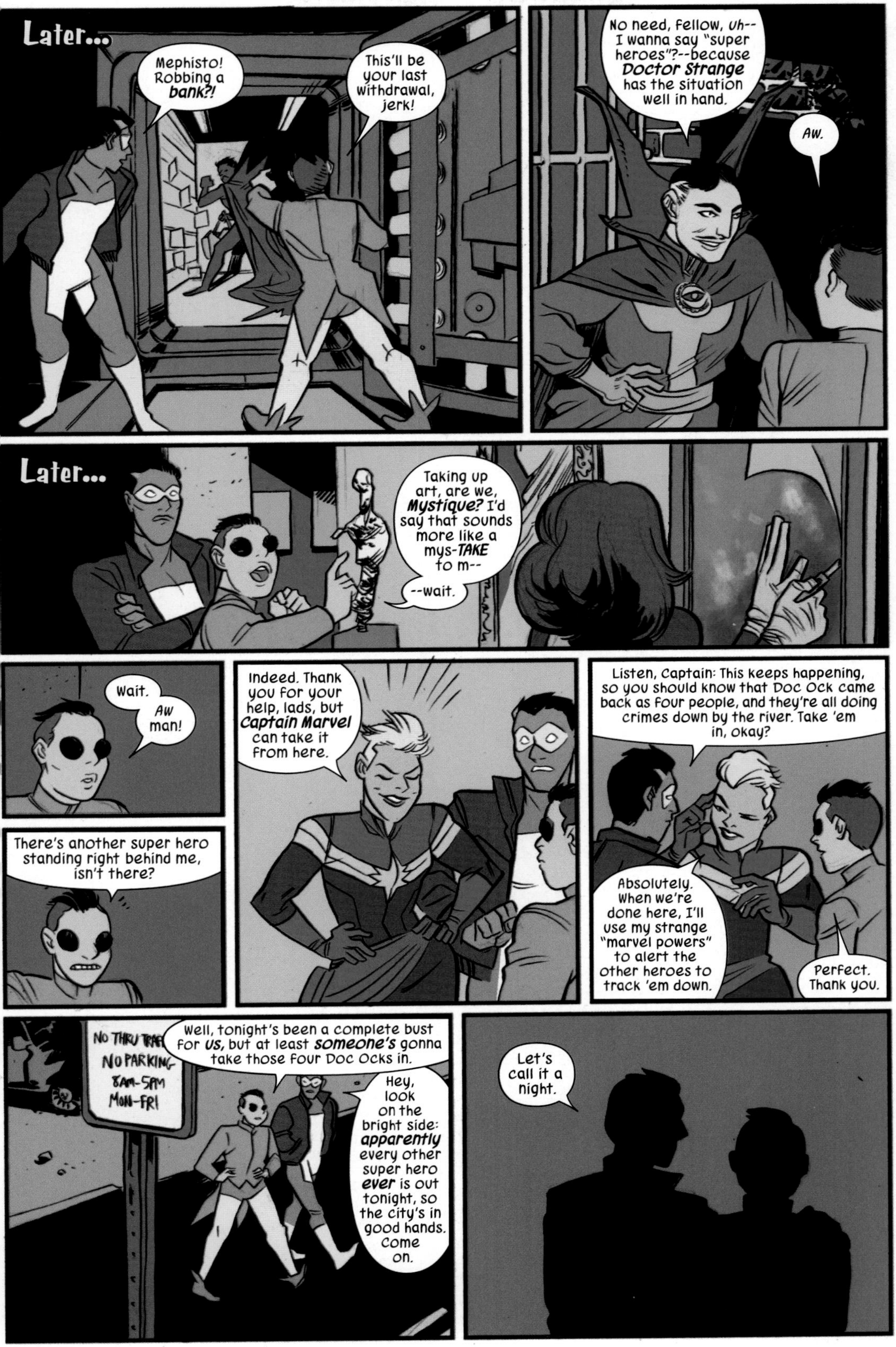

Later...
Mephisto! Robbing a bank?!
This'll be your last withdrawal, jerk!
No need, fellow, uh-- I wanna say "super heroes"?--because Doctor Strange has the situation well in hand.
AW.
Later...
Taking up art, are we, Mystique? I'd say that sounds more like a mys-TAKE to m--
--wait.
Wait.
AW man!
There's another super hero standing right behind me, isn't there?
Indeed. Thank you for your help, lads, but Captain Marvel can take it from here.
Listen, Captain: This keeps happening, so you should know that Doc Ock came back as four people, and they're all doing crimes down by the river. Take 'em in, okay?
Absolutely. When we're done here, I'll use my strange "marvel powers" to alert the other heroes to track 'em down.
Perfect. Thank you.
NO PARKING
8AM-5PM
MON-FRI
Well, tonight's been a complete bust for us, but at least someone's gonna take those four Doc Ocks in.
Hey, look on the bright side: apparently every other super hero ever is out tonight, so the city's in good hands. Come on.
Let's call it a night.

The next morning...

BANG BANG BANG

Tomas! *Wake up!*

What?! What's going on?

This.

Dude, did you sleep in your costume?

I got *dressed quickly* when I read what I'm trying to show you; please read it *immediately* before offering further questions!!!

I don't-- why wouldn't Spidey bring the Goblin in?

Because, Tomas:

That wasn't Spidey.

"Remember how our 'Spider-Man' last night didn't *swing* in--he *walked* in, like anyone else. And he never actually webbed *anything.* He *couldn't.*

"Because he was just some *regular chump* in a *costume.*

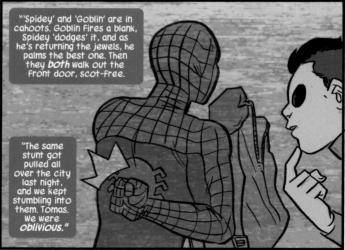

"'Spidey' and 'Goblin' are in cahoots. Goblin fires a blank, Spidey 'dodges' it, and as he's returning the jewels, he palms the best one. Then they *both* walk out the front door, scot-free.

"The same stunt got pulled all over the city last night, and we kept stumbling into them. Tomas. We were *oblivious.*"

It must be fun to be a headline writer in the Marvel Universe. I bet it's never boring. You probably get to use a 72pt font any time you want and don't even have to wait for a moon landing to give you the excuse.

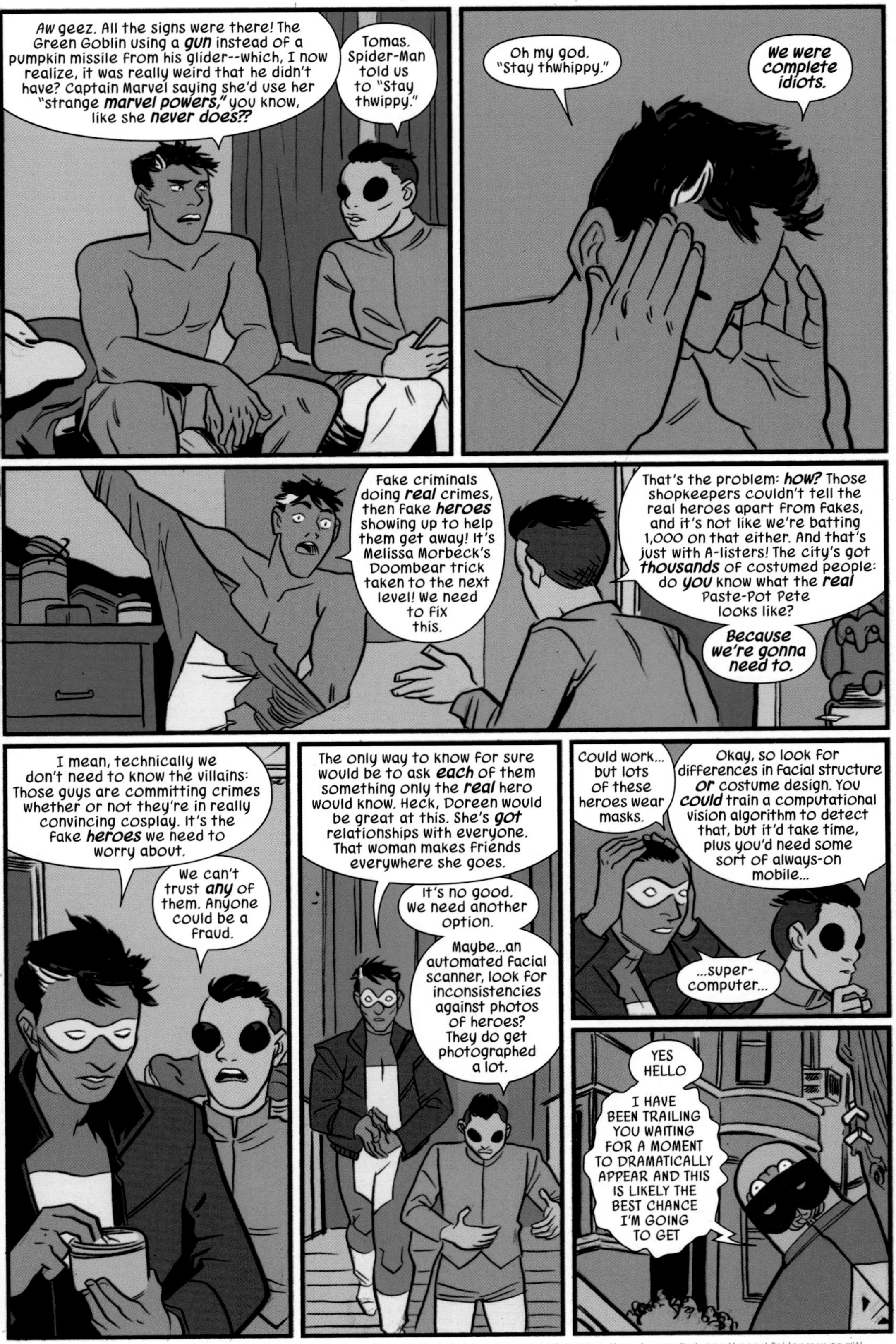
Aw geez. All the signs were there! The Green Goblin using a gun instead of a pumpkin missile from his glider--which, I now realize, it was really weird that he didn't have? Captain Marvel saying she'd use her "strange marvel powers," you know, like she never does??
Tomas. Spider-Man told us to "Stay thwippy."
Oh my god. "Stay thwhippy."
We were complete idiots.
Fake criminals doing real crimes, then fake heroes showing up to help them get away! It's Melissa Morbeck's Doombear trick taken to the next level! We need to fix this.
That's the problem: how? Those shopkeepers couldn't tell the real heroes apart from fakes, and it's not like we're batting 1,000 on that either. And that's just with A-listers! The city's got thousands of costumed people: do you know what the real Paste-Pot Pete looks like?
Because we're gonna need to.
I mean, technically we don't need to know the villains: Those guys are committing crimes whether or not they're in really convincing cosplay. It's the fake heroes we need to worry about.
We can't trust any of them. Anyone could be a fraud.
The only way to know for sure would be to ask each of them something only the real hero would know. Heck, Doreen would be great at this. She's got relationships with everyone. That woman makes friends everywhere she goes.
It's no good. We need another option.
Maybe...an automated facial scanner, look for inconsistencies against photos of heroes? They do get photographed a lot.
Could work... but lots of these heroes wear masks.
Okay, so look for differences in facial structure or costume design. You could train a computational vision algorithm to detect that, but it'd take time, plus you'd need some sort of always-on mobile...
...super-computer...
YES HELLO
I HAVE BEEN TRAILING YOU WAITING FOR A MOMENT TO DRAMATICALLY APPEAR AND THIS IS LIKELY THE BEST CHANCE I'M GOING TO GET

Yes, sadly, that wasn't the *real* Spider-Man, which means Spidey's latest catchphrase is not "Stay thwippy." However, there is a small chance the real Spidey may go with "Thwips to meet you, see you next thwips," and we here at Squirrel Girl Headquarters will definitely keep you appraised of any developments in that area.

Brain Drain!

YES IT IS I

AFTER THE ENIGMO SITUATION, I UPGRADED MY VISUAL PROCESSORS, WRITING A COMPUTATIONAL VISION ALGORITHM VERY SIMILAR TO THE ONE YOU JUST DESCRIBED

IT SCANS FACES AROUND ME, PERFORMS SEARCHES, THEN BRINGS UP A DISPLAY ONLY I CAN SEE WITH NAMES AND BIOS

HELLO DETECTIVE MICHAEL CORSON, BORN: 1979, OCCUPATION: NYC POLICE, SPOUSE(S): NONE

HOW ARE YOU

Uh...

"IT HAS MADE ME AMAZING AT PARTIES"

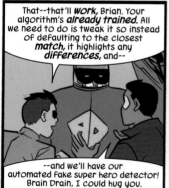

That--that'll **work,** Brian. Your algorithm's **already trained.** All we need to do is tweak it so instead of defaulting to the closest **match,** it highlights any **differences,** and--

--and we'll have our automated fake super hero detector! Brain Drain, I could hug you.

THANK YOU. YOU MAY PROCEED

Oh.

Uh, all right.

I guess we're doing this.

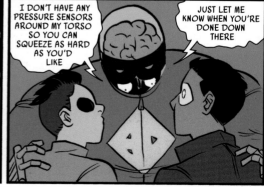

I DON'T HAVE ANY PRESSURE SENSORS AROUND MY TORSO SO YOU CAN SQUEEZE AS HARD AS YOU'D LIKE

JUST LET ME KNOW WHEN YOU'RE DONE DOWN THERE

DETECTIVE MICHAEL CORSON, HOW DID YOU ENJOY THAT STEAK YOU POSTED A PICTURE OF ON SOCIAL MEDIA THREE DAYS AGO? I NOTICE THE PHOTO EARNED A TOTAL OF TWO LIKES AND I HOPE IT WAS AS HASHTAG TASTYSTEAK AS YOU ANTICIPATED

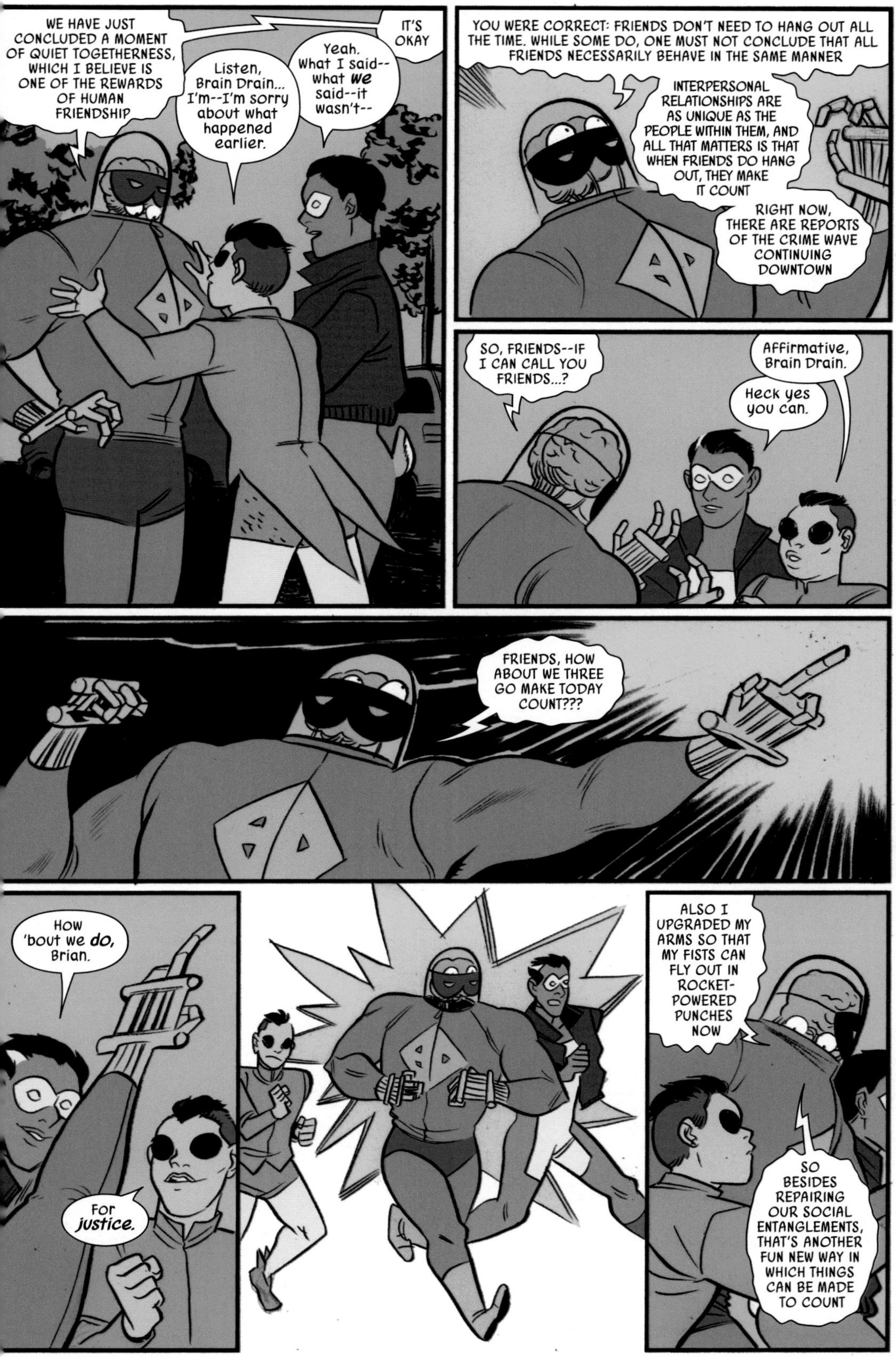
WE HAVE JUST CONCLUDED A MOMENT OF QUIET TOGETHERNESS, WHICH I BELIEVE IS ONE OF THE REWARDS OF HUMAN FRIENDSHIP
IT'S OKAY
Listen, Brain Drain... I'm--I'm sorry about what happened earlier.
Yeah. What I said--what *we* said--it wasn't--
YOU WERE CORRECT: FRIENDS DON'T NEED TO HANG OUT ALL THE TIME. WHILE SOME DO, ONE MUST NOT CONCLUDE THAT ALL FRIENDS NECESSARILY BEHAVE IN THE SAME MANNER
INTERPERSONAL RELATIONSHIPS ARE AS UNIQUE AS THE PEOPLE WITHIN THEM, AND ALL THAT MATTERS IS THAT WHEN FRIENDS DO HANG OUT, THEY MAKE IT COUNT
RIGHT NOW, THERE ARE REPORTS OF THE CRIME WAVE CONTINUING DOWNTOWN
SO, FRIENDS--IF I CAN CALL YOU FRIENDS...?
Affirmative, Brain Drain.
Heck yes you can.
FRIENDS, HOW ABOUT WE THREE GO MAKE TODAY COUNT???
How 'bout we *do*, Brian.
For *justice*.
ALSO I UPGRADED MY ARMS SO THAT MY FISTS CAN FLY OUT IN ROCKET-POWERED PUNCHES NOW
SO BESIDES REPAIRING OUR SOCIAL ENTANGLEMENTS, THAT'S ANOTHER FUN NEW WAY IN WHICH THINGS CAN BE MADE TO COUNT

I RECOVERED MY COSTUME FROM THE TRASH CAN I'D LEFT IT IN; IT IS LUCKY FOR ME THAT THIS CITY'S CUSTODIAL SERVICES ARE NOT AS RUTHLESSLY EFFICIENT AS, IN A MORE PERFECT WORLD, THEY COULD BE

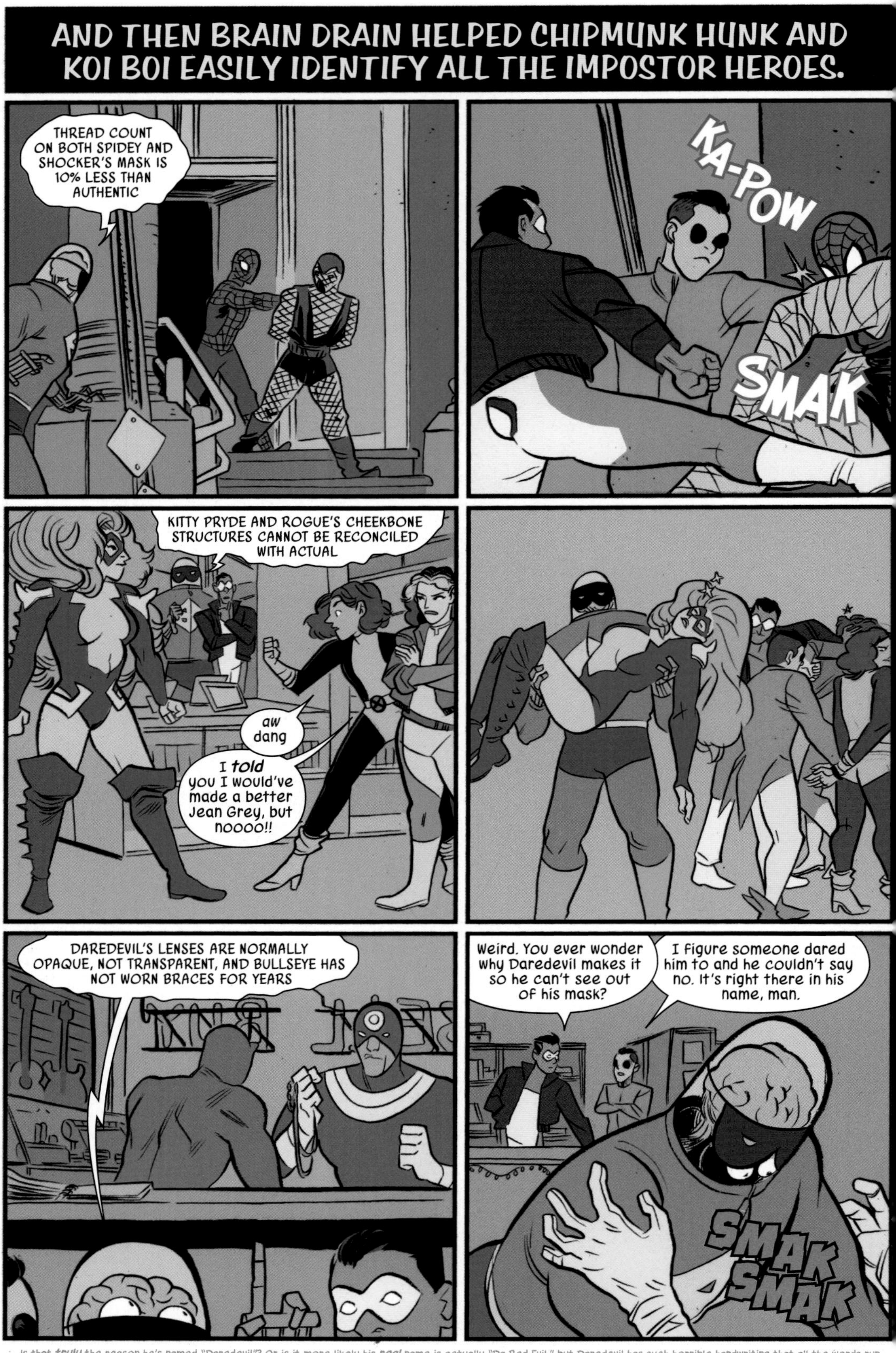
AND THEN BRAIN DRAIN HELPED CHIPMUNK HUNK AND KOI BOI EASILY IDENTIFY ALL THE IMPOSTOR HEROES.
THREAD COUNT ON BOTH SPIDEY AND SHOCKER'S MASK IS 10% LESS THAN AUTHENTIC
KA-POW
SMAK
KITTY PRYDE AND ROGUE'S CHEEKBONE STRUCTURES CANNOT BE RECONCILED WITH ACTUAL
aw dang
I *told* you I would've made a better Jean Grey, but noooo!!
DAREDEVIL'S LENSES ARE NORMALLY OPAQUE, NOT TRANSPARENT, AND BULLSEYE HAS NOT WORN BRACES FOR YEARS
Weird. You ever wonder why Daredevil makes it so he can't see out of his mask?
I figure someone dared him to and he couldn't say no. It's right there in his name, man.
SMAK SMAK

Is that *truly* the reason he's named "Daredevil"? Or is it more likely his *real* name is actually "Da Red Evil," but Daredevil has such horrible handwriting that all the words run together, and that, combined with crippling shyness about correcting anyone, means we never found out the truth...*until this very moment???*

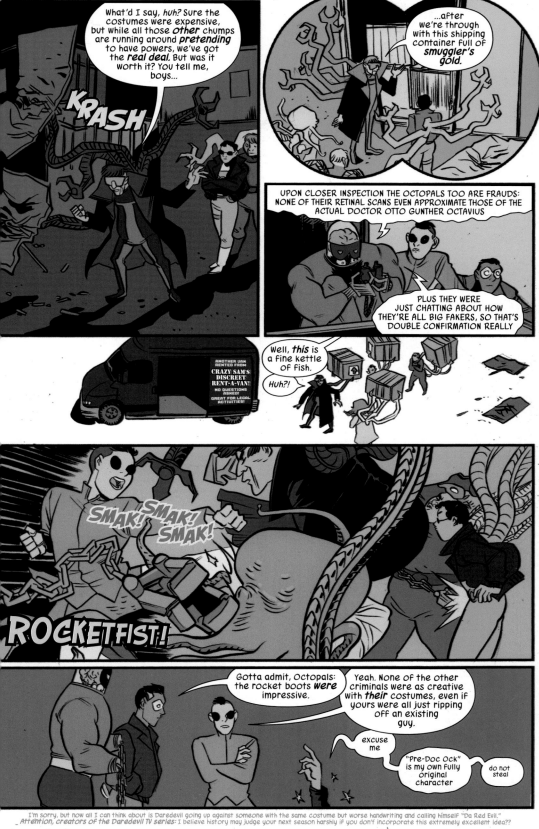

I'm sorry, but now all I can think about is Daredevil going up against someone with the same costume but worse handwriting and calling himself "Da Red Evil."
Attention, creators of the Daredevil TV series: I believe history may judge your next season harshly if you don't incorporate this extremely excellent idea??

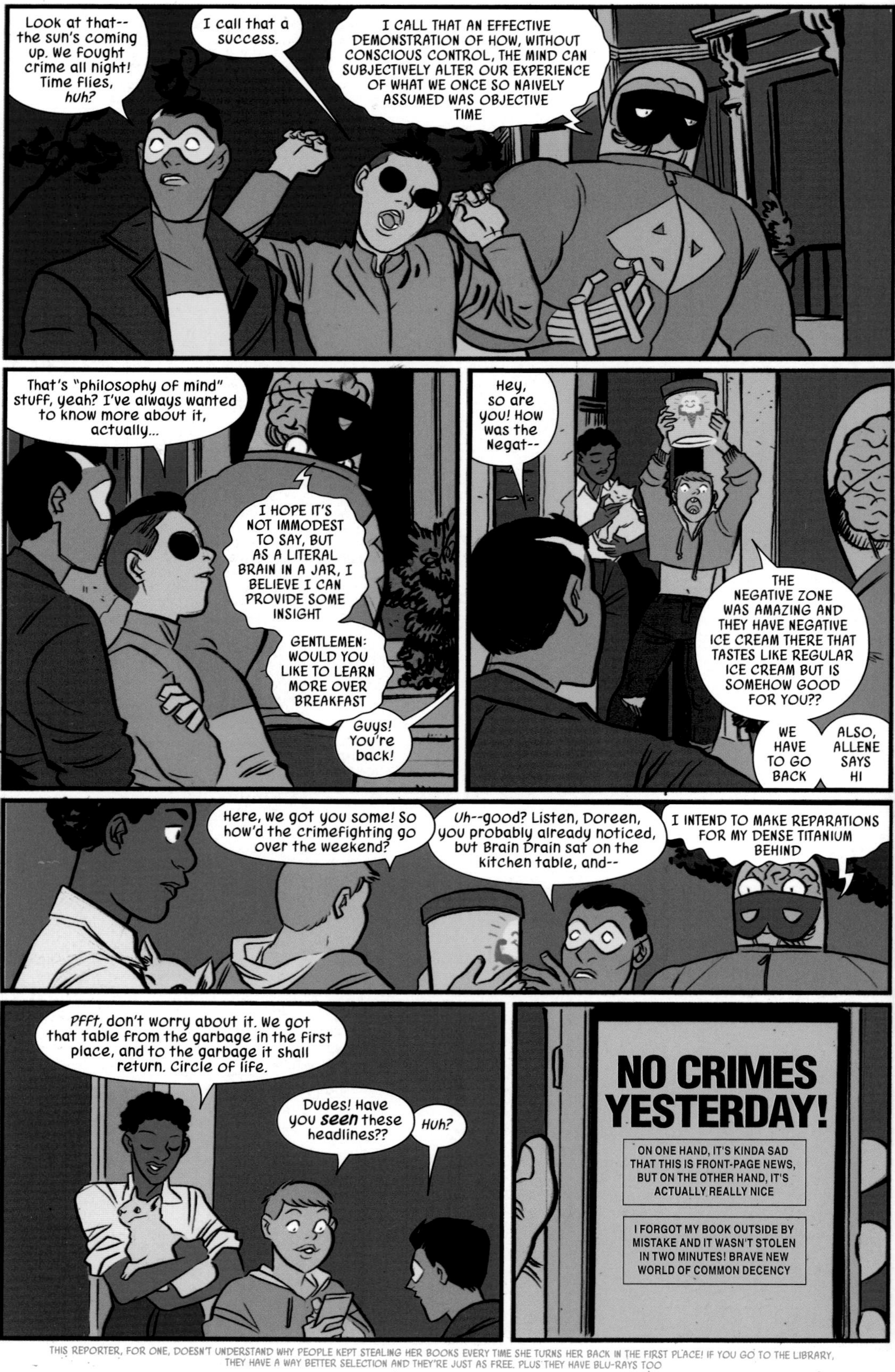
Look at that-- the sun's coming up. We fought crime all night! Time flies, *huh?*
I call that a success.
I CALL THAT AN EFFECTIVE DEMONSTRATION OF HOW, WITHOUT CONSCIOUS CONTROL, THE MIND CAN SUBJECTIVELY ALTER OUR EXPERIENCE OF WHAT WE ONCE SO NAIVELY ASSUMED WAS OBJECTIVE TIME
That's "philosophy of mind" stuff, yeah? I've always wanted to know more about it, actually...
I HOPE IT'S NOT IMMODEST TO SAY, BUT AS A LITERAL BRAIN IN A JAR, I BELIEVE I CAN PROVIDE SOME INSIGHT
GENTLEMEN: WOULD YOU LIKE TO LEARN MORE OVER BREAKFAST
Guys! You're back!
Hey, so are you! How was the Negat--
THE NEGATIVE ZONE WAS AMAZING AND THEY HAVE NEGATIVE ICE CREAM THERE THAT TASTES LIKE REGULAR ICE CREAM BUT IS SOMEHOW GOOD FOR YOU??
WE HAVE TO GO BACK
ALSO, ALLENE SAYS HI
Here, we got you some! So how'd the crimefighting go over the weekend?
Uh--good? Listen, Doreen, you probably already noticed, but Brain Drain sat on the kitchen table, and--
I INTEND TO MAKE REPARATIONS FOR MY DENSE TITANIUM BEHIND
Pfft, don't worry about it. We got that table from the garbage in the first place, and to the garbage it shall return. Circle of life.
Dudes! Have you ***seen*** these headlines??
Huh?
NO CRIMES YESTERDAY!
ON ONE HAND, IT'S KINDA SAD THAT THIS IS FRONT-PAGE NEWS, BUT ON THE OTHER HAND, IT'S ACTUALLY REALLY NICE
I FORGOT MY BOOK OUTSIDE BY MISTAKE AND IT WASN'T STOLEN IN TWO MINUTES! BRAVE NEW WORLD OF COMMON DECENCY

THIS REPORTER, FOR ONE, DOESN'T UNDERSTAND WHY PEOPLE KEPT STEALING HER BOOKS EVERY TIME SHE TURNS HER BACK IN THE FIRST PLACE! IF YOU GO TO THE LIBRARY, THEY HAVE A WAY BETTER SELECTION AND THEY'RE JUST AS FREE. PLUS THEY HAVE BLU-RAYS TOO

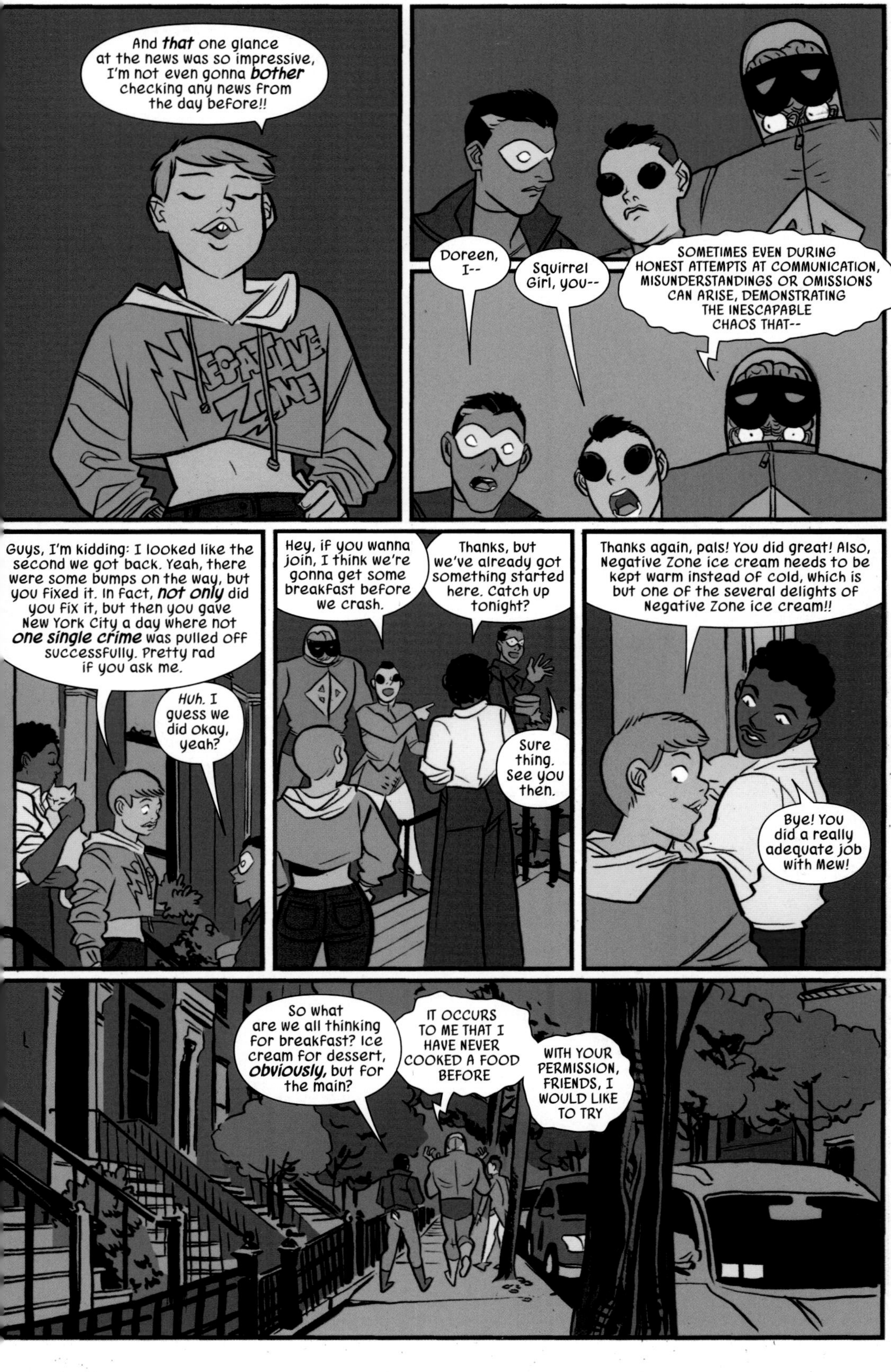

And *that* one glance at the news was so impressive, I'm not even gonna *bother* checking any news from the day before!!
Doreen, I--
Squirrel Girl, you--
SOMETIMES EVEN DURING HONEST ATTEMPTS AT COMMUNICATION, MISUNDERSTANDINGS OR OMISSIONS CAN ARISE, DEMONSTRATING THE INESCAPABLE CHAOS THAT--
Guys, I'm kidding: I looked like the second we got back. Yeah, there were some bumps on the way, but you fixed it. In fact, *not only* did you fix it, but then you gave New York City a day where not *one single crime* was pulled off successfully. Pretty rad if you ask me.
Huh. I guess we did okay, yeah?
Hey, if you wanna join, I think we're gonna get some breakfast before we crash.
Thanks, but we've already got something started here. Catch up tonight?
Sure thing. See you then.
Thanks again, pals! You did great! Also, Negative Zone ice cream needs to be kept warm instead of cold, which is but one of the several delights of Negative Zone ice cream!!
Bye! You did a really adequate job with Mew!
So what are we all thinking for breakfast? Ice cream for dessert, *obviously,* but for the main?
IT OCCURS TO ME THAT I HAVE NEVER COOKED A FOOD BEFORE
WITH YOUR PERMISSION, FRIENDS, I WOULD LIKE TO TRY

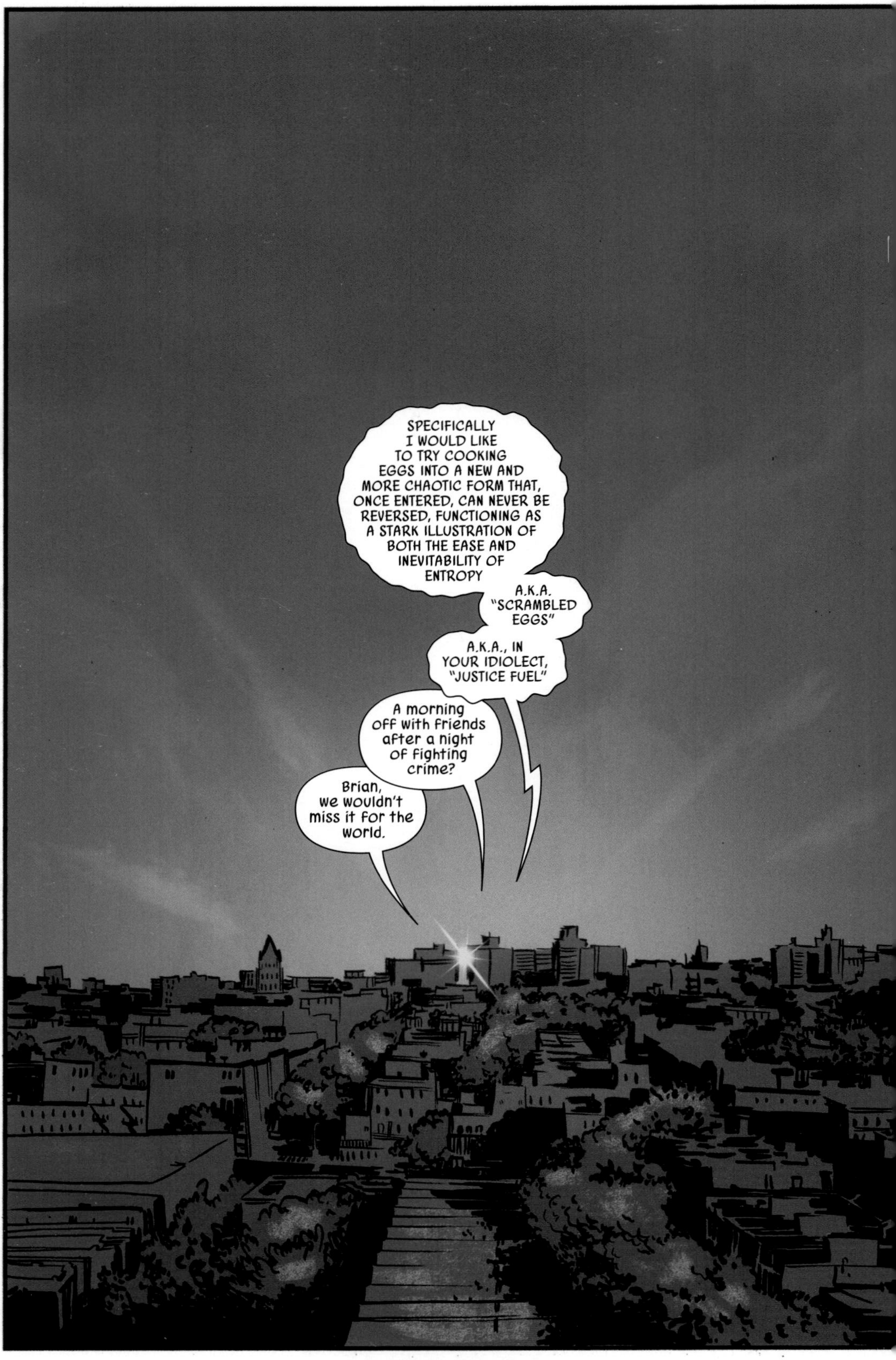
SPECIFICALLY I WOULD LIKE TO TRY COOKING EGGS INTO A NEW AND MORE CHAOTIC FORM THAT, ONCE ENTERED, CAN NEVER BE REVERSED, FUNCTIONING AS A STARK ILLUSTRATION OF BOTH THE EASE AND INEVITABILITY OF ENTROPY
A.K.A. "SCRAMBLED EGGS"
A.K.A., IN YOUR IDIOLECT, "JUSTICE FUEL"
A morning off with friends after a night of fighting crime?
Brian, we wouldn't miss it for the world.

THE END.